The Temple
Dancer

The Temple Dancer

A Novel of India

JOHN SPEED

St. Martin's Press ❧ New York

This is a work of fiction.
All of the characters, organizations, and events portrayed in this novel
are either products of the author's imagination
or are used fictitiously.

www.stmartins.com

Map by Virginia Norey

Design by Sarah Gubkin

LIBRARY OF CONGRESS CATALOGING-IN-PUBLICATION DATA

Speed, John.
The temple dancer / John Speed.—1st ed.
p.   cm.
ISBN-13: 978-0-312-32548-0
ISBN-10: 0-312-32548-7
1. India—History—1526–1765—Fiction.   2. Travelers—Fiction.   I. Title.
PS3619.P438T46 2006
813'.6—dc22

2005044422

First Edition: August 2006

10 9 8 7 6 5 4 3 2 1

CGGG

For Jean, who inspired it:

More eunuchs, and the Sultana unwrapped

MAJOR CHARACTERS

The Dasanas:

LUCINDA DASANA — A young Portuguese woman raised in Goa; heir to the Dasana fortune

CARLOS DASANA — Lucinda's uncle, manager of the Dasana trading interests in Goa

GERALDO SILVEIRA — A profligate cousin of the Dasanas, and a distant heir

VICTORIO SOUZA — Lucinda's maternal uncle, manager of the Dasana trading interests in Bijapur

In the Caravan:

JEBTHA DA GAMA — A Portuguese settlement man, often called Deoga

KURSHID PATHAN	A *burak* of Bijapur, sometimes called Munna
SLIPPER	A eunuch
MAYA	A young temple dancer (*devadasi*), recently enslaved, a nautch girl

In Goa:

HELENE	Lucinda's maid
CARVALLO	General secretary to the Dasanas
ADOLFO	Carlos Dasana's valet

In Valpoi:

FERNANDO ANALA	A Christian trader. Also called Brother Fernando
SILVIA ANALA	His wife

In Belgaum:

LADY CHITRA	Mistress of the Lake Palace, former concubine to the sultan of Bijapur
LAKSHMI	Chitra's companion, a child

In Bijapur:

SHAHJI	General commander of Bijapur's armies
WHISPER	An old eunuch. The Royal Khaswajara (manager of the royal household)
WALI KHAN	The grand vizier, chief minister to the Sultana
MOUSE	A eunuch in service to Victorio Souza
THE SULTANA	Widow of the former sultan
IBRAHIM ADIL	The heir to the throne of Bijapur, a boy

Others:

GUNGAMA	Maya's guru, thought to be drowned, now appearing in dreams
BANDITS	Of the Three-dot clan and of the Naga clan
A CHEAP JEWELER	In Bijapur
SHAHEEN	Pathan's housekeeper and steward

AUTHOR'S NOTE

In India, all journeys change the traveler.

This novel tells of a journey between Goa and Bijapur, a journey I made myself a few years ago. Shepherds still walk the old roads through Sansagar Pass. The golden bell of Santa Catarina still rings. Fullers still spread the bright silks of Belgaum along the lakeshore. Beneath the great dome of the Gol Gombaz, schoolchildren play in the whisper gallery.

But in the course of three centuries, much has been lost. To build their navies, the Portuguese, Dutch, and English cut down the great teak forests that dominated the Deccan Plateau. That changed the weather: Gokak Falls no longer roars. The steps of the old temples around Lake Belgaum now lead to dry ground instead of water. Instead of palaces, only piles of stone remain.

This story is part of a larger epic that took more than twenty years to write—the history of the final years of the Mogul Empire and the rise of the Marathis under the highwayman Shivaji. The first volume of that epic topped 2,400 manuscipt pages. With the help of my agent, Jean Naggar, and the skillful efforts of Maureen Baron, I managed to pare that down to about 800.

But it broke my heart! Da Gama, Lucinda, Pathan, Slipper, and Mouse called to me from the discarded pages. Happily, Jean suggested a framework for that story, and encouraged me to write it as a separate book, and St. Martin's Press agreed to publish it as an introduction to the larger epic.

Researching this novel proved difficult. Source documents on the Moguls and Marathis abound—victors love writing history. But the losers remain silent—and by 1657, Portuguese India had been crushed, and Bijapur was failing. No one writes tales of their defeat.

I based my picture of Bijapur on Mogul records that were clearly biased. Lacking firsthand accounts of Goan society, I sought help from transport records, which were carefully preserved and provided knowledge of living conditions in 1657. My firsthand examination of period artifacts and architecture led to many aspects of the way I depict Portuguese and Bijapuri culture.

I based Lucinda's clothing on the styles of Lisbon society in 1648–50, since it would take a few years for fashion to reach Goa. The dress and deportment of other characters were inspired by contemporary paintings, and by source descriptions of Portuguese traders at the Mogul court.

The use of cosmetic arsenic as a murder weapon was inspired by a series of killings in the English colony of Jamestown a few years before the time of this story. The Flying Palace was inspired by a 1712 woodcut in an exhibit at the Berlin Dahlem gallery.

The prosecution of the Pepper Wars is described in an excellent monograph by Alfons van der Kraan: *A Baptism of Fire: The Van Goens Mission to Ceylon and India, 1653–54.* Interested readers may also enjoy the fascinating *Sufis of Bijapur, 1300–1700: Social Roles of Sufis in Medieval India* by Richard Maxwell.

My descriptions of Maya's dancing may not square with current versions of "Bharatnatayam," but in fact that school of dance is of rather recent origin—the British wiped out Indian dance, and its current "classic" form is only a reconstruction based on sculptures and the written word. There is reason to believe that dance in 1657 was far more flamboyant than its staid reconstruction.

I have freely included some historic personages in this story, notably the Sultana, Wali Khan, and Shahji. The other characters are entirely fictional.

A novel such as this cannot be written without help. My writing coach,

Michael Wolf, the greatest listener I have ever found, helped me to realize the themes that drive my tale, and my fellow authors at his writer's workshops, with their demanding critiques, inspired me to do my very best. My driver, guide, and friend, Ali Akbar, showed me his India, a magical and difficult place most westerners never see, and opened the doors of mystic Islam; I hope he will forgive me for basing Pathan on him. To them all I extend my totally inadequate thanks.

My wife, Barbara, gave me the greatest gifts of all. I am in awe of her unflagging confidence and insightful comments. Most important, she creates in this turbulent world a home of beauty and serenity—a creation that inspired the Lake Palace of Belgaum. Ultimately this book would not have existed without her.

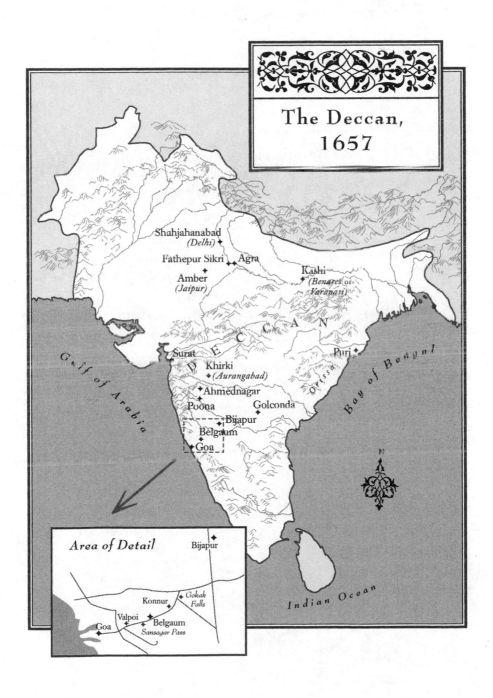

The Deccan, 1657

Shahjahanabad
(Delhi)

Fathepur Sikri   Agra

Amber
(Jaipur)   Kashi
                        (Benares or
                         Varanasi)

D E C C A N

Surat

Khirki
(Aurangabad)

Ahmednagar

Poona   Golconda

Bijapur

Belgaum

Goa

Gulf of Arabia

Orissa

Puri

Bay of Bengal

Indian Ocean

Area of Detail   Bijapur

                 Gokak
         Konnur   Falls

Valpoi

Goa   Belgaum
         Sansagar Pass

Part One

The Howdah

PORTUGUESE CANTONMENT
Goa, India
1657

Satisfied that her face looked perfect, Lucinda Teresa Emilia Dasana dipped a pheasant's tail feather into a crystal vial and touched a milky drop of belladonna to the corner of each eye. "Aya," she said, dabbing at a tear before it stained her powdered cheek, "I can't find my *arsênico.*"

Across the room, her maid folded Lucinda's dressing gown. "It's all gone, my *bebê.* I meant to tell you."

Lucinda, blinking as the belladonna blurred her eyes, bit her bottom lip in frustration. Then she smiled patiently at her maid, not knowing that one of her front teeth was speckled with vermilion. "Aya, the box was right here. Where have you hidden it?"

The maid, Helene, as if unaware that Lucinda could not see, shook her head and kept on folding. "You should not be using that terrible paste, little one. It is very bad for you. Better that it's gone."

"I'm not your little one anymore. I'm a woman. A lady. And you are my maid now, no longer my nurse. So bring me my *arsênico,*" Lucinda said.

Helene, whose name before she became a Christian had been Ambalika, muttered something in Hindi. "I am not a bitch in heat," Lucinda whispered angrily. "And I have said, we will speak only Portuguese. Now bring it."

Helene looked suddenly very old. Lucinda, her eyes blurred by belladonna, did not see this change, but she heard Helene's weary sigh. Lucinda's heart ached, but she remembered herself, and her new station in the world, and said nothing. Helene, meanwhile, reached beneath the feather mattress and brought out a tiny silver box. "Don't use too much, please," Helene said in Portuguese.

"I'll use what I want," Lucinda answered, and took such a large pinch of the red paste that Helene gasped. Having gotten the effect she wanted, however, Lucinda only touched a little to her tongue. "There."

"You shouldn't take this poison. If your mother were here! That red stuff only will make you sick and you are so beautiful without it."

"You only say that because you love me. I need it—I must not be seen with dark skin."

"What's wrong with dark skin?"

Lucinda lowered her eyes, regretting her words, for of course Helene was dark as shadow. "I'm sorry, dear one," Lucinda said in Hindi, and though Lucinda could not see it, Helene smiled. "You know my cousin has just come from Macao. I haven't seen him in years," she went on in Portuguese. "I must look my best. It's fashionable to be pale. All the Lisbon ladies use *arsênico* these days."

Helene snorted. "So they are pale, yes. But they are not pretty, not like my *bebê*. Why all this fuss over a cousin? What would your mother say, our lady rest her soul? You are pledged! If your father were alive . . ."

But Lucinda had stopped paying attention. Through the window that looked to the sea, a salt breeze carried the sounds of Goa: the cries of street merchants in Hindi and Portuguese, the blare of gongs and drums from a nearby Shiva temple, and on top of all, the golden cathedral bell of Santa Catarina, tolling the hour.

The breeze whispered through Lucinda's upswept hair. She swirled a stiff silk shawl over her shoulders. "How do I look?"

Too young, thought Helene. Too young to wear a corset laced so tight, or a bodice cut so low. Oh, what will people think? The pupils of Lucinda's eyes, now huge from belladonna, glistened: dark, inviting, like hidden pools lit by moonlight. "I suppose you look all right," Helene said at last.

But Lucinda had not waited. Already she had found the door, already reached the stairs to her uncle's office. Until her father's death the year before, the halls had glowed, bathed in lamplight. But the arrival of Uncle Carlos changed all that. He hated waste; he would stamp through the halls, snuffing out candles with his fingertips. "Thrift!" he'd shout to anyone in earshot. "Economy!" But in the dimness, Lucinda's deliciously dilated eyes could see perfectly. Still, she edged forward with one hand pressed against the wood-paneled walls, for the *arsênico* was making her feel light-headed.

◉◉◉◉

Carlos Dasana glared across his table, awash with papers, and wagged a heavy finger at his young relation. "Don't you realize the trouble you are in?"

Geraldo Silveira shifted in the hard wooden seat—perhaps to adjust his coat, perhaps to hide the amusement in his eyes. His long fingers played with the lace cuffs of his shirt. "I apologize, Tio Carlos . . ."

"Don't insult me with your apologies! You killed a man, Aldo! You can't apologize for murder! Dueling in the streets! They hang men for this!" Carlos pounded on the heavy wooden table so hard that a pile of papers bounced into the air. "And the husband you killed was your own cousin!"

"I only found that out after, Tio. I apolog . . ."

"For the love of God, hold your tongue! If it had not been for me, Aldo, you'd be locked in the stocks, getting your feet roasted. And then to Lisbon and the gallows, that's what. You owe me a debt!"

Carlos drummed his fingers on the dark wood table and considered the young man. "You're too handsome. You've been spoiled. All mothers spoil their children, but my cousin went too far, rest her soul. And your useless father . . ."

"He was a good man, Tio." Geraldo's eyes flashed, but he kept his voice calm. "You can't blame him."

"Did I ask your opinion? I'll blame who I wish! Your father was a rounder and a fool. Like you, too handsome for his own good. Learn from his mistakes, Aldo." The older man stopped glaring at the youth and tugged his mustache. "But I blame myself as well. I have indulged you too much. I should have . . ."

Carlos Dasana stopped short, rubbed his brow with his heavy fingers, and sighed. "You can't live like you have no future, Aldo! Keep your *fonte* in your pants. You can't bed every woman you see just because you get a tingle. Not if they're married, for the love of the Virgin! Those you keep your hands off! Otherwise people end up dead!"

"With luck, only the husband, Tio."

Carlos Dasana's eyes bulged, and a vein began to pulse across his forehead. Geraldo leaned forward, worried that he might have a fit, when Dasana burst out with a roaring laugh. "Only the husband, eh?" He struggled to frown. "Why not take a bayadere, for the love of the Virgin? They're cheap enough, and better than any wife, eh?"

Geraldo leaned back and looked straight into the older man's eyes. "Where's the sport, Uncle?" His sharp face slowly opened into a sly grin.

Ah, he's a Dasana, all right, Carlos thought. "Look here, Aldo, I've intervened on your behalf. You've been placed in my custody. Sent to Goa instead of to the gallows."

Geraldo lowered his head. "Tio Carlos, I wish to thank you . . ."

Carlos snorted. "Don't. Before you're done, you might wish for the gallows! To be frank, you couldn't have come to Goa at a worse time." He leaned back in his chair. "After twenty years of combat, the Pepper Wars are over, Aldo, and the blasted Dutch have won."

"You can't be serious. Surely the Portuguse fleet . . ."

The old man sputtered. "The fleet? Have you looked in the harbor? Do you see a fleet anywhere? They're gone! Gone to Brazil! We've handed all Asia to the Dutch, but now, now we must do everything to save precious Brazil! Face facts, Aldo! Lisbon has abandoned us! Goa is lost! The Dutch have strangled us. Only a few *dhows* will even try to run that blockade."

Carlos Dasana shook his head. "Our countrymen flee like rats. They take what they can carry and run, the cowards. Only a few hundred Portuguese remain in Goa. Even the goddammed priests have gone, most of them."

Dasana hesitated, as if his next thoughts were too painful to voice. Geraldo seemed to sense this. He leaned across the table. "Come, Tio. I am not a child to be toyed with, nor did you bring me here from kindness. What do you need of me?"

Carlos blinked and bit his lip. "You're right. I need someone I can trust. Someone of my blood. The Pepper Wars have wiped us out. The Dasanas are near ruin."

It took a moment before Geraldo could reply. "I don't believe it!"

"My brother, rest his soul, made a mess of things. I don't know if I can repair them. We're out of cash. We have goods, Lord yes! Factors full of goods. But the Dutch have us by the balls. We can't trade, Aldo, and without trade we're dying." Dasana leaned close to him, his voice now a harsh whisper. "How much do you know about the country of Bijapur?"

"Those Muslim devils? Only that they have been our enemies for a hundred years. First those infidels surrendered Goa to us, and then they attacked us! They massacred our colonists, and they slaughtered our women . . ."

Dasana waved his hand. "That's in the past. Forgive and forget."

"Tio Carlos!"

"Enemies are a luxury for the rich, Aldo. We're broke. We'll take all the friends we can buy. Now, listen, Aldo, listen well. We have one chance to change things." Carlos glanced around the room, as though spies might be anywhere. "The sultan of Bijapur died about a year ago. His heir's only nine years old. Bijapur's gone mad. The widow queen, the Sultana, has come out of the harem to try to rule. It's unheard of . . . a complete disaster. So now the Sultana has agreed to appoint a regent, and there lies all our hope." The older man arranged himself in his chair. "This is why I have brought you here. I have a job for you, Aldo."

Geraldo sat up straight, eyes hooded and watchful. Carlos noted this, and continued: "The Dasanas have one final throw. If our man becomes regent, he'll give us a trade monopoly in Bijapur for eight years."

"Our man? Who is our man?"

"Wali Khan, the grand vizier of Bijapur." Carlos bit his lip. "He should get the regency. He should—but it won't be easy. He's got the Sultana to contend with, and she's a handful. And then there's the army—armies are always a problem—but this is even worse because the commander's a Hindi, and Hindis are unpredictable. Worst of all: eunuchs. The Khaswajara is a eunuch. He'll have all his brothers plotting for him. Even so, despite it all, Wali Khan will win. He should win. He must."

"What have you done to persuade him, Tio Carlos? How have you brought him to our side?"

"Do you think it was easy? *Baksheesh*. Bribing. There is no other way. . . . Wali Khan is too powerful to threaten. So it must be a bribe, and a great one. The man has refined tastes. The bribe must inspire him, not insult him." Carlos allowed himself a small smile. "We've managed to procure a certain item for him—something unique. Something he covets. Aye, something he covets more than life. A half a *lakh* of hun we paid—that's equivalent to forty thousand rials." Geraldo's eyes grew wide.

"Our bribe comes all the way from Orissa, Aldo—that's the length we've gone to get it—and arrives by dhow today if the wind is right. Then off to Bijapur within the week. I want you to go with the caravan. We've hired the best settlement man in Hindustan—a fellow named Da Gama. You may have met him, he's a distant relation." Geraldo shook his head. "Well, Da Gama's the best: he's honest, he's dull, he has no imagination or ambition, but he's deadly and ready for violence."

"He sounds a perfect fit, Tio."

"Dammit, Aldo—I'm relying on you! I need you to keep your eyes open."

Geraldo lowered his head so Carlos could not see his smile. "I shall study him, Tio."

Carlos gave him a withering look, as if doubting that Geraldo had ever studied in his life. He sighed. "I'm going to have to shut down this house. For a while, at least. We'll lose face, of course, but it can't be helped."

"You're returning to Lisbon?"

"Not to Lisbon. To Bijapur. Like it or not, the fates of the Dasanas are intertwined with our old enemies." Carlos looked into his nephew's eyes with unexpected frankness. "I don't know how I'm going to tell Lucinda. She's lost her mother, her father—now to lose her home . . ."

"But isn't Lucinda pledged to be married?"

"That's off!" Carlos barked. "The bastard heard about our business problems and . . ." Carlos's voice broke off suddenly. Geraldo thought he was choking. "I love that sweet girl," Carlos mumbled. He tugged a dark kerchief from his sleeve, wiped his eyes, and gave his nose a shaking blow. "You must not say anything to her, Aldo. Not a word about the bastard dropping the engagement. I'll tell her when the time is right. And nothing about moving to Bijapur, either! She'd rather die than leave Goa." Carlos examined the kerchief and then wiped his eyes. "Keep your mouth shut around her, do you hear? She's fragile. She's become as a daughter to me."

Again Carlos blew his nose, but this time, to Geraldo's relief, he stuffed his kerchief away without a glance. "Well, it's business. It can't be helped. In the meantime, you'll accompany the bribe to Wali Khan. You and the settlement man. That's why I brought you here. Don't fail me. Earn my trust. Succeed and you'll have my gratitude. Fail, and I'll send you to Lisbon and the gallows. Do we understand each other?"

Geraldo nodded.

"Very well. I'll say no more. You're my cousin's only son. Who else can I trust? We need that monopoly . . . and the bribe is the key! Our only hope is getting her to Wali Khan. She's worth a fortune, so keep your eyes open! Tell Wali Khan that if he becomes regent, then she's all his."

Geraldo's brow furrowed. "She? Do you mean a ship, Uncle?"

"Not a ship—what gave you that idea? I mean the bribe! She's a bayadere, boy . . . a nautch girl, the finest whore that's ever been!"

❧❧❧

The door opened, and as a wave crashes on the shore, Lucinda burst in, her white dress an explosion of brightness in Tio Carlos's dark office. A fragrance of jasmine and roses surrounded her as she floated across the carpet on silk-slippered feet. At the door, a sheepish-looking secretary lifted his hands hopelessly and Carlos shook his head and waved the man away. They had as much hope of stopping a cyclone.

"Uncle, dearest!" Lucinda sang, swirling toward the table. The old man rose and placed a respectable kiss on his niece's proffered cheek. "And this must be Geraldo!"

"Yes, I've just come from Macao," said Geraldo, standing.

"This is your cousin, Lucinda Dasana," Carlos said formally. His brow furrowed at seeing them together.

Geraldo swept into a bow. Lucinda returned a long curtsy, but though she lowered her head, her eyes stayed fixed on her cousin's face. Her vision was still blurred by the belladonna, but in the dark room she noted that he was tall, that his shoulders were wide and his hips narrow, that his face was tanned but his eyes sparkled, that his teeth when he smiled were brilliant white.

"I should never have known you," Geraldo said, his gaze roaming over her. "You were six when last we met. I put a toad down your dress, if I remember right." His eyes gleamed when he said this and she blushed.

"I'm sure you never did, or I'd remember and hate you. Anyway I'm grown now." Lucinda laughed, turning so the pale light of the office's single window caught her face.

"Remember, she's pledged," Carlos said pointedly, "so don't get any ideas."

"Uncle!" cried Lucinda. "We're cousins."

Geraldo seemed to have thought about the question. "Technically, she's right—we are cousins, but many, many times removed. We might even marry if we wished." His dark eyes peered deep into Lucinda's.

"I said she's pledged," Carlos said firmly. "Remember what I told you!"

"Who is the lucky man?" Geraldo asked. His eyes danced so when he asked that his question seemed impertinent. Lucinda turned away again, her face burning.

"Marques Oliveira, a former minister to his majesty," Carlos answered for her, a hint of warning in his voice. "A great man."

"I hope he is handsome," Geraldo said. "A woman like you deserves a handsome husband."

"His portrait is handsome," Lucinda stammered. "We haven't actually met."

Carlos didn't like the turn of this talk. "Of course he's handsome! He's rich, isn't he?"

"My very best wishes," Geraldo said. But this time when he bowed he fastened his eyes on her, and this time, through her misty eyes, she looked back. As he swept upward Aldo grasped her hand like a tiny bird in his long fingers and gently brushed it with his lips. "Let us be good friends, cousin, now that we have found each other once again." She felt his mustache tickling her knuckles. "I'm about to go to Bijapur. Would you like to come along?"

Carlos sputtered as he leaned over his desk. "What are you saying, Aldo? I never . . ."

But Lucinda had already heard, and when she turned to Tio Carlos, her face pale with *arsênico* and her eyes limpid with belladonna, beseeching him, it was more than any uncle could resist, even an uncle as strong-willed as Carlos Dasana. "Please, Uncle, please. You promised I could visit Tio Victorio!"

It was a good idea, Carlos had to admit: sending her to Bijapur now would make it simpler to close down the house. But he disliked any idea he had not thought up himself. So of course Carlos said no at once. Then no again, and then once more, no.

The trip would not be easy, Carlos warned. And Bijapur was not like Goa. Victorio, her uncle who managed the Dasanas' Bijapur factor, was old now and often ill. These objections merely fired Lucinda's resolve. One by one Geraldo countered them, and each time Lucinda would beg again, each time more plaintively than before.

"Very well, little one. You may go. But you'll do what you're told, yes? And follow orders for a change?"

"Oh yes, Tio Carlos," Lucinda answered, tiptoeing to kiss his rough brown cheek.

Then the *arsênico,* or her corset, or the excitement seemed to overwhelm her, and her pale face grew even paler, and her eyes fluttered, and she fainted into her uncle's arms.

My God, thought Carlos as he caught her, she looks pale as death. By the Blessed Virgin, he thought as her breasts heaved and her dark curls spilled across his arms, she's a grown woman. You truly are a Dasana, my dear niece, he thought; and the Dasana women are as beautiful and dangerous as gold.

He glanced at Aldo, and then back at Lucinda who even now was stirring in his arms. What have I agreed to? Carlos thought.

May the Blessed Virgin save us from our relatives.

☙☙☙☙

The shallow-keeled dhow scudded over the gray seas, clinging to the rock-edged shore. The captain's eyes were everywhere: to the dark and threatening sky and the twisting monsoon winds, then on the steersman beside him, pressed hard against the shuddering rudder, to the triangle sail that furled and luffed as his sailors heaved the boom, and again and yet again upon the thirty-gun privateer at the harbor mouth, its tricolor flag bright against the black clouds.

Would she follow? Would she fire? As the dhow swung into the harbor and the waves of the Arabian Sea tried to hammer it against the moss-furred rocks of Arguin, the captain peered at the warship. If she was turning to fire, there was little he could do. The Goans wouldn't help him—they had no ships to fight her.

"She's turning away, Captain!" the steersman cried at last.

The captain watched a long time before he accepted the steersman's conclusion. "Yes, Allah be praised! Bring us to Goa quick as you can and get us away from these damned rocks." The captain couldn't hide his relief. He moved to the forward hatch and shouted down. "Senhor Da Gama! We've made it! We're through! You can come up, now. All of you can come up!"

A pair of shrewd brown eyes appeared in the shadows below, and a burly Portuguese *soldado* clambered up to the deck. The captain placed a hand beneath his arm, but Da Gama shook it off. He carried a wide-brimmed hat. "Where are they?" he asked. The captain pointed to where the privateer had turned south at full sail.

"She's heading for Malabar, I bet," the captain said. "They can't see us from here. In any case, we'll be in range of Goa's guns before they can reach us. We're safe as we'll ever be."

Da Gama's leathered face followed the Dutch privateer with a cautious, irritated look. When he at last felt sure of the captain's reasoning, he jammed the hat on his dark, graying hair. "You were right, Captain," Da Gama said with a bow. "I should never have doubted you."

The captain acknowledged the farang with a nod and a shrug. "The Dutch don't care about an old dhow, so long as they don't see any Portuguese on deck. I tell you, the Pepper Wars are over, senhor."

"Maybe," Da Gama answered as respectfully as he could. But I'd like to see a treaty first, he thought. His heavy boots clattered on the teak deck as he stomped to the stern. With a nod toward the steersman, he looked back across the gray-green Sea of Arabia, where waves crashed against the jagged rocks of the harbor mouth.

Bright green against the dark sky, coconut palms swayed in the monsoon winds that swirled beneath threatening clouds. Any minute another deluge might start. Da Gama took off his hat and leaned into the breeze. But when the steersman lifted his chin toward a cluster of gulls soaring just overhead, Da Gama jammed his hat back on. The last thing he needed now was gull shit in his hair.

At last, as if he'd come to some decision, he turned his back to the wind, and faced his destination: the bright walls of Goa.

For the first time in his life the sight of Goa left him cold. How many years had he been in Hindustan now—twenty-five? Twenty-seven? And never a trip back to Lisbon . . . no, he'd never looked back. But Hindustan grew tiresome, more trouble-filled each day.

Da Gama knew that this moment would be the last time he'd be able to relax for a long while—once the dhow landed, he'd be in a constant flurry of tedious, irritating activity. Such was the life of a settlement man. He worried that he was getting too old for so much trouble, and worried also that he was too poor to stop.

He turned to face the prow, and his hand flew to his *pistola*. Where he had expected to see the gates of Goa he found instead a one-eyed gull floating inches from his nose. The old steersman cackled. "Go ahead and shoot him, senhor! Maybe it will scare his friends away. I'm sick of their mess! It's easier to clean their blood than to clean their shit!"

Da Gama cursed, pushed the gun back in his belt, and batted a fist at the gull's yellow bill. The old bird gave a nonchalant flap and rose sarcastically just out of reach, to join a dozen other gulls that hovered overhead. With beaks open to the sea wind exposing blood-red tongues, the gulls hung motionless above him as dangerous as knives, a few yards from Da Gama's unprotected face.

He hated the gulls of Goa: their piercing eyes, their bellies black with salt mud, their cawing as harsh as an open wound. They reminded him of the palsied beggars who stalked the urine-soaked streets of Lisbon. As a boy he'd been their perfect target. He ran, he hid, but even so, the boy Da Gama often found himself surrounded by shattered, angry faces, his trembling hand shaking cruzados into their snatching fingers.

But he was far away from Lisbon now, and dangerous now himself. He carried six double-barreled *pistolas* on his wide belt and was so fast with them and accurate that he could have killed a dozen gulls before the first dead wings flopped to the deck.

Still he hated the gulls of Goa. They were but the first of Goa's troubles. Goa was ringed with troubles, like the circles of hell.

❧❧❧❧

The dhow approached the docks. As the steersman tacked against the wind to slow it, it began to shriek like an old lady in ecstasy. The ship was, after all, only teak timbers lashed together with ropes of hemp.

Da Gama leaned against the railing, watching the captain bark out orders. From time to time he snapped a leather thong for emphasis. Sailors scurried in practiced chaos. Soon the ship groaned against the worn pilings of the pier. Da Gama turned and waved at a cluster of ragged boys waiting expectantly at the dock. The birds flapped off, disappointed.

"*Baksheesh! Baksheesh!*" the boys cried, extending their hands. "Christian!" they cried, when they saw he was a farang, pointing to wooden crosses they'd strung around their necks. They'd seen plenty of farangs before.

"Fetch me three *palkis*!" Da Gama shouted. "Good ones!" He tossed a *tanga* toward the boys, as a man might skip a stone. They all ran off at once, snatching at the boy who'd caught the coin. Da Gama knew they'd soon be back; dozens of palanquins would be waiting for him on the dock, with boys and bearers with hands out for *baksheesh*; just as he knew without looking how the steersman now eyed him, hoping for *baksheesh* as well.

Baksheesh be damned, Da Gama thought. In Hindustan, everyone stuck out his hand. At first it had been only Hindis, but now even farangs had caught the disease. And there was never an end, never! Give the watchman a tanga for opening a door, and he'd stick out his hand again for closing it behind you.

Nowhere was the practice more obnoxious than Goa.

In Goa, *baksheesh* was no longer a request; it was a demand, even a threat. One had to think ahead: Am I likely to see you again? the diner must consider as he looks at the waiter. Do I really want to find a glob of your phlegm clinging to my tankard next time I drink here?

Already the cargo hatch was open. Thin, bare-chested Hindis humped great sacks of Cochin peppercorns from below, while the captain watched and swore. With each thump as they landed on the deck, the sacks exhaled a spicy, tang-filled cloud. A young sailor began to sneeze, and the old hands laughed.

Da Gama moved to the rear hatch and called, "Senhor Slipper, come up! We've docked!" The only answer was a miserable, high-pitched moan. Da Gama chuckled. "You'll feel better once you're on land, senhor!"

Da Gama glanced along the docks. Two elephants walked in lazy unison through the city gate, their mahouts ignoring the curses of the oxcart drivers stuck behind them unable to pass.

Without waiting for the gangplank, Da Gama leaped to the pier. Nearby a sailor eyed him icily—the gangplankwallah, no doubt, now realizing that

Da Gama's jump had just cheated him of his *baksheesh*. He didn't think I'd make it, Da Gama thought, pleased with himself.

On the dock a gaggle of boys mobbed Da Gama. They pointed to the crosses hanging from strings on their necks. "Hello, brother! Hello, Christian!" they shouted in Portuguese. They pointed to the palanquins, whose bearers waited eagerly beside them. "*Palki* to city only three rials! Christian!"

"Two rupees only!" Da Gama roared in Hindi. Some of the boys cowered in surprise; others more insistent pressed closer, holding up their crucifixes. Da Gama scowled, pushing through them. He strode down the pier, past mounds of shiny green-skinned coconuts stacked like polished cannon-balls, past gulls arguing with skinny cows over some scrap of garbage. Thin, dark-faced men with fierce, determined eyes staggered past, backs bent beneath huge gunnysacks holding twice their weight of cinnamon.

Da Gama frowned. The port was busy, to be sure, but not as busy as it ought to be. If he needed further proof that the Dutch were strangling the Portuguese trade, here it was: the dismal movement on the dock, far slower than it should have been, particularly at this time of year, right after the monsoons. The pier should be sagging with goods. But no.

Suddenly Da Gama found himself surrounded by the dock boys, who swept him as in a wave toward the palanquins. As the *palki*wallahs called and gestured, Da Gama noticed a tall, turbaned Muslim watching the scene with dry amusement from a few yards off. "Pathan!" Da Gama shouted, spreading his arms with delight.

With the *palki*wallahs and boys following, Da Gama strode over and gave Pathan a bear hug. The Muslim was tall, and Da Gama's wide-brimmed hat pushed into his face, which helped him disguise his pleasure. "*A salaam aleichem,*" Pathan whispered.

"And what am I to say now? *Aleichem salaam?*" Da Gama laughed. Of course he knew the answer.

The clamor of the boys and *palki* bearers around them grew unbearable. Pathan glared at the crowd. With just his look the turmoil stopped, and one by one the boys and men stepped back.

"How do you do that? I can never make them go away!" Da Gama said.

"They think you are not dangerous, sir," Pathan replied. "If they knew you as I do, you would have no difficulty."

Da Gama shrugged. "That explains it. When I was your age I was dangerous, maybe. Now I'm just an old man. They see right through me . . . while you are still blinded by excessive respect." Pathan bowed his head politely. "I see you are too courteous even to laugh at my jokes. Now tell me, friend, what brings you to this godless city?"

Pathan's face revealed little. "That which brings you, sir, brings me as well," he answered.

Da Gama frowned. "I'm only here to do a settlement for the Dasanas."

"I am here for that same settlement," Pathan said quietly. He stared blankly into Da Gama's frown.

"The settlement in Bijapur? You're the *burak*?"

"Yes. For the grand vizier, yes," Pathan answered. Da Gama nodded. "Both you and I, sir, chosen for this same settlement." The Muslim watched Da Gama for his reaction.

"The thought worries me."

"It worries me as well, sir. Though I lack your experience, I too have a reputation, undeserved as it may be. And I did not expect to find you here." He lowered his turbaned head. "But the journey may prove diverting. Perhaps I shall find some way to repay my debt to you."

Da Gama snorted. "That again? How long will you plague me with your gratitude? I told you, it was nothing. A trifle. Any man would have done the same." Pathan lifted his head. "Now tell me, what do you know about the settlement?"

"Very little. The grand vizier said I was to be sure the goods arrived intact. He would say no more. He is cautious of spies."

Da Gama gave a low whistle. "Ah, my friend, my friend, my friend. The wind has blown trouble your way." He nodded toward the dhow. "Here comes our problem now."

A short, heavy ball of a man stumbled down the gangplank. Though he reached out for help, none of the sailors offered a hand.

"What, him?" asked Pathan.

"No." Da Gama lifted his chin toward the deck. "Her."

ᴄᴏᴄᴏ

She was small, but the sunlight glancing from her silver shawl gave her a regal grandeur. As she turned, the sea breeze pressed against her silken garments, revealing for an instant each curve of her body. The sailors on the deck rose as she passed. When she reached the gangplank, a half-dozen hands went out to help, but she needed none. She smiled her thanks and stepped from the dhow with stately grace.

The small fat man bounced down the pier in front of her, his clumsiness exaggerated by the woman's flowing steps. The cinnamon bearers dropped their sacks and gaped; the cows lifted their sad eyes to watch; gulls flapped into the air and hovered around her head like attendants.

Da Gama alone seemed unaffected. He strode toward the *palkis*—no one now seemed to notice him—chose one at random and clapped its roof noisily, calling out, "Hey! Whose *palki* is this? Hey!" As if sleepwalking a half-dozen bearers stumbled toward him, eyes fixed all the while on the woman dressed in silver. Near the end of the pier the fat man's turban came undone. He stopped walking to rewind it, so now the woman came on alone.

As the glistening pulp of a ripe mango slips beneath its peel, her hips, round and luscious, swayed against her skirts. The dock fell silent except for the jingle of her ankle bells. She glanced into the eyes of every man she passed, a look both haughty and beckoning. Her long-lashed eyes, cinnamon-brown and flecked with gold, promised and teased

When she reached Da Gama, she looked at him as if there were no other man in all the world. The breeze carried a hint of her perfume. "Is this my *palki*, sir?" Though her face was young she had a woman's voice: dark, suggestive, twining like the tendrils of a vine. Every man close enough to hear could imagine her lips brushing his ear, whispering his name.

Da Gama reached out to her. Grasped by her hand so delicate, his fingers looked swollen and enormous. She slid into the palanquin like liquid, and tugged its curtains closed. As the *palki* bearers moved in a daze to take up their burden, Pathan made his way to Da Gama. "Her? Is she the one, sir?"

"Oh yes," Da Gama answered. "That's our problem."

۞۞۞

"But not Bijapur! You said we'd go to Lisbon, *bebê*. Bijapur! Why would anyone want to go to Bijapur? It is just like Goa, only uglier!"

"We're going, and that's that," Lucinda answered. "It is not your place to give opinions, Helene."

"Such words! It was I who brought you up!"

"I am a woman now, Aya. You must be more respectful." But Lucinda's voice was not too harsh, for from Helene's unending complaints she had gleaned much about Bijapur—about the cannon at its gate, bigger than a house; about the dome of Gol Gumbaz, largest in the world. These facts Lucinda would slip into her talk when in the company of Tio Carlos or cousin Geraldo.

"You know quite a lot for a girl who's never left Goa," Geraldo whispered. But something in the way he said it, in the luster of his bright black eyes, or the way the corner of his lip curled in a half smile, sent a tiny shiver through her, like he was talking of another kind of knowledge altogether. Often when they spoke she'd end up blushing.

But she had little time for socializing if she were to be ready in three days. From the storage barn, servants humped dusty trunks up the narrow staircase to her bedroom. "Only two, my dear cousin," Geraldo told her, and despite her protests and her pleading, she ended up sending all the rest back down, saving the two largest for the trip.

"I could fit my house in here," Helene complained, "and my brother and his family could fit into this other." But Lucinda wondered how she'd squeeze in everything she needed.

Petticoats, corsets, linens of all kinds—Helene took these folded from the dresser, unfolded each one with a shake, then muttering in Hindi, refolded and packed them. The dresses were brushed and wrapped in yards of muslin against the dust. Stockings and garters, and then shoes, shoes of all kinds. And bed linens, and towels, and precious soaps from Lisbon. "The Virgin knows what you will find in that heathen city, *bebê,*" Helene said. For Bijapur was a Muslim kingdom. Even so, Lucinda let out a little *hmmmph,* as though she were too sophisticated to care.

In truth, she'd seen only a few Muslims—pilgrims mostly, loading onto boats bound for Mecca, viewed from far away. Only three regularly visited her uncle's office. They always stared at her, and one—only one— bowed stiffly when he passed her in the hallway. It felt dangerous when they were about, like when the snake charmers sat outside your house and you worried that one of the cobras might escape. Lucinda would wait by the window in her room, staring down into the street until she saw them leave. They rode horses—muscular Bedouins with flaring nostrils and bright, skittish eyes and coats that glistened like they had just won a race.

One day, after growing frustrated with Helene's impossibly slow packing, Lucinda burst into her uncle's office. "But I can never be ready in time, Tio!" she cried, managing to squeeze out an affecting tear.

"Don't go then! All the better!" Carlos had answered. He said it sincerely, of course, but stiffly. His table was neat today, his shirt starched, and he sat upright in his seat. Lucinda looked around, suddenly aware that he had guests.

One was a Portuguese *soldado*—middle-aged, paunchy, with ill-kept clothing and an amused demeanor—who slouched casually in one of Carlos's big wooden chairs, a glass of brown wine balanced on the carved lion's head of the arm. He twisted around for a better look at Lucinda, lifting himself half-sideways with a nod and hearty grin, as though this were the best courtesy he could manage. A half-dozen *pistolas* poked out from his wide leather belt.

The other man was already on his feet: tall, slender with a face shaped like an almond, and skin the color of polished teak. He wore a tightly wound turban. His bright eyes and long, narrow nose made Lucinda think of a hunting bird. Lucinda tried to hide her surprise. The man was Muslim.

"Lucinda, please greet my guests. This is Captain Pathan, of the court of Bijapur." The Muslim lifted his folded hands to his chin. His face, Lucinda realized, had a self-important air that was really quite annoying. She made him a very brief curtsy, but he didn't seem to comprehend its hinted insult. Or if he did, he was too smug to care.

"You've met this other rascal before, though you probably were too young to remember."

"I knew your father, Lucy," the soldier growled, finally managing to place his well-worn boots on the floor, and approximate a gentleman's bow. "You were a baby. He was a good man. A great man. I see you've turned out well. Beautiful like your mother." She realized that his eyes, which had seemed sleepy when she first saw them, were shrewd and full of life. His face was so unguarded that she blinked and nearly forgot to curtsy in response.

"Watch out for him, niece, he's a charmer of the old school," her uncle laughed.

"But, Uncle, you haven't said his name," Lucinda said.

"Jebtha Albuquerque Da Gama at your service, Lucy," the man said, lifting his bowed head. "Or should I now say, Senhorita Dasana?" He took her hand in his sun-browned fist and kissed it with a tenderness she had not expected.

"I'd be pleased if you'd still call me Lucy," Lucinda said, surprising herself.

"Good, good," her uncle said, as if wanting to be on with business. "Well, now you've all met, and I daresay you'll know each other better by the end of the trip. But I forget—you can't manage to be ready in time? Wasn't that what you came to tell me?"

"Me? No, Tio Carlos! I'll be ready, of course! In fact, I must be going. So nice to meet you all!" Da Gama kissed his fingers in a wave as she left, but the Muslim, Captain Pathan, just stared at her, his lips pursed like he'd bitten something sour.

ⓒ๏ⓒ๏

On the eve of their departure, Carlos Dasana set a feast. Lucinda sat at the end of the table as hostess. As usual, Dasana's secretary, Carvallo, sat to her right, next to his fat wife, Maria, who had painted her face with oil and lead oxide. *Arsênico* could only do so much to improve the complexion, and past a certain point lead was needed, for it not only whitened the face, but was thick enough to fill the pits and gaps of age. Supposedly. Why doesn't she do something about her hair then, thought Lucinda—use a lead comb, at least, to darken the gray.

On her left sat the *soldado* she'd met a few days before, Da Gama, the adventurer who said he'd known her parents. He'd had a bath and a shave, and his queue was oiled and tied in a bow, but despite his clothing, which was proper, and his manners, which were pleasant, he looked out of place amid the china and crystal. He seemed almost to be seated in a taverna, as though the blown-glass goblet in his leathery hand were a metal tankard and the tiny roasted pigeon on his gilded plate were a haunch of boar.

At the other end of the table Tio Carlos sat next to Geraldo, who had the polished look of a man freshly barbered. From time to time he glanced Lucinda's way, arching an eyebrow or tilting his head as if to say—you and I, we understand, we two. Every time he did this, Lucinda gave a little start and forced herself to look elsewhere. It was as though he could see into her heart.

The party might have been perfect except for the last guest, who sat across from Geraldo, the Muslim captain Pathan. He perched uncomfortably on his chair, his head held higher than the others. Such a conceited man, Lucinda thought. He drank only water, frowning as the wine flowed freely at the table, and he seemed especially disturbed whenever Lucinda raised the wineglass to her lips. Why should I care what you think, Lucinda thought, glaring at him. Even so she watched in fascination while he ate, using only his fingers, but with more delicacy and refinement than some of the men who struggled with their forks.

"Senhor Dasana says that you're still worried about the arrangements," Carvallo said to Da Gama, talking past Lucinda.

"I'd prefer to be taking Portuguese *soldados.*"

"You won't need them. This is Hindustan, Da Gama—*baksheesh* means more than arms. You of all people should know that. Bribes are so much more effective than guns, particularly these days. Besides, the *burak* has four or five men with him."

"We should send our own men, and not rely on Muslims," Da Gama scowled.

"Well, you've got Geraldo. And you, of course, the great Deoga himself. Isn't that sufficient?"

Man-talk, Lucinda thought with a sigh. She took a long drink of wine and glanced at Pathan, realizing that he'd said not a word all evening. As if sensing her gaze, he looked back at her, and she saw his frown as he watched her drink. Smiling at him, she held out her goblet for a refill.

Suddenly she realized that the men were talking about Pathan.

"I don't understand why you're so concerned, Da Gama," Carvallo said. He seemed to be goading Da Gama.

"Because he's their best *burak.* They wouldn't have sent him unless they thought there'd be trouble."

Carvallo was about to speak. Then he thought better of it and dabbed his lips with a napkin. "And that's why we sent for you, sir. Aren't you supposed to be the best as well?"

"Maybe." Da Gama shook his head. "Maybe I'm not the best, just the last. Everyone else is gone, or dead."

"Gone where?" Lucinda said cheerily. This conversation was getting very dreary.

"Gone to Lisbon, Lucy," Da Gama answered. "Or to Macao, some of them. We're just handing Hindustan to the Dutch."

"Oh, Hindustan is so tiresome. I wonder what Macao is like?" Of course the men then began to tell her, and she nodded and laughed and shook her curls as though she cared. But her attention was suddenly brought back when Carvallo and Da Gama began whispering about Geraldo. Trying to be discreet, she listened hard.

"So Carlos paid off his Macao debts?" the *soldado* asked.

Carvallo, the perfect secretary, merely shrugged. "You'd be amazed if I told you what he owed. And he's run up more in Goa, if you can believe it, just in the few days he's been here."

Da Gama took a long pull of wine. "I remember being young," he said, smiling at Lucinda, who pretended to be uninterested. "What about his family?" Da Gama asked, but something in his manner made Lucinda wonder if he didn't already know.

"A bad lot, for the most part. They left him little, and what he had is gone, I expect."

"Well, it doesn't pay to be his relative, I can tell you that much," Da Gama said, leaning forward. "He's bad luck. People die around him. In Lisbon, three of his cousins died in one month." Carvallo raised an eyebrow, and Da Gama tilted his head for emphasis. "That man he killed in Macao was his great-uncle."

"But I heard he was a young man."

Da Gama leaned back, took a drink of wine and shrugged. "A distant relative. It's complicated. Genealogy's a hobby of mine."

This caught Lucinda's attention. "Why is that, senhor?"

Da Gama smiled and shook his head sheepishly. "Because of my name, Lucy. I had hopes, don't you know. I dreamed that I was related to Vasco Da Gama. I hoped I was a missing heir and unspeakably rich."

"And?"

"And I'm not," Da Gama said with dancing eyes. "I have the same name, Lucy, but a different family entirely. Related to the Dasanas, in fact. So while it is my good fortune to be your cousin, sadly, I must work for a living."

"Master Carlos plans to bring the boy into the business," Carvallo said after a pause, staring at Da Gama as if studying his reaction. "He'll stay in Bijapur and work with Master Victorio."

A darkness fell across the *soldado*'s face. "Tell him to watch his back," he said at last.

Whose back? Lucinda wondered. But just then Tio Carlos raised his glass. Servants scurried to fill the goblets of the others while Pathan glowered. "Tomorrow, you leave for Bijapur. May the Blessed Virgin grant a pleasant journey to you all!"

"Long life and health to you, Tio Carlos," Geraldo answered, clinking his uncle's glass. Around the table all lifted their goblets and mumbled agreement.

All but Pathan, who stared fiercely at his water glass and scowled.

That night Tio Carlos came down with a flux so terrible that a doctor was summoned, and later a priest. Lucinda heard the commotion and hurried to her uncle's room, but Carvallo assured her that she could do nothing. She saw Geraldo seated in a corner by the door, his face in turmoil. "He's shown such kindness to a poor orphan. What am I to do if he should die?" he said. She placed a hand on his shoulder. He grasped it, and lifted it to his cheek and then kissed it before looking away, his dark eyes brimming with tears.

By morning the household was in an uproar. Pathan had brought the caravan to the door at dawn, as originally planned. Of course an argument had started in the hallway, for the servants had decided on their own that the master was dying and the journey was off. "You must do something, *bebê*," Helene told her as Lucinda dressed.

Lucinda threw on a painted linen dressing gown as she looked through the window. Muslim horsemen stood in the street, along with several bullock carts. But they were dwarfed by a great bull elephant with banded tusks, his gilded headdress glittering in the morning sun. The curtained howdah on the elephant's back came up nearly to her window. It looked like a miniature house: its curved green roof held up by red lacquered uprights, its carvings gilded with gold leaf, its platform flowing in silks and edged by a railing of polished brass.

"What's all the fuss?" she said as she came down the narrow staircase.

"Ah, Mistress Dasana," Carvallo said. "Your Hindi is much better than mine. Explain to this numbskull that your uncle is sick and the departure must be postponed."

Lucinda felt small as she walked toward the *burak*. Pathan's robes were crisp and his sword hilt sparkled. His face, always dour, seemed to burn with resentment. She took a deep breath and stood as tall as she could. "Captain Pathan," she said in Hindi, "what Senhor Carvallo is trying to say . . ."

"I understand completely, madam," Pathan answered, his voice much softer and gentler than she expected. "But what can I do, I ask you? I have a duty to perform, do you see? If I succeed or if I fail, I care not. But I am told to leave today and duty compels me to try. Please forgive me if I disturb the peace of this house."

"What does he say?" Carvallo demanded, but for the moment Lucinda ignored him.

"Then you understand, Captain, that my uncle is near death, and we must postpone . . ."

"I understand nothing of the sort, madam. My men checked with the servants; they tell me that your uncle has much improved."

Lucinda looked at Pathan's steady gaze and found herself irritated once more by his smug demeanor. She was about to argue, but instead turned to Carvallo. "What is Tio Carlos's condition?" she asked in Portuguese.

Carvallo bowed, "Much better, senhorita."

"Then why do we postpone?"

Carvallo seemed taken aback. "It does not appear seemly, senhorita . . ."

"Has anyone asked your uncle's wishes, madam?" Pathan asked quietly in Hindi.

Now it was Lucinda's turn to be surprised. "I will do this," she answered. With a glance to Carvallo that she hoped would indicate her command of the situation, she burst inside and hurried upstairs.

She found Geraldo sleeping in a chair by her uncle's door. "He's been there all night," the valet, Adolfo, told her as he led Lucinda inside.

"Come in, niece," Carlos said. The wave of his hand seemed to take all his strength. His face was pale from being bled, but his eyes were bright and he beamed at her with love.

She explained the situation. "The caravan must leave at once," he told her. "Things are not good, and I fear any delay."

"Yes, Uncle," Lucinda answered, placing her hand on his. His skin felt thin, cool and slightly damp. He'd been cleaned, and his hair combed back, but even so a smell of vomit and feces hovered in the air. "We'll go then as you say."

"Wait," Carlos said placing his other hand on hers. She saw the white bandage on his forearm covering the wound where the doctor had bled him. "They thought I was dying last night. They said it was poison. Bah. Too much wine for an old man, that's all. But when the priest placed the chrism on my forehead, do you know what I thought?"

Lucinda hid her surprise. No one had told her about the priest. "What, Uncle?"

"Not about my sins or the Virgin. No, I thought about you." A tear glistened on his cheek. "You're so perfect, Lucy. So pure. Family is everything. I see that now more clearly than ever. You're all I've got now, dear one."

"And Geraldo, Uncle."

"What?" Carlos said, blinking as if he'd been asleep.

"Geraldo . . . He's family too, isn't he? And Victorio, your brother, don't forget him."

He stared at her for a long time before he finally answered. "My brother-in-law, yes." His hand moved from hers. "Yes. I only meant . . ."

"Yes, Uncle?"

He sighed and closed his eyes, and for a frightened moment Lucinda thought that he had died. Then he mumbled, "I thought you'd understand."

"I do," she answered.

Carlos waved his hand. "Go now. Carry my good wishes to Victorio. Enjoy your journey."

"Thank you, Tio Carlos." She leaned over and kissed his forehead.

"One thing," he gasped as she was about to leave. "Da Gama. Be careful. Don't trust him."

Lucinda started when she heard these words. She yearned to hear more, but she could see that her uncle was weak, too weak to talk, and if the truth were told, she was anxious to start her adventure. "Yes, Uncle," she said brightly. "I'll be fine."

Outside she shook Geraldo's shoulder. "Get up. We're leaving."

"Will he be all right?" Geraldo said, his face grave.

"It will take more than flux to kill Tio Carlos," she said. But Geraldo's face seemed full of worry, not relief.

ͼϿͼϿ

When a Goan said, "We'll leave at dawn," everyone understood it was a figure of speech. By the time goodbyes had been said and trunks unlocked once more to be stuffed with an assemblage of forgotten items, dawn had long passed. The Muslim horsemen had unfurled their prayer rugs toward a west-facing wall. Then the trunks had been loaded and tied onto the bullock carts, then untied and unloaded, and loaded once more, and now the sun was high and the animals thirsty and impatient.

She was so used to Goa and its cascade of unexpected delays that Lucinda couldn't understand Captain Pathan's increasing frustration. Pathan sent servants for water for the animals, but the Goans, used to a siesta, moved so slowly he at last sent his own men.

Then the elephant defecated in the street, and there was no one to clean it up, for Dasana's servants had by that time wisely disappeared to shady corners, and, after the insult of carrying water, the Muslim guards ignored their captain's soft request and he had not the heart to make it a command. Eventually some nobodies came and carried off the mess in wide baskets that they balanced on their heads, but the stink lingered.

Da Gama, who might have helped, for some reason sat in the shadow of a doorway, letting Pathan fend for himself. "He's had more luck so far than I would've, Lucy," he explained when Lucinda questioned him. He seemed amused by it all. Lucinda wondered if he'd been drinking.

As for Geraldo, after his sleepless night, he had given orders not to be disturbed until all was set, and napped in his room with the drapes closed.

As noontime came, instead of being on her way, Lucinda found herself arranging lunch for the travelers. Fortunately she stopped the servants before the platters of cold meats left the house, sending them back to the kitchen where she had the ham and beef placed on separate plates, for the Hindi Christians despite their conversion would not eat cow, and the Muslims would not eat pig. The Portuguese, of course, ate anything.

By the time the golden bell of Santa Catarina struck two, it seemed that all was prepared. She sent Helene to be sure everyone was gathered up for travel, and then Lucinda took a moment for herself and hurried back to her uncle's room. Before she turned the corner she heard shouting.

She nearly ran into Geraldo being shoved by Tio Carlos's angry valet. Despite Geraldo's size and strength, he seemed no match for the toothless valet's righteous anger. "Adolfo," Lucinda said. "Explain this!"

"He was trying to sneak into the master's bedroom, senhorita," Adolfo said, giving Geraldo's chest another angry push.

Geraldo, to Lucinda's surprise looked shocked, guilty even, not angry or amused as she would have expected. "I only wanted to say goodbye," he said, holding out his hands to her helplessly. "Who knows when I'll see Tio Carlos again?"

"He was up to no good," the valet insisted. "Look what I found on the floor by his feet!" Adolfo cried, opening his fist below Geraldo's nose, and then showing it to Lucinda: a tiny silver box.

"My *arsênico*!" Lucinda said.

"Poison!" Adolfo cried, waving the box. "Villainy!"

"So now you accuse Senhorita Dasana?" Geraldo said, snatching the box from the valet's palm. "You say my cousin poisoned our uncle?"

Adolfo's mouth formed into a wide, toothless O. "That's not what I meant!"

"Come with me, Lucy," Geraldo said, taking her arm firmly and guiding her away. Over his shoulder he called, "I will send a very stern letter to my uncle about this insult to his niece."

"Come back," Adolfo wailed, waving an empty fist.

"How old is that fool?" Geraldo said, his dark eyes burning.

"He must be sixty, maybe seventy years old."

"Well," Geraldo said with a sigh as if to calm himself. "Maybe that explains it."

"He's been with Tio Carlos for ages. Don't be too harsh with him."

"You're right, as usual, Lucy. I'll let it go this time." When he smiled, his teeth gleamed in the sunlight like pearls. "Forgive my temper. I care about you too much, I suppose." He pressed her arm gently, and handed her the box of *arsênico*. "This is yours, I think. I'll meet you downstairs."

As he strode off to his room, Lucinda tried to settle the jumble of her thoughts. And while an older or a wiser woman might have wondered about Geraldo and his sneaking, or the mysterious appearance of her silver box at Geraldo's feet, Lucinda's mind still reeled from the way he said he cared about her. The way he called her Lucy echoed in her ears just as a golden bell will vibrate softly for hours.

ଓଚ୍ଓ

At last all was ready. Lucinda was giving one last goodbye to Carvallo and his wife when she heard Helene screaming in Hindi near one of the bullock carts. A crowd formed, blocking her view, but she heard women's voices calling each other terrible names. Da Gama waved for her to come over.

There stood Helene, hands on hips and feet planted firmly on the ground, pointing and shouting at someone Lucinda could not well see. "She's your servant, Lucy," Da Gama said, urging her forward.

Lucy finally saw that the other figure, though it spoke with a woman's voice, was not a woman as she had supposed, not unless it was a woman dressed as a man, and a short and fat one at that.

"What's wrong, Helene?" she demanded in Portuguese.

Helene's face was twisted in anger and disgust. "First that jackal dog tells me I must ride like a sack of flour in a bullock cart!" she snapped back in coarse Hindi, pointing angrily at Captain Pathan, who stared skyward and said nothing. "Then they tell me I must ride with this *hijra*! I am not to be insulted so! Let her walk!"

"Please, Aya, please calm down," said Lucinda in Portuguese, walking toward her.

Helene pulled away. "*Nahin!*" she answered angrily. "I'll not travel with a *hijra*!" With that she crossed her arms and sat on the ground.

The other—man or woman, whichever it was—looked over to Lucinda with a round face full of hurt and sadness. "It is my cruel fate to be treated so, madam," the piping voice said—a voice, Lucinda thought, more like a child's than a woman's.

Of course, then she realized. In Hindi, *hijra* was a word said in answer; it meant "neither this nor that." Now as she looked at the strange figure standing sadly near her maid, it dawned on her. "*Hijra,*" she murmured.

"A *mukhunni*, madam, if you please," the figure said in offended Hindi, lifting his head high. "That is the proper term. I was a eunuch of the first rank in the seraglio of the sultan of Bijapur. And I am a he, obviously, not a she!" Helene rolled her eyes.

Not knowing what else to do, Lucinda made a small curtsy, which the eunuch answered by lifting his hands to his forehead. "Excuse my bad manners," she said, knowing from Helene's teaching that apologies were always the best place to start a conversation in Hindi. "You are the first . . . er . . ."

"*Mukhunni*, madam," the eunuch answered, lifting his head high and exposing a tiny neck. "It means 'short-tusked' and is the proper greeting for one deformed as I."

While he stared at her, Lucinda became aware that the circle that had formed to watch the argument had now begun to critique her. She could hear the whispers.

Her maid, seated grumpily on the ground. A eunuch dressed in silks, waiting proudly as if daring her to speak. The Muslim captain staring at her with disdain. The chuckling eyes of Da Gama. The whispers of the circle.

Would no one help her?

And just then she felt a firm hand grip her arm gently, and heard a whisper. "I'm here with you."

It was Geraldo.

Geraldo snapped his fingers at Helene. She looked up, offended. "Stand up, now, woman, and get into the cart as you're told," he said in perfect Hindi.

Helene's eyes grew wide. "Not with that *hijra*. I will not."

"You'll do what your mistress commands," Geraldo said. His voice, though soft, hinted at harsh action.

Now all eyes turned to Lucinda, who whispered to Geraldo, "But, cousin, why is that eunuch here?"

"He's here to look after the . . . the cargo," Geraldo whispered back.

Of course, Lucinda would later regret that she'd never inquired about the caravan's cargo. But on hearing Geraldo's reply, the answer to the problem burst into her head. "Very well then. If you will not ride together, then one of you must travel with the cargo."

At this Helene's eyes grew wide, but the eunuch, to Lucinda's amazement, burst into a wide, relieved smile. "Oh thank you, madam, thank you," he squeaked. He hurried off, but then returned and haltingly pressed Lucinda's hand between his chubby palms. "I never expected such courtesy from a farang. Forgive me." With that he puffed toward the elephant. Lucinda stared at her hand.

"As for you," Lucinda said to Helene, squeezing her face into a frown, "how dare you make such a scene in front of everyone? To refuse to ride with someone—why? Because he is a little different? Christian charity teaches us to love others, not condemn them." She might have said this in Portuguese, but instead she spoke plain Hindi, determined to embarrass Helene for her defiance. Helene glared back furious. Lucinda eyed her coldly. "We are none of us free of fault, Helene. But I won't stand for insolence. You will remain here, Helene."

"But my little *bebê*! How . . ."

"No more! You've heard me. Get your baggage from the cart and go inside!"

Lucinda waited. She expected an immediate apology, but none came. A moment passed, and then another, but still Helene was silent. In fact, while they waited for her maid's luggage to be removed, Lucinda noticed a coy, triumphant look in Helene's dark eyes.

Now what have I done, Lucinda wondered. What do I do without her?

Before she could change her mind, however, Captain Pathan urged everyone to take their places. He turned his horse toward Lucinda. "You ride up there in the howdah, madam," he said in Hindi, nodding toward a silver-ornamented ladder leaning against the elephant's side. She looked back desperately at Helene, but Pathan stepped between them. He said to her softly, "That was justly done and wisely, madam. To show respect for our fellows, even those who differ from us, that is the Prophet's teaching. You make me ashamed, madam."

"You? Ashamed? What of?" she answered in surprise.

His voice seemed strained. "Here I am in the land of Christians, I who should show the tolerance enjoined by the Prophet. But I berate, I criticize, I condemn. Because you are a little different from me. Because you worship the Lord one way and I, another."

They had reached the ladder, and Pathan slipped smoothly from his horse, taking her arm to help her up. Her heavy skirts, flounced with padded hoops to emphasize her tiny waist, bunched over her little shoes, and she was glad of his touch, reassuring but firm.

"I am the man. I am the Muslim. Yet here I must be learning from a Christian, and a woman. And so I am ashamed."

"Well," said Lucinda. "That's very nice, I suppose."

For the first time that she could remember, Pathan smiled. It was not a smile like a Portuguese. There was something more difficult about it, as though pleasure were earned, not free, but more relaxed, as though once earned that pleasure could be savored. "You are most tolerant, and most wise, madam. It is my privilege to be your escort."

By now she'd reached the top of the ladder. The mahout rose from his seat on the great beast's head, and stood with his bare feet on the elephant's ears. He thrust aside the howdah curtains with his pointed brass *ankus;* with his other hand took her firmly by the arm. Few men ever touched her so: his grip felt strong and dry.

"Please enter, madam," Pathan called from below.

For suddenly Lucinda was frozen, staring into the howdah. They can't be serious, she thought. I can't be expected to ride here. Not here. Not with them.

There on the cushions and throws, behind the silk curtains that billowed in the ocean breeze, sat the eunuch, smiling and bowing. And next to him, half-naked, it seemed to Lucinda, sat the cargo.

A bayadere, she thought. A nautch girl. A common whore.

From below Captain Pathan gazed at her with something close to reverence.

Well, I wanted an adventure, she thought.

With the mahout and the eunuch's help, she clambered in.

ଔଔଔଔ

"This is the nice farang woman I spoke of," the eunuch said to the bayadere, his high voice bubbling. "Come in, come in, come in," he told Lucinda. "Isn't this nice? Our own little house." Then with his pudgy hands he took Lucinda's, offering more enthusiasm than support, and fussed with the curtains as she crawled to take a seat on the howdah floor. "And she speaks Hindi," the eunuch added, as if he'd never stopped speaking to the bayadere.

He beamed at Lucinda. In the muted sunlight that filtered through the howdah's silk curtains, Lucinda saw that the eunuch had an odd face, as though the face of a slender boy had been swathed in rolls of custardy fat.

She could make out the pointed, dimpled chin that seemed to swim amidst an ocean of jowl.

"There should be a nicer way to get up here, don't you think? Undignified to make one scramble so." He leaned over and poked his head outside the curtain, giving Lucinda a view of his billowing form, like a fat little boy's, blown up like a balloon. "Move the ladder, Captain; move it now; we're all aboard." His large bottom wiggled as he called.

Lucinda saw the bayadere make the subtlest nod to indicate the eunuch's outlandish form, as though they as women could share a joke.

"Now maybe we can go," the eunuch said as he sat down again, his jowls flushed pink. "Waiting around all day. Do we have nothing better to do with our time?"

"It's all one," the bayadere said softly. Her face seemed utterly serene. Lucinda noted that she was younger than she first thought—about Lucinda's age, in fact. On her lap she held what seemed to be a bundle of palm leaves.

"Now: introductions first, I think," said the eunuch. "This is my new mistress, the famous *devadasi . . .*" but the bayadere cut him off with a barely perceptible lifting of a finger.

"You must call me by my new name, my nautch name, or how shall I get used to it?"

"No, mistress . . . ," the eunuch protested, but again she silenced him, this time by closing her eyes.

"I am Maya, a nautch girl, that is all."

"But mistress, she should know. You were . . ."

"I was many things. But now . . ." she lowered her eyes with a sigh "I am Maya the nautch girl." She greeted Lucinda by lifting her folded hands. Lucinda was about to say something when from outside the howdah's curtains, the unseen mahout called out, and the elephant lurched forward. Lucinda spilled backward, into the profusion of cushions scattered everywhere.

"We're off," the eunuch exulted.

Lucinda had just managed to right herself when the eunuch extended his pudgy hand to help her. He seemed offended that she did not take it, even though now she had no need.

Maya lowered her eyes and whispered to herself. Laughing at me, Lucinda thought, but then she changed her mind. No, she's praying, saying a mantra for the journey, Lucinda decided. When she looked back the eunuch was staring at her with eager, merry eyes.

"My name is Slipper," he told her earnestly.

"Maybe you should tell her *your* real name," Maya said.

"Oh, what difference does that make now? In a few days we'll be home and no one cares what I used to be called." He blinked at Lucinda and turned away, whispering to Maya. "Anyway, that was supposed to be our secret."

"*Ahcha,*" Maya answered, wobbling her head. "Forgive me. I won't mention it again."

CQCQ

The elephant trumpeted. Lucinda had forgotten how the great beasts swayed when they walked—the howdah lurched like a boat on a windblown sea. "It takes some getting used to," Slipper said, as if reading her thoughts. "But it's so much nicer up here than in one of those dusty old bullock carts. We have cushions," he added, waving his hand toward them as if Lucinda had not already tumbled among them, "And nice shade. And food." He uncovered a basket of custard apples, grapes, and sweet limes with a pleased flourish. "And of course, company, which is the best comfort of all."

"Yes," said Lucinda pleasantly, and again she caught the glance of Maya's amused eyes. "Can we open the curtains? I'd like to see."

"Well, yes," Slipper said, but it seemed clear the suggestion disappointed him. He reached along the roof of the howdah, lowering gauze screens for privacy before opening the side curtains. "I won't do the front," he said. "Who wants to see the mahout's old back anyway?"

Lucinda thought about insisting, but held her tongue. There was much to see.

Outside, the caravan was turning a corner, leaving behind the palm-lined shore and the whitewashed houses of the farangs, heading for the eastern gate of the Goa walls.

The elephant was in the middle of the procession. Ahead of them, led by Pathan, rode four Muslim guards. Some bullock carts followed the howdah, then Da Gama and Geraldo riding side by side.

Somehow, Lucinda had imagined that the procession would be grander.

But it was exciting even so, to ride on the back of a great elephant in a rich howdah, led by horsemen carrying long, bright spears.

Behind them, the tower of Santa Catarina faded into the sea mist. Ahead Lucinda saw the shambling huts of the Hindis that ringed the Portuguese cantonment. The road narrowed here, for the ramshackle buildings, many of them cobbled together from materials salvaged or stolen from the farangs, connected in a haphazard sprawl that paid little heed to traffic. The guards shouted for pedestrians to make way, and raised their spears toward any that hesitated. Amidst the shouts and taunts somehow the caravan muddled through.

"Let's see," Slipper said. "What shall we talk about?"

Lucinda paid him no attention, for slowly they approached the eastern gate. The howdah was nearly as high as the thick stone walls, where bored-looking *soldados* patrolled with flintlocks.

Since she'd been brought to Goa, barely older than an infant, she had not left the boundaries of the city. All her life she'd heard stories of outside, and from those tales had constructed an imaginary world, full of brave princes, and bandit kings, and glittering palaces; all the foolishness that might fill a young girl's fancy. After her parents' deaths, Tio Carlos had made her his ward and then installed her as the lady of his house, and she had forced herself to realize that those thoughts had been only the fancies of a girl. Even so, her heart pounded as she approached the gate, for beyond them lay a world of which she'd only dreamed.

The gatekeepers rang the big bronze bell and swung wide the elephant gate. Before passing through, the mahout made the beast slow almost to a stop; he then stood up on the elephant's head and measured the archway until he was sure the howdah would squeak through.

"Such a big elephant," said Slipper, looking at Lucinda with a sort of reverence. "You must be very important."

"I assure you I'm not," Lucinda answered.

Once through the gate, they moved slowly through a sort of tunnel. From platforms on the walls of the gateway, *soldados* leered, for from their high perches they could see the women clearly. Cannon barrels aimed straight at them.

"They use this turning place to prevent the ramming of the inner gate. It's such a nuisance. All this trouble, yet how often are they attacked?"

Slipper sighed, as though he'd seen it all before. Lucinda tried to appear as though she too knew all about this.

The elephant moved slowly, reluctant despite the mahout's murmured words and the prodding of his *ankus,* for the beast had to negotiate a tricky bend around a narrow corner. And even when this was managed, they faced one last gate.

The *soldados* swung the heavy doors wide. Lucinda held her breath as the elephant lumbered through, but of course there was no magic world beyond the last gate, only a wide sward of yellowing grass where the trees had all been cleared for defense. A few hundred yards later, the road disappeared into the shadows of a forest, a tangled jungle of teak and mango and jackfruit and palms. Above their tall branches, she could see blue shadows of the distant hills.

"Ugh, what's that smell!" exclaimed Slipper. He crawled to the other side and leaned out to look.

Maya glanced outside, then returned her gaze to the bundle of palm leaves in her lap. "A nobody village," she said. It was the first time she'd looked up since they started moving.

Lucinda looked. She thought at first it was a field of grassy mounds—then she realized that she was looking at low huts roofed with mudgrass. The rotten smell was carrion: hides drying, bones boiling, the smell of old death.

"You call them nobodies?" asked Slipper, sounding irritated.

"It is their lot in this life to be unclean. No one may touch them. To touch a nobody is to be polluted."

"Why? What's so wrong with them?" the eunuch insisted.

"It is their karma to clean latrines and tan hides, to do all those things that must not be done and yet still must be done," Maya answered. Lucinda felt that she was humoring her like a child.

"They deserve better than to be stuck out here," Slipper scowled.

"Who would want this smell in the city? Besides, they have their own foods and their own wells, and they come and go as they please to do their work."

Slipper frowned at the mud-hut village. "They're so filthy. Almost like they're made from dirt." When he saw a pig drinking from a puddle where two babies played, he turned away, and his eyes glistened.

"What's wrong, Slipper?" Lucinda asked. "Surely this is the way of the things, even in Bijapur."

The eunuch looked back, serious for a change. "It's not the same. You'll see when you get there. I've seen Hindis run to get a bath if a nobody's shadow even touches them. In Islam, all living things have souls. We are made pure by the fire of the Lord's compassion."

He stared back at the village and spoke almost to himself. "I'm lucky I'm not a Hindi. This is where I'd be sent, don't you see? The Hindi law says that eunuchs must live among the nobodies. But even the nobodies won't have us. The eunuchs must live outside the nobody village. They must wear women's clothing, they must be called 'she.' They must have no wells, but drink water from the gutters. Children throw rocks at them. If I were Hindi, this would be my village. These pitiful filthy souls? They would be my neighbors. It is they who would despise me. Don't you understand?"

He looked at Lucinda with searching eyes, and she turned with a sort of horror to gaze once more upon the nobody village. But by this time they were nearly past the place, the people, and the huts now nearly indistinguishable from the brown earth. And a breeze, sweet with forest dampness, blew the stench away.

"Well," said Slipper with a sigh. Then taking a custard apple, he looked up smiling. "So. Who's hungry?"

⊘⊃€⊙

Upon entering the dense, overhanging trees, Lucinda at last felt as if she had entered a different world. Damp stagnant shadows replaced the hot sun. Even the caravan's clatter seemed muffled by the leaves.

Lucinda grew used to the rhythmic roll of the elephant's shoulders beneath the howdah floor. In all directions she saw nothing but dark leaves and branches. The patches of sky that peeked through the foliage looked white as linen. She heard the whispers of wind and the chatter of a thousand birds; she smelled the mold and dampness of the forest floor, and the warm, grassy smell of the elephant's body.

"Why do you keep looking out?" Slipper asked. "There's nothing to see."

Lucinda took a while to realize that Slipper was addressing her.

"Leave her alone, Slipper," Maya said. "Can't you see she's happy?" Lucinda nodded gratefully to the nautch girl, surprised that she of all people would understand her feelings. "Have you seen much of the world?" Maya asked. Lucinda shook her head. Maya's eyes drifted back to the stack of palm leaves on her lap. "Well, there we are similar, you and I."

Lucinda gave her a surprised glance, but did not contradict her. She leaned out over the edge of the howdah, though the forest here looked just the same as the forest a hundred yards back. "But aren't we going to talk?" Slipper sighed.

From the front of the line, Captain Pathan looked back and saw Lucinda peering out. Frowning, he peeled his mare to the side of the road, and waited there for the howdah to catch up. "Keep the curtains closed, madam," he told her, trotting along beside it, but Lucinda looked away and pretended not to hear. "Madam, for your safety," he insisted. She ignored him.

Frustrated, Pathan rode back, and sent Da Gama to the howdah. "How are you all doing so far?" the *soldado* called.

Slipper crawled forward to answer, his pale jowls showing blotchy pink patches from the effort. "Hello, Captain," he said in Hindi. "Why do you wear so many guns?" For at each of Da Gama's hips hung a *pistola* with its grip facing backward, and he wore two broad belts that crossed in an X over his chest, where he had tucked half a dozen more.

Da Gama laughed and answered in Hindi. "I have more in my bag, Senhor Eunuch. Better having too many guns and not needing them, eh?"

"Are you worried about wolves, Captain?" Slipper asked. His tiny eyes opened wide.

Da Gama lifted an eyebrow. "That is so," he said. "I'm worried about wolves." He nodded toward the curtains. "Keep the curtains closed, eh?" he said. Then in Portuguese, he added, glancing at Lucy, "Better for everyone that way, eh, Lucy?" With that he trotted back to the end of the line.

With unexpected agility, Slipper quickly started to pull the curtains, but Lucinda held out her hand to stop him. "He was only teasing you, you silly!" she said. "You don't really think that wolves will see us?"

"He wasn't speaking of wolves," said Maya.

Sensing danger without really understanding it, Lucinda removed her hand. Soon Slipper had closed them in.

ⓒⓄⓒⓄ

The howdah was much darker now, and Maya took the palm leaves from her lap, touched them to her forehead, and placed them on a square of silk beside her.

"What are they?" Lucinda asked.

"Can you read?" Maya asked, handing them to her.

Of course, a book, Lucinda realized, as she glanced at the writing on the palm leaves. They'd been sewn together across the top. "I can't read this language," she answered as she handed it back.

"It's the Gita," Slipper said. "She reads it all the time."

"You know this book?" Maya asked. Lucinda shook her head. "Our most sacred text," Maya continued as she folded the thin volume in its silk cover. "Bhagavad Gita, the Song of the Adorable One."

"That means her god," Slipper put in, his lips pursed in disapproval.

"You think our god is different from yours?" Maya asked. Slipper seemed about to snap an answer, but Maya's eyes were so gentle that instead he merely blinked. "When Mohammed said there was but one god, did you think he meant one different from mine? Or from hers?"

"Whatever you say, mistress," Slipper replied, though to Lucinda the eunuch looked unconvinced, even angry.

Maya smiled. "In this book, the Lord says, 'When the wick of righteousness burns low, I take on human form.' Isn't that what Christians believe as well?" She cocked her head at Lucinda, who at this moment was uncertain what she believed.

"That's not what we think," Slipper answered, as if for both of them, before Lucinda could say a word.

"Perhaps I misunderstood," Maya replied, her face now so still it looked like a mask.

"I thought only your priests could read," Lucinda said to Maya after an uncomfortable silence.

Maya turned her eyes from the eunuch. Lucinda could sense that it took her some effort to breathe calmly. "Yes that's true, for the most part. Some of the merchants read, of course, but not Sanskrit, not the language of the gods. But for some reason, reading is taught to us *devadasis*, to the dancing women of the temple." She laughed, but her eyes were serious.

"You know it's funny—only the brahmins say these words aloud, but I never met a brahmin who has actually read these books. They learn reading, when they're boys, but they prefer to memorize the scriptures, by repeating the words their guru says. Sometimes those words they memorize are completely different from what's in their books."

"I'm glad I never learned to read," said Slipper.

"But if women are not to say the words aloud, why do they teach the dancing girls to read?" Lucinda asked.

"I've often wondered that myself. Maybe because the texts we *devadasis* must study are too boring for the brahmins to bother with: the *Natya Sutra*, the book of dance, for example, or the *Kama Sutra*, the book of love. Maybe because so many of us *devadasis* end up sold to the Muslims, where the brahmins know we'll have no access to the scriptures." She shook her head ruefully. "But of course that seems unlikely, doesn't it? If they really cared about our welfare, they'd not have sold us in the first place."

Now surely Lucinda had known before this that Maya was a slave, but for some reason the bayadere's words hit home with unexpected force.

"Please don't look shocked. It is your family that has bought me."

"What?" Lucinda stammered.

"It is nothing special," Slipper said, sensing her discomfort.

"What difference should it make to me—to any of us? It is but one more life: Now I'm a slave. . . . Have I not been a king? A tree? A dog? A nobody? I've taken birth a million times and will be reborn a million more."

Lucinda said nothing. She had often heard the local merchants blaspheme this way. But Maya was so pretty, with skin nearly as fair as hers, and so young, just her own age, and it disturbed Lucinda to realize that she was no more than some man's property.

"He's a slave as well, you know," Maya said, indicating Slipper with her eyes.

Slipper sat up as tall as he could. "There's no shame in being a slave, miss. It's not what you are, but how you act that makes the difference."

"Yes," agreed Maya. "That is what the Gita teaches us as well." Her eyes sparkled as though she found the eunuch's discomfort amusing. "Otherwise I should not have offered myself for sale."

"You *offered* to be a slave?" Lucinda gasped.

"Why not? As Slipper says, there is no shame. Our temple had been nearly destroyed by floods, and the *shastri* had hinted that he could get a good price for me. I'm sure it saved the temple."

"What about your family?"

"I've been an orphan for as long as I remember. And my guru died. She was all my family to me, and she disappeared in the floods. So why not? Why do you look so shocked?"

"I had no idea," Lucinda answered.

"You thought that I was born a slave, as you were?"

Lucinda's hand covered her mouth. "How dare you! I'm a free woman!"

"Are you?" Maya said softly. "Have you a house? A purse full of gold? Do you go where you please? Take a lover when you wish, or none at all?"

Lucinda answered with a frown.

"Please forgive me, then," Maya replied. "I thought you were like all the other farang women—some man's property with no freedom of her own: a virgin, maybe, offered to a rich man to unite two fortunes, or a wife whose only value is in manufacturing sons."

"I forgive you," Lucinda answered. In the silence that followed, she found herself becoming aware of the endless rocking of the dark, shadowed howdah, and wished that she could be once more on solid ground.

"I don't feel well," Lucinda said at last. "I have a headache." She leaned over onto one of the cushions, fluffed her hooped skirts over her ankles and squeezed her eyes tight. But she could feel the stares of the other two. The howdah rocked, creaking like a boat tossed by the waves. In a few minutes she was asleep.

 enenene

When the endless sway of the howdah stopped, Lucinda woke. "Where are we?" she asked.

"We've come through Valpoi, and we've just stopped at someone's house," Slipper answered, looking perturbed. "And we passed right by a perfectly satisfactory inn, too."

Lucinda was the last one to inch down the silver ladder propped against the elephant's flanks. Slipper stood to the side, speaking seriously to Maya, who tried not to look too annoyed.

The wide, comfortable courtyard overlooked a deep valley. The sun was just setting, and its red rays colored the mountains to the east. Hindi servants hoisted luggage and hurried it inside. Da Gama came over to Lucinda. "Your uncle arranged that we should spend the night here. This is the house of Fernando Anala, one of your father's trading partners."

"I don't think I ever met him," Lucinda answered.

A tall Hindi wearing a shiny silk turban appeared at the door of the house and came down the verandah. "My master wishes to greet you," he said in passable Portuguese. With that he gave a stiff but correct farang bow, even giving his fingers a little flourish as he spread his arms. Rising, he looked at Lucinda, Da Gama, and Geraldo, and with a sweep of his hand, motioned them toward the door. The others understood that they were not invited. Even so, Lucinda glanced at Maya, letting her embarrassment show. Maya nodded, unconcerned.

The servant led them down a dark corridor lit by high-flamed candles, to a great hall, nearly empty except for a thronelike chair at the far end. He bowed them through and latched the double doors behind them.

The clack of Da Gama's boots on the wooden floor echoed from the high ceiling. Beside the throne a half-dozen torches burned so bright that it was hard to see who sat there. A mastiff resting at the man's feet stood and growled as Da Gama approached, but the man clapped once and the dog sat.

When they reached the throne, Da Gama bowed, sweeping his broad-brimmed hat. "I am Jebtha Da Gama at your service, senhor. Here are Geraldo Silveira and Lucinda Dasana. Your friend Carlos Dasana sends his best wishes." Geraldo bowed as well, and Lucinda gave a curtsy.

The man rose in answer. He was much smaller than Lucinda expected. "In the name of the Blessed Virgin and of Jesus Christ our Savior I welcome you to my humble dwelling." He had a thin voice and an unrecognizable accent. When he came forward to greet them, leaving the harsh glare of the torches, it took Lucinda a moment to puzzle through what she was seeing.

Fernando Anala was a Hindi.

☙◦☙◦☙

He wore the clothes of a Portuguese trader—the long coat, knee breeches, leather shoes—in fact he was dressed almost exactly like Geraldo, but with more gold braid. But he himself was tiny, dark, delicate—clearly a Hindi.

She had seen Hindi women in European dress, but never a man. He reminded her of an organ-grinder's monkey.

"I am Fernando Anala at your service," he said, now returning Da Gama's bow. "I say that name with pride, for it was given to me when I became a Christian. But you must not call me senhor . . . as we share one Father; you must call me Brother Fernando." With that, Anala walked to Da Gama and put his tiny arms around the *soldado*'s chest. "Brother," he said, embracing him. Da Gama looked too shocked to move. Anala then reached Geraldo. "Brother," he whispered. Geraldo had recovered sufficiently to embrace him back.

Anala now came to Lucinda. She could not take her eyes from his, which glistened in the torchlight, radiant against his dark skin. He seemed hesitant but excited as he placed his arms around her waist. "Sister," he sighed, nestling his head against her breasts. His thinning, perfumed hair had been pulled back into a queue, and Lucinda found herself looking straight down on to his dark scalp while he clung to her.

He stood there for a long time, stepping away only when Da Gama cleared his throat. Even then he kept Lucinda's hand sandwiched between his palms. She had always thought of her hands as delicate, but in his tiny ring-covered fingers her hands seemed huge and clumsy.

"My wife, Silvia, is also a Christian, of course," he said. His eyes fixed on Lucinda. "She is honored that you will be her guest tonight. She waits for you in the guesthouse." His fingers rubbed Lucinda's palm. "I'm sure we men would only bore you with our talk."

Lucinda lowered her eyes and nodded.

"There are other women in your party?" He did not let go.

"Just the bayadere," Da Gama said. Anala blinked as though the word eluded him. "The nautch girl, I mean. The *devadasi*."

At the last word, Anala's head flew up. "You have a *devadasi* with you? No one told me." He seemed upset. Lucinda seized this opportunity to slip her hand away, but still he held on. "I should have been informed."

"The blame for the secrecy is mine, senhor. She's a gift to the grand vizier."

"*Ahcha. Baksheesh.*" He hissed when he said the word. Anala lifted his dark face to Lucinda's. "Bijapur is full of sinners. A city of the damned. Muslims have the blackest souls." He leaned toward Lucinda as if revealing a confidence: "A Muslim will keep a dozen wives and a hundred concubines."

But it seemed to Lucinda as if Anala were sizing her up for a place in his own harem. "Well, we must save souls, not condemn them. What better way to save a soul than trade, eh? In trade we find the vehicle for redemption." He leaned so close to Lucinda that his ear nearly touched her breast. "If I had not begun to trade with farangs, sister, my wife and I would still be damned today, instead of glorying in Our Lord's salvation."

"How nice for you," Lucinda replied. Anala would not let go her hand.

Soon Anala had tallied everyone: Maya and Slipper, he decided, would be entertained by his wife, while Pathan would join the Christian men for dinner. There was some hope, Anala said, that the three Christians could save his soul. The arrangements settled, Da Gama and Geraldo made sweeping bows as Anala approached them, and managed this way to fend off another embrace. Anala once more pressed his head against Lucinda's breasts. "Sister," he said fondly. "My servant will see to your comfort," he told them all as they left. "We say the rosary in here before supper."

"Oh good," Da Gama managed to say.

⋐⋑⋐⋑

The silk-turbaned servant led Lucinda across the courtyard and opened the door for her, saying, "Good evening, senhorita," in perfect Portuguese. The room was spacious, dominated by two big canopied feather beds that stood in the center of the room. Lucinda saw her smaller trunk had been placed near the end of one of them. Wooden chairs stood stiffly against the walls, as if no one had ever sat there, and here and there a small table and the odd chest.

Maya was already there. On the carpet she had spread out a few of her belongings from her floppy cloth bag. Lucinda wondered whether that one bag was all of Maya's luggage.

Maya nodded toward the beds and lifted her eyebrows. "So this is how farangs sleep," she said softly. "I will be too frightened to sleep so high. How do you not roll off?"

"You don't roll off. You sink into the feathers like a big pillow. It's very comfortable."

"Comfortable for farangs. Not for Hindis. I shall sleep on the floor."

"Our host and hostess are Hindi," Lucinda said. Maya looked up, but when she saw that Lucinda was serious Maya giggled. "I was surprised as well," Lucinda went on. "The man calls himself Fernando, so who would know? And he dresses like a Portuguese. I haven't seen the wife. Anyway, she will be eating with us here."

Lucinda circled the room as she spoke, but stopped when she noticed something unusual on a table. A sort of shrine, she decided; amidst a scattering of white grains of rice, a single silver lamp; lying next to it a crucifix, the head and hands stained red by *kumkum*. "What is this?" she said, almost to herself.

Maya came to her side and looked. "She must love this god very much."

"Well, no Christian would treat a crucifix this way."

"No, she is Christian. But not like you are Christian." Maya looked suddenly concerned. "You say she's eating with us? Where will Slipper eat?"

"With us, of course."

"That will not be pleasant. I must speak to Deoga."

"Who is Deoga?"

Maya looked at her, confused. "Senhor Da Gama. Do you not call him Deoga as well?"

"No," Lucinda replied, equally confused. "What is Da Gama to do?"

"Look here; look at this woman's *puja*. She is Hindi. She will not eat with a *hijra*."

"Why don't we ask her first?" Lucinda suggested.

Maya looked at her as if suddenly seeing her heart. "You speak Hindi so well that I imagined you understood our ways as well. Of course she'd agree."

"Then where's the problem?"

"She would say so only to be polite. It would be most unkind to impose so. Like asking her to eat in a latrine."

Lucinda's face twisted. "But why?"

"Don't worry. Deoga can fix it. He's very good with these things, once you tell him."

"How do you know this?"

"Didn't we sail together in a dhow for three weeks?"

Lucinda nodded. But a second later she began to wonder—Maya's answer any number of interpretations. So of course she changed the subject. "But don't you eat with Slipper?"

"I do a great many things that Hindi women do not do, and before long

I shall do a great many more. You know why as well as I do. Let us not speak of it again. I will tell Deoga and that will be enough."

"You seem very certain."

Maya smiled. "He is a good man. Haven't you seen that?" A moment later she was out the door.

☙◦◦❧

Da Gama, of course, understood, and did what Maya asked. After a wearying hour standing beside "Brother" Fernando, intoning rosary after rosary in front of a particularly gruesome crucifix, Da Gama persuaded him to invite Slipper to the men's supper. At first their host had been reluctant, but with Da Gama repeatedly imploring, Anala's concern for Slipper's immortal soul overcame his distaste at eating with a *hijra*. "A Hindi would never agree," he told Da Gama. "It shall be the proof that I am reborn a Christian."

"Your actions reflect well on Christ," Da Gama assured him.

Anala's servant found Slipper in a small courtyard by the stables, at evening prayer with the other Muslims. Pathan's guards laughed when they heard Slipper being invited. "What shall I do?" Slipper asked Pathan.

"You must accept. I'm sure the Christian considers his invitation to be some sort of honor."

"Will there be forks?" the eunuch asked. "I've wanted to try eating with a fork."

"Forks, yes," the servant replied. "Also wine."

"Wine . . ." Slipper said dreamily. "Tell him I shall come."

☙◦◦❧

The dining table was lit by a chandelier. The sideboard was crowded: a platter of roasted chickens the size of pigeons, a mutton haunch, a loin of pork, each rubbed with pepper and coarse salt. The steaming meats glistened; juice trickled onto the pewter platters. Beside them stood gravies and sauces fragrant with wine and herbs, crisp round loaves of yeasty bread, and a bowl of butter. If not for the bowl of rice and dal and a plate of mango pickle, they might have been eating in Lisbon.

The men sat in chairs (Fernando's seat a few inches taller than the others), used forks, ate from porcelain. A pair of waiters, dressed as farangs except for bare feet and turbans, served them with unexpected skill. "How did he get all this stuff?" Geraldo whispered to Da Gama. But Da Gama was too busy eating to answer.

"Don't I get a glass of wine?" Slipper asked in a piping voice after a few minutes. "Everyone else has one."

"Not the *burak*. Muslims, I assumed . . ." said Anala, looking miffed. But he recovered, and with a flick of his delicate fingers, directed one of his servants to bring a glass.

Slipper drank the whole glass before the servant had time to step away, and held it out for more. Soon his round cheeks flushed in a mottled patchwork. He gave up trying to use his cumbersome fork, and like Pathan ate with his fingertips, washing down his food with big gulps of wine. One of the servants took to hovering near him, pitcher in hand.

Soon Slipper could barely speak for giggling. One of his eyelids began to droop. Fernando kept trying to bring the conversation around to theology, but Slipper brushed each effort aside with a joke, often lewd.

Finally, to everyone's surprise, Fernando leaped from his chair. "I can turn my other cheek no longer," he shouted. His voice was not much lower than the eunuch's. Even Slipper grew quiet, sensing the fury radiating from Anala's tiny form. "You will make no more sport at my expense, *hijra,* or at the expense of my beloved Lord Jesus Christ!" Fernando stabbed the air with a fork for emphasis.

"Your Jesus?" Slipper struggled to his feet. "Yours? I won't be scolded by a Hindi! Particularly not by a counterfeit farang like you! I'm a Muslim, not some Hindi infidel! I knew about Jesus while you were still kissing some idol's plaster ass!" With that the eunuch drained his glass, and with an attempted dignity stumbled from the room. As the waiter shut the door behind him, they heard a great clatter from the hall beyond, but no one moved.

Fernando whipped a kerchief from his sleeve and patted his dark forehead, then pressed the cloth to his lips as he regained his composure. The gesture was so perfectly European that Geraldo nearly laughed out loud. "Insolent *hijra!*" Ferando's delicate fingers pressed the kerchief back to his sleeve. "As if he knew anything about my beloved Lord Jesus Christ."

"But he does, you see," Pathan said softly. "He is a Muslim, though he drinks. You must certainly know that we Muslims hold Jesus in great reverence." But a glance at the others made it clear that none of them knew any such thing.

"Is this true?" Fernando asked Da Gama.

"How would I know, senhor? But this fellow is a *burak,* and a prince as well, and I have never heard him lie."

Pathan turned to Fernando. "Does not your faith teach forgiveness, sir? Here is a chance for you to forgive. That *mukhunni* . . . that *hijra* as you call him . . . lives a life that might be pitied. Stolen from mother and home, cruelly maimed when he was child. He has no home, no family. All his life he lives with women, cleaning them, dressing them, doing all their bidding. Can we be surprised that he acted so foolishly here? What does he know of the company of men? Rather it is for us men to pity him and forgive."

Fernando stared at Pathan. Perhaps he hoped to find a flaw in his words, so he might reveal his better knowledge of the love of Christ.

But he found no flaw. At last Fernando raised his hands to his forehead. "You are right, sir. He was not ready to accept the treasure I tried to offer him. His is the greater loss. I will forgive." Fernando sat again, and slowly the dinner went on.

⊘⊃⊘⊃

While Maya went out to find Da Gama, Lucinda changed into her dressing gown. Helene had thoughtfully folded it at the top of her trunk. It had been hard to take off her dress and unlace her corset by herself, and Lucinda now very much regretted sending Helene away.

But thinking of the incident in Goa brought the memory of Pathan's eyes, lustrous and troubling; a memory she quickly set aside.

After Maya returned, servants came in with lit candles, and unrolled a linen sheet over one of the colorful rugs near the wall. Not long after, Silvia entered, a short round woman wearing a Portuguese dress. Her black hair, shot with gray, she wore in long braid wrapped into a bun. She had a wedding ring, but around her neck she also wore a Hindi's marriage necklace.

She saw Lucinda first and smiled, friendly but nervous. But before she greeted her visitors, Silvia made a slow circuit of the room, pausing for a moment near the *puja* table. Lucinda watched as Silvia's fingers darted from her lips, to the silver crucifix, then to her heart. After that she *namskar*ed to each of her guests, and then, with an awkward flouncing of her skirts, sat beside them.

"It is an honor and blessing to welcome my sister Lucinda to this house," Silvia said in halting Portuguese.

"It is a blessing and honor to be here, my sister in Christ," Lucinda answered. Then she said in Hindi, "But we must be thoughtful of our companion." She nodded to Maya.

Silvia's expression changed to one of surprise and relief. "My husband told me you spoke Hindi, but I thought that he was joking." The idea of Brother Fernando joking with his wife had never crossed Lucinda's mind. Silvia leaned toward Maya. "A Christian woman who speaks like a civilized person. How remarkable."

"She is remarkable in many ways," Maya answered. Lucinda felt her cheeks burn as the women looked at her.

But Silvia seemed to have a question that would not wait. She turned to Maya, her eyes round and wide. "Are you truly a *devadasi*?"

Maya shrugged. "Whatever I was once is in the past."

"You will always be a *devadasi*! It is a blessing to have you in our house." Silvia's round face glowed in admiration, but Maya humbly turned aside. Lucinda tried to hide her puzzlement. So Maya was a temple dancer? What of it? But she said nothing.

Soon servants brought in dinner. Before Silvia and Maya they set china plates: rice, vegetables, dal, and dahi. Then the women waited politely while Lucinda was served.

Someone had made an effort to cook Portuguese food in her honor. Her plate held cabbage boiled to a thick paste, and in a pool of congealing fat, an unidentifiable sphere of meat, fire-blackened until it looked like an enormous bolus.

"I knew you would not want your food half raw, the way men eat it," Silvia said.

"You are very kind."

All of them stared in silence at the dreadful plate. "Would you like a fork, sister?" Silvia asked politely.

"My digestion is unsettled," Lucinda answered. She glanced at the servant, who whisked the plate away, holding it at arm's length as she carried it from the room.

The other two women looked relieved. "Perhaps some rice and dahi? Very soothing, I think." Silvia nodded and one of the servants scurried to fetch a plate. The white grains floating in the white curds actually looked rather appetizing, Lucinda thought. She did her best to scoop up the mixture with her fingers, Hindi fashion, since Silvia had not given her a spoon.

What a strange collection they were: She and Maya so similar in age and appearance, so different in background. She and Silvia, like a pair of mismatched bookends, dressed in Portuguese clothing but talking in Hindi. It wasn't that Silvia looked uncomfortable in her clothes so much as she looked lost. She wore the Portuguese dress as one might wear a costume to a fancy ball.

They talked little until the plates were cleared. When they did at last begin to chat, Silvia wanted mostly to speak with Maya. Even though Maya did her best to include Lucinda, somehow the subject always steered to temples and idols, and gurus and *shastris*. Lucinda could do little but listen.

"But Maya cannot have always been your name," Silvia insisted.

Maya shook her head. "It was given to me by that *hijra*."

The two women shared a scowl. "What was it before?"

Maya set her face, as one preparing to feel the doctor's knife. "Prabha."

Silvia sighed and closed her eyes, looking as if someone had placed a sweetmeat on her tongue. "Do you know this word?" she asked Lucinda. "It means light; the light that surrounds the head of the Lord. It is one of the names of the Goddess."

"Which goddess?" Lucinda asked.

Silvia looked confused. "There is but one."

Maya placed her hand on Lucinda's. Lucinda tried to hide her surprise. So many people had touched her since she left Goa. "That one goddess has so many forms. Surely you have seen the goddess Lakshmi?" Lucinda nodded; the goddess of wealth—even some of the Portuguese shopkeepers kept her idol in a tiny shrine. "Prabha is one of her names."

"My name was Uma. That name too means light—the light of serenity." Silvia smiled, remembering. Then she sighed and turned to Lucinda. "I suppose your name means something, too?"

"Yes," Lucinda answered slowly. "Lucinda too means light."

Later, there had been an awkward moment when Slipper burst into the women's room. He staggered and lifted his pudgy hands to the women, nearly toppling over, as if this were some difficult balancing act. No one knew what to say, least of all Slipper. "I'll go to sleep now," he slurred at last, and with that stumbled out of the room. Soon they heard him snoring outside the door. Though his speaking voice was high as a woman's, his snores were deep and rasping as an old man's.

"And he pretends to be a Muslim," Silvia humphed. "They're just the same. All of them, just the same."

As the evening went on, Lucinda noticed that Silvia's conversation recalled the way her father discussed money—he would talk for hours, discussing everything and anything else before finding the courage to touch the subject. But from her circling talk, it seemed to Lucinda that Silvia too had some topic she wished to bring up but was too embarrassed to say.

The candles had already begun to flare and gutter before Silvia at last revealed her target. "Why have you done it?" she asked Maya in a whisper. "Why have you become a nautch girl?"

"What does it matter now, auntie? What's done . . ."

"Don't humor me. I'm too old for it. Tell me."

A darkness such as Lucinda had never seen fell across Maya's face. The nightbirds chattered outside, a dog barked, in the stable courtyard the elephant yawned, and Slipper's snoring sawed outside the door. A half-dozen times Maya took breath and seemed about to speak. "What was left for me?" she said at last.

"Tell me, daughter. Tell me." Seeing Silvia cradle Maya's hand so gently, Lucinda recalled the nearly forgotten memory of her own mother's touch.

"You know I was a *devadasi*." Silvia nodded. "I was at the Paravati temple in Orissa. My guru . . ." here Maya halted, letting out a tiny sob. Silvia stroked her hand. "My guru said I might go to the Shiva temple. She said I might do *seva* there with the *sadhus* and *siddhas*."

Lucinda knew that *sadhus* were mendicant monks: beggars, most of them naked with matted hair so long that the dirty, braidlike locks fell to their knees. She didn't know what *siddhas* were, or *seva*.

Silvia, oddly, seemed conscious of Lucinda's ignorance. "*Seva* means work; work for god," she whispered to Lucinda, while her hand stroked Maya's arm.

"It was good, you know. The training was difficult, but the work made it all worthwhile. In the morning I would dance for the god; in the evening I had congress with the *sadhus.*"

In less than a day, Lucinda had all but forgotten that Maya was a whore.

Well of course she'd had congress with them, Lucinda realized. Of course. That was her work. But Maya's wistfulness and regret made Lucinda realize that Maya thought she was doing something worthy, not something shameful. Maya spoke of having congress as a nun might speak of giving alms.

Silvia sighed. Lucinda expected her to pity or to scold. Instead she said: "You were most fortunate, daughter. Why ever did you stop?"

"There was a flood. The temple was damaged. There was no money, so I offered . . ."

"Is that really why, daughter?"

Maya's cry began as a low moan and ended as a wail. She pitched forward, shaking her head and sobbing. "My guru was gone. She was swept away in the floods." Lucinda could not resist reaching out to Maya, patting her back while she sobbed.

"Who was your guru?" Silvia asked.

"Gungama," Maya said. The name set off a new round of sobs.

"Gungama?" Silvia whispered. Her face grew pale and her eyes wide.

"Did you know her?" Lucinda asked, as Maya tried to still her sobbing.

"Of course I know her. My father was one of her patrons. She's famous throughout the world." Silvia seemed shocked that Lucinda had not heard of her. "But she's not dead."

Maya sat up. She seemed to have cried all her tears away. "Auntie, she drowned eight months ago."

"But she didn't," Silvia insisted. "She slept in this very house last month."

ଓଈଓଈଓ

Looking up from his port wine, Geraldo glanced at Fernando Anala and once more experienced a moment of confusion. Anala's face was so perfectly

Hindi—the dark, alert features, the bright, perfect teeth—but to see it emerging from a lace-trimmed shirt and a Portuguese coat awash with gold braid—each time Geraldo looked up, he was taken aback.

They had been discussing the upcoming leg of the journey through the Sansagar Pass. Pathan seemed unable to avoid bringing up his concerns, though clearly he and Da Gama had discussed the matter already. "Should we not have more guards, sir? Are we not in danger?" he asked Fernando.

Fernando glanced at the farangs before answering. "What does Senhor Da Gama say?"

"What I say is, the hell with guards. They only attract attention and you can never have enough, not really, not if the bandits are determined. Half the ones you hire will be spies." Da Gama took a long pull on his port while Pathan shook his head.

"Still one must make provision against misfortune. One must plan even if one does not expect trouble," Fernando said.

"My friend plans to offer *chauth* to the bandits." Pathan looked seriously at Fernando as he spoke.

"There's really only one clan active at the pass this time of year," Fernando said carefully. "His plan could work."

"The Three-Dot clan, you mean," Da Gama said. "They'd just as soon take your money peaceably as rob you. So we'll pay them and the hell with it. *Baksheesh, chauth,* extortion, call it what you will. We'll pay through the nose, but they won't attack." Da Gama turned to Pathan earnestly. "And why not? The key is keeping the cargo safe." Pathan nodded noncommittally but didn't appear convinced.

"Other than the pass, the route is safe enough," Fernando agreed. "But how will you find them, the Three-Dot clan? If you don't pay—in advance—your plan is useless."

Da Gama eased against the leather back of the big wooden chair. "They'll find us, I have no doubt."

"If this were my responsibility . . ." Pathan muttered.

"But it's not," Da Gama replied. "Your responsibility begins when we reach Bijapur. Until then, you're only here for the ride, so try to enjoy yourself." He leaned to Fernando. "The only thing worse than a settlement man is a *burak,*" he said with a wink.

"Is it not unusual to have both settlement man and *burak* on the same journey?" Fernando asked.

"Very," both men answered in unison. At this, at least, they laughed.

Geraldo said. "For some time I've been wondering—What is a settlement man? Exactly what does he do? I have been too bashful to ask." Da Gama laughed out loud. "My shyness is well known, sir!" Geraldo protested.

Pathan held up his hand like a mullah about to teach a lesson. "When they first came here, the farangs were not used to our ways, sir. They could not distinguish between a promise made in earnest, and a polite agreement that would never come to pass. This ignorance caused many difficulties, not only for the Portuguese but for their trading partners as well."

Pathan continued. "Eventually, the Portuguese developed a solution: When a trade was to be settled they sent a man along to assure that the settlement took place as promised. Or more precisely, as the Portuguese believed it to have been promised. At first, settlement men were little more than hoodlums. Threats—or violence if threats failed—this was their only tool. But that was years ago, eh, Deoga?"

Da Gama nodded. "Violence may solve some problems, but it causes new ones. Settlement men learned this, and adapted. We developed subtlety."

"For example?" Geraldo asked.

"Compromising. Offering terms. Imploring. Pleading. And if those should fail, other means of influence. Settlement men consider the men they deal with. Each man has a weakness; each fears something . . . censure . . . poverty . . . a secret coming out. Some call it intimidation, but a settlement man calls it persuasion, and it's very nearly as effective as drawing blood. Only rarely these days must I hold a *pistola* to some fellow's head and cock the hammer."

Geraldo frowned as he considered the implications of Da Gama's words, then lifted an eyebrow. "Oh, but you're having your joke, cousin."

A silence fell over the room. Finally Fernando said, "It cannot be a happy profession, brother. Nor one easily reconciled with the teachings of our Lord Jesus."

"No," Da Gama said. "A settlement man is no more than a whore. Except whores earn more money. I travel constantly. Sleep comes hard. There's . . ." Again he sighed . . . "an element of fear. Most settlement men don't last long. Most quit. The rest die."

"But not you, sir." Geraldo's voice was troubled.

"Your uncle is the best settlement man the Portuguese have," Pathan put in.

"The oldest, maybe," Da Gama said ruefully.

"Only the best can last so long," Pathan said. "Among *buraks*, Deoga is a legend."

"And what, pray tell, is a *burak*?"

Da Gama snorted. "A *burak* is a Bijapuri settlement man. It's where the Portuguese got the damned idea."

Pathan shrugged. "Except that we are not so subtle, we *buraks*. Old ways are best. Blood is always persuasive."

For a long time then, the conversation stopped. Da Gama and Pathan were locked in a fierce and burning gaze.

At last Da Gama broke the silence. "Anyway, you needn't worry about it, Aldo. Settlement men are a dying breed. The Dutch are taking over, the Dutch and the goddamned English. Most of the Portuguese are gone already."

Fernando could scarcely contain his shock. "The Portuguese gone? This cannot be. What of my contracts?"

Da Gama shook his head. "Sounds like you may need a *burak* of your own." He placed a heavy hand on Fernando's birdlike knee. "Look here, brother, don't worry. There will always be trade. There's still the Dutch."

"But don't they speak a different language?"

"German, I think," Geraldo said encouragingly.

"German!" Fernando took a big gulp of his port. "Are they Christians, at least?"

"Of course," Geraldo said. "Just not the same kind as us."

Fernando nearly choked. "There are different kinds?"

The rest of the evening did not go well.

❀❀❀❀

It took Lucinda some time before she realized what all the fuss was about. Slowly she understood that Maya had only allowed herself to become a slave because she had given up hope, because she thought that her teacher, her guru, was dead.

Silvia's news, apparently, changed everything.

If you're a whore, thought Lucinda, what difference who you whore with? But to Maya and Silvia, it made a great deal of difference indeed. They spoke of the grand vizier of Bijapur—a man of high position, Lucinda knew—as if Maya were expected to have congress with a dog.

"Run away," Silvia whispered. "Tonight!"

Maya's eyes flashed for a moment. "No," she said at last, "they'd come after me. Deoga. The *burak*. The *hijra*. Too many people have an interest. They'd never give up."

They sat in silence. "What about death?" Silvia whispered at last.

"How?" Maya said.

Lucinda gasped.

Maya ignored her. "How?" she asked once more.

Silvia looked into the quivering shadows. "A knife?"

Lucinda could stand no more. "No! No!"

"Hush," Silvia ordered. "This is your fault!"

"Mine?"

Maya placed a hand on each woman's arm. "Do not let yourselves be troubled. This is God's fault, or mine. Not hers, not anyone's."

Silvia winced at Maya's words, and then turned to Lucinda, looking up from under her bowed head. "In the name of Jesus' mercy, forgive me, sister."

"Nonsense. Of course." Lucinda regretted how irritated her voice sounded, but charged ahead anyway. "But why kill yourself? Why not escape?"

Silvia looked up as if surprised that Lucinda would take Maya's side. Maya shrugged. "I have said that it is impossible."

"Impossible tonight, maybe. Impossible from here, maybe. But not impossible forever."

Silvia considered this. "She is right, sister. The gods will provide a chance someday. You must be ready! Do you have a knife? You may need one. I will get you one, easy to conceal."

"No," Maya answered abruptly.

"A knife's too obvious," Lucinda agreed. "You need something subtle." Her eyes brightened. "Poison."

Maya sat up straighter.

"*Ahcha,*" Silvia sighed, suddenly interested. "But where would one get poison?"

"I have some," Lucinda said. She told the women about her *arsênico*.

"Fetch it! Fetch it!" Silvia commanded.

"We've plenty of time for that, sister," Maya said. "See how sleepy she looks? Go to bed, sister. You can show me later." Gratefully Lucinda climbed the bed stool and sunk into the featherbed. The other women hardly noticed, and despite their whispers, Lucinda dissolved into a bottomless sleep. Slipper's rattling, sputtering snore, however, leaked through the chamber door into her consciousness, and all night she dreamed she was pursued by bears.

ⓒⓄⓒⓄ

Lucinda woke to see through a high window the dawn begin to pink the sky. Maya and Silvia stood together facing the *puja* table, whispering a chant. Lucinda waited until they were finished before she said, "Good morning."

"Did you sleep well?" Maya asked. Her eyes were bright as if polished by her tears. She looked surprisingly fresh, though the other bed had not been slept in. Lucinda wondered if they'd stayed up all night or slept on the floor.

"I slept well, thank you."

Through the high window, they heard a high-pitched retching followed by a barking cough and a pitiful moan. "Slipper," Maya explained, looking pleased with the eunuch's discomfort. "He's been in the latrine for over an hour."

"Who will help us dress?" Instantly Lucinda regretted not voicing some concern over Slipper's health, but the two women seemed not to care.

"I won't let him touch me, so it's no great loss," Maya said. Her answer surprised Lucinda.

"And as for farang clothes—I'm sorry, sister, but no *hijra* will be of any use to you," Silvia said. "They have no stomach for it."

"Maybe . . ." Lucinda stammered, suddenly feeling very helpless, "maybe you could send your maid after you have done with her?"

Silvia frowned. "I dress myself. How hard is that?" But her face softened when she looked at Lucinda. "I know . . . you think you can't do it yourself. But only because you will not try! Even so, I myself will help you."

Lucinda nearly jumped off the bed to hug her. "Thank you, thank you."

Breakfast was a kind of pancake mixed with onions and spices, unex-pectedly delicious. Lucinda washed it down with a creamy cup of water-buffalo milk. If Helene could see me now, she thought.

Dressing, however, was a disaster. Silvia helped as best she could, but she herself had never worn a corset, nor ever learned to tie a proper bow. She and Lucinda together could barely master the corset laces. The fit was too loose, and there were knots that Lucinda knew she would never be able to untie. But after the two were done wrestling with Lucinda's dress, the final effect looked good enough that Silvia stood back and smiled in satisfaction.

"Now for the hair," Silvia said.

Oh, God, thought Lucinda.

❧❧❧❧

Two unexpected events occurred before they left. After making their farewells, Maya and Lucinda climbed the silver ladder to the howdah. Slip-per was nowhere to be seen.

As the mahout helped her mount, he gave Lucinda a big grin, showing a single front tooth. "Have you seen the *mukhunni*? Do you know where he is?" he then asked. Lucinda shook her head. Maya, already seated among the cushions, seemed unconcerned.

The horseman had mounted, and all were forming up to leave. Brother Fernando and Silvia stood by to see them off. Lucinda had just started to wonder if Slipper would be left behind when she saw him. He walked with careful, uncertain steps, like a girl learning posture by balancing a pitcher on her head. The stair to the courtyard in particular seemed difficult, and he winced with every footstep. He looked neither left nor right, passing Fernando and his wife without a glance.

Lucinda was surprised therefore when Slipper changed direction and slowly spiraled back to face Brother Fernando. With awkward, painful dig-nity, Slipper bent his knees to the bare ground, and then got on all fours. Lucinda thought he was going to vomit. But instead he slowly stretched forward, until his face was in the dust. "I acted shamefully, sir," Slipper's high voice came, muffled, but loud enough for all to hear. "You showed me kindness and I repaid you with discourtesy. I beg you to pardon me."

Fernando, who had maintained until now a stolid countenance, seemed shocked. "Get up, get up!" He grabbed the eunuch's hand and tried to pull him, but it was hopeless.

"Not until you forgive me; only then will I rise!" Slipper wailed. Good Lord, he's crying, Lucinda thought.

"Yes, yes, I forgive!" Fernando said. "Now stand! Stand!" Then he jumped back so suddenly, Lucinda wondered if Slipper had tried to kiss his feet.

Maya gazed at the morning clouds, ignoring the scene.

Slipper struggled to his feet and brushed the dust from his clothes. He seemed ready to prostate himself once more, but this time Fernando shooed him away. With many low bows, Slipper took his leave.

"It was well done, sir," the mahout whispered as Slipper clambered into the howdah.

"Oh, master, please make the elephant walk smooth today." He collapsed on a heap of cushions.

The other unexpected event happened as the gate to the courtyard was opened.

A wolf was standing there.

At first Lucinda thought it was Fernando's big dog, but when the animal staggered through the gates, its eyes wild, foam falling from its jaws, she realized it was a wolf, and a sick one.

One of Pathan's guards shot an arrow through its belly, but instead of dying, the animal raced around the courtyard in a blind rage. The horses skittered as the wolf snapped at their heels with its yellow teeth.

Maya slid next to Lucinda. "We are safe up here," the mahout said. "My friend fears nothing. The wolf cannot hurt him." Even so he rubbed behind the elephant's ear and whispered calming words.

The horses danced and bucked, kicking at the sick animal. "How do the riders hold on? What if they fall?" Maya whispered.

Fernando hurried Silvia into the house.

After a few minutes that seemed like an eternity, the wolf fell to the ground, exhausted. The horsemen rode up, arrows fixed in their bows, backing away whenever the wolf spasmed. Da Gama aimed his *pistolas* at it, but for some reason no one shot.

Then Pathan dismounted and fetched a *pistola* from Da Gama's saddle-bag. The *burak* walked calmly to stand over the shivering wolf. He fired. The wolf's head imploded and its body shuddered.

Pathan shouted that all was well. He had a couple of his guards carry the carcass to the woods outside the gate.

Fernando's door opened, but he did not come out again. Instead he pushed his small, lace-trimmed hand through the opening and waved his kerchief in farewell.

Slipper snored through it all.

Part Two

Bandits

Soon the howdah resumed its relentless sway. Maya had taken up her usual position, her palm-leaf book on her lap; Slipper snored curled up nearby, a ball rolling in the cushions. Lucinda watched the house of the Analas disappear behind the trees that lined the road. Soon there was nothing to see, only trees and more trees, and Lucinda shut the curtains and made herself as comfortable as she could.

There was nothing to do except to sit. Lucinda wished that she had brought some needlework, something. She glanced at Maya, and wondered whether she should bring up the subject of *arsênico,* but the bayadere seemed so totally absorbed in reading that Lucinda held her tongue.

Someone had placed a bowl of fruits in a corner of the howdah, but they were unfamiliar. Lucinda finally chose one that looked something like a custard apple, but when she cracked the papery skin with her thumb, the insides were brown and she put it back without tasting it. She glanced around, and found Maya looking at her.

"Must you stare?" Lucinda said.

"I have been thinking," Maya said. "Yesterday, we talked about being a slave."

The memory of that conversation made Lucinda feel cold. "Let us speak of something else," Lucinda said.

"Indulge me for a moment."

Lucinda closed her eyes, steeling herself for another insult. Maya seemed to find it difficult to speak, and when she did at last her voice sounded distant and sad. "I was rude. I hurt you under the guise of speaking truth. Maybe I spoke cleverly, but I did not speak truthfully, for truth does not injure." Lucinda's face softened at the unexpected words. "A month ago I danced for the gods; now I am a slave. My thoughts tangle like wet string. My mind is such a tumult that I scarcely know what next I'll say."

Lucinda grew very still and considered Maya's vacant face. At last she said, "I understand."

"Do you? Maybe you do. In any case, I of all persons should be capable of controlling my words."

"I forgive you," Lucinda answered.

Maya nodded, but when she looked up again, her face had an amused superior look. "Christians like to forgive, I think. This is what your god teaches you, yes?"

"It is a blessing to forgive. Don't Hindis forgive?"

"We apologize, of course, and accept apologies," Maya said. "Maybe it's not the same as Christians. The Gita teaches only by placing all our actions, good and bad, at the feet of the Lord can we hope to escape the never-ending web of pain we feel and cause." She looked expectantly, but Lucinda did not know how to answer. "No, I see it is not the same," Maya said at last, and without another word returned to her book.

Lucinda framed a half-dozen replies, but all were in Portuguese. Apparently courtesy and polite conversation counted for little to a whore. She began to long for the prattle of Slipper, odd as the eunuch was. He at least seemed to share some sense of etiquette. But at that moment the eunuch stirred in his sleep and gave a long, trumpeting fart.

Maya rolled her eyes and threw open the curtain. "How typical of a *hijra*!"

"Well, he can't help it!" Lucinda's voice was harsh, and she realized that she was still disturbed by Maya's halfhearted apology.

"What can't he help?" Maya seemed ready for an argument.

"He can't help being a eunuch."

The fat of Slipper's cheeks spilled toward his pillow, so his face looked awkward and unbalanced. He breathed through his mouth like a child, and a dab of drool glistened at his lips. Maya shook her head. "No, I suppose he can't help that, can he?" She frowned and leaned back in her cushions.

What an impertinent woman, Lucinda thought. She ignores me for hours, but expects me to drop everything and talk with her whenever she wants. She opened her curtain.

The sky was clear blue, and the sun high and bright enough to cast dark, clear shadows. Black monsoon clouds hung in the far distance; someplace, probably, the monsoon rains still fell, but here the season was ending. Their road had been cut into the stone face of a long, sloping mountain. To the left the hillside inclined toward a broad river valley. Sunlight sparkled on the river's surface. Everywhere spread a carpet of vegetation in a thousand shades of green.

A moan interrupted her reverie. Lucinda turned to find Slipper sitting up. He made a few feeble attempts to retie his turban. "I'm so thirsty," he said to no one in particular.

The water pitcher was right beside Maya, but she did not move. Finally Lucinda leaned over to fetch him a cup, which he drained in a gasping gulp. He turned to Lucinda, but didn't thank her. "Can't you feel that the howdah sways differently now?" he said. "The elephant strains with each step."

"I hadn't noticed."

"Oh yes," he answered brightly. "We've been going uphill for the better part of an hour."

"I thought you were supposed to be asleep," Maya said without looking up.

Slipper ignored her. He sat with his eyes closed, rubbing his temples. "I should never drink, never. Oh, I am a fool."

"You very much impressed me, Slipper." The eunuch looked up at Lucinda. "It took some courage to apologize as you did. I was touched."

"Oh, that," Slipper said, with a wave of his hand. "Mere playacting, I assure you. As if I would ever apologize to such a one as that. Neither Christian nor Hindi! He is the true *hijra*! And I should apologize to him? Let him apologize to me!"

"But I heard you!" Lucinda protested.

"Captain Pathan suggested it. He said that my behavior had made

Deoga lose face. He was right, of course. So I made the drama. Did you like it?" He selected a piece of fruit—one of those same brown fruits that Lucinda had refused—and sucked noisily on its soft flesh through a hole he poked in its skin. He was starting to feel better, which meant, to Slipper, that it was time once more for pleasant conversation. He was good at this. In little time Lucinda had forgotten her irritation and had started chatting amiably once more.

She became aware of that he was leading the conversation somewhere. His direction was subtle but persistent. A dozen roundabout questions of Lucinda's clothing; about her shoes of brocade silk; about the lace that frilled her bodice.

Suddenly Lucinda understood. "You want to know about my corset, don't you?"

"One has so little opportunity to explore the question," Slipper replied, blushing.

"You needn't be embarrassed." She had learned that corsets were a source of endless fascination to most Hindis, but she had expected it would be Maya who asked her, not a man.

Lucinda explained the garment in some detail, to Slipper's obvious delight: how the linen tube laced front and back, ringed with channels round its length. "Some have their stays sewn in permanently, but in the one I'm wearing, the stays can be removed. Silvia and I removed half the stays this morning, for we couldn't manage to tighten it like my maid, Helene."

"Are they really made of bone?" Slipper asked.

"A sort of bone, from a great fish common near my homeland."

"I am an educated man. I know about whales," Slipper said, looking peeved.

"I am sure you do, senhor, but I regretfully forgot the Hindi word." Lucinda was pleased to see that Slipper at last looked a little embarrassed. "Some of the ladies of Goa use stays of twisted broomstraw, for they are both cooler and cheaper, but Helene insists that I wear whalebone."

"But doesn't it hurt when you breathe?" Slipper asked.

"It's quite comfortable; in fact. I feel strange without it."

"It presses you tightly . . ." Slipper seemed about to say more, but then delicacy overcame him. Lucinda lifted her arms to show the flatness of her bosom and the narrowness of her waist, the smallness emphasized by the fullness of her skirts.

"And your men? Is that the shape that they desire?" Slipper asked.

"I assume it must be. I doubt if anyone has ever asked them."

Slipper closed his eyes, as if trying to envision the garment Lucinda described. "Someday you must let me undress you, madam," he said at last.

This comment caused Lucinda to stop short. She'd gotten used to thinking of Slipper as a man—a strange man to be sure, beardless and ball-shaped, with a voice like a boy's. It occurred to her that Slipper did not think of himself so. Why hadn't she recognized earlier how much he acted like a woman, she thought. It's all so obvious: how he fusses over the curtains and the cushions, how he whines about the journey as though he were a hapless, helpless victim, how he lives for conversation, or more to the point, for gossip. Now his request to undress her—what man would say such a thing?

☙ ❧ ❧

Not long after, the caravan stopped so the Muslims might pray. Slipper made a show of getting down from the howdah, demanding that the ladder be brought even though the mahout told him the elephant could lower him. "I've seen you riding on the trunk, sir. That is for mahouts and little boys, not for a *mukhunni* of the first rank."

With much puffing, he worked his way down the ladder, and after the mahout too had joined the prayer, Maya came over to Lucinda. Now she wants to talk, Lucinda thought bitterly, so I suppose I, of course, must listen.

Maya glanced toward the clutch of men facing west toward Mecca, and sighed to Lucinda. "I wanted to speak with you alone, away from the presence of my captor."

Lucinda blinked. "Your servant, you mean? I thought you were his mistress."

"That monstrosity? He is my jailer, nothing less. I wanted to warn you. Do not trust him. He is wicked and treacherous. Hear me: do not trust him."

Lucinda frowned as though amused. "But he's such a silly . . . so eager to please."

"So he tries to appear. But you must ask yourself—who is it that he seeks to please? I assure you, it is not me, and much less is it you."

Lucinda blinked, uncertain. "But to call him a monstrosity . . ."

"Those like him, they are not persons anymore. You heard how we Hindis keep them apart. . . . Their souls are broken with their bodies. They cease to act like men."

Lucinda shook her head. "Your words are too harsh."

"My thoughts were gentle, not so long ago. I no longer have that luxury." Maya leaned forward, glancing round her. "You know about the Brotherhood?"

"Well, I've heard of it," Lucinda answered, looking doubtful.

"What you've heard is true, and more besides. Beware."

But at that moment a rustle of the curtains and the sound of huffing made it clear that Slipper had returned.

"Sharing secrets?" the eunuch asked when he regained his breath.

Before either could answer, however, Geraldo's face appeared at the curtains of the howdah. "How are you ladies faring?" He cast a long appraising look at Maya.

"Geraldo, hurry up," came Da Gama's voice in Portuguese. After hours of Hindi, the language sounded like music to Lucinda.

"I'll just ride here with my cousin for a while, if I might, Captain," Geraldo answered lightly. He winked at Lucinda.

"All right," Da Gama said, "ride there until we get to the dharmsala. I'll lead your horse." They could hear Da Gama cursing softly as he rode off, and the sound of the silver ladder being stowed.

۞۞۞

"This seems a pleasant place to ride," Geraldo said in his flawless Hindi.

"How have you two learned to speak our language so well?" Slipper asked while they waited.

"My cousin, I think, speaks much better than I," Geraldo said. Lucinda pretended to hide her face and they all laughed. "My father's second wife, my stepmother, was a Christian Hindi woman. She was beautiful, but she spoke not a word of Portuguese, and my father spoke no Hindi. I was young then, and much more agreeable; so I learned Hindi at her very attractive knees. Of course, for the rest of my father's life, I had to translate for them both: arguments, love talk, everything."

"Your stepmother still lives?" Slipper asked politely. But Geraldo only shrugged as if the question were meaningless. "Well, what about you, madam?" the eunuch asked Lucinda, quickly changing the subject.

The howdah lurched as the caravan began to move, and everyone but Geraldo grabbed for something as the floor jostled into its rocking rhythm. Geraldo, who'd spent much time at sea, sat upright easily, smiling at the discomfort of the others.

"My mother died young," Lucinda said. "My father always hired Hindi governesses, and I must confess I won their affection by learning their language. But this knowledge has come in handy, as you see."

"All of us, orphans," Slipper remarked softly.

"So, does everyone know about where we're headed?" Geraldo asked amiably.

"Bijapur!" Slipper answered, like an eager pupil.

Geraldo laughed and Lucinda saw him steal another a glance at Maya. "I meant our route today. . . . We've been heading east, over the coastal plain. We're a few miles from a high mountain range called the Western Ghats. You probably saw the mountains in the distance yesterday."

"Do the mountains look like steps, sir?" Slipper asked for "ghat" also meant stairway.

"Alas, senhor, if only the mountains were shaped like steps, our journey would be easier. Bijapur lies in the middle of a wide plateau—very much hotter than this part of Hindustan. To reach the city, we must climb those Ghats. But they are not steps; the roads are steep and treacherous. See how much slower we're travelling today than yesterday."

In truth none of them had noticed . . . the road looked much the same as ever, though the hillside had grown much steeper of late. "There's an especially difficult road ahead, through a narrow pass. But Deoga says we will stay at a dharmsala tonight and face the pass tomorrow."

Slipper pursed his lips. "A dharmsala." His tone was disappointed.

"Why do you call him Deoga?" Lucinda whispered in Portuguese.

"It is what the Hindis call him; I don't know why. I've just picked it up in talking with them." Geraldo's teeth showed beneath his well-trimmed mustache. "This is the first I've spoken in Portuguese all day."

"Yes." Lucinda sighed, feeling the tension fade from her shoulders. "Speaking Hindi constantly is quite exhausting. It's a pleasure to talk with you."

"And with you, Lucy," Geraldo said. His eyes bored into hers and she turned away, wondering if she were blushing.

"What are you talking about?" Slipper demanded in Hindi.

☙✦☙✦☙

By late afternoon, the caravan reached the dharmsala. Unlike inns, dharmasalas were provided by the government, free of charge. The dharmsalas of Bijapur were famous for their austerities, yet merchants travelling with goods preferred them to inns because of their safety. The gates were locked at night, and only opened in the morning after the guests had checked their possessions. Anyone found with someone else's goods would be arrested or even killed on the spot.

Da Gama and Pathan quickly got the caravan settled: the horses were stabled, women safely stowed in the plain guest houses, food cooked, dinner served.

The master of the dharmsala was just about to lock the gates when two well-armed horsemen rode up. After a little discussion and a little *baksheesh,* the master fetched Pathan. "Bring your purse, Deoga," Pathan said, and the two of them went to meet the riders.

Pathan hung back, letting Da Gama make the arrangements. Da Gama considered the faces of the riders, their rings and earrings, their richly liveried stallions, their shining weapons. "Can I trust you to guarantee our safe passage?"

The bandit with a dark scar across his flat nose had been doing most of the negotiating. His hand curled around the emerald-covered handle of his dagger. "The courtesy of the Three-Dot clan is well known. Some small token of your respect, that is only fitting. Do you think we have no honor?"

It took a quarter of an hour to haggle the precise size of that small token of respect.

"Ask for proof," Pathan whispered when a price had been set. The riders glanced at each other, and then the one with the scarred nose peeled back his sleeve and showed Da Gama three black dots tattooed in the crease of his elbow.

"What do you think?" Da Gama asked Pathan, who simply shrugged. At last, Da Gama counted out a pile of golden rials.

"Have a pleasant journey," the rider told him, rolling down his sleeve.

"You're not accompanying us?"

"Do we look like guards?" The rider snorted. "You'll be safe enough. We'll be watching."

"But you won't see us," his companion said. Without a bow, without another word, the riders wheeled their horses and rode off.

"Now do you see why I wanted to have our own guards, Deoga?"

Da Gama looked helplessly at Pathan. "Shall I tell you why we hired no guards? Dasana couldn't afford them. He gave me barely enough to cover this bribe. If it weren't for my family obligation to my cousins I should never have taken this job." Da Gama stalked off, leaving Pathan staring speechless.

Finally the dharmsala master came and waved them both inside before he locked the gate. The sun set and the moon glowed behind great silver clouds.

꧁꧂꧁꧂

"Tonight you sleep like a Hindi," Maya said as she and Lucinda looked at the small dharmsala room they were to share. Two quilted bedmats had been tucked into opposite corners of the room. "Have you slept on the floor before?"

Does she mock me? Lucinda wondered. "This will be my first time."

"So many first times. So many new experiences for both of us," Maya said, moving toward one of the mats without looking at Lucinda.

I wonder if I make her as uncomfortable as she makes me, Lucinda thought. She struggled with the brass latch of her large, leather-bound trunk. With a final grunt, the latch opened, the sound echoing like a gunshot from the high whitewashed walls. Maya meanwhile spread on her bedmat her few possessions from the cloth shoulder bag she carried. Lucinda compared them to the piles of clothing and linens heaping from her trunk. "I envy you, Maya," she said quietly.

"Do you?" Maya replied, just as softly, without looking up. She pulled a pair of roughly finished wooden boxes from her bag.

"What are those?" But Maya hid them underneath the quilted cotton coverlet without a word. "Aren't we friends?" Lucinda demanded.

"You are the daughter of my owner," Maya answered without looking up.

Lucinda looked up, shocked. "No, I'm not!"

"You deny it? It is your father who bought me!"

"My father's dead!" Lucinda sighed. "Who told you this?" The look in Maya's flashing eyes told Lucinda everything. "Slipper . . ." she said.

Maya muttered something under her breath. "Look, if you want," she said, pushing the wooden boxes toward Lucinda. Inside the smaller box was a cloth bag. Out of it spilled a sort of golden net, strung with beads. Lucinda held it up, spreading her hands. "A headdress?" Maya nodded. "How pretty. And so heavy!" The beads caught the flickering lamplight; some clear glass, others white.

"The person who gave it to me said it belonged to my mother."

"*Ahcha,*" Lucinda said, gently setting it back. "And this?" Lucinda started to open the long box.

"My father's, that person said. Who knows? I like to think so, anyway."

As Lucinda lifted the wooden cover, she saw a broken sword. "This is a farang blade."

"I think my father might have been a farang. I remember so little, but I seem to remember the man who lifted me over his head, his face so pale and his pale eyes. And a white shirt full of ruffles. Only farangs wear shirts like that."

"Was your mother a farang as well?"

A tear slid down Maya's cheek tracing a glistening path. "I remember a cold night, and a woman pulling me into the forest. I don't remember much about her, but she wasn't a farang. She wore a sari, wet with blood. I remember that she fell asleep and I could not wake her. I pushed leaves into the wound beneath her breast. When she stopped bleeding, I thought I had healed her. But she then grew cold."

"You poor thing! How old were you?"

Maya's voice was steady, but now tear after tear spilled down her cheek. "Two, maybe? Three? I left her there, in the night, on the bare ground. I spread more leaves over her, like a blanket. She was so beautiful, so still." A sob escaped her. "I left her," she choked.

"You were a child!" But Maya covered her face and Lucinda sat silent. Then a golden glint in the sword box caught her eye. Lucinda lifted out a golden rial, rudely sawn in two. "What's this?" she asked. But Maya did not hear her for sobbing, and Lucinda set it down without another word.

The elephant, too big for the dharmsala stables, stood near one of the guesthouses, lit by the flames of a small fire. Bits of ash danced like fireflies into the starlit sky.

Despite the dharmsala guards, Pathan had stationed his own men at key points of the compound. He found his way to the fire. Soon Da Gama and Geraldo came. Da Gama had brought a few saddle blankets from the stables; he and the others sat on them tailor-fashion. All but the mahout, who squatted on his haunches, keeping his hands pressed against his lips as if blowing them for warmth, occasionally pushing twigs toward the flames with his bare toes, as nimble as a monkey's. Each time he did this, Geraldo blinked in amazement.

The faces of the men, lit from below, took on an eerie glow. There was little talk: instead the men focused on the flames, which they watched in tired, silent fascination.

Finally, huffing as if at the end of a race, Slipper joined the circle. The farangs slid apart to make him room, but Pathan and the mahout did not move. With a number of grunts and sighs Slipper sat and tucked his fat legs beneath him. He held his pudgy hands toward the flames, and rubbed them together enthusiastically. "Well, well," he blinked. "What a cozy night!"

The men might otherwise have eyed each other in silence all night, but Slipper's piping voice acted like a lubricant. He turned from face to face with happy appreciation, asking polite questions and nodding open-mouthed as if astonished by the answers. Whenever someone made an observation, Slipper glanced at the others, offering everyone a chance to respond, like an auctioneer encouraging a bid. When anyone spoke, he let out a tiny happy sigh.

Soon Geraldo was telling of the whores of Macao. "They're tiny as dolls! I went to one, I swear, she had a *calha* no bigger than the neck of a wine bottle; I swear, I could barely stick my little finger in!"

"Sounds like a perfect fit for you!" Da Gama said.

"To the contrary, she nearly fainted when she saw the size of my *fonte*. She had to pry herself open with her thumbs to get me in. When she sat on me, I thought I'd split her in two. Each time she moved, the suction! Madonna!"

Slipper's tiny eyes glowed as the tip of his tongue circled his lips. "You should let me give you a shampoo sometime. Many men enjoy it."

The deep laughter of the circle died away, and all eyes turned to Geraldo, awaiting his response. "You are most kind to offer," Geraldo answered. And the others, knowing that they would be traveling with both the eunuch and the young farang for many days, hid their smirks.

"You should go to Macao, Deoga," Geraldo said to Da Gama. "There if you had but one rial you could buy yourself a dozen whores."

"If I had forty thousand rials, I'd buy a nautch girl," Da Gama answered. He nodded toward Maya's room. "That one, and no other." Da Gama lifted an eyebrow to the others. "But I don't, so I won't. Anyway, she's young enough to be my daughter. My granddaughter for that matter. My dream is to find a feather bed, and a nice fat aya."

"What's stopping you, uncle?" Slipper asked sympathetically.

Da Gama frowned. He didn't like artificial pity, particularly from someone he considered inferior. "What's stopping any of us, eh, senhor eunuch? Nothing but money. Gold slips through my fingers like water through a sieve. Like everybody, I'm poor." He nodded ruefully toward Pathan. "Like everybody but this fellow, eh?"

Pathan's eyes narrowed. "If you wish for money, my friend, you need only ask. I owe you much."

"You owe me nothing. Certainly not money. That would be too easy," Da Gama answered. "Someday, maybe, I will ask a favor." Pathan solemnly lifted his hands to his forehead.

The mahout cleared his throat. "You want money? Just find the Web of Ruci. They say a farang hid it, somewhere near here. So maybe a farang would have better luck finding it. Maybe a farang would know where to look." Slipper gave the mahout a particularly unpleasant look.

"What's the Web of Ruci, sir?" Geraldo asked.

The mahout's eyes glowed. "When our sultan married, may his soul be in Allah's care, the *mukhunni* Brotherhood commissioned a wedding present." He looked to Slipper as if seeking confirmation, but the eunuch said nothing. "What the hell else do eunuchs do with their money, anyway? They've got no families, no expenses. I'll tell you: they use wealth to buy power. The Web of Ruci was *baksheesh* for the sultan—a wedding headdress; a net of diamonds and pearls the size of pebbles."

"Diamonds that big?" Geraldo's eyes widened.

The mahout's faced glowed in the fire's flames. "Everyone who saw it marveled. The jeweler called it the Web of Ruci, the Web of Effulgence. Then, poof, it disappeared."

"What became of it?" Geraldo asked.

"No one knows. The *mukhunni* were fools: they entrusted a settlement man to transport it to Bijapur, a damned farang. He never arrived, and the Web of Ruci disappeared. The eunuchs have searched for it these fifteen years without success." The fire crackled, and behind them, the elephant groaned in its standing dream.

"If you believe the stories, maybe," Pathan said softly.

Slipper held his hands out. "The Web is real. I myself held it with these very fingers. They were not so fat then." The eunuch sighed. "If you want to know, I was one of three brothers who was to fetch the Web. We had travelled in secret to the farang's house. That night the house was attacked. We heard shouts. One of us ran for guards, but the bandits had gone by the time they arrived. The farang was dead and the Web was gone. Our Brotherhood looked after his son, but the wife and daughter had fled into the jungle. We never found where they went. Of course we never found the Web."

"Well, then, what's the mystery? The bandits took it."

Slipper's face grew unexpectedly dark. "No— they never got it. They thought the Brotherhood still had it. We caught one or two and persuaded them to speak."

"The Brotherhood is well known for its persuasive powers," Pathan observed dryly.

"Well, if they didn't take it, what happened to it? Anyway by now the headdress has been broken up," Geraldo said, "and its jewels sold individually."

"No," Slipper said. "It's too beautiful for that. To destroy it so would break your heart." He lifted his pudgy hands to the fire as if they were very cold. "We think the farang hid it, or that he gave it to his wife to hide. We have spent many years seeking it." His tiny eyes grew bright. "But it is too beautiful. It cannot hide forever."

Da Gama chuckled, the dimming fire etching his face with shadows. "Many have searched for the Web, Geraldo. It is a pleasant recreation. A few years ago, I myself searched that very jungle. Why might I not be the lucky one?"

"Did you find anything?" Geraldo asked. Da Gama's silence answered him.

"Someday, someone will find it," Slipper said, almost to himself.

"If ever it was," Pathan put in.

"I said I held it," Slipper protested.

Pathan's eyed the eunuch, but his head did not move. "Yes. That is what you said."

Slipper looked back, and then stood up with a grunt. "Time I went to bed." He bowed to everyone except to Pathan and padded into the shadows, and the others followed. Only Pathan and Geraldo remained, gazing at the hot embers and low flames.

"You don't believe him?" Geraldo asked Pathan when Slipper was out of earshot.

Pathan shrugged. "I don't believe anything that eunuchs say, not anything, not ever."

Geraldo considered this in silence. At length he stood, bowed and turned to leave when Pathan spoke. "That farang woman . . . your sister?"

Geraldo looked back. "My cousin, sir."

Pathan's serious eyes met Geraldo's. "Do you find her attractive?"

"Some find her so." Geraldo waited, but Pathan did not answer, and Geraldo did not bother to bow again.

☙☙☙

Next morning, Lucinda cracked open the dharmsala door. She expected to find Slipper snoring outside the room as usual, but there was only the breakfast that one of Pathan's men had left discreetly on the porch. Maybe last night's rain had driven the eunuch off, she thought.

An unexpected shower had fallen in the night, leaving the air clean and brilliant. In the dawn light the rain-spattered courtyard sparkled like a thousand jewels. The red roses and magenta bougainvillea leaped toward her eyes, framed by the brightness of the whitewashed walls. From the mountains came a breeze so fresh it seemed never to have been breathed before.

"Chilly," Lucinda said as she latched the door. Maya was nearly finished dressing, and her skin had a golden glow that made Lucinda think she'd bathed in cold water. "You're so pretty!" The words tumbled out unexpected. Maya lowered her head, embarrassed, and Lucinda blushed. "I'm sure everyone tells you so."

"That is what a mother says to a little girl or a father to his daughter. Maybe a husband says this to his wife. Priests raised me in a temple. They never used the word."

"But you must know," Lucinda said.

"I know I fetched a high price, particularly with the merchants." It took Lucinda a moment to work out what Maya meant. The nautch girl had taken a vial of kohl and touched a black application stick to her eyes. She looked up at Lucinda, blinking tears. The black powder settled against her eyelids and cleared the whites, making her strange, gold-flecked eyes seem even larger. "Do you want some?" Maya asked. Lucinda hesitated, then took the vial. Maya helped her touch it to her eyes; her soft hand felt full of vitality.

"I thought you . . . had . . . *sadhus* . . ."

"Blink," Maya said. As she closed the vial and put it in her bag, she spoke without looking up. "*Sadhus* were the better part of my duties. They had true commitment—forsaking all, yearning only to be one with the Goddess. For them I was a grateful vessel. But merchants are how the temple made its money. Of course they'd pretend a little, wearing a white garment or smearing themselves with ash." Maya said no more. She had taken another box from her bag, tiny, maybe made of silver, and opened it to reveal a red paste.

"Do you take *arsênico*?" Lucinda said with surprise.

"This is my *kumkum*," Maya answered. She moistened her third finger and touched the color, then pressed it to her forehead.

"Does it mean something, that dot?"

Maya laughed. "In some castes it does. I have no caste, so to me it's just a dot." She then turned warily to the pile of clothing on Lucinda's trunk: her corset, drawers, hose, petticoats and dress and who knew what besides. "We'd better get you dressed as well. I myself will help you."

"It could take a while. Let's eat first."

They alternated eating and getting Lucinda into her complicated clothing. It took some effort to get Lucinda dressed. The corset in particular was difficult. In the end they had to take out all the stays to get it laced. The door latch rattled, but it was locked from inside. "Come, come, hurry!" Slipper's voice piped outside the door. "Everyone is waiting!"

"Never mind him," Maya told Lucinda.

"I'm waiting." Slipper said impatiently through the door. Lucinda patted her clothes into place and closed the trunk. She opened the door. "Hurry, hurry," Slipper told her.

"You go first without me, dear. I really must rebraid my hair." Ignoring the eunuch, Maya shut the door behind Lucinda.

Not even acknowledging Lucinda, Slipper blinked at the closed door, his mouth forming a small pink O in his enormous face. "She'll pay for this!" he whispered as he walked Lucinda to the howdah.

The morning sun shone so crisp that even the cheap gilt of the elephant's traveling livery gleamed.

After another ten minutes of Slipper pounding at her door, Maya walked across the courtyard with Slipper beside her. With exaggerated politeness he pointed out puddles in their way. With one hand she lifted the hem of her sari over the mud, with the other she held a long loose fold of sari cloth over her head. The creamy silk, edged with red and gold, framed her golden skin and gleaming hair. "It isn't right, mistress, for everyone to see you thus. It's time you began wearing a veil," Slipper hissed.

"There's time enough for that when we reach Bijapur," she answered. Still, she kept her eyes down, and held the sari to shield her face, but as she walked she determined to remember forever the feeling of the breeze soft as rose petals against her cheek.

Slipper glared and clucked his tongue. As he tiptoed across the muddy courtyard, he heard a servant making rude remarks. Unable to contain himself, he turned and gave the fellow a grateful smile.

Near the elephant stood Da Gama and Pathan, conferring in hushed tones. Da Gama gave Maya a sweeping bow. Such a strange man, thought Maya. None of his clothing seemed to fit; any moment some new bit of pasty flesh might show.

Pathan for his part did not lift his hands as would have been polite, but merely nodded. Noting the Bijapuri's arrogance, Maya ignored him, turning instead to Da Gama. "So, Deoga, how shall our travel be today?"

"Excellent, madam," Da Gama smiled. "We have a good road; the rain is gone. Easy travel."

"So it seems. You fear no . . . trouble?"

Da Gama glanced at Pathan, but he had turned his cold eyes elsewhere, content to ignore Maya as much as she ignored him. Da Gama smiled warmly. "I think we'll be fine. Captain Pathan has sent some men to scout ahead, to be sure that the road is not too slippery after last night's rain."

"I place my trust in you, Deoga," Maya answered as she melted Da Gama with one of her special smiles and made her way to the elephant's silver ladder.

"You should not speak to him so familiarly," Slipper whispered as he held the ladder for her. She did not answer, but hurried to the howdah. When she passed through the silk curtains, Maya found Geraldo already there, chatting with Lucinda, and although they both tried to hide it, she saw the longing in their eyes.

"Geraldo was just telling me about our route," Lucinda told Maya. "We go through the Sansagar Pass today. He says it won't be easy."

"The mountain road gets rather narrow in places," Geraldo said, turning his dark eyes toward the nautch girl. "It could be difficult. Elephants have a rough time, I'm told, particularly after a rain."

"It wasn't much of a rain," Lucinda said.

"Most times it's heavier in the mountains."

"Are there bandits?" Maya asked quietly.

Geraldo's face darkened. "Who told you that?" Maya shrugged. "Yes, it's true," Geraldo answered. "But Deoga has made arrangements. I'm sure we'll be fine." Still, a chill had fallen on Geraldo's attractive face.

⊙⊙⊙⊙

Puffing with the effort, Slipper now heaved himself into the howdah. Once seated, he yanked the curtains closed, glaring at Maya, glaring at Lucinda, then smiling shyly at Geraldo. With the mahout's *hut-hut* the elephant's walk began, and with it the rolling lurch of the howdah. The elephant's footsteps made no sound—they heard only chittering morning birds, and the talk of the riders and the clip of their horses' hooves, the deep, arrhythmic clunk of the elephant's lucky bell.

"Let's open the curtain," Lucinda suggested. The sun was brilliant; the trees and grass and ground sparkled like emeralds. Ahead of them dark mountains loomed like black fingers. The road, as Geraldo had suggested, was getting narrow. Whoever had built this road, hundreds of years before, must have had a difficult time. They had scraped it from the living rock of the mountainside: a sheer rock wall on one side, a narrow road of stone scraped flat, and then a sheer drop where the mountainside continued.

A deer appeared in the brush, took a long, terrified look at the procession, and dashed off. The caravan toiled upward. At one point they squeezed past a couple of women placing flowers on a rock painted bright orange. "What are they doing?" Lucinda asked.

"Hindis," snorted Slipper. "They worship stones."

"No! Do they?" Lucinda looked at Maya for an answer, but the nautch girl had buried her face in her book. Slipper glared at her, then snatched the curtains closed.

Growing uncomfortable in Slipper's icy silence, Lucinda began to prattle on about nothing. A memory popped into her head: the children's puppet shows that Uncle Victorio had put on when he visited Goa. As she talked about the beautifully crafted dolls, Lucinda's memory stirred—Princess Colombina, graceful, lonely, cold as ice; the jester Arlequim wretched with love for her. The stories were meant to be funny, and of course the children had hooted and laughed at the jester's misfortunes, but as she spoke, Lucinda realized that even then, her child's heart had stirred at the pangs of ill-starred love.

Slipper's mood improved as Lucinda spoke. He seemed eager to hear everything; his eyes gleamed like black beads. Even Maya looked up from her reading. Soon Geraldo brightened, and joined in, remembering the fox prince, so sly and debonair. "But the fox always confused me!" laughed Lucinda. "Was he a hero or a villain? You could never be sure!"

"I suppose he hardly knew himself," Geraldo answered.

It seemed only a few minutes had passed when the howdah lurched to a stop. Geraldo now threw all the curtains wide. They stood at the foot of the ghats. A great battlement of black craggy stone leaped into the air ahead of them, so high that it blocked the morning sun and left them in shadow. Geraldo moved casually to a seat near Maya, and pointed with his forefinger as farangs do, not caring that it was impolite. "You can just see the road there," he said, loud enough for all to hear, yet Maya felt that he spoke to only her.

In the midst of the mountainside Maya saw a deep cleft, like a stone curtain ripped in two. They stood at the narrow juncture between two cliff faces, above the stream that had over the years cut them in two. Far below ran the chattering stream, now brown and turbulent from last night's rain.

Their road led into this fissure, a narrow pathway that seemed scarcely wide enough for a man to walk. The road clung to one side of the sheer rock walls, and disappeared behind an overhanging crag.

"You can't mean we're to go up there," Lucinda said, her eyes wide.

"I'm sure the captain knows what he's doing," Slipper put in. But his eyes too had grown as big as marbles.

Geraldo laughed. "You are all too nervous. You'll be fine. I'm sure this beast has walked this road a hundred times. Elephants are more sure-footed than horses, you know."

"Do you say that to relieve us?" Lucinda asked. "When all the horse-men fall to their deaths, will we not be next?"

"And just look, just look!" Slipper pointed to a pair of mountains to the rear. "Those are forts. Bijapuri forts! You can see the green flags."

"I can't see flags," Lucinda said.

Slipper sniffed. "They're there. We have reached Bijapur." The eunuch leaned toward Maya as if teasing her, but his eyes were cold. "And now you must obey me." Maya did not reply.

Geraldo laughed. "We're not to Bijapur just yet, Master Eunuch. Bijapur is miles away."

Slipper lifted his nose. "General Shahji would disagree. All these lands belong to Bijapur."

Captain Pathan rode up to the elephant and spoke to the mahout. Then he looked into the howdah. "Senhor Silveira," he called, his expression guarded. "Please come down and join us. From now on the howdah is off limits."

Geraldo bristled but kept calm. "I asked Da Gama's permission."

"You did not ask mine." With that Pathan whispered a few words to the mahout and then wheeled his horse back to the head of the line.

Geraldo shrugged. "A self-made man, I understand," he said to Lucinda.

"I think he's very rude," Slipper told him.

Geraldo crawled to the edge of the howdah, and stood carefully on the elephant's back. "Can't you help me?" he asked the mahout, but the elephant handler had suddenly gone deaf, and steadfastly stared straight ahead. "That's what Pathan was talking to him about," Geraldo whispered in Portuguese to Lucinda. "No ladder. I'm being punished." He kissed his fingertips to his cousin, gave a carefree nod to Maya, and then slid down the elephant's flanks.

"What a handsome man," Slipper said as they watched him stride off. "Pity he's such an awful cardplayer."

"Who told you that?" Lucinda asked.

Slipper smiled. "Oh, I learned it for myself. He lost ninety-three *tangas* to me last night. He said he'd pay me when we get to Bijapur."

"Well, now you have two things to look forward to," Maya said.

☙☙☙☙

As they waited at the foot of the ghats, Slipper passed the time by telling tales of bandits. He seemed to have an endless supply. The bandits of his stories had some similarities: they were all young, all handsome and virile. Many were princes living in exile. Their hearts—stolen in an instant by the sight of a beautiful woman—drove them to reckless action: kidnapping sometimes, or secret meetings within the harem walls. Maya managed to focus on her reading, while Lucinda listened in rapt attention.

"What's the delay?" Slipper said, looking around irritably. "It's almost time for prayers." He crawled to the edge of the howdah and looked out. "Why aren't we moving?"

"It's not like Bijapur is going anywhere," Maya said softly.

"Well, neither are we," Slipper sniffed. "It's those scouts. What has become of them?" The eunuch glared at Maya. "I'm sure they're Hindis."

"I thought they were Captain Pathan's men?" Lucinda said.

Slipper snorted. "For a price, a Hindi will do anything, even pretend to pray. They have no principles." He called for the mahout to bring the silver ladder.

First they'd waited while Da Gama and Pathan arranged and then re-arranged the order of ascent along the trail. Then more waiting while they debated whether they should proceed without word from the scouts.

Da Gama wanted to go up the pass at once. He pointed to the sky, which had changed from hazy blue to bright gray, and to a heavy black cloud that had curled around the opposite peak, which seemed to grow larger and darker even as they watched. "If we don't start soon, we'll get caught in the weather," he said to Pathan, his voice growing loud enough for all to hear. "And we can't stay here. There's no shelter."

Pathan answered softly, but his demeanor suggested that he had his own worries. He knew the scouts, and their failure to report troubled him. So they waited. Flies began to buzz around the elephant's flanks as the sun heated the air. After the noon prayers, Da Gama tried once more. "How long have you known those scouts, Pathan?"

"I think long enough. There must be some trouble or they would have returned by now."

Now Da Gama's frustration showed. "You send out scouts before sunrise, and of course they'll nap before they come back . . . probably asleep right now," he said, smiling to show that he meant this in a friendly way. "Hell, I could use a nap myself."

"Maybe that is the way of farang scouts," Pathan replied.

Da Gama changed his argument. "Forget the sky. What if the scouts were lost or hurt? Shouldn't we go to their aid?"

At last Pathan agreed.

❀❀❀❀

"No lunch!" Slipper announced when he crawled back into the howdah. As they got closer to Bijapur, Lucinda noticed, Slipper seemed to act less like a servant, and more like a guest, and a demanding one at that.

"Odd that we've seen no traffic come the other way," Lucinda said, almost to herself.

"Not odd, not odd at all," Slipper answered, looking very pleased with himself. "The Sultana has banned trade with Goa. Didn't you know? Haven't you wondered why you've been sent away from home?"

Lucinda stared at the eunuch.

"Often you speak when you should be silent," Maya said to him.

Slipper pretended he did not hear. Amid the shouts of guards, the elephant began to move. Slipper jostled the women as he yanked the howdah curtains shut. "It is better if you do not see the dangers of the road."

"We'll be fine," Lucinda answered coldly, with a confidence she did not feel. She'd seen the drop before the curtains closed, and the unsettling fragile trail carved along the mountainside.

The howdah rocked slowly, as if the elephant now measured every step. If she hadn't known the danger, the slow rocking might have lulled her to sleep, but as it was, she felt in her stomach each step the elephant took—from the moment he lifted his heavy toes, until the howdah's bump as the beast's foot next touched solid ground. And with the next step it all began again. After a few minutes, Lucinda's back was damp with sweat.

Just then the howdah lurched to an unexpected halt. Slipper crawled, and with eyes squeezed tight, opened the side curtains. He steeled himself, looked out, and drew back, clutching his heart dramatically, his face pale. Unable to speak, he merely nodded, wide-eyed, toward the scene beyond.

Here the road was so narrow that its edge could not be seen for the elephant's flanks. They seemed poised for a violent drop to the bottom of the chasm hundreds of feet below. They could see through misty shadows the churning stream they'd seen at the entrance to the pass. Scrawny trees poked sideways from the rock wall, clinging precariously, their gnarled branches swaying in the constant breeze, looking so tiny from the howdah's height that Lucinda's head began to spin. "Lord help us," she said in Portuguese.

Maya put down her book to see for herself. Perhaps the shock of the others prepared her, for she gazed calmly into the chasm. She even leaned out of the howdah, and looked up and down the trail.

The road was no longer wide enough for two horses to walk abreast safely. At the head of the caravan, Da Gama was waving to the men to press into single file against the cliff face, making enough space for Captain Pathan to walk back to the elephant, stepping carefully along the terrible outer edge of the trail.

Pathan spoke brusquely to the mahout. Last night's rain had done more damage than expected, he told him, and the road ahead was wet and ragged. "My friend will manage," the mahout answered, rubbing his hand over the tiny hairs that bristled from the elephant's head and scratching its great ears as if it were a puppy.

Pathan looked worried. "Maybe we should go back," he said.

"And how should we do that, sir?" the mahout answered.

He was right, Maya realized. There was scarcely room for the elephant to stand; certainly none for it to turn around. She knew that elephants could walk backward, of course, but behind them were the oxcarts that could never manage such a feat.

"In any case, go slow," Pathan said. The captain inched back to the front of the line, where he mounted and shouted the order to proceed.

Slipper leaned to close the curtain, but Lucinda glared at him and he sat back. When the howdah lurched as the elephant began to move, Slipper yelped. "This is very dangerous. Someone should do something."

"What do you want done?" Maya asked. "Accept your fate."

Slipper glared at her, but his face grew white.

They fell silent, and in the silence they became anxious, attentive to each jolt and jar, glancing to each other for reassurance.

The mahout tapped the elephant to a halt. On the road ahead, a young girl in rags approached, a jug balanced on her head, leading a string of goats. Just before she reached them, however, she vanished down the side of the chasm. "Has she fallen, sir?" Slipper gasped.

In answer, the mahout pointed to the road's edge. A narrow pathway leading off from the road wound to the bottom of the chasm, only wide enough, it seemed, for a child to walk. "There are many such pathways, here," the mahout said. "They lead from this road to the water below. Look, you can see her village." In the depths of the chasm, in an elbow of the river, they saw a half-dozen huts of grass. Lucinda realized that she had seen others earlier, but thought that they must be bushes.

The mahout gave a *hut-hut*, and the elephant began once more his slow march up the canyon road. The breeze through the chasm became a wind, and the wind grew damp. The curtains of the howdah slapped and sighed as it gusted. Dark clouds swelled.

Then the front right corner of the howdah platform caught on something. With a snap like tinder breaking, the whole front of the howdah lifted, and the elephant let out a groan. They all tumbled. Slipper slammed against the howdah's low brass railing. Grabbing anything—cushions, curtains—they waited, breath caught, hearts pounding.

The mahout shouted his commands now—he who rarely spoke, but directed his beast with taps of his heel and the point of his *ankus* now shouted. With another whining groan, the elephant took a hesitant step backward. Released from where it had caught on the rock, the howdah thudded back into place.

The curtains had swung shut in the muddle. Ignoring Slipper's protests, Maya opened the ones nearest her, and Lucinda the front curtains.

The road had narrowed even more, if possible. The howdah's right side had a long, bright gash where it had scraped against a high outcrop of rock. The cliff face was a foot away or less. The elephant's right flank pressed against the wet black stone. "The road has crumbled here," the mahout said, as if it were his own fault. "It was not this way when we came from Bijapur."

The line had halted, and the riders twisted in their saddles to see what had become of the howdah. Pathan dismounted and hurried toward the elephant. "Is everyone all right?" he called.

"We're well, Captain," Lucinda answered. Pathan then began a tense discussion with the mahout, pointing to the road ahead, even walking to certain places to point out where the edge had collapsed in the rain.

In the meantime, Slipper poked his head out the rear curtain. Behind him came Geraldo riding a pony, who gave him an encouraging wave. "How is the ride up there, senhor eunuch?" he called. "Remember, I promised to pay you in Bijapur . . . but first you must get there, eh?"

"If ever I get home I shall give half my winnings to the poor!"

"Fine, fine!" Geraldo laughed. "You can start with me!" Then he looked seriously at the eunuch. "Look, don't worry. Everything is fine. There's plenty of room. How's my cousin, eh?"

"She's taking things well, sir. The best of any of us, sir," Slipper answered. His eyes widened as he saw how the chasm fell off just inches from Geraldo's side. "I must go back inside, sir."

"Go with God," Geraldo said in Portuguese as the eunuch disappeared.

๛๛๛๛

The mahout let the horses get a few lengths ahead before he urged the elephant forward. As they neared the outcropped rock again, he stood on the elephant's head. Leaning his back against the howdah, straining with the effort, he twisted it enough so that this time the howdah just squeezed past. Still its edge scraped against the stones, sending a rasping screech into the air. Slipper covered his ears. "There, that's the worst of it," the mahout said, but his face lacked any confidence.

Like a drunk tiptoeing in the dark, the elephant chose each step with worried care. But the mahout was right, they'd passed the worst . . . for a while at least. The wind had grown cold now, but dry, and at that moment it blew away the mountain mists. Lucinda wished she had a warmer shawl. Then a hole broke through the dark clouds, and the sun bloomed above them, and they saw it all: the churning sky framed by great steep walls of glistening black stone, the brilliant green of the brave trees that clung to the sides of the chasm, and far below the white foam of the rain-glutted stream.

"What's that?" Maya asked, pointing with the fingers of her hand politely together.

Below the road a few yards ahead, a narrow shelf of brownish rock bowed out from the chasm wall, forming a shelf about twenty feet long. This shelf looked almost like a second, lower road, although there seemed to be no way to access it other than by jumping.

"That can't really be another road," Slipper whispered.

"No, it's just an outcropping," Maya said. "But look."

She nodded: behind a scraggly bush lay what appeared to be a white sack. Something soft and brown was spilling from it.

"It's a body," Lucinda whispered as the image resolved in her mind.

"One of the scouts," Maya said.

As if he'd heard, the mahout halted the elephant again. Captain Pathan once more hurried toward them.

Maya changed places so she could better see the very front of the line, and soon Lucinda was by her side. "What's that ahead?" Maya asked her softly.

The answer was what Pathan had come to tell them. "There's a barrier on the road," he said quietly.

"What kind of barrier?" the mahout asked.

"It might be man-made." Pathan licked his lips as he glanced at the women's faces, clearly uneasy to speak in front of them. "There's blood on the road. The scouts are dead." Pathan's eyes, dark as steel, found Lucinda's in the howdah. "Close the curtains," he said.

At that moment they heard Da Gama giving orders to ready weapons. The mahout's face turned ashen. "We must get out of here."

"You know yourself there's no way back," Pathan replied.

"The bandits in these hills are killers, Captain."

"Arrangements have been made. Bribes paid. It may only be a terrible mistake. Besides, we have nothing worth stealing." But in answer, the mahout simply turned and lifted his chin toward the howdah.

"They'd be insane to try," Pathan muttered.

"There seems to be no shortage of insanity today, Captain. Should we unload the passengers?"

Pathan thought about this and shook his head. "There's no way to get them down safely, is there? Besides, they're in no more danger in the howdah than out of it." He looked up again. "I said to close the curtains of the howdah!" He spun on his heel and hurried to the front.

"Do you pray in your religion?" Maya asked Lucinda as they pulled the curtains closed.

"Yes."

"Then pray now."

಄಄಄಄

Somehow, as the mahout urged the elephant forward, Maya found her fingers wrapped around Lucinda's hand. She was almost surprised to see Slipper—in the excitement she'd nearly forgotten him—huddled against an upright of the howdah, the fat of his jowls pale and quivering.

The elephant turned its head, his old gray eyes looking balefully at the mahout. But then the mahout spoke to him, and he began to move, slowly and reluctantly.

Lucinda pulled the curtain open just enough to peer out. The road ahead of them was empty, for the horsemen had crossed the roadblock and now huddled on the other side, eyes peeled, bows poised. Below she saw the crumpled bodies of the scouts on the stone shelf, and beyond that the endless chasm.

Then the howdah's roof collapsed.

A boulder fell on them.

It splintered the lacquered roof and smashed through the floor. The roof pitched backward like an opening clamshell, and suddenly the women were in the open air. They heard Slipper scream, but his face was hidden by the broken roof.

"Bandits!" screamed the mahout, pointing upward. "Get down!" He pushed Maya's head to the shattered floor. Pathan's men lifted bows, and Da Gama shot with his pistols. Pops and roars echoed between the stone chasm walls. "They have guns!" the mahout yelled.

Maya looked up in time to see a hail of stones pouring from a ledge above. She pushed Lucinda beneath what was left of the ruined roof and shoved her to the floor, then threw herself across her. The stones rained down, snapping against the howdah floor, thudding when they struck the back of the unprotected elephant.

A stone the size of a loaf of bread hammered Maya's left shoulder. She lifted her head as in a dream. Her arm, she noticed calmly, was useless—she could not move her hand.

Around her the action seemed to happen far away. The shouts of the soldiers and the roar of their guns might have been a mile off. She looked up and saw bandits above her: there were two of them. They were dancing.

One pattered backward, arms lifted forward, until he stepped back where she could not see. The other bandit burst upward, spun on his heel, and then leaped into the air, one hand extended outward, the other hand pressed against the hole blown through his chest. Not dancing, Maya realized. Dying. The bandit dove past the elephant in a graceful arc. Then his head struck the edge of the road, and he spun like a pinwheel as he dropped into the fathomless chasm.

But the elephant heaved and Maya spilled backward before she could see the bandit land. Spooked by the attack, the beast lifted his front feet from the ground and waved them in the air. The mahout tumbled into the howdah beside Lucinda. Behind the broken roof they again heard Slipper call for help.

Balanced on his hind legs on the narrow road, the elephant began a slow, colossal turn until he actually faced the side of the mountain. His front feet crawled along the mountain wall, as if he hoped to climb up its face.

"He's trying to turn around, but there's no room!" the mahout shouted. And as if to prove this, the beast lurched backward, and his left rear foot stepped off the road and slipped into nothingness.

Flailing with his forelegs, the elephant crashed down. In the howdah, they tumbled and clung desperately. The women and Slipper screamed.

Somehow the elephant managed to break his fall, and now he clung desperately to the road. But at this place, the road pushed away from the cliff, and so the elephant's hindquarters could find no purchase. His head and forelegs pressed against the mountain face, while his rear legs hung off the road and pedaled uselessly in the empty air.

Maya, without even thinking, scrambled from the howdah, slid over the beast's gray shoulders and fell on the broken road.

There was nothing to hold the elephant from sliding off the road. Though his legs churned in the air, his hindquarters slowly dropped into the chasm. Only the bulk of the beast's belly against the road's edge slowed his slide. His forelegs pawed the sheer black stone of the chasm walls like a dog scratching a door, but found no place to cling.

The howdah had pitched forward and leaned on the beast's great head like a broken hat. "Hurry! Come, come! Hurry!" Maya screamed, reaching for Lucinda, for the mahout. The mahout tried to push Lucinda to safety, but she clung desperately to the howdah's broken railing, looking into the chasm in horror. More gunshots cracked the air. The elephant struggled, and the road's edge crumbled beneath him. He slid backward, squealing like a puppy, eyes wide, trunk straight with terror.

The howdah disappeared. Maya shrieked.

But the elephant did not fall. Somehow the beast managed to hang on with his forelegs, though his belly was following his hindquarters into the chasm. His chin rested on the road between his forefeet, and his trunk swept wildly near Maya, as if he might hold on to her to stop his fall.

Maya could not tell what had become of the howdah. She managed to peer over the road's edge and saw that somehow the howdah still clung to the elephant's back, suspended by a single strap. And she saw Lucinda, Slipper, and the mahout still clinging to it.

Maya staggered forward. The mahout, head bleeding, began to climb to her. Clutching the elephant's bell strap in one hand, the mahout then reached back to Lucinda with the other.

Maya stepped up to the road's edge, between the elephant's right front foot that slipped and struggled, and his gold-banded tusk. "Stop moving!" she told the elephant.

Taut as a bowstring, the mahout strained to lift Lucinda to Maya's waiting hand. The elephant seemed to sense the moment, and let off flailing his useless rear legs, holding breathlessly still.

But just when their hands were inches away, the howdah's straps gave way and Maya, in horror, watched Lucinda spill off into the endless air.

☙🙙🙚🙛

But Lucinda did not drop to her death. Instead she struck an outcropping of rock—not enough to stop her, but enough to slow her down. From there she slid in a hail of gravel to the rock shelf they'd seen earlier. Lucinda collapsed a few feet from the bodies of the scouts.

Maya's thoughts were broken by the cries of the mahout. He was standing on the very edge of the howdah platform, whose straps had tangled at the elephant's rear knees.

Looking tinier than ever, the mahout was struggling to lift Slipper to safety. The eunuch scrambled mindlessly upward, feet nearly knocking the mahout from his precarious perch. Maya leaned over the chasm, taking the elephant's tusk in one hand for leverage, and reaching as far as she could with her other, still numb from the falling rock.

"Give me your hand!" screamed the eunuch.

"I can't move it!" she cried. "My arm is broken."

For all his size, Slipper shinnied up the elephant's neck, grabbing rolls of gray skin in his pudgy fists. With the mahout pushing him from below, he climbed with unexpected vigor. His tiny eyes nearly popped from his head. The eunuch reached the great beast's neck and grabbed Maya's numbed hand.

As he twisted and pulled, feeling returned to Maya's shoulder, and her arm exploded in agony. Pain seared through her and darkness swarmed across her eyes. Somehow she managed to hold on. Slipper, scrambling past her, stepped on her leg when she fell to the ground.

The elephant at that moment gave a small lurch backward, as though something were tugging on his tail. His eyes gaped so wide Maya saw them ringed with white. He let out a tiny sound, like the sigh of a frightened child.

"Hurry!" Maya called, grasping the tusk once more and leaning toward the mahout. "Hurry now!" The mahout stretched to his full length, reaching his hands toward her.

But at that moment, the elephant slipped again, his forefeet and chin sliding backward just an inch, and on his back the mahout staggered, grabbing a gray ear to break his fall. "Please!" Maya shouted, reaching toward him.

But the final slide had begun. The elephant's tusk began to move, and Maya herself dropped to the ground to keep from falling with it.

She watched as the elephant's wide eyes softened, then closed. Then he slipped backward, slowly but smoothly, until only the tips of his forefeet and his trunk remained on the road, like a child peering over a table. Hopelessly Maya reached toward the mahout, and he for her.

Then the elephant dropped silently into space, his huge legs waving slowly as he hurled downward through the open air. The mahout pressed his cheek against the elephant's gray head, and looked at Maya as he fell.

She turned away so she wouldn't see the end, and covered her ears so she would not hear. When at last she stood and looked around her, she heard Slipper's high-pitched whimper, and also the shouts of the men. They were pointing to the ledge where Lucinda had fallen.

A bandit on a skinny mountain pony rode along that ledge. How had he gotten there? He looked up to the guards and gave a loud, taunting laugh, then wheeled his pony to where Lucinda lay. He jumped off and pressed a hand against her heart. Satisfied that she was alive, he threw her over the pony's back, and leaped on the saddle behind her.

A bowstring twanged, and an arrow clattered against the stones just inches from the bandit's head. "Put up your weapons," Da Gama screamed. "You might hit the girl!"

The bandit's laugh turned into an animal-like howl. He pushed his pony toward the edge of the ledge. Maya screamed, and the bandit then looked up at her. She saw his eyes gleaming like a demon's. Then he jammed his heels into the pony's flanks. There was a kind of a trail down the chasm walls, nearly impassable, but somehow the bandit twisted and turned his pony along it in an endless slide.

When he reached the stream at the bottom of the chasm, Lucinda's white dress looked like a dot of paint in the shadows.

The bandit waved in triumph as he galloped off.

☙☙☙☙

Lucinda dreamed she was back in the nursery, rocking.

Sometimes she dreamed herself cradled in Helene's warm arms; sometimes she dreamed she rode her painted hobbyhorse. The constant rocking rhythm felt so comforting.

She woke to find herself slung across the back of a sweat-foamed pony. A thick arm curled around her waist. Her head bounced against the pony's flank and with each footfall pounded with exquisite pain. Somehow she managed not to cry out. Some undiscovered part of her, desperate for survival, warned her.

She tried to gather her wits. Where was she? What had happened? The last thing she remembered was clinging to the broken howdah as the elephant slipped from the road. The haze around that memory began to clear:

before that, she recalled, bandits cast stones upon them from above. But hadn't their attackers been shot?

For a moment she imagined that she was being carried to safety.

Then at one particularly rough step, she let her head flop as if unconscious, to face the rider's leg. The saddle and the stirrup told her all: cracked leather and dry wood, the saddle of a bandit, not the tended livery of the horsemen of the caravan.

Lucinda kept her head down and bit back the pain. That her captor did not know she was awake was an advantage, she reckoned, and she would need every advantage she could muster.

They traveled slowly now, scarcely faster than a man might walk, thrusting through high grass that grew along the bank of the brown, turbulent stream. It occurred to Lucinda that it was the same stream she'd seen from the chasm's edge. If she'd fallen from that height, it was no surprise that her head hurt.

The pony's chest thrust the grass aside, but with each step the blades snapped back and stung her face. The rider slapped the pony with a long switch, digging his heels furiously into the animal's flanks; even so, the animal could hardly go faster. The rider whipped the pony only out of hatred, Lucinda sensed.

I am lost, she thought. Her head throbbed. Nearby, Lucinda heard the rushing stream, and realized how thirsty she was.

Suddenly the man leaped from the saddle without waiting for his pony to stop. He tied the reins to a nearby tree and strode around the small clearing. Lucinda feigned unconsciousness and watched.

He was small and squat with a filthy turban and a scraggly beard. A long knife hung from the sash of his dust-stained robe.

Two more men appeared, also dressed in filthy clothes, so similar they might have been a uniform. One had long mustaches instead of a beard, but otherwise they resembled each other. Maybe all three were brothers. They spoke oddly accented Hindi, not what Lucinda was used to, but she could make out enough to understand.

The rider fell to his knees before the others. "It was horrible," he wailed, his voice cracking, "Hamfist and Rat Tail got killed. I nearly died myself. Where are the others? Don't tell me they're dead, too?"

"Take it easy. We'll recover soon enough. Then we'll get revenge," the mustached one said.

"Was there no treasure?" snarled the other. "What have you brought there on your pony?"

"A farang woman. I captured her."

"She's not dead?"

"Not yet. We can ransom her."

"Or take revenge," the mustached one suggested.

"Or both," said the other.

"I can't do it, not now," the rider wailed. "Not with my brothers' death cries in my ears."

"Rest then," the mustached one said. "We will revenge them for you."

As the mustached bandit headed for the pony, Lucinda willed herself to act. With all her strength she pushed off the pony's back, intending to run. But she slipped on the wet jagged gravel at the stream's edge and collapsed, twisting her ankle. She saw that her hands were bleeding. She rolled onto her back just in time to see the mustached man run toward her.

"Look who's awake!" he cried. He flung himself down and grabbed a handful of her hair, twisting it until Lucinda whimpered. She thrust out her bleeding hands, hoping to scratch his eyes, when she heard a cold dull ringing sound. Somehow she recognized it at once, a steel blade unsheathed, and before she could move, she felt a blade pinching her throat.

Lucinda got very quiet. The splashing of the wild stream against its banks mixed with the wheezing of the bandit, the smell of the moist earth mingled with his horrid breath.

"No one's going to hurt you," the bandit said. His pig eyes gleamed.

"She's a farang! She don't understand!" the other bandit called.

"Give me a hand," the mustached one answered.

A new world of helplessness spread before Lucinda. It's one thing to be helpless as one tries to lace a corset or to mount an elephant, quite another to be helpless as a bandit pushes a black steel knife against the flesh of your throat while his brother comes to join him.

"What's under those things?" the seated one asked, nodding to her skirts.

"Legs, I expect," the other answered. He threw the skirts toward Lucinda's face, then pawed through her petticoats. "Shit, what is all this?"

"Just use your knife, idiot," the seated one cried, lifting himself to see better and unconsciously pressing his knife blade harder against Lucinda's throat. She could smell his skin, sweating with excitement.

"Shut up," said the other. Lucinda heard again the ring of steel, and felt a cold blade slide along her torso. The blade sliced through her petticoats and corset. She felt damp air on her naked belly. The bandit's thick fingers gripped her thighs.

"Nice," he whispered, his eyes widening. "You did good!" he called to the one who'd brought her, who still knelt sobbing a little way off.

"Shouldn't we wait for the others?" he sniffed.

"Plenty for everyone," muttered the other as he knelt at Lucinda's feet. "Hold her still."

Behind her head, the mustached one jerked forward to place his knees on her shoulders. "Feel that?" he whispered, sliding the flat of the blade softly on the skin of her neck.

"She don't understand a word!" the other told him.

"She gets the idea."

Lucinda could look up and see the mustached bandit's face, puffed and sweating, blotting out the sky. Or she could look between her legs, and watch the other struggling to pull down his pants. She chose to close her eyes.

"Come on, come on," she heard the bandit above her yell.

"Give me a second!" the other replied.

"What's taking so long!"

"I'm not hard yet!"

"Goddammit! Then let me go first!"

"No!"

Suddenly the weight came off Lucinda's shoulders. She looked up to see the mustached bandit leaping toward the other, knife in hand. As the two brothers wrestled, she dragged herself along the stream bank, no longer conscious of the pain in her hands or head, or the gravel tearing into her back.

"Look what you've done now! She's getting away!" the kneeling one cried out.

Their fight was forgotten as the bandits came back to Lucinda, now panting and grimed with sweat. Lucinda's efforts had only served to move her to a place less comfortable, if possible. A sharp-edged rock poked into her shoulders. Her head hung limply backward—she was too exhausted to hold it up.

At least they had let go of her hair.

"Hold her down while I go," the mustached one said. She watched him tugging on the tiny sausage between his legs.

The other bandit swung over her to sit on her chest. He put a knee on each of her shoulders, and pressed his heavy buttocks against her corseted breasts. "Hey, look. I can have her mouth!" he said.

"If you're not too soft for that, too," the mustached one answered. "Now hold her while I get it hard."

Lucinda felt his sausage rubbing on her thighs, and kicked out as hard as she could. She must have hit something, for the man groaned. A heavy fist slammed into her belly.

For the first time, as if the pain had freed her voice, Lucinda cried out.

"That's right," the bandit sitting on her shoulders said. "Open wide. I've got something for you."

Then his head dropped to the ground beside hers. Its eyes rolled back in a kind of ecstasy: its lips throbbed though no sound came.

Above her, blood exploded in a fountain from the bandit's now headless neck.

Lucinda clamped her eyes shut against the spray of blood. The bandit's lifeless body fell across her.

Blinking through the blood that fogged her eyes, she looked up, and to her wonder saw Pathan.

He walked past her without a glance, curved sword raised, advancing slowly on the mustached bandit, who scooted on the ground, pants down, hands raised, whimpering. Pathan moved with stately slowness, with unearthly calm.

"Behind you," Lucinda said.

The third bandit had stopped crying. He raced forward with a shrill war cry, a long knife in his outstretched hand.

As though moving in water, Pathan turned to face him. With an unearthly languor, he dropped to one knee. Pathan's curved sword arced slowly along the bandit's leg, and a chunk of thigh sailed through the air like a child's ball. The bandit's knife slipped harmless past Pathan's ear, and the bandit fell first to his knees, then in screaming agony to his belly.

Ignoring for a moment the mustached bandit, who struggled to pull his pants back over his bare ass, Pathan closed on the fallen man, step by slow step. Raising his sword with both hands like an ax, he brought the blade down across the bandit's spine. The body shuddered at Pathan's feet.

Pathan had to place a foot on the man's back in order to remove his sword. Meanwhile the mustached bandit, his pants on at last, half-ran, half-crawled toward the tethered pony.

How can Pathan move so slowly, Lucinda wondered. The bandit was frantic: fumbling at the pony's bridle until he finally remembered his knife. He cut the traces and leaped on the saddle just as Pathan arrived.

The bandit wheeled, waving his long black knife, but Pathan stood as if frozen. His sword seemed barely to move, yet somehow as the pony galloped past him, the bandit's hand fell to the ground by Pathan's feet, still clutching the knife.

The bandit screamed at the sight of his bleeding stump as he galloped off. Pathan reached down and threw the severed hand into the water.

Then there was only silence, and the rushing sound of the stream against the rocks.

☙☙☙

Lucinda became aware of the bandit's blood growing sticky on her face, of the weight of the headless body that had fallen across her legs. What should a woman do, knowing that a severed head lies inches from her own? Lucinda stared into the clouds, but the memory of the dead bandit's face would not go.

The bright sun peeked through, and she heard Pathan's footsteps. "Please, madam," he said. "Close your eyes and do not move until I say."

Lucinda squeezed her eyes. Her head pounded. She felt the weight of the lifeless body shift, and started as though she'd been kicked. "Please stay still, madam," Pathan grunted as he dragged the body away.

"Your eyes still closed, madam, please," Pathan said. She heard him come beside her, heard the gravel shift next to her ear and knew he'd picked up the bandit's head. Unable to restrain herself, she watched as Pathan waded into the stream carrying it by its filthy hair, and heaved it into the water.

Then Pathan drooped down, his hands to his knees. He vomited into the stream, once, twice, and shook his head slowly. He took his sword and rinsed it in rushing water, and heaved once more. Then he scooped some water from the stream and rinsed his mouth. At last he stood again, took a deep breath, and stripped off his shirt, which he swirled in the water. Then he wrung it out, and came back to Lucinda.

Though he set his face Lucinda could tell he was horrified by her appearance. "Madam, madam," he whispered, "please, I mean you no harm." He stooped near her and began to dab her face with his wet shirt. At each touch she startled, and each time he whispered, *"Shhhh,"* as though she were a frightened animal.

When he began to wash her forehead, she winced and pulled back. "I'm sorry, madam," he whispered. With exquisite care he touched the hurt places with his fingertips. "This is not so bad, madam," he told her, his face serious. "Is this your only injury?"

It was as though she could not speak. She glanced toward her twisted ankle. Pathan nodded. *"Shhhh, shhhh,"* he said again.

The first thing he did was to move her torn skirts to cover her. Still terrified and furious, but also suddenly grateful, Lucinda could not find words, and so said nothing. "Now I must look, madam," Pathan said, softening his voice. "I mean you no harm. I assure you I have seen the ankles of many women." Even so, she shivered when he touched her.

"Shhh, shhhh," he said once more. He probed the leg and ankle with his fingertips. "Forgive my rudeness, madam, but I must remove your shoe." With a little effort he tugged the silk slipper from her foot. "Now also the stocking," he said, scarcely breathing.

Lucinda whimpered when he slid the torn gauze stocking from her leg, not with pain, but from the memory. "Your ankle is only twisted, I think, and it will heal. This is not so bad, madam, not for one who had such adventures. The angels of Allah were with you."

He looked at her earnestly. "Madam, did I come to you in time?"

Remembering, remembering it all, she closed her eyes. "You were the angel, Captain. God sent you."

Pathan covered his face with his hands, and when he looked back at her, tears stained his cheek. *"Ishwar-Allah,"* he said—what God wills.

"There are others, Captain."

"Eh?"

"The bandits. They said they were meeting others."

"Yes," Pathan said. "We saw others ride away. We must get to safety."

"Is any place safe?"

Pathan turned as though her words had startled him. He took her hand. "With me, madam." His palms, which she thought would be rough, were smooth and soft.

"We must be going," Pathan said. He left her for a moment and scouted around the clearing, but came back disappointed. "There are no horses here. They must have come by foot."

"I don't think I can walk, Captain."

"I shall carry you, madam." He scooped her into his arms and stood, grunting only a little. "You are light as air."

Lucinda put an arm around Pathan's neck and smiled at his lie.

✿✿✿✿

When she looked up from the falling elephant, Maya saw Geraldo's mount rearing and whistling in terror. Geraldo clung to the beast's arching back as it bucked and skittered toward the packhorses.

But then her mind went blank, and her vision exploded in a thousand stars. Only when she fell backward did the pain come. Above her she looked into the quivering face of Slipper. "Bitch! Bitch!" he screamed. His fat cheeks flared scarlet, and he shook his hand as if the blow he'd given her had broken his fingers. "You nearly killed me!" He continued to shriek, but in a language she did not know.

She had fallen on her bag. She felt the corners of her wooden boxes poke against her skin, and also the stones of the road that cut into her back. She was too tired to stand, and feared that if she did Slipper would strike her again. Her arm hurt.

With an almost languid slowness, she turned her face from the eunuch. From this position she could again see Geraldo and the ponies as they stumbled down a narrow embankment road. Whether he drove the pack ponies before him, or was being dragged behind them, she could not tell. His hands flailed the air, for he had lost the reins.

More shots rang out, mingling with the ringing in her hurt ear, and Slipper's incoherent shrieks. The bitter smoke of Chinese powder drifted over the rain-wet rocks.

"Get up! You whore, get up!" Slipper shrieked, lifting his hand to strike her again. "We're going to die, you bitch!"

She blocked his blow and scrambled to her feet. "Where is Deoga?" she cried. She could barely hear her own voice for her ear ringing.

But Slipper's face had suddenly gone ashen, and his eyes wide. She turned and saw what he saw: another bandit, driving his pony for them at full speed, holding his wide sword like a scythe for their necks. She threw herself against the eunuch, pitching Slipper on to the road just as the blade whistled above their heads.

The bandit galloped forward, heading straight for one of Pathan's horsemen. The guard held his sword as steady as a lance, but his bedouin crabbed and cantered. He wanted to attack but his horse wanted to flee, and so they churned uselessly; and all the while the bandit and his pony drove forward like a shot arrow.

The guard's bedouin reared just as the bandit galloped past, and the bandit's wide sword sliced through the horse's belly. A spray of blood erupted from the gash. The guard slid from his saddle as the bedouin collapsed beneath him. The bandit wheeled round for a new attack.

Before the guard had looked up, the bandit's wide sword hacked halfway through his neck.

A shot rang out, echoing from the cliff walls. Maya swung her head around, but could not find the source. She pushed herself from Slipper. The eunuch covered his head with the tails of his shirt, clutched his ears, and sobbed.

The bandit struggled to tug his sword from the guard's neck. The bedouin shuddered and died. Blood still pumped from the wound in its belly, a scarlet stream that inched along the wet stones toward Maya and Slipper.

Another shot rang out, pinging as it ricocheted from the nearby rocks. The bandit managed to yank his sword free. His eyes had found Maya's. She saw that his eyes were empty, that a coldness flew from them like knives that sought her heart. Later she remembered the dirt on his stubbled cheeks, the sinews that pulsed in his neck. At that moment she saw only his eyes black as death. Once they found her, the bandit's eyes never left hers. She could not understand why he looked at her with such fury.

Another shot. Both the bandit and Maya glanced toward the sound. It was Da Gama, riding toward them. He held his reins high in his left hand, in his right hand a gun. He dropped the smoking *pistola* like an empty husk and let it fall to the road without a glance, then reached behind into his saddlebag for another.

Again he shot. The bandit's pony collapsed—Da Gama's round had shredded through its hindquarters. The bandit flailed to avoid getting pinned beneath it. The wild-eyed pony dragged its lifeless rear legs, whistling and screaming. Its cries drowned out even Slipper's mindless wails.

As though the pony's shrieking infuriated him, the bandit turned and slammed his sword into its neck. The pony squirmed and twisted and died. Steam rose from the blood on the bandit's sword as he turned to face Da Gama.

Maya saw that Da Gama had again dropped his smoking *pistola* and readied a new one. The bandit's eyes had once more locked on her. She drew back as he marched relentlessly toward her with his wide blade held high. His cold rat eyes bored into Maya's. Despite herself, Maya could not look away.

Then the bandit's face disappeared. For an instant in its place she saw a red pulp, like a sponge dipped in paint, and then the bandit's head exploded. He spun and fell like a broken doll. His stained sword clattered inches from her feet in the puddle of bedouin's blood. She never heard the shot, although she could hear its echo still ringing through the canyon.

Once more Da Gama dropped his empty pistol to the road and took out a fresh one. Maya hardly recognized him now; his friendly, bemused look had disappeared; instead she now saw a face grown fierce, bared teeth clinched tight. Da Gama dismounted cavalry style, swinging his leg over his horse and sliding to the ground while he kept his *pistola* level. His head spun at every tiny sound.

Da Gama glanced at her and nodded. Keeping watchful, he sidestepped to the body of the guard, and bent down to check the pulse. Only when he was sure the horseman was dead did he make his way to Maya and the weeping Slipper. There was no need to check the bandit.

"How badly is he hurt?" he asked. But he kept his *pistola* high and did not look at either of them, only snatching glances as he scanned the rocks. At their feet, Slipper had fallen into breathless whimpering, but he still clutched his shirt ends over his head. His pink belly quivered as he sobbed.

"I don't think he's hurt at all," Maya answered.

"Scared, then," Da Gama said. He shot a quick glance at Maya. "And you?"

"I twisted my arm."

"That all?" She nodded, and he seemed to understand though his eyes were elsewhere. His left hand fished in a pocket and produced a kerchief. "You've blood on your face. I don't think it's yours."

Maya wiped her face as Da Gama moved to the road's edge and looked down.

"Shit," he said.

Maya peered down—the plummet took her breath. A long way down she saw the twisted body of the mahout, and below him the carcass of the elephant, its gray belly split open like a fruit. "Alive?" she whispered.

"It doesn't matter," Da Gama replied. There was no sign of Lucy, nor of Pathan. Maya stepped back from the edge, horrified, grateful to still be alive. Da Gama's face looked broken by the sight. "Can you help me with the eunuch?" he asked her.

Together they tugged Slipper's plump arms and staggered down the road. Da Gama led them to a place where the road widened, and an over-hang of rock formed a kind of shelter. The last of Pathan's guards lay there, stretched beneath a saddle blanket, breathing hard. An arrow protruded from his eye.

"Is he dead?" Slipper whimpered.

"Nearly," Da Gama said. Da Gama once more turned to the road, with *pistola* held high. "You stay here. I'll just get my horse," he said.

"Let me come with you," Maya said, and after a moment's decision, Da Gama nodded.

"Did you see anything of Geraldo?" he asked as they walked. Maya told him how he and the packhorses had galloped down an embankment road. The information was just one more item that Da Gama would have to sort out later.

They found Da Gama's mare pacing nervously around the bodies of dead men and horses. He gentled it and led it from the blood-soaked rocks. "Let's get back to the eunuch," he said.

"What about Lucinda and Captain Pathan?" Maya said. When she said the names, they hung in the air, like names of the newly dead.

"I don't know," Da Gama said.

"Are we in danger still?"

"I don't know. I don't know what's going on. My plans have all gone wrong. I made a big mistake coming here." As they walked back, Da Gama stooped from time to time to pick up a *pistola* he earlier had dropped.

When they neared the overhang, Slipper shuffled to them on his tiny feet. "He moaned at me!" he wailed. "How can he moan with an arrow in his eye?"

"Yes, yes," Da Gama answered angrily. He tethered his horse and sat near the injured man, smoothing his hand over the horseman's forehead. "There's nothing we can do for him."

"If he hasn't the sense to die, then kill him!" Slipper whispered.

"No. We don't do such things." Slipper sniffed and huddled a little way off. Da Gama reached into his pack and handed a *pistola* to Maya. "Ever work one of these?" She shook her head. "Pull this back until it locks," he said, pointing to the flint-hammer. "Then point it and pull here." He wrapped her small fingers around the *pistola*'s oiled grip, and glancing at her face as if to check her resolve, not her understanding. "I've got to reload."

"Do you think we're still in danger, Da Gama?" Maya asked.

His silence told her everything.

He hauled the saddlebag from his horse's back and sat near a flat rock. He took out five or six loaded *pistolas* from the bag and laid them in a line; next to them the fired pistols that he had not dropped. "Listen to me," he said as he worked. "You have to be steady to hit the target, especially from a distance." He opened a small leather bag of shot, and a flask of Chinese powder. "If you really mean to kill someone, let him get close to you."

Maya took this in without a word. "I didn't expect this," Da Gama muttered as he reloaded. He might have been talking to himself. "This, after we paid them off! You can't trust even thieves these days." His hands moved quickly, angrily. A stiff brush down the barrels of the fired guns. One or two had misfired; these he poked at but heaved away.

Only when she saw the fury with which he hurled those useless *pistolas* against the mountain wall did Maya realize the depth of his fears, and of her danger. Da Gama took up the other *pistolas* and began to load them: powder down the barrel, followed by a twist of cotton torn from a dusty wad. He had begun to sweat. He tamped the powder, taking a hurried glance over the road. Then the shot. This was more elaborate: Da Gama placed a round between his teeth and bit down on it, then wiped it dry on his shirt. He pressed the now misshapen round into the iron barrel, grunting with the effort it took to push it with the tamping stick. His hand slipped and he gashed a knuckle. He topped off the firing pan with a final dose of powder, and placed the loaded *pistola* in the line on the flat rock. Then he started on the next. When he finished there were nine, and also the one in Maya's hand.

After the horror of the bandits' deaths, Da Gama's work, so unexpectedly precise, comforted Maya. Slipper had crept into some nearby bushes, where he squatted and grunted with his efforts. She tried not to watch.

Da Gama's mare pranced nervously. Thunder rumbled in the distance and the sky grew dark. A huge drop of rain splattered at Maya's feet, and another, and another. Da Gama gathered up his *pistolas* and shoved a couple into his belt and the rest into his saddlebag. "Cover the hammer with your hand," he said to Maya.

Rain pelted from the sky in big, stinging drops. "Oh, Allah!" Slipper cried as he ran up to the others, tugging on his silk trousers. "What more can go wrong?"

Then they heard the hoofbeats.

෴෴෴

Lucinda's dress hung in tatters. Clinging to his bare shoulders, Lucinda felt Pathan's fierce breath and the effort of his running. Lucinda wished that she were lighter. She could hear the sound of hoofbeats growing louder.

"We're not far from the others now," Pathan told her. They came to a turn in the road. "Here," he panted, his voice little more than a gasp.

But when they made the turn, Pathan slowed and nearly dropped Lucinda. Before them was a body, facedown, a deep gash across its back. The relentless sound of hoofbeats approached. Pathan stepped over it. "Do not look, madam," Pathan said, recovering his wits.

Lucinda did close her eyes, but only for a moment, and only after she had looked, and then only out of sorrow. She could no longer hide from what faced them. There were more bodies on the road. "Dear God," Lucinda whispered as they passed.

At last Pathan slowed, and stopped. They had come to a narrow landing. A neem tree, growing horizontal from the cliffs above them, gave a little shelter. "If any of our people survived, they have fled, madam. I'm sure that some got away. We can pray so. But for now we are on our own, I fear." He nodded to some rocks near the grove. "Let me help you down, madam."

"I can walk if you will give me your arm to lean on," Lucinda answered. With Pathan's help, she limped to a nearby rock and falteringly sat down. "What will you do now?"

Pathan looked away, his face hard. "I don't know, madam." Thunder rumbled in the distance.

He took off his turban and quickly wound the long cloth tightly around his left hand. Then he unsheathed his sword. "The poet says life is a caravan, madam, and we sleep, he says, in many different tents. Tonight maybe we shall sleep in a new tent, madam." He looked very small in the mountain shadows, his bare torso muscular and taut, but too slender for what was to come. His hair fell to his shoulders.

The hoofbeats echoed around the cavern walls around the bend in the road.

"Madam, maybe . . ." Pathan looked at her hard, refusing to be distracted by the sound of the oncoming horses. "Meeting you has been a great pleasure and a great lesson. If you wish it . . . when I have fought to my last breath for you, I mean, and only if all hope is gone . . . if you wish it . . . I could see that no more hurt would come to you. . . . Do you under-stand me?"

Lucinda stared at his anguished face, and slowly the meaning of his words came clear. "Do not say such foolish things, Captain."

"We have passed the time for foolishness."

"Somehow you will triumph. I know it." He gave her one of his rare smiles. She saw more clearly than ever that smiling was hard for him. "Have no fear, dear captain, as I have none."

But now the hoofbeats were too loud for any more talk.

⊘⊘⊘⊘

When she was little, Lucinda had seen a demon painted on the wall of an old temple: wild-eyed, misshapen, red-skinned, horrible. Blood dripped from his fanged jaws. She only saw it once, just a glance, but the image had been planted. It haunted her dreams. Over time the nightmare demon be-came more human, and more frightening. Some nights she'd wake to find

Helene shaking her out of her screaming, for in her dreams the demon was advancing, more human now and more terrifying than ever.

It was that face Lucinda now saw. The bandit had cinched a leather braid around the stump of his wrist to slow its bleeding. He must have pulled it tight with his teeth, for blood stained his face and streaked his shirt. Even his hair was sticky with blood. His eyes burned with pain and hate. He had wrapped his reins around the bleeding arm; in his good hand he held as a club a heavy branch of dead wood. Ropes of foam hung from his pony's muzzle.

Pathan placed himself directly between Lucinda and the bandit. The sun glistened on the sweat of his shoulders; Lucinda could see each twist and ripple of his muscles as he swung his sword in slow circles. His long hair fell and hid his face. Lucinda wished that she might see his face just once more, just once, but he did not turn around.

She thought that the bandit would cry out before he attacked, but he spurred his mount without a word. Pathan raised his sword, but the bandit clubbed the blade with the branch. Pathan's curved sword whirled from his hand and clattered down the embankment. When Pathan spun around, Lucinda saw the terror in his eyes and covered her mouth to keep from screaming. She crawled to the chasm's edge, and saw the blade glittering far below.

The bandit wheeled on the narrow road and drove back for another attack. This time, Pathan ducked the branch as it swung at him. He leaped up, and grabbed the bandit's shirt, nearly toppling him. But the bandit hung on; and Pathan hung on behind him, half-dragged as the pony galloped madly on. The bandit swung at him with awkward blows until Pathan tumbled against the stones.

Pathan staggered to his feet while the bandit watched. The braid had loosened on his stump, and blood now seeped from it with every heartbeat. His eyes had the brutal stare of a dying tiger.

The bandit spurred his pony. It had reached a full gallop when the bandit's club smacked Pathan's side. Pathan arced through the air with the force of the blow, sliding on his belly when he fell. He struggled to lift his head.

Again thunder rumbled, and shadow filled the sky. A raindrop so large it felt like a splattering egg struck Lucinda's face. The bandit wheeled around once more. Blood from his stump had stained his pants now. Rain began to pelt the road, each drop spraying into the air as it struck the stones.

Too desperate to heed his danger, Pathan pushed up to his feet. The rain pummeled him; his long hair hung in wet streaks across his shoulders. He tried to walk, but staggered, barely keeping his feet. He could not focus his eyes but stared half-blind into the distance. Twenty yards away, the bandit faced him.

Lucinda watched in horror as the bandit spurred to a gallop. Pathan did not move; he seemed unaware of the danger. Get down, get down, she whispered in Portuguese. How could he even be standing after the blows he had taken?

The bandit came on, swinging his club. Pathan staggered blindly. Then the club struck his head, so hard Pathan's feet left the ground. He slammed to the road, flopping onto his back landing so close to the road edge that one of his arms hung in the chasm air. Pathan's body shuddered and grew still.

"Pathan!" Lucinda shrieked. Her cry was lost in the bandit's scream of triumph. "I have won! I have killed him!" The bandit's face was deathly pale, the wild eyes rimmed yellow. Another man might have collapsed from losing so much blood, but the hate that coursed through the bandit's veins kept him alive.

He dropped the branch club and ran toward Lucinda. Come on, she thought as she hobbled to her feet, fists clenched. I'll hurt you before I die.

But she hadn't counted on the bandit's spirit, which seemed on fire despite his injuries. As he passed he grabbed her arm, and by some trick twisted her so she ended up sprawled across his pony once more.

"You are mine!" he crowed. Lucinda bounced against the beast's hot flanks. He pressed her down so that she could not move. She smelled the bandit's blood, and saw Pathan's body, and she wept.

❧❧❧❧

"Get ready," Da Gama said. "Use the mare for cover." He propped his *pistola* on the horse's rump. Maya swallowed hard and followed his example, sighting down the barrel toward the sound of the hoofbeats.

"Shoot! Shoot! Why don't you shoot!" Slipper screamed.

"There's nothing to shoot at, eunuch."

At that moment the rain abruptly stopped. Where there had been before a cascading tumult there was now sudden silence. The air fell still, and the approaching hoofbeats echoed from stone to glistening stone.

"Shoot!" Slipper whispered. The bandit's pony swung into view. "Shoot!" he screamed.

"No!" Da Gama shouted. "Hold your fire! He has Lucy!"

"Shoot him, whore!" Slipper bawled into Maya's ear.

"Didn't you hear Deoga?" she answered. But Slipper's face was livid, and he grabbed for her *pistola*.

"Give it! Give it! I'll show you cowards how to shoot!" In an instant he wrenched the pistol from Maya's grasp and raised it toward the road.

"No!" screamed Deoga. He grabbed the eunuch's arm just as Slipper pulled the trigger. Da Gama fell backward beside him.

"I'm hit! I'm bleeding!" Slipper screamed. Clutching his fat cheeks, he stumbled back toward the bushes and fell to his knees. His face was covered with blood.

But not his own. His shot had pierced the eye of Da Gama's tethered mare. A stillness fell over the animal. It sagged on its hooves, and canted slowly sideways, as if made from moist clay. Da Gama dropped his *pistola* and pushed against it. His posture reminded Maya of the way a heartbroken man leans against a wall and sobs. Slowly she realized that the beast was collapsing, and Da Gama was trying to keep it from crushing them both. She leaped away, but at that moment the horse toppled over, trapping Da Gama's legs.

Da Gama howled as the horse toppled on him. Maya hurried over and leaned her back against the carcass, but Da Gama could not free his legs. "I don't think they're broken, but I can't get out," he whispered through clenched teeth. Maya didn't need to ask if it hurt. Da Gama's eyes, however, had now swept down the road back to the approaching pony.

"Look! Look at this!" The bandit's voice was a dull rasp. "This is justice, this is! Look!" He slid from the pony and grabbed Lucinda around the neck. "This is pretty justice. All day you've been killing my brothers, but now there will be justice. I will kill your daughter, bastard, and then I'll kill you." He shoved Lucinda forward, using her body as a shield. Somewhere he'd found a knife.

"I paid, you son of a bitch!" Da Gama shouted. "The *chauth*! The *baksheesh*. Goddamnit, is there no honor anymore?"

"It is I who paid, all day, but you'll pay now, that's certain. You'll pay, she'll pay. Everyone will pay."

"Can't you shoot him, Deoga?" Maya whispered. "Let me get you a *pistola.*"

Flinching and gritting his teeth, Da Gama checked the range. "Not from here. I'd as likely hit Lucinda."

The bandit shoved Lucinda forward. Da Gama watched in agony, fearing the bandit would cut her. She lifted her hands to him. Da Gama's face grew hot.

"So, papa: Can you kill me before I kill her?" The bandit's face was pale, and his eyelids and lips drooped. "Throw me your sword."

Da Gama couldn't do it, not by himself. Maya helped him unbuckle his belt, and tossed the sword, scabbard, and all. "Do you want more money? Is that what you want? Can't we work a deal?"

"I'll have all your money soon enough." Staggering, the bandit pulled Lucinda to some rocks. From there he had a comfortable view of Da Gama struggling under the dead horse, and Maya beside him. He yanked Lucinda to her knees: she whimpered with the pain. He was fading, but was still strong enough to hurt her.

"Throw away your guns."

"I can't move, you bastard. Let her go!"

"You do it," the bandit said, glaring at Maya. Da Gama gave a grimacing nod. Maya crawled behind him, picked up the leather bag of *pistolas* that were just beyond his reach. "Throw them here," the bandit called.

"They might go off!" Da Gama said. The bandit twisted Lucinda's hair for answer. When he heard her whimper, Da Gama's face grew hard. He nodded, and Maya from a crouch threw over the guns. But she kept one hidden behind her back.

"That's a good papa. Now—unfinished business." Saliva mixed with the dried blood on his cheek as he sneered at Da Gama. "Business before pleasure. I lost a hand over this bitch. I hope she's worth it."

There was little left of him but hate, but his hate was strong and Lucinda was exhausted. The bandit twisted her arm until she could do no more than fall. Her nightmare of the river began again. Worse this time. Wet this time, dirtier this time. Worst of all, Pathan dead this time.

Stained by his own blood, half-dead, the bandit showed no imagination. He placed a knee on each of Lucinda's shoulders to hold her down and gripped his knife between his teeth. He began once more to tug at his pants.

"Stop it!" Da Gama cried. He sounded in agony.

"Oh, papa. Just enjoy the show," the bandit said. He meant to shout, but his voice was no more than a whimper. His belly was streaked with blood, and he could barely find his shrunken lingam. Finally his hand was working at it, and at his own touch his head fell back in a long, growling grunt. "That's good. That's good."

"Wait," Maya said, rising from Da Gama's side. "Let me show you what a nautch girl can do."

The bandit's eyes flickered from Lucinda to Maya and back. "What's your game?"

"Am I not pleasing? Let her go, and I'll give you pleasure."

"You're crazy." He blinked at Maya. His eyes were having trouble focusing.

"After I've pleased you, take me with you."

"What about him?" the bandit nodded to Da Gama.

"Kill him if you like. He's nothing to me."

"You really a nautch girl?"

"Oh, yes," Maya sighed. Her arm ached, and her ear rang, and as she walked her vision spun, but she forced her face to an elegant serenity, and she moved as graceful as flowing water. "I won't fight. Why should I? How often does a slave get to have a real man? A man like you . . . a bandit prince? I'll be your slave. I'll do anything you ask." Maya had covered half the distance. "You could make me beg. A man like you could make me beg." By now the bandit was lost in her eyes. "Let her go. Take me."

The bandit leaned back on his heels, freeing Lucinda's shoulders. Sliding across the wet road, Lucinda crawled away. Tatters of her skirts tugged under the bandit's heels, but only for a moment, and then she was free.

But the bandit never stirred—he seemed too tired to rise. His lips had turned blue, and a thread of saliva hung on his chin. "It's getting cold," he said. His mouth hung limp as he stared at Maya. Blood seeped from his wrist stump in viscid drops.

Maya waited until Lucinda had crept away. "I know you," the bandit whispered through chattering teeth.

Then Maya walked calmly until she stood over the shivering bandit.

From the folds of her sari where she'd hidden it, Maya lifted a *pistola* and raised it level with his eyes. Then she fired.

The bandit's head imploded and his body shuddered.

☙☙☙☙

As the shot's echo faded, Slipper came crashing through the bushes where he'd hidden. "Murderer! Murderer!" he screamed. He fell to his knees and sobbed.

Maya dropped the *pistola* like an empty husk. Taking Lucinda's arm Maya helped her walk to Da Gama. Lucinda threw herself on his shoulder and sobbed. Da Gama grimaced.

Once more they heard horses—louder this time, lots of horses. They looked up. Dreadful silence fell as the sound thundered closer. "We'll never fight so many," Maya whispered.

Around the bend came a dozen glossy bedouins, and on their backs a dozen soldiers carrying bright lances with green pennants flying. The horses' livery sparkled. Behind them came Geraldo on his pony, standing in his stirrups, grinning and waving, leading one of the pack ponies. Da Gama waved back, despite the pain.

Their leader of the new horsemen, a solid-looking fellow of about Da Gama's age, raised his hand, and the horseman drew around him in a crescent, facing the three travelers and the dead horse. The leader took a long, slow look around the scene before he spoke. "I am Shahji, general commander to the Sultana, queen of Bijapur," he said. His soft voice echoed through the silence.

Behind one of the soldiers rode a tall man with a bare chest, and long black hair still wet with rain, for he had wrapped his turban around his hand.

"Pathan," Lucinda whispered. Ignoring her pain, she stumbled to him.

Part Three

Lake Palace

The night she arrived at the Lake Palace of Belgaum, Maya dreamed of her guru Gungama.

General Shahji had led them over the mountains, reaching the Belgaum pass just at sunset. Their destination lay below, touched by the golden sun: a low white palace on a green island in a wide lake. A narrow causeway crossed the lake to the palace. The setting sun cast long shadows as they reached the palace gates. A silver-haired monkey watched solemnly.

In the courtyard, Shahji barked out orders. Clothes and hot food came, doctors were sent for. Injured, frightened, filthy, dazed, the remnants of the caravan had kindness showered on them. The mistress of the palace had baths prepared for Lucinda and Maya, and made up soft beds for them.

Maya's room had a narrow balcony that overlooked the lake, in the heart of the valley of Belgaum. On the shore, she could see fires flickering before houses hidden by shadows. By the light of the cloud-hidden moon she saw mountains in the distance. Then she blew out her butter lamp, crumbled onto the bedmat and slept.

She found herself in a grove of trees, in bright sunlight. Nearby a fountain of milk flowed into a gently lapping pool. But as she looked, the pool of milk became enormous. Its shores melted away, and it stretched before her larger even than the ocean. Miles away, she saw an enormous, cone-shaped mountain rising from the foaming waves of milk.

As she watched, a great blue lotus flower floated toward her across the surface of the milk, like a living boat. When it reached her, its petals unfolded. Seated in the center of the flower was her own guru, Gungama.

My dear guru! Maya cried. Gungama was tiny as ever, as wrinkled as ever, but radiant, her skin lustrous, her sari like hammered gold. Maya wept to see her; her mouth fell open and to her surprise she began to sing. The stars danced. Gungama lifted her hands, and water poured from her palms. A tiny blue flame flickered between her eyebrows.

When the song was done, Gungama smiled. She spread out her arm, and it was as though she had unfurled a sheet of black gauze into the wind. It fluttered like a great shadow onto the ground at Maya's feet, and in the shadow, as if from a great height, Maya saw the Belgaum palace. In the courtyard of the palace was a line of horsemen, and in the line was Da Gama, dressed in jama *robes like a Hindi.*

"Give him what is yours," Gungama said, pointing to Da Gama.

And at that moment, Maya woke.

She did not hesitate, no, not even to dress. In her shoulder bag she found the small, unfinished wooden box and took from it the plain cloth pouch it held. Pulling a coverlet from the bed over her shoulders, she ran barefoot from the room. The coverlet spread out behind her like a cape, and her black hair went flying. She was in the courtyard in an instant. The padding of her feet echoed softly from the silent walls.

It was just as she had seen in the dream: there in the courtyard were Shahji's men in a line, preparing to leave. Da Gama was indeed dressed in *jamas,* but he still wore his heavy farang boots, which gave him a clownish air. He was leaning from his saddle to shake Geraldo's outstretched hand. The sky glowed, a cloudless gray, pink at the horizon. Roosters crowed. She raced across the white marble tiles.

"Ho, ho, what's this!" Da Gama laughed as she approached. Some of the riders snickered, until a fierce glance from Shahji stopped them.

Breathless, Maya reached up her pouch. "Take it, take it, uncle, take it," she gasped.

"But what is it?" Geraldo demanded. He seemed ready to take the pouch from Da Gama's hand.

Maya snatched it back and clutched it to her chest. She'd forgotten the young farang. "It is for him alone." She raised her face to Da Gama. "Just take it, uncle."

Da Gama frowned. He reached for the pouch, and his big, leathery hand brushed her slender fingers. "What is it?"

"A secret, uncle."

Da Gama glanced at Geraldo, who shrugged and shook his head. Da Gama hefted the small bag testing its weight. "What secret does a nautch girl keep?" He began to open the pouch, but Maya placed her small hand on his to stop him.

"What you hold is as dear to me as life." Da Gama frowned at her. She leaned up to him and whispered desperately, "Keep it for me. Do me this favor. I have no money to offer, but I can give you pleasure, uncle. If that's what you want."

Da Gama's face grew serious, his eyes smoldering. "Don't tempt me, child. I'll keep it for you. Don't make stupid offers. I might take you up on them, and then where would we be?"

Maya grabbed Da Gama's stirrup and pressed her forehead to the toe of his boot. "How then shall I thank you, uncle?"

Da Gama's cheeks grew hot. "Stand up for one thing. Just pray for me. God knows I need it."

She raised her hands. "Be blessed in your journey."

At that moment, Shahji gave a piercing whistle, and the guards rode through the green gate of the courtyard, and along the narrow causeway that led across the lake. Da Gama turned and waved many times.

Geraldo came up to stand just inches from Maya's side, watching them depart. In the cold morning air she could sense the heat of his body. "What was in the pouch?"

"It is his now. You must ask him." As she watched Da Gama ride away, Maya's thoughts raced. From the fire to the pot, from the pot to the fire— what difference does it make? I may never see it again, or him.

At least they won't have it, the filthy *hijras*. But what will they do to that poor farang if they find him with it?

I'll pray for us both, uncle, she whispered. When Da Gama passed into the mists, she walked off and did not look back.

⊙⊙⊙⊙

One of the servant women, seated at the edge of the courtyard, nodded to her and offered Maya some of the simple breakfast she was cooking. Maya realized she was famished. She ate a *paratha* and another.

As Maya wiped her fingers, she saw an open *palki* come on the road across the lake. As the bearers came closer she saw who they carried.

Slipper.

Was he ashamed at the fuss he had made, he who had never been injured? Why bother to ask?

Maya turned to walk off. Slipper called to her from the *palki,* again and again. The servant woman tugged her hand and nodded toward the *palki* until Maya sighed and turned to face him.

The bearers set him down, and Slipper lifted a pudgy languid hand so the *palki*wallah could help him up. He came straight for Maya, chattering with his high-pitched voice.

The doctor, he told Maya, was a true master who had brought Slipper back from the brink of death, but now he was fine. Then the doctor had recognized that Slipper was worthy of honor, and had begged the eunuch to ride to the palace in his *palki.*

About Pathan, of course, Slipper had nothing to say. Nor did he ask for news about anyone else. He was a *hijra,* only a *hijra,* and he squawked like an ugly old bird. It took little time before he was squawking at her.

"You are hiding it! I saw it fall from your bag at the pass. Where is it, where is it?" Soon he was screaming "Tell me, tell me!" Maya did not even look up.

This set him flapping. "You . . . you . . . woman!" he howled.

His blow exploded in her head. There were no stars this time, just a thudding pain. The side of her face felt dense; cold like a block of iron. Her back teeth ached. Then he struck her again, this time with his left hand, and she fell over. Like a pig on tiptoe, Slipper danced beside her. "Tell me, tell me now or get another!" He kicked her side, but the curved toe of his slipper slid across her waist and so did not hurt too much. He danced some more. "Tell me!" Now he lifted his foot over her head, ready to bring it down on her ear.

Then with a scream, Slipper fell backward and rolled like an air-filled bladder over the marble tiles of the courtyard. And near where he had stood, Maya saw Geraldo, his dark eyes flaming. Geraldo had thrown him, Maya realized.

He held out his hand and helped Maya to her feet. Then he strode to the wailing Slipper and kicked him so hard his fat belly lifted from the ground and fell back with a thud. "Get up," he ordered.

Slipper struggled to his hands and knees and crawled backward, his bottom wiggling and his forehead scraping the tiles. His turban had once again come undone. "Please, please, sir, oh please, dear uncle, please!" Geraldo placed his foot where the *hijra* could see it. "No!" the eunuch cried. "You must not! She's a thief! She has stolen . . ."

"What has she stolen?" Geraldo asked quietly.

Slipper's fat cheeks, red and blotchy, quivered. Then his mouth began to flap but no sound emerged. And then Slipper began to cry. His face curled up, his eyes creased, and his lips quivered. But then he filled his big lungs and let out a wail that filled the courtyard like a horn.

"What has she stolen? Speak!"

But Slipper could not control his wailing. Geraldo spat and hauled him to his feet. "This is how you treat a woman? You are an abomination!" One of Slipper's curl-toed slippers flipped from his feet as Geraldo dragged him off. The eunuch reached back helplessly but Geraldo, furious, dragged him even harder. Both of them were sweating, both grunting with the effort. Every time Slipper wailed, Geraldo gave him another furious heave, and so they tumbled toward the green gate of the palace.

"Out! Out!" Geraldo placed his foot against the eunuch's enormous buttocks and shoved him through the gate. Slipper tumbled to the drive in a sobbing heap. The young farang, teeth bared and eyes blazing, motioned to a dazed old gatekeeper to swing the gates shut. Slipper lay in the dust and screamed like a goat when the knife strikes its neck.

The gatekeeper moved too slowly to suit Geraldo. The farang pushed him aside, slammed the gates shut and latched them himself. The poor old gatekeeper looked more dazed than ever.

Slipper's pathetic screams attracted attention. Servants came and stood staring at the green gate as if to see through it. Some children scurried up a ladder of lashed bamboo and looked over the wall. To Slipper's wailing the children added their thoughtless laughter, and then their mothers shouted and scolded, and from the gardens the peacocks began to trumpet, and at that same moment temple gongs clashed and clanged. Geraldo, who stood at the latch, lifted his hands to his ears and began to laugh.

Geraldo went to Maya. She still knelt on the tiles, catching her breath. She realized with embarrassment that she was still wearing only her thin nightdress and the coverlet. Her head hammered with each pulse beat and her belly felt cold and dark. Geraldo stooped beside her, looking very regal in his borrowed *jama* robes. When he touched her face, his fingertips were soft, more gentle than Maya expected. The way he peered at the side of her face made Maya feel uncomfortable, as though she were a dead thing. She tried to catch his eyes, but he saw only her bruises.

"It could be worse. You'll be fine. He didn't hurt you badly."

Her eyes blazed. "Your goods are still intact, you mean. How very fortunate for you."

Geraldo inhaled harshly, and his face grew pale, and he got to his feet so furiously Maya thought that he too might strike her. "You say that? You? After I defended you?" Suddenly he bent down and came up with the eunuch's curl-toed slipper. "This is how you treat me?" He shook the slipper a few inches from her face. Then he ran toward the gate and hurled it over the wall, as if he hoped to cast it in the lake. "Maybe the eunuch was right," he muttered, facing her again. There was sorrow in his face as well as anger. Then Geraldo spun on his heel and stalked off.

Yes, thought Maya, glaring at him, there is no good in me. Now you know the truth.

But by the time Geraldo's shadow passed the threshold of the guest-room door, Maya regretted what she'd said.

☙☙☙

The temple bells stopped clanging. From the other side of the courtyard, Maya heard a *thump, thump, thump*. She looked up to see Lady Chitra, the mistress of the palace, approaching pulled forward by the eager little girl. She wore a long shawl that spread behind her like a golden cape. With every other step, her walking staff banged the white marble tiles of the courtyard. Despite her staff, she moved as smoothly as a ship on calm waters.

As she came, the servants and children stopped shouting. They huddled in groups and edged toward the doors. Outside the gate Slipper kept up his screaming.

"Halt," came Lady Chitra's voice, harsh and dry as a sour raisin. "What is that racket?" She rolled her *r*'s when she spoke, giving her words a majestic, antique quality, as though she had learned to speak from an ancient queen. The servants rolled their eyes at one another and tiptoed toward the doors. "Do not think I cannot find you! I am not so blind!" Lady Chitra raised her staff and turned slowly until her sightless eyes faced Maya. As she pointed the staff directly at her, Maya got the impression that Chitra somehow could see, despite her filmed, unfocused eyes. "You! What is this disturbance?" But the little girl, Lakshmi, tugged at Lady Chitra's hand, and the woman stooped while Lakshmi whispered excitedly into her ear. Lady Chitra came up slowly, and placed the tip of her staff on the ground. "You are that *devadasi* from last night."

Maya nodded, then remembered herself and said aloud, "Yes, madam."

"Do not be formal with me, child. We are more sisters than you know. What is all that screaming?" She lifted her staff toward the gate without turning her head from Maya.

"It is one of our party, a *hijra*. He just returned from the doctor's house. The farang Geraldo, who you met last night, beat him and threw him out the gates."

"A *hijra*." The word as Lady Chitra said it had a dark malevolence, and her eyelids tensed and her filmed eyes rolled. But Maya thought the woman was trying to conceal a smile. "How did he come to beat a *hijra*, that fine young farang, eh?"

"Because the *hijra* was beating me."

"*Ahcha*. And why you?"

"The *hijra* wanted something that I used to have." Lady Chitra grunted encouragingly. Little Lakshmi's eyes grew big, as they flickered from Maya to her mistress. "Some trinkets of my mother's."

With a sigh, Lady Chitra closed her blind eyes and lifted her face so the warm sun fell upon it. "Worse than snakes are *hijra*s," she hissed. She nodded toward the gate, and the little girl began to guide her there. "Are you not coming?" Lady Chitra called. Maya realized it was a command, not a question. She rose and followed.

"Open," Lady Chitra intoned when she reached the gate. Outside, the wailing had become a blubbering sob, like the crying of an exhausted child. The old gatekeeper unlatched the wide gate and pushed it open. Instantly the wails began again. The girl pulled Lady Chitra forward.

"Begone from here, *hijra*! Begone!"

Maya expected Slipper to scream, or to fall at Lady Chitra's feet and beg mercy—in fact almost anything except what came next. The eunuch clapped his fat hands over his gaping mouth and stared at the woman with wide eyes. His right foot still was bare, though his curl-toed slipper lay on the ground nearby.

"Begone!" she cried once more.

Slipper peered at her, blinking, as if realizing at last that Chitra was blind. This seemed to suggest a course of action to him. He held his mouth still more tightly, and began to tiptoe backward, away from the gate. By chance his foot bumped against the empty slipper, which had landed on the road. He squeezed his fat foot into it, though his eyes never left Lady Chitra.

He crept backward like a fugitive, finally reaching the causeway. Halfway across, he glared at Maya, and his face burned. He shook his fist at her, and then turned and bustled to the other shore, his fat buttocks jiggling in his *jamas*.

The girl tiptoed to whisper into Lady Chitra's ear. The woman rose with a satisfied smile. She turned and said, as if to no one, "Let the gate stay open, but call me if the *hijra* dares return." The gatekeeper bowed low as she passed, as though she could see. Then the little girl led her to where Maya was standing, and she said, "Sister *devadasi*, the dear goddess has brought you to me. Come and join me in my rooms, and tell me all."

"I am not dressed," Maya answered.

"I can wait," came Lady Chitra's reply.

ෙ౧౧ෙ

So began Maya's friendship with Lady Chitra.

It was only while Maya was changing into a borrowed sari that she realized that once more, her life had changed. Only a few days ago she had been dancing for the Goddess every morning and every night, in the company of a dozen sisters. Wrenched from that life, she had gotten used to the endless lassitude and irritations of traveling as a slave with a *hijra* for a companion. It usually took a while for Maya to set her feelings in order. Days, sometimes months. This time it dawned on Maya suddenly that with Deoga away, and with Slipper banished, she was on the brink of a new freedom. She buried that thought, planning to consider it later, and finished dressing.

In the part of the palace farthest from the main courtyard, Lady Chitra's rooms fronted an astonishing garden, filled with fountains and towering trees, and flowers—roses, jasmine, tuberoses. The garden looked across the lake, bordered only with a low wall more suited to sitting than protection. The breeze that spilled into Lady Chitra's rooms swirled with fragrance. Peacocks walked there, and parrots darted from tree to tree.

Lady Chitra's rooms were large, even grand. In the corners of each of her rooms were heaps of tuberoses that sweetened the air with perfume. In the lampstands and hanging lamps, Persian rose blossoms of deep violet had been placed where wicks should be. Chitra had no use for flames, but she loved the peppery scent of musk roses.

In a cage which hung from the ceiling a white parrot eyed Maya suspiciously.

Near the blind mistress of the palace sat her eyes: the quick-faced little girl Lakshmi. Seven years old, maybe eight, no one cared, for she was only an orphan who had worked in the palace kitchens until Lady Chitra discovered her talent for seeing and describing. Lady Chitra adored the child, and had secretly begun to teach her *natyam*, holy dance.

The women sat on a carpet spread as for a meal with white muslin sheets. Servants brought cups of chilled melon juice and plates of plain chapatis on a tray, and lit cones of incense. As they set things down, some of them tried to catch Maya's glance. They nodded to Lady Chitra and lifted their eyebrows and rolled their eyes and shook their heads. Maya ignored their bad manners.

Lady Chitra said nothing until the servants left. She sat with a straight back, not leaning on a bolster, or reclining like the little girl. "The frog awaiting the sunset before he calls out his love," she said softly, as though forgetting Maya were there. "The cock watching the sky for the light of dawn. The hawk who holds his cry until the ferret rests." She turned her rolling, sightless eyes to Maya. "Now speak, and hold back nothing."

So Maya began to relate her story: the death of her guru in a flood—how she thought that Gungama had been killed. Being sold to the farangs. The journey over oceans and mountains. Finally the bandit attack. Chitra stopped her often, demanding that she leave out no detail, however small. Chitra was not satisfied until Maya had even included in her story her last night's bath, and her dream of her guru, and finally her encounter with Slipper in the courtyard. Maya did not tell the part about the headdress.

"Of course you have considered suicide, and murder, too," Chitra pronounced when she had finished. Maya acknowledged this with silence. "Those are vanities, child. They cause immeasurable suffering in this life and all future lives. Who knows, perhaps you have been given this harsh portion because of misdeeds in some past life."

"What if I run away?" The words escaped from Maya's lips before she had a chance to stop them.

"Ah, sister," Chitra answered. "The farang is gone, the *hijra* is gone, and the gate of this palace is easily opened. But I tell you, you would not escape. They would follow you and bring you back. You are too valuable."

"Is there no way out? If I had known that Gungama was still alive . . ." Tears splashed from her cheeks.

Then with her sightless eyes drifting, Chitra lifted her hand. But instead of words of comfort, she began to tell of her own harsh life. Lady Chitra had been head concubine to the sultan of Bijapur, Maya learned. A concubine to the sultan, and before that a nautch girl, and before that a *devadasi.* But this information came out slowly, in a whorl of words majestically intoned.

It took a while for Maya to realize that Lady Chitra was crazy.

ᑫᓕᑫᓕ

Lady Chitra's rambling story sounded all too plausible to Maya, given the similarity of their histories. She came from the southern reaches of Hindustan, and her parents had given her to Kanyakumari, the Goddess as bride and virgin, whose temple overlooked the southern seas. There Chitra had studied *natyam,* temple dance. Eventually she too had come to be a vessel.

Slowly Lady Chitra came to realize that it was this part of her training that most engaged the *shastri.* Dance, which meant everything to Chitra, was only a vehicle for the *shastri* to train his vessels for repeated congress. Chitra rebuffed him. When she was fifteen the *shastri* sold her to some Golcondans, who in turn sold her to the eunuchs.

Or as Chitra called them, cursing them, the Brotherhood. It was as though she spoke of demons.

The Brothers, Chitra said, had mocked her and tortured her, forced her to do all kinds of unspeakable acts that to Maya seemed impossible, particularly for eunuchs.

So Chitra patiently explained that there were many kinds of eunuchs: shaved eunuchs who had cut off both testicles and lingam, usually at a young age. These, Chitra told her, were barely human.

Most eunuchs had merely had their testicles sliced off as they approached puberty, and still had a lingam like a shriveled sausage; these were the more docile. These eunuchs laughed often, and were easy to frighten.

But then, Chitra said, her face strained, there were crushed eunuchs.

It was Chitra's portion to have been sold for a concubine at the time a war was ending. The eunuchs who had bought her made a specialty of crushing.

The eunuchs had bid for a company of captured soldiers. One by one, the Brothers took the prisoners to a tent and crushed their testicles with a mallet and a block. Their screams, she said, were unendurable.

Crushed eunuchs, Chitra explained, were most often used as harem guards, not as servants. Still, the women of the harem greatly desired to acquire crushed eunuchs as slaves, for they were still like men in many ways. They kept their low voices, and much of their strength, and most important, they could still have congress. They were better than men, for they did not squirt like thoughtless men, who shrivel up and sleep and leave their women frustrated. Instead, if properly aroused, crushed eunuchs stayed stiff a long, long time. This provided for vigorous congress.

Chitra herself could confirm this. She said this bitterly. She had not been a lonely, well-heeled harem wife, protected by a rich husband. Chitra was the prisoner of those new-made *hijras*, those bitter souls who had recently been men. At night, a gang of them would snatch Chitra into a tent. There she'd be passed from *hijra* to *hijra*, another picking up as soon as the first began to droop.

Though the crushed *hijra* could get their lingams stiff, there was of course no finishing them off. They thrust and thrust and thrust without a hint of pleasure until they found themselves exhausted. Then they would vent their fury on her with cries and blows, and when they tired even of that, would pass her on to another of their kind. Dozens of them would spend the frustrated night ramming away, then striking her, sometimes until she bled, all the while cursing her and cursing their fates. In the morning she would be forgotten, depleted, marked, and sore. The crushed eunuchs, smelling of wine and vomit and sweat, would still be weeping.

ೞೞೞೞ

Lady Chitra hated the Brotherhood. Eunuchs, she told Maya, control the world in secret, using blackmail and money and cruel plots. She blamed them for all sorts of things: famines, wars, even droughts and floods.

They had untold wealth. Chitra told Maya of visits to torchlit caves filled with jewels and gold. There the eunuchs dressed her as a queen and did unspeakable things with her and with each other. They forced her, and forced her to watch, and called it training. "I could see then," she said softly. "Sometimes I wish I'd gone blind earlier."

"Do you know the types of congress of the mouth, sister?" Chitra said in her dry, throaty voice, as if suddenly changing the subject.

Maya looked up in surprise. "Vatsyayana says that there are eight ways, sister, to bring a man to paroxysm with the mouth: Nominal Congress, Biting the Sides, Pressing the Outside, Pressing the Inside, Kissing, Rubbing, Sucking the Mango, and Swallowing," Maya recited methodically. "Scratching and Striking, and Biting with the Teeth may also be done with this type of congress." She had of course memorized this and dozens of other passages of the *Kama Sutra.*

"You are well informed, sister. And how many of these forms have you attempted?"

Maya blanched. "None of them, sister. They are unclean! Only *hijra* and unchaste women . . ." Maya let the thought drift, slowly realizing Chitra's point. And it was like a cut made with a razor . . . slowly darkening Maya's thoughts like a spreading bloodstain.

"The Brotherhood had a special purpose for me, sister. The sultan of Bijapur required an heir. He had . . . varied tastes, none of them likely to produce offspring. But the Brotherhood had a plan, and I was part of it."

Lakshmi had taken Chitra's golden shawl, and moved silently to the shadows where she folded it with care. Other little girls might have run and played or been bored, but Lakshmi's big bright eyes stared ardently at her mistress, stroking the folded cape as one pets a cat. Chitra's lacquered staff lay at her feet, glistening in the sunlight.

"Now that I am blind, I see it all. When I had my eyes, I could see nothing." Maya was about to answer, but Chitra lifted her hand before she could speak.

Maya saw the strange, dark mark on Lady Chitra's palm, like a magenta star, or—Maya thought a moment later—like an evil eye.

"The odd thing is that we fell in love. Yes, I did things. I satisfied the sultan's rude desires as the Brotherhood forced me to." Chitra's voice sighed, and she almost whispered. "I would have done those things anyway, for him. He was beautiful, and so kind. And he loved me." Cares seemed to fall from Chitra's face, and Maya could see the beautiful young nautch girl that the sultan loved.

"Is that all they wanted, sister? That you should do those unchaste acts to satisfy him?"

Chitra's face grew stony. "Do you think so? You are quite naïve. No, for each act, always there was something; some price, some favor, some little wish that I was to exact. So I sold to my dear love what I would have given gladly. That was the price the Brotherhood demanded."

"But why did you agree, sister?"

Lady Chitra's voice, usually so formidable and majestic, grew as weak as a little girl's. "You have no idea of what they may do, sister. But I fear too soon you will."

"But how could these unchaste acts produce an heir, sister? Didn't you say that was what the Brotherhood desired most?"

Lady Chitra however had begun to weep. She said nothing as the tears stained her cheeks. At last she waved her hands, and Lakshmi instantly rose. The girl took Maya's hands and pulled her swiftly from the room.

ଈଓଈଓ

Lakshmi tugged Maya through the courtyard with the same timid strength that she used with Lady Chitra. Without a word, she pulled her through

Chitra's garden. At the far end was a door so small Maya had to stoop to pass through it. Before Maya had crossed the threshold, Lakshmi had taken hold of her hand again. Along a narrow dirt path that hugged the brick wall of the garden, Lakshmi tugged Maya, sometimes walking backward and staring at her with terrified pleasure.

A few yards from the end of the wall were a half-dozen mud huts with peaked thatch roofs, like conical hats. Some of the huts had been decorated with whitewash: *Oms, swastiks,* geometric designs. Small dark women in faded saris squatted on the open ground, peeling onions and chopping pumpkin. They wrinkled their faces familiarly when Lakshmi passed, and stared at Maya but said nothing.

Around the rough door of the last hut someone had drawn a design of whitewashed diamonds. In the center of each diamond was a bright red spot of *kumkum.* Lakshmi slipped through this door, into the darkness of the hut, and Maya followed.

Her eyes adjusted to the shadows. The inside walls had been whitewashed. Maya could probably have touched both sides if she stretched her arms. The dirt floor had a shiny green, well-kept look from being swept and painted with cow-dung slurry. On opposite sides of the hut were two thin mats, one of them short—Lakshmi's mat, Maya guessed. "Who sleeps there?" Maya asked. "Your mother?" But Lakshmi shook her head.

At the foot of Lakshmi's bedmat stood a small wooden trunk. As the girl opened it, her eyes rarely left Maya's. Then she handed to Maya a tiny pair of painted slippers as a baby might wear, some ribbons, and with great shyness, a doll made with bright silk rags.

Maya received each item like a precious gift. When she was Lakshmi's age, she herself had a box like this in her kitchen hut in Orissa. She admired the slippers and ribbons, examining them with delight, then setting them with care upon the bedmat. Then she lifted the doll as one might lift a toddler, holding it gently beneath the arms. "What is your name, little girl?" she asked. But the doll didn't answer. Maya gave it a stern, disappointed look, and asked again.

"Uma," Lakshmi whispered, answering for the doll. It was the first time she had spoken.

"What a pretty, pretty name for a pretty little girl."

Lakshmi held out her hands, and Maya gave her the doll, which Lakshmi cradled in her arms. Maya watched her for a minute, and then one by one removed a few bangles from the dozens she wore on her wrist. It took a while; for they were small, and she had to squeeze the bracelets past her knuckles. "These are for you and Uma."

Lakshmi solemnly placed them on the doll's rag arm, one at a time. Then, glancing guiltily at Maya, she slid them onto her own wrist. She then locked the doll and everything else back into the wooden box.

Near Lakshmi's hut was a storehouse with a wide, flat roof. The girl led Maya to a ladder and climbed to the top. Around them, servants glanced up and then looked away again, unconcerned. Maya understood their looks. When she had been a girl, she too could do as she pleased: everyone considered her someone else's problem.

A little girl in a short dress and bare feet had no trouble negotiating the flexing bamboo ladder, but for Maya, holding her sari and climbing in smooth-soled sandals, each step was an adventure. When she reached the top, Lakshmi pulled her down beside her. Her little legs dangled over the edge of the roof. She took out a handmade sack and poured a pile of cashews into her dusty palm, and offered one to Maya.

From here, Maya could see much of the palace grounds, and across the lake, the bustling city of Belgaum, in fact the whole valley ringed by mountains. It was noon; the lake was peaceful as a mirror, and the sunlight was silvery and diffused, casting gentle shadows. A family of monkeys lounged in a cavity in the wall a few yards away, a mother nursing a cute black-eyed baby.

Lakshmi leaned against Maya as if she were a bolster, one leg flipped casually over the other. She stared up at Maya and solemnly offered her cashew after cashew.

"You're happy here, aren't you, Lakshmi?" Maya said, combing the girl's hair with her fingers. "But sometimes, maybe not so happy." Lakshmi merely watched as Maya spoke. "Maybe you think about running away; maybe to that city across the lake. Maybe you just think about running on and on and never stopping." Lakshmi's little bare foot ticked up and down as she listened.

"But where would you go, little one? Who would care for you? What would become of you, all alone in that big world?" Maya's eyes drifted over the peaceful lake as clouds scudded across the sky.

"Maybe you think to end it all. Could your next life be any harder than this, you think?" Lakshmi's foot stopped moving. The girl slipped her hand around Maya's fingertips. But Maya seemed hardly to realize that Lakshmi was still there. "Is there no way out? No way but to live in endless suffering, or to die?"

As if in answer to this question, Maya saw the form of Geraldo stepping into the courtyard far below. Her face grew brighter and more serious. Something Chitra had said, she now realized, had been a hint to her, pointing to the way out of her dilemma. "Maybe the answer lies not in being good, but in being selfish."

Maya looked down to see that Lakshmi's face had grown troubled. The young woman stroked the girl's cheek. "Pay no attention to me, child," Maya smiled.

But Lakshmi had lived too long with Lady Chitra. When someone told her that, she worried twice as much.

ⓔⓢⓔⓢ

Lucinda woke beneath a light coverlet in the darkness of an unknown room. She rose slowly, for her head felt thick, and winced when she tried her weight on her hurt ankle. She was wearing a dressing gown of cotton lawn that tied around her waist with a ribbon. She couldn't remember where she got it.

Near her bed she saw an old crutch, its head wrapped in faded rags. She had a vague memory of an old hakim looking at her gravely and leaving it for her last night. She took it and hobbled toward the wedges of brightness glowing along the sides of a dark curtain near her bed. Drawing back the heavy drape, she found not a window as she expected, but a stone archway as wide as the room, leading to a shallow balcony.

The balcony extended beyond the palace wall and gave an impression of floating in space. An exquisite vista spread in a coral haze before her, a wide lake in a valley framed by sheer shadowed mountains. On the other shore Lucinda saw forests of dense shadowed greens, and vibrant fields bright and soft as velvet as tiny shoots peeked from the ground. The lake water glittered.

Living all her life in Goa, used to city streets and sea winds, Lucinda had no words to describe what she saw. It was like a dream, she thought, like the magic country of bedtime stories. The Beautiful Lands, she had called them to herself as a child; but now they stood before her.

She could taste moisture on the caressing breeze, even taste the smoke of cooking fires. On the far shore she saw a string of shining water buffalo, small as toys, wading along the lake; and near the forest's edge, a pack of gray-backed monkeys loping in a line.

Where was she? Where were her clothes? How had she gotten here? Where were the others? Just then she heard a soft voice behind her. "Isn't it a beautiful sight?"

It was Maya.

"You're all right!" Lucinda said. "Where am I? Where's Da Gama? Where is everyone?"

Maya did not seem to feel the need to answer her questions. "Lady Chitra sent me to see you. Your trunk was destroyed, lost and broken in the chasm. Lady Chitra sends her regrets, and asked me to bring you this sari—never worn, so far as I can tell." Maya held out a thick square of silk, folded flat.

The news of her belongings seemed unimportant at the moment. "Captain Da Gama?"

"He left this morning with General Shahji. He came to see you earlier. Do you remember?"

"No. Shahji was the man that brought us here, yes? And what about Geraldo? Did he go as well?"

"He stays here with us."

"Captain Pathan?" Lucinda asked. But she couldn't bear to hear the answer, and hobbled back to her bed, and sat down heavily. She felt herself in pieces, as if slashed by a knife. One part of her controlled her body: that part could speak, perhaps even think; another part of her, hidden deep inside the first, was a broken bundle, terrified.

Maya sat beside her. "You don't remember? After the bandits, we were discovered by General Shahji, and he and his guards brought us here. It's Shahji's summer palace. Very rich. Very beautiful."

But Lucinda had stopped listening as soon as Maya had said "bandits." The gentle light of the room began to dim before her; her mind's eyes stared instead into a vile face, half-mad and evil; cold and stony ground pressed against her back. She leaned against the crutch.

Maya touched her arm with distant friendliness and nodded toward the folded sari. "The silks of Belgaum are famous." She shook the square of cloth, which unfurled with a snap; a six-yard length of light, stiff silk the color of sand at sunset, its edging dense with gold-thread embroidery, the main body dotted with tiny, multicolored designs.

"But I am a farang. How can I wear a sari?"

"I can help you," Maya said. "It is so easy. First let's comb your hair."

Lucinda felt nothing, thought of nothing as Maya rubbed her dark hair with scented oils, then gently combed it and braided a ribbon through it. She had never worn it so. Her braid was much longer and heavier than she expected. With Maya's help, she stood, placing her weight on her good foot, and let the bayadere wrap her with the sari.

First she swirled over Lucinda's head a gauze blouse light as air. It barely hid her breasts, and left Lucinda's belly bare. Strange to be dressed without proper underclothes, just a wisp of gauze; no slip, no corset. With quick, sure motions, Maya folded the sari around her bare hips, hanging the cloth in nine pleats over her outstretched fingers, then quickly tucking it into place to form a generous skirt. The other end of the sari, heavy with gold embroidery, she lifted across Lucinda's chest and then tossed over her shoulders.

"You look like a princess," Maya said, looking her over with unexpected directness.

Lucinda lowered her eyes. "Is there no petticoat? Are there no fasteners? No pins? No buttons? What holds it on?"

Maya moved around her critically, here pressing in a fold, here straightening an edge. "You worry too much," she said. Taking care with her hurt ankle, she placed Lucinda's small feet into silk slippers with turned-up toes. Again she stepped back and admired the effect. "You look quite presentable. No one would know you were a farang. Would you like some lunch?"

Suddenly Lucinda realized that she was hungry. Maya helped Lucinda to hobble across the marble-tiled courtyard toward a wide pavilion that overlooked the lake. By now the sun had risen high, and the white tiles gleamed. "We're here in the women's section," Maya explained as they slowly neared the pavilion. "On the other side of the pavilion are the men's quarters. We'll get lunch there on that verandah, which the two sides share."

With the bright mountain sun, the stiff silk, the braid, the crutch, the slippers with the turned-up toes, Lucinda seemed not to know herself. She seemed to float above the courtyard watching a strangely dressed young woman hobble forward, held up by a nautch girl who might have been her twin.

ʘʘʘʘ

The wide pavilion stretched in a semicircle, its sandstone archways overlooking the western shore. "I can't get over how you look," Maya said softly.

Lucinda glanced at her unfamiliar clothing. "Don't I look all right?"

"You look very different in a sari," Maya answered.

Lucinda thought about this for a moment, then turned to face the bright waters that sparkled in the noon sun. "What do you know about this place?"

"We're in Belgaum, about seventy miles from Bijapur. General Shahji often spends his summer here. Shahji has given part of this palace to the late sultan's first concubine, Lady Chitra. We met her last night. Do you remember?"

"No." Lucinda's gaze drifted over the water. A part of her still seemed asleep, but some other part she hardly knew drank in the sight of the palace grounds. "It's so quiet. So vast. Not like home, all city streets and bustle." She looked down, embarrassed. "Now you will think me unsophisticated. I came to Goa as a child and never left its walls."

Maya considered her. "Jewelry," she said. Lucinda arched an eyebrow, not understanding. "Jewelry. You asked how you looked. You need jewelry with such a fine sari. Bracelets. A necklace. With a rich sari like that, you should wear a headpiece as well, maybe a teardrop pearl resting on your forehead." Maya traced Lucinda's brow with a delicate finger. "Do farangs have such things? I think not."

It was odd to feel her touch. No one ever touched her face. At the stroke of Maya's finger on her brow, Lucinda looked up, shocked. She had the odd sensation of the disjointed parts of her memory colliding back together. Suddenly her eyes welled up with tears. "I have nothing, nothing. My trunk had everything. My jewels are gone, my clothes. I had brought nearly everything I owned. Now it's gone, gone, everything is gone."

While Lucinda sobbed into her palms, Maya's face passed through many changes: first concerned, then irritated, finally serene. "You think you have had misfortune," she whispered. "But I tell you that this is good fortune. The gods cannot place their gifts into a closed fist. First your hand must be emptied, then the gifts may be received. We poor fools call this loss, and we suffer, but it is the blessing of the gods."

Lucinda looked into the nautch girl's eyes. "Do you believe that?"

"I have to." She covered Lucinda's hand with her own, her many bangles clinking as they slid down her arm. "Here," Maya said suddenly. With an effort, she squeezed a few bangles from each wrist. "Wear these."

Lucinda gave a soft laugh. "They'll never fit! Look how small your hands are!"

"Nonsense. Our hands are just the same size. Let me help you." She took Lucinda's hand and rubbed her knuckles until they relaxed; the bracelets suddenly slipped over onto her wrists.

Lucinda shook her hand and the bangles jingled merrily, but her face grew dark. "What do you remember of . . ." she let the words hang in the air.

Maya studied her face carefully. "I remember the elephant; I remember it slipping from the road, over the cliff's edge into the chasm." She looked back at Lucinda. "The mahout."

"The bandit," Lucinda whispered. "His mouth dripping spittle."

"Let me see your leg," Maya said.

The words were so unexpected, it took Lucy a moment before she lifted her foot and swept her sari skirts to the side for Maya to see. "Captain Pathan said it was broken."

"It's not," Maya said as she smoothed the ankle with strong fingers. "You couldn't walk on it if it were."

"It hurts," Lucinda insisted.

"You just think it does," Maya answered, stroking the bones. She looked into Lucinda's eyes. "You want it to hurt."

"I don't!" She stared back at Maya. "What are you doing?" Maya's fingers made her ankle feel longer, softer somehow. Lucinda closed her eyes, strangely transported by the warmth, but only for a moment.

"Close your eyes." Maya's face was so confident that Lucinda could not disobey. The image of the bandit tore into her mind, but she kept her eyes tight. "There," she pouted.

"Better," Maya said, as if she could see into Lucinda's dream. "Let your mind wander."

Fascinated despite her reservations, Lucinda kept her eyes shut and did as she was told. She found herself again by the stream, again in terror. Tears streamed from her eyes. Then, suddenly, she saw not the bandit's face, but the captain's. Her eyes flew open. "Pathan," she cried, leaping to her feet.

"Yes." Maya's hair clung to her damp face. She looked exhausted. "Yes, we must help him."

ᏩᎣᏋᎧ

A moment later they were hurrying through the courtyard, Lucinda walking as if her ankle had never been hurt. "Wait," Maya said as they passed her own door. She stepped inside and returned holding a tiny enameled jar. "Hold still," she said; and with the stick on the jar's stopper placed a drop of blackness into each eye. "Kohl," she told her as Lucinda blinked. "It will clear the whites. You don't want Pathan to see you with your eyes red from tears."

Impulsively Lucinda took Maya's hands. "When you show me such kindness, how shall I keep from crying even more?" With their shoulders pressed together, they walked across the causeway.

Belgaum was a warren of winding old streets and alleys. Maya asked a half-dozen people in the town before a boy helped them find the house of the hakim. The boy kept glancing over his shoulder, holding himself very tall and looking very serious. Wisps of fuzz had just begun growing on his cheeks and upper lip, and he would one day be handsome. Lucinda wondered if he were married.

The old hakim came and stood blinking as the two women came to his door, as if hoping they were a dream that would vanish if he could just wake up. "You may not be here," he told them at last.

"Don't be absurd," Lucinda answered. "We won't leave without seeing him."

The hakim blinked his old eyes once more. "You are a farang! But dressed so? It can't be!"

"We will see Pathan now, sir," Lucinda insisted. Without waiting for permission, she stepped past him. He was too frail to put up much resistance. Maya shrugged and followed. "Where have you put him?" Lucinda asked.

"But he is near death," the hakim said, now reduced to pleading.

"That is why we have come," Maya answered softly. The hakim grumbled, but then led them to a small dark room. Smells so crowded the air that Lucinda recoiled when she started to enter. Smoke, herbs, urine, and excrement hung in the darkness like an unseen fog. Maya stepped past her and found the clasp of the shuttered window. "No, he must have darkness!" the doctor hissed. Maya ignored him and pushed aside the shutter. Light streamed through in a single beam; the rest of the room stayed hid in shadow.

In the sudden sunlight Maya saw Pathan, limp as a broken doll. One of his hands poked from beneath his rough blanket, looking unnaturally pale. "Come," she said to Lucinda as she knelt near his head, but Lucinda could not move; no, she could barely breathe.

"His head is broken, see?" the hakim said, pulling aside a dingy bandage. "Here behind the ear." He pointed with a twiglike finger.

"Why is there no blood?" Maya demanded.

"It means he will die."

"Quiet. He'll hear you," Lucinda whispered.

The hakim merely shook his head. "The fresh air will disorder his spirit," he murmured as he moved to shutter the open window. "Not that it makes any difference."

"Leave it," Maya said. She had placed her fingers over Pathan's ear.

"You will kill him! His blood will be on your hands, not mine."

"You've found someone else to blame for his death, you mean," Lucinda said.

"Be quiet both of you!" Maya whispered. Something in the set of Maya's chin unnerved the hakim, and he shuffled quickly from the room.

"Can you fix him?" Lucinda sat beside Maya, fumbling with her unfamiliar sari skirt. "Say you can."

"He's very far away. I can hardly find him." Maya's eyes were closed, as if she were listening for a faint sound.

Lucinda wrapped her arms around Maya, pressing her cheek near her ear. "Help him, help him," she murmured.

As Lucinda clung to her, Maya slowly probed Pathan's head. "Be very still," Maya whispered. Lucinda held her breath. She could feel Maya's heartbeat. She stood that way for what seemed like hours. Sweat began to pour from Maya's body, and from her own.

Then Lucinda heard Pathan give a rattling groan. "He can't have died," she cried.

"No, he lives." Maya slumped to the floor beside his bed.

Lucinda sat near Pathan's bedside. Maya had gone outside to catch her breath.

Pathan would open his eyes for a moment and then close them as if the light made him dizzy. Finally he blinked at her. "Madam," he whispered.

Lucinda felt suddenly terrified at the prospect of speaking to him. "You're thirsty. Let me fetch you some water," she whispered, standing up.

"No," Pathan said. "Sit beside me."

Lucinda pulled her sari back into place as best she could, feeling almost naked. She patted her hair and tried to keep her breasts covered with her elbows. The bangles Maya had given her clinked on her arm. She was careful not to touch him. "Is the light too bright for you, Captain?" she said. She hated the formality she heard in her voice.

"I love the light, more than you can imagine." He reached out for her hand. His long fingers curled around her palm, dark against her pale skin. "I was in a place of darkness. I thought I would never see the light. Then I heard you calling me."

Lucinda's fingers trembled in his hand like the heart of a caught bird. "It was Maya who called you, Captain."

"It was your voice I heard, madam," he answered, looking at her with bright, burning eyes. "Your voice that led me to the light."

She gazed at him for a long time. "You're thirsty, Captain. I'll get water." As she took her hand from his, her eyes drifted to his mouth, to his lips.

She had strength enough to turn her head, but she could not find the strength to leave his side. His long fingers again found her open hand. "How different you look, madam, dressed so." Lucinda felt herself blushing, but did not move. He slowly drew his thumb across her palm. "So different, yet I always would know you. Always." Lucinda could not help turning toward him. The silence of the room seemed to roar in her ears. "How blind I was, madam. I have looked at you so often, but seen only your farang garments, and never saw the woman. Forgive me, I beg you."

She found it difficult to speak. "You saved my life and nearly lost your own. There is nothing to forgive." His eyes were wide, dark. And she knew that her eyes were speaking to him, speaking words she dare not say aloud.

She pulled back her hand, knowing that she must leave. "I'll be back soon, Captain."

His eyes never left hers. "Come back quickly."

Once outside she leaned against the wall clutching the cold pitcher to her breast. It took her a long time to find her breath.

⊙⊙⊙⊙

She looked up to find Maya and the doctor staring at her. "He's awake," she said. She was certain that they could see her trembling. "I'm getting him some water," she added, holding out the pitcher as if hoping it would distract them.

"I will take care of this," the hakim said. Perhaps Maya had said something to him, for he no longer seemed so unfriendly. In fact, his old eyes crinkled at Lucinda, in what she understood was meant to be a smile.

Maya gave her a knowing look. Again Lucinda felt her herself blushing.

Maya gave a short laugh. "Slipper's gone."

"Dead?"

Maya laughed again. "No, not dead. Gone. He tried to beat me this morning, and your cousin Geraldo kicked him out of the palace. The hakim tells me someone gave him a ride to Bijapur. He's gone, sister."

"No more Slipper? Whatever shall we do?" Then Lucinda laughed with Maya.

But the hakim scowled when he returned. "You laugh at him, but I think you should not laugh. If he is the one I think, he is a dangerous fellow. Very nasty."

"We know he is nasty," Maya said. "But why dangerous?"

"I've heard tales. I will say no more." He glanced at the windows as if fearful spies were lurking there. "But if he has gone to Bijapur, I say beware." With that he took the pitcher to Pathan's room.

"Beware of what?" Lucinda asked.

But before anyone answered, the hakim cried out. "What have you done to my patient?" Pathan was drenched in sweat. The hakim began to take his pulses, first his neck, then his wrists.

"His pulse will tell you. He is strong and growing stronger," Maya said. "But he will sleep for many days."

"How can you know this?" the hakim asked skeptically.

"But he was talking to me. Holding my . . ." Lucinda cut her thought short.

"He woke because he felt your presence," Maya said. "Now he will sleep."

"Will he be all right, sister? Did you cure him?"

"I just took his pain away. It will help him heal."

"But what happens to it? Where does the pain go?" Lucinda looked at Maya with concern. "Do you take it on yourself?

Maya did not answer.

"But will he be better?" Lucinda asked, suddenly worried. "All better?"

Maya nodded. "Yes, all better, except that he will remember nothing."

"Maybe not," Lucinda sighed. "But I will remember. Everything."

☾☽☾☽

As she walked back to the palace, holding Lucinda's hand, Maya considered the idea that had come to her, sitting on the roof with Lakshmi. If it worked, she realized, it would solve all her problems. And once she had seen the solution to her problems, Maya embraced it. It was not as extreme as killing, herself or someone else, not as uncertain as running away. Not so terrible, she reasoned, yet it would destroy her value with a single stroke.

She could hardly know the consequences of her decision, or how much pain she would cause herself.

At the entrance to the wide, common verandah of the guest quarters, Maya saw Geraldo. The young farang, pacing the length of the balcony that overlooked the valley, glanced up at her grumpily, and then turned away. He seemed not even to notice Lucinda.

He's still sulking, thought Maya. Even so, he looked rather dashing in his borrowed *jamas*. What will he do when he discovers my plan?

As the women drew near him, Maya favored him with her most fetching smile, and a long look that promised much.

❧❧❧❧

After rinsing her breasts in rose water, and combing her hair, and rubbing sandalwood paste on her wrists and ankles, Maya dressed in a fresh sari of bright green edged with gold. She dabbed a single dot of bright red *kumkum* between her eyebrows, and blinked a dab of kohl into the corner of each eye.

As she made to leave, she paused briefly before a small bronze statue of Durga riding her tiger. Oh, Goddess, she thought, what do you think of my plan? If it is not your will, let me fail. If it is not my guru's will, let me fail.

❧❧❧❧

Maya's bedroom had tall, narrow double doors of dark wood. Opening one just a crack she peeked through. As she expected—as she hoped—Geraldo lounged in the verandah, leaning on a column near the entrance to the women's quarters. Maya's smile was like a lotus flower; Geraldo yet another bee driven mad by its fragrance.

It was not such a great step, Maya reasoned, to go to the verandah, nor such a great step to speak with him. Before she had time to reconsider, she stood near his side.

Of course he insisted on sulking, and Maya could barely keep from laughing at him. But this did not distract her from her purpose. "Oh, sir," she said. The deep tang of sandalwood paste floated in the air whenever she moved.

Of course he would not answer her at once, and as she waited, she looked out over the lake, touched by the purple shadows of the setting sun, its surface a green so dark it looked nearly black. At last she heard him sigh, and she turned to him with practiced coyness. "Are you still very annoyed with me?"

She was shocked to see how his face hid so little, so different from a Hindi: he was naked to her. His emotions floated on his skin like paint: she saw not just his anger, but his desire. His burning eyes seemed deeper and darker than most men's, contrasted by his pale skin which glowed in the sunset light. He breathed deeply, through clenched teeth, as though each breath were an effort. "Oh, dear, you are still very angry."

"Should I not be? I showed you kindness and you insulted me."

"You speak the truth, and I am ashamed." That much was true—Maya regretted what she had said earlier, just as she regretted what she was about to do. The best duplicity, she knew, was mixed with a measure of honesty.

Her words, her downcast eyes, the closeness of her body, which seemed to set the air trembling, the sandalwood paste and her own natural, dark perfume began to confuse his senses. "Well, you were upset," he said, a little hoarsely. "That eunuch could irritate a stone."

When she smiled up at him, her look was so forthright, he gulped. He glanced around: The veranda was empty. The corridors silent. They were alone.

She let the solitude enfold them. "If I asked most sincerely, sir, could you forgive me?" She bent her head, and then lifted her gold-flecked eyes to him ever so slowly. Geraldo seemed to have trouble swallowing.

The green silk of her sari rustled as Maya raised her small hand and placed a single finger on his chest. Her voice whispered like a breeze: "You could maybe forgive your Maya? If she were very good to you? If she did her very best to make it up to you?" Geraldo's eyes watched as Maya's finger traced a tingling path across his shirt, and slipped past the closure of his *jama*, and then touched his skin.

"This is not right," Geraldo said. His voice was husky. Even the crows had stopped their cawing. Silence fell everywhere like the night around them.

"Right or wrong? What is to stop us?" She leaned forward and lifted herself so her lips were a breath away from his ear. "Do you not want what I want?" Her hand reached out and glided over his.

She was trembling, or he was.

It was not such a great step from the verandah to the men's quarters, nor from there to Geraldo's room, nor from his door to the cushions of his bed.

And only after they had clasped and unclasped; only after the moans and slaps of flesh thrusting into flesh had risen and dissolved in the dusk-cooled air; only after their sighs had mingled with the scent of sandalwood and sweat; only after she caught her breath and Geraldo slept, while she stroked his cheek that gleamed like metal in the last light of the setting sun; only then did Maya discover the unexpected flaw in her designs.

Part Four

Meetings

After two days rocking in the back of a farmer's cart, Slipper saw a miracle. After two days of eating only chapatis and bananas, and hearing only talk of drought and scarecrows and dung, Slipper trembled, as one trembles at the sight of a prison door swung wide at last. He held his breath for fear that even breathing would make the vision disappear. But the farmer by his side only swore when he saw it, clapping his fists to his head in frustration. He loved whining, Slipper had discovered. "By the Prophet's beard! Did I not say that Allah the all-merciful hates farmers! Is this not the very proof? This is your fault, eunuch! You have brought bad luck!"

"Me, sir?" Slipper's tiny eyes widened.

They had come nearly to the crossing of the Bijapur road when they saw it. Slipper, despite his weak eyes, could just make out the sight, just ahead of a line of wagons and carts and herders with cattle, bunched up motionless at the crossing.

"I bless all the angels," Slipper whispered to himself. But the farmer jumped from the cart, holding his head as if it would explode. Slipper jumped down as well. Already other travelers were lining up behind them, just as annoyed as the farmer. Finding others more willing to listen to his miseries, the farmer ignored his passenger, and Slipper pushed through the crowd until he came to the crossing itself. But he held back behind the line of people waiting there—he did not want to be seen just yet.

❡❡❡❡

Beneath the wavering shadows of huge-branched trees that canopied the crossroad, a dozen guards, tall, dark-skinned, powerful, barred the road. Their lances bore the green tassels of the harem eunuch guard.

Crushed eunuchs, Slipper saw at once. So many of them, he thought, hardly able to contain his pleasure.

To the south, he could hear a procession approaching. First came the tinny sound of small cymbals clanging, and then the blare of herald trumpets. Soon the musicians came into view, a bored lot of crushed eunuchs, walking in a listless approximation of a march. Slipper despised them for their indifference. More eunuchs followed, carrying pennants of Bijapuri green.

After them came the Guard cavalry, riding lively bedouins on shining saddles of gilded leather, the silver bosses of their shields glinting in the sun. Their horses—all geldings of course—pranced scornfully before the annoyed onlookers who waited at the crossroads, just as their riders eyed the peasants with disdain.

Surrounded by his bodyguard, the captain of the Guards followed on a tall blood bay. His bodyguard carried unsheathed swords. Next came the captain's servants holding in their outstretched hands caskets of his jewels on velvet pillows. A young Abyssinian eunuch (cut, or even shaved, thought Slipper with approval) walked beside the captain's horse, lifting a huge peacock feather fan on a long pole to shield his head.

Behind the captain, came the elephants. Five, ten . . . Slipper was too dazzled and too happy to keep count. He gaped at the ornamented howdahs, the curtains closed so the riffraff might not see in, and let himself imagine who was sitting inside.

Slipper waited breathlessly, and then, to his delight he saw it: the Flying Palace of the Sultana. Only a few roads in Bijapur were wide enough to accommodate the Flying Palace, for it took four matched elephants, walking in unison, to manage it. Two walked side by side in front, two side by side behind. Each beast had a special harness tied round its midsection. Stout ropes strung from each harness attached to the corners of a sturdy platform as large as the foundation of a temple. Wooden walls rose from the sides of the platform, above them a roof; painted to give the illusion of a palace hall of stone, with columns and arches, and even a glittering silver dome above all. The Flying Palace was two stories tall, with a breezy balcony over the royal suite below: bedroom, kitchen, bath, even a toilet. The walls were bossed with shining stars and crescents, gilded, and silvered. Hovering on its long ropes, held at perfect level by the careful elephants, the palace appeared to float. One could not imagine a structure so large moving so, hovering in the air—it defied logic, and many who saw it felt a wave of vertigo.

When the palace passed, Slipper could hold back no more. He pushed through the crowd. The caravan was far from over: more elephants and closed howdahs, more guards, and, of course, the whole train of carts and palanquins and wagons that made up the Sultana's suite. He thought for a moment about thanking the farmer for his ride, but then snorted at his thought.

He would need no longer to be courteous nor kind. Slipper was going home.

೨೦೦೨

The eunuch guardsman looked confused when a ball-shaped eunuch appeared amid a crowd of farmers and traders. "Let me through, you fool," Slipper shouted. "I must speak to the Khaswajara!"

"Get back with the others. Who do you think you are?" The guard's voice was rough. He must be new, Slipper thought. He wondered if the eunuch master had done his job right when he made him.

"Who are you to treat me so. Take me to Brother Whisper at once!"

The guard startled. "Nobody calls him that, you lout—not in public, anyway."

"I call him that, fool! He is my brother and my friend. In the name of the Sultana, take me to him!" Slipper could now see the end of caravan drawing closer. In desperation he hurled himself at the eunuch guard's feet. "Brother!"

To the fury of everyone at the crossroads, the caravan was halted. Runners hurried messages to the Flying Palace and back. The guards at the crossing had to brandish their lances as the crowd grew restless. At last a eunuch dressed in robes as bright as the noonday sun came gracefully down the road, along with two finely outfitted guardsmen. At the sight of him, patches of color formed on Slipper's wide cheeks, and he began to tremble.

The eunuch, very fair and sophisticated, dripped with pearls: necklaces, earrings so heavy they hooked over the tops of the eunuch's ears, strands of pearls that looped through his gold embroidered turban, so large that they clicked together with his every swaying step. He examined Slipper as if he were a dead bird he'd found in the marble courtyard of the harem: something unexpected and not very pleasant. "Oh, dear," he sighed.

"Brother!" Slipper's voice was choked, and he lowered his eyes as the other eunuch approached. "My name . . ."

"You have no name. I do not know you." He turned the eunuch guards and lifted his hands sadly. "We came in error . . ." He began to walk away.

Slipper gave a whimper that changed into a wail. He tried to leap forward, but the guards had anticipated this, and they blocked his path with crossed lances. "No! Wait! Don't go! I have found it!" Slipper cried out.

At this the other turned slowly. "Found it? Where? Tell me."

"No." Slipper's voice was firm. "To Whisper, only to Whisper."

The other considered this. After a moment, he glanced at the guards. As soon as they lowered their lances, Slipper lurched through. "And say my name! Say it!"

The other eunuch, taller, younger maybe—but with eunuchs, who could tell?—calmer, and certainly better dressed, looked at Slipper, with his turban, as usual, unraveling, with his threadbare silks now travelworn and stained. Slipper pulled himself up to all his small height, and lifted his nose in a gesture so haughty that the guardsmen struggled not to laugh. "Say it," Slipper said again.

"Nawas Sharif," the other said, after a long pause.

At the sound of his name, Slipper closed his eyes like one tasting an old, delicious wine. "Ali Nawas Sharif," he demanded softly.

The other took now a longer time. The words seemed to pain him. "Ali Nawas Sharif," he said at last.

With the guardsmen behind him, Slipper walked to the Flying Palace. The hoisting ropes hung limp: the elephants had set the palace on the ground.

Two footmen holding long horsehair whisks stood beside a set of silver stairs, set down only when the caravan halted. At a glance from the bejeweled eunuch, the guards bowed to Slipper as he mounted. Unseen hands pulled the velvet entry curtains wide, and Slipper was swallowed up in shadow.

A moment later, the footmen took away the stairs. *Hup, hup,* the mahout captain called. The four matched elephants each took three steps outward; the hoisting ropes groaned, and the Flying Palace lurched into the air.

The elephants marched forward with slow steps. The caravan began to move.

Slipper had come home.

☙❦❧❦☙

Slipper did not mind the wariness of the brothers who attended him. He understood—how could he not? But he snapped at them anyway, as demanding and fussy as any concubine, and why not? They bathed the road dust from his face and hands with rose water and brought linens, and how long had he been deprived of such necessities? They found silk *jamas* that would fit him, and he snapped insults while they pulled his arms through the sleeves and smoothed the thin stiff silk across his corpulent shoulders.

"I need jewels," Slipper fussed. "Bring me rings, good ones. And a necklace. Where is Whisper?" he demanded. "Bring Whisper to me now." Knowing all the time of course that these attendants would do no such thing at all.

After washing and dressing and fussing, the elegant eunuch that had met Slipper at the crossroads reappeared and shooed the lesser eunuchs away. The two stared at one another; the only sounds the creaking of the walls and the groaning of the ropes, and outside the occasional muffled trumpet of an elephant. Though the room gave the impression of being a room in a palace, the floor sometimes lurched, as though they stood in an enormous boat with great waves rolling underneath.

"The Khaswajara will see you now." He waited for a moment, and then added, "Brother." The word seemed to take much effort.

"I remember this room, these walls, those sounds," Slipper said softly.

"Nothing has changed much since you . . . went away," the other replied.

"I have changed."

❀❀❀

They mounted the narrow staircase that led to the upstairs breezeway. On one side, Slipper's hips rubbed along the wall, on the other they hung out over empty space. He leaned into the steps, pressed his hands on them, and so came into Whisper's presence looking rather furtive and uncertain.

"Leave us," Whisper said to the other eunuch.

His voice, as always, sounded hollow, rasping—and as always, so soft that Slipper had to strain to hear. For some reason, Whisper wore no turban, and his fine, colorless hair, dry as bleached straw, drooped to his narrow shoulders. He was as thin as Slipper was fat, brittle as an old reed, his face a thin skull lined with skin dry as parchment. Finally he turned to Slipper, and blinked like a bird.

"How many years has it been?" croaked Whisper. The floor lurched, and Whisper nearly fell. He looked so frail, so old, thought Slipper, that he might shatter if he landed hard.

"Nine, I think. How old is the heir? You had just been named Khaswajara . . . how many years is that?"

"Ten years, then." Whisper shook his head wistfully, and motioned for Slipper to follow to a comfortable alcove. "How have you been, brother?"

"How do you expect, brother?" Slipper's words were soft, but his tone was venomous. "You yourself gave the order."

"It was the Brotherhood council that decided, not I," Whisper murmured. "Blame them, not me."

"You were part of the council."

Whisper shrugged as he sat near the gauze-curtained window. His bones creaked. "It was for your own good, brother, and the good of the Brotherhood. Surely you saw that? Surely you see that now?" Whisper motioned to a cushion facing his. "You say you've found it." His rasping, shallow voice could not disguise his eagerness.

Slipper sat heavily. No food, he noticed, no drink. "Not much welcome, brother," he pouted. "I shall want a great deal better treatment than this." Slipper laughed, like the laugh of a nasty boy. "I should tell you everything now, I suppose, so you can take the Web, and thus cast me aside?"

"You should tell me so your exile may be ended. It was you that lost the Web in the first place, brother."

"That's not true!"

"But that's what the council found, and so it is true, brother." Whisper's leathery lips parted to reveal his long teeth. "But now you've found it again, so what difference is there?"

Slipper leaned back. "I'll want a post of power. Not in the harem, either. A real one, this time. In the court."

"It can be done."

"A house of my own. Not just rooms."

"Yes."

"Jewelry. My old jewels back. That woman who brought me here, he was wearing one of my rings! I want it returned, everything returned, and a full accounting!"

"Yes, yes," came Whisper's answer. "All that and more." His big eyes were bright. "You found it?"

"Yes," Slipper sighed, leaning back. He thought about demanding something to drink, but in truth he was as eager as Whisper. And so, with no more delay, he began to tell the story of Maya.

◦◦◦◦◦

On the cold ground of the courtyard of the fort, Shahji's soldiers snored in brown blankets, like great locusts in cocoons. Da Gama's eyes flew open at first light, though the western sky was still filled with stars. He rose from his borrowed bedroll and pulled on his heavy boots. The damp morning air chilled his skin.

Da Gama took his bearings. He had been on the road with Shahji's men for nearly a week. Now it seemed to him most foolish that he had decided to travel to Bijapur with Shahji. He should have gone alone.

General Shahji had been on tour of review when he and his men rescued the caravan. That night, when Da Gama said he had to get to Bijapur, Shahji suggested joining them. "Ride with my guard. Take a few extra days," Shahji had said, "Visit a few forts with me, and arrive in Bijapur rested and safe."

He did not need to add, you'll arrive in the company of the commander general. That would give a certain cachet to Da Gama, and right now Da Gama needed all the cachet he could get.

They were close to Bijapur now—a few hours' ride; they could get there today. Da Gama began to worry. He should not have delayed. But he had enjoyed the delay, a fact that worried him even more. Instead of facing the questions and anger of Senhor Victorio, Da Gama had enjoyed the company of Shahji, and his life of rugged ease.

Da Gama had heard of Commander Shahji, of course; he knew that he was a wily and ferocious soldier who'd once been a rebel, who had made peace and become the general commander of Bijapur's armies. He hadn't expected a man of Shahji's background to be so cynical and yet so friendly, so strategic and yet so practical. It was clear why Shahji had been named commander, despite being a Hindi.

When they'd reached the first fort Da Gama had asked permission to sleep outside with Shahji and his men. After his initial surprise, Shahji agreed. "Real soldiers hate a roof," Da Gama had told him. Shahji kept his face impassive, but his eyes had the look of man who had found a friend.

On this morning Da Gama caught the scent of bread frying. He sniffed a few times, guessed the direction, and walked away from the sleeping soldiers. A few yards behind the main barracks was a squat brick kitchen. As Da Gama approached, a dozen gray crows flapped from the ground and into the wide mango tree. A yellow dog snarled at him, but stopped when Da Gama growled back.

When Da Gama ducked through the low kitchen door, he saw a few women working near a small fire, peeling onions and grilling chapatis. Sparrows flew through the window, fluttering onto the low rafters. One of the women looked up and tossed Da Gama the flat bread she was cooking. He snatched it from the air.

"You want a real soldier, just find the kitchen." From a dark corner, Shahji grinned at him. "There's butter here." Da Gama sat beside him, stretching out his muddy boots in front of him. He knew it was impolite to stretch one's legs, but he didn't care. It made him happy. He didn't know the next time he'd be happy.

Using his punch dagger, Shahji scooped a mound of butter from a clay dish onto Da Gama's chapati. "Don't tell me you don't like the stuff," Shahji said. "I can see well enough that you do."

"No, I like it enough," Da Gama laughed. "What plans have you got, General?"

Shahji looked him over. "We're on our way back to Bijapur. Our inspection is done." Shahji paused. "You're starting to get worried, Deoga.

You're beginning to wonder if you did right, leaving that young farang in charge back at Belgaum." With a shrug and a tentative nod, Da Gama allowed that this might be so. "You see, you are not very hard to understand. I myself wonder if you were wise to do that."

Da Gama stared at Shahji for a moment. "Why do you say that, sir? He is a sort of hero, is he not? He was the one who went for help. He was the one who found you and your men. If he had not found you, we might all now be very dead."

Shahji lifted his eyebrows. "Take some more butter, sir," he said. "That man of yours, I think he was not running for help. I think he was running away. We had heard the shots and were already coming to investigate. One of my men had to chase him to bring that youth around." Shahji gave Da Gama a moment to let this sink in. "Maybe you should have put the eunuch in charge."

Da Gama looked back, blinking.

Shahji nodded seriously and went on, "I myself was most surprised to see that eunuch with you. He had been a very respected fellow at the sultan's court. He was the Khaswajara's right-hand man. You know what this word means, Khaswajara?"

"I know," Da Gama said. "Are you sure it is that same one?"

Shahji nodded. "He got into some trouble at court. *Hijras* ... who understands their ways? He must be back in Whisper's good graces or he'd still be banished. He might have the Sultana's ear as well." Shahji chuckled and gave Da Gama's shoulder a pat. "Hey, listen, Deoga, what do I know, eh? I'm only a simple soldier, just like you. Maybe that Geraldo fellow will do everything right."

"Who can say? But what can I do now?" Da Gama answered, shaking his head. "Done is done. Geraldo is family. If I left anyone else in charge, my masters wouldn't understand." Da Gama tore a piece of bread, but chewed as though it had no flavor. "If Pathan were not hurt, it would have been an easy choice."

"Yes," Shahji agreed. "Prince Pathan's a good man. And quite rich, if the gossip is to be believed, but he'd rather be a soldier than a noble. Makes you wonder, though. Why would a rich man want to be a soldier?" Shahji stood, and gave a howling, stretching yawn that made the women round the cook fire stare and laugh aloud. "Today, Deoga, you get to Bijapur! Come, we'll wake the others."

ᏻᏻᏻᏻ

"You farangs don't come here, do you? Not to the interior of Hindustan," Shahji said to Da Gama as the day's journey wore on. "Mostly you cling to the seaports, like swimmers frightened to get too far from shore."

"Yes, General. My travels on the Deccan Plateau have been all too few. Much of this is new to me," Da Gama agreed. His imaginary map of Hindustan consisted of a coastline and a few mountain passes that led to nearby trading cities, islands in his sea of ignorance. He had not really understood the sweep of the country; how beyond the moist green mountains like those that sheltered Belgaum stretched an endless dry and fissured plain, punctuated here and there by green fields and shadowed forests, a boundless expanse of rock-strewn earth more tedious than any ocean.

The horses' heads nodded heavily and they breathed hard now as their road wound upward under the relentless sun, always upward. By the light of last night's sunset they had first seen on the horizon the high plain of the city of Bijapur. Now its far-off shadow taunted them, refusing to come closer no matter how long they rode.

Da Gama missed the sweet, soft sea winds of the coast. Here the air smelled like hot metal and parched his tongue and the wind blew blister dry, so dry he did not sweat despite the heat. Though he drank from his bronze canteen, the water now sour and tepid, his thirst never ebbed.

Shahji had made a special point of riding near Da Gama on this last day of the journey, asking brief, careful questions that Da Gama answered with good humor. He enjoyed the general's company. He noticed that Shahji seemed to feel more comfortable with him than he did with his own men. At first Da Gama had thought that this was the typical tendency of an officer to isolate himself. Then he realized that Shahji was an immigrant to Bijapur, a former enemy who made a lucrative surrender and had been named commander. Da Gama guessed that Shahji, like himself, felt like a stranger, and sought the comfort of the company of another stranger. Also, of all the travelers only he and Shahji were non-Muslims. He wondered what Shahji had done during prayer times before he had Da Gama to chat with.

Despite their growing familiarity, however, Shahji did not speak entirely freely. While he offered his opinions about court politics and scandals, about the extravagance of the courtiers and the treachery of eunuchs, he skirted military matters.

Even so, Da Gama got a vague understanding about the Malve forts to the northwest and how those forts gave Bijapur dominance of the western trade routes. He pieced together that Shahji had been a rebel general who had managed to control enough of that territory to bring Bijapur to its knees, and had chosen at last an honorable alliance instead of constant war.

Now Shahji was rich, now he had power, but always would he be a stranger to the Bijapuris, and always suspect. Few men could be his confidants, Da Gama realized; and this explained, maybe, why Shahji seemed so determined to be friendly with Da Gama.

The general seemed particularly interested in the details of the bandits' attack on the Goan caravan, and he asked Da Gama about it several times. At first Da Gama wished that his Hindi was better, for he assumed that Shahji had not rightly understood him, but slowly discovered that Shahji wanted as full a description as he could give.

Shahji's questions began to circle especially around Slipper—how had he come to be part of the caravan in the first place? Da Gama explained that Slipper had arrived at Orissa just about the time he'd picked up the nautch girl, sent to accompany her on her trip to Bijapur. Yes, said Shahji, but how had he found out about the nautch girl in the first place? Had he been sent by Carlos Dasana, or by someone in Bijapur? Who arranged for him to get to Orissa so quickly? Da Gama, sadly, could not answer to Shahji's satisfaction.

"But what difference does it make, General?" Da Gama asked. "He's only a eunuch."

Shahji considered Da Gama's face for a long time before he answered. "Tell me why you say that."

"Well, I suppose he's sort of a lady's maid or something, isn't he? Don't eunuchs tend the women, just as grooms tend the horses?" Da Gama felt suddenly very foolish.

"Is that what you suppose?" Shahji lowered his voice to a whisper, but his eyes burned. "Eunuchs are a disease. Like tapeworms they attach themselves to the noble and the rich; like ticks they bloat on others' blood. They have no children to provide for, no heirs to fret over. This, they claim, makes them objective and less apt to steal. It is but another of their endless lies.

"Soon they manage the harem, soon the servants, then the household, even the family business. Every great household has its Khaswajara and soon no one can stir except with his approval.

"They seduce the women with obscene tricks and the men with drink and opium and abominations. Their tongues are agile, and their ears are quick. Who else knows the most intimate details of their masters' lives? Who else listens with such rapt attention?

"Eunuchs have no religion, no country, no family, no friends. Like rats who build a city in a sewer, they've established a society all their own, a brotherhood of secrets, of borrowed wealth and stolen goods, populated by children kidnapped and then maimed. Like moles they make their vile plots in hidden burrows. From behind a curtain they move the world as a puppet master moves the hands of a doll. Their brotherhood is dark and powerful, and in Bijapur, Slipper was one step from the greatest power of all."

Da Gama found himself whispering in answer. "What power is that, then?"

Shahji seemed to consider carefully, glancing around him almost involuntarily as if checking who could hear. "The power I speak of is held by the vilest *hijra* in Bijapur, the sultan's Khaswajara, the eunuch Whisper, who even now vies for regency, for the control of the heir, and through him control of the kingdom. Slipper was his second in command, but he disappeared a few years ago, and no one has heard of him until now."

Da Gama considered what Shahji had said. He'd heard similar tirades by Hindi traders too drunk to mind their speech, but rarely from a sober man, and never from one otherwise as clear-headed as Shahji. Stumped for a reply, he said, "Do they all have such foolish names?"

"Names designed to fool the foolish. Their real names they tell to no one." Seeing Shahji's dark, frowning eyes, Da Gama felt concern growing in his heart. Maybe I did wrong to leave them all in Belgaum, he thought, to leave them all alone with that eunuch Slipper.

Shahji seemed to read his thoughts. "He is no danger, farang, or at least not much of one; not by himself, not without his cohorts. Clearly he has some interest in that nautch girl though. So if you must worry, worry for her. He had no designs upon the others, I would guess, or you would know by now—nor on you either, or he'd have come along."

"I never would have permitted it!" laughed Da Gama.

But Shahji's face was stern. "He'd have come, like it or not, permitted or not. He'd have found a way."

At that point, Da Gama almost told Shahji about the nautch girl's small pouch, now tucked into a secret pocket of his coat, how Maya had begged him to keep it as though she feared for her life. Almost he told him, but he held back.

ೞೞೞೞ

By the time the sun reached its fierce zenith, they could see in the distance the dark basalt walls of Bijapur. The road grew busier with each mile, the dull clank of cowbells now always in the air. They passed a line of bullock carts, each piled mountain-high with sugarcane stalks. Straddling the sugarcane like charioteers, drivers with long reins and long whips drove the exhausted bullocks at a gallop. They passed huts of mud and grass. Naked children ran along beside them, holding out their hands.

As they stopped for afternoon prayers, Shahji nodded to a road that snaked through the hills to the south. "That road leads to Gokak Falls," he told Da Gama. "The Sultana goes there often. Have you seen it?"

"Once, in the dry season. Even then, a most impressive display."

"You should see it now, after the rains." Shahji's heavy face bore a thoughtful frown. He began talking with an unexpected urgency, as if he'd been thinking for a while and had finally made up his mind to speak. "Look, Deoga, there's some things you should know. In Bijapur you may not find what you expect."

With that, Shahji began to tell him of Victorio Dasana's recent fortunes. "He no longer lives in his great house. He's lost a lot of money playing Fives with Wali Khan, the vizier. Wali Khan has moved him into some rooms at the palace, but whether out of friendship or just to keep an eye on him until the debt is paid, who can tell?"

Shahji lowered his voice. "I know you're worried about what he'll say when he finds out about the attack." Da Gama answered with a shrug and Shahji went on. "He's lost a lot of influence, Deoga, so I don't think he can do much. But if you should have trouble, I will do what I can. In fact I'd be less worried about Victorio than about Whisper, the Khaswajara."

Da Gama stared at Shahji, suddenly more worried than ever.

"As I say, farang, I will do what I can to protect you. In the meantime, many people will wish to speak with you. Avoid them if you can. Say as little as possible, less if there are eunuchs around. Keep your wits about you." Shahji nodded toward the shadowy hills of Bijapur. "We'll be there soon. Try not to worry. Soldiers worry too much. Anyway, in a few hours you can stop worrying about what might happen, because then it will be actually happening." He chuckled as if he'd made a joke.

☙☙☙☙

But it took longer to reach Bijapur than Shahji expected. When the sun disappeared behind the black clouds of the western sky and the dark walls of Bijapur turned dusky rose in its light, they still were miles from the great gate. Here the plain was dotted with farms. In the darkening air, fragrant with smoke, lamps and fires glowed in the distance. Shahji sent a rider ahead at a gallop to tell the city gatekeepers to wait for his arrival.

At last the basalt walls loomed over them, lit by torches. As they approached, the muffled sounds of the city drifted over the stone parapets. They turned left on the perimeter road; along its shoulder gypsies and tinkers stared up from their tents with glowing eyes lit by tiny dung fires.

The soldiers patrolling the gateway stood at a rigid salute when they saw Shahji, but he merely waved at them without a look as he coaxed his mount through the small horse portal embedded in the massive wooden gates. The horsemen twisted through the entrance maze and then were on the wide thoroughfare of the great city of Bijapur.

Directly ahead of them sat the monstrous cannon, Malik-e-Maidan, the biggest gun ever made, straddling the road like a beached whale. Its barrel glinted in the rising moon, an opening so wide a horse could walk straight in. "It's only been fired once that I know of," Shahji said, riding back to Da Gama's side. "They shot off some poor fellow—he had got caught mounting one of Wali Khan's wives. They shoved him right down the barrel like a cannonball! The roar was fantastic—I couldn't hear for days; smoke so thick I nearly choked! They found the fellow's body four miles from here, and everyone still argues whether he died from the firing of the cannon, or from the fall. I hope it was from the fall. I like to think of him, soaring across the plains, enjoying in his last breath a sight no other man had ever had."

The street they rode was so broad that it took Da Gama some time to realize how many people they passed. A narrow Goan street would have been packed. Food stalls and taverns bustled, for the Bijapuris were liberal about drink despite the Prophet's admonitions, and music and laughter and the smell of hot meat and cheap wine mingled in the lamplit night.

Shahji lifted his chin to point out another wall ahead of them. "That is the palace, the home of the sultan and the court. It is where I live, and also now where your man Victorio must live." Shahji smiled to Da Gama. "Look here. Stay with me tonight. It will give you a chance to rest and orient yourself before you face Victorio." Da Gama took only a moment before bowing his head in gratitude.

❀❀❀❀

Shahji's palace—he called it his "cottage"—stood just inside the palace gate. Grooms appeared and helped them from their horses, but Da Gama clung to his bags with such vehemence that Shahji laughed. Inside the vestibule, a pretty young woman ran forward and placed her head on Shahji's feet. He stood above her for some time, clasping his hands at his chest, then raised her and introduced her to Da Gama as his wife. Da Gama gave her a sweeping farang bow and was rewarded with a delighted, carefree laugh. She looked about sixteen, Da Gama thought.

A servant came to show Da Gama to a guest room, but Shahji followed, only leaving when he was sure of Da Gama's comfort. After he left, Da Gama locked the door and glanced around the walls as though worried that someone watched him. Then from his saddlebag he fished out the small bag Maya had given to him, and held it in his for a long time, remembering his promise. Then he undid the knot and spilled its contents on to the bed.

Inside was a glittering spiderweb, a dazzling net of pearls and diamonds the size of peas.

❀❀❀❀

Next morning, Da Gama woke to a soft knocking on his door, and a girl whispering his name. Before he could get up, the door creaked open. It was not a girl, but a young eunuch that slowly entered. "Who are you?" De Gama demanded.

The eunuch jumped back with an exaggerated start. "I thought you were asleep, sir, forgive me!" he squeaked. "I am a *mukhunni* associated with the household of Senhor Victorio Souza. He wishes me to bring you to him as quick as I can. I've brought fresh clothing for you, sir. My name is Mouse."

Perhaps the eunuch got his name from his eyes, which were big and long-lashed, or from his nose, which twitched when he tried to keep still. But Da Gama guessed Mouse's nickname came from his left hand, which peeked from his billowing sleeve: the hand was brown and withered, and covered by what looked like a layer of downy fur.

Mouse floated into the room in that silent way that eunuchs had. At the foot of Da Gama's bed, he placed a set of farang clothes: a fresh pair of stockings, a clean shirt, and pants. His boots had been cleaned and blackened. "Shall I help you dress, sir?" Mouse inquired.

"I can dress myself, eunuch," he said. A look at Mouse's shocked, gentle face made Da Gama regret his tone. Even so, the hell with him, Da Gama thought. "Give me some privacy." Mouse bowed until his forehead nearly touched the floor, and slid off toward the door. "No, wait," Da Gama called. "Is there a bathing room here, senhor?"

"You should wait until we go to your uncle's rooms at the Gagan Mahal, sir, where the bath water is piping hot always."

"I'm a *soldado,* my boy. Cold water's fine." So Mouse led Da Gama down the narrow hallway to a tiled room, scarcely more than a drain and a bucket. "This will do." From a tap, he filled the bucket—ice-cold water, stored in a cistern on the roof, Da Gama guessed—and poured it over his head. Then another bucket, and another. All the time he cursed his soldier's bravado. All I had to do was be agreeable, he told himself, and I'd be bathing in hot water. Piping hot always.

Shivering, he wrapped himself in a muslin sheet and returned to his room, leaving a wet trail on the marble floor. Mouse sat next to the door, and lowered his head when he passed. It took some time after he dressed before the warmth returned to his skin.

Da Gama gathered up his things and threw the saddlebags over his shoulder. He did not need to look to know that Maya's headdress was no longer among them. Outside, Mouse tried to carry his bags, but Da Gama refused. The eunuch looked crushed. He walked as though trying to hide his withered hand from Da Gama's sight. It looked like a gesture he had practiced often. The eunuch jabbered pleasant nonsense as he followed Da Gama down the corridor. That was Slipper's habit as well, Da Gama remembered. Maybe eunuchs couldn't keep their mouths shut.

They found their way to the central courtyard. Shahji's palace—his cottage, Da Gama corrected himself—was simple and elegant, and the walls of burnished plaster glistened like gold in the morning light.

Shahji stood near the outer door. "I'm glad you finally got up, farang. You slept well?" He didn't wait for an answer, but threw an arm around Da Gama's shoulders and led him away from Mouse. "I don't usually allow eunuchs in my house, but he had clean clothes for you and would let no one else touch them. Did I do wrong?"

Da Gama shook his head. "I am indebted to you, General, and will always be."

"Remember—what help I can give to you is yours. I'll be watching, never fear." The general's face furrowed, and he dug into his pocket. "Here is a hundred hun."

Da Gama eyes grew wide. "I don't need money, General."

"Then take it only to humor me. Pay me back in a month. You may find this more useful than you think." He clasped the coins into Da Gama's hands and lowered his voice. "In the meantime, remember my words, eh? And have a *paratha* before you go." With that he marched out the door, giving a general's vague wave behind him.

Da Gama, smiled, picked up one of the fragrant pancakes, and tilted his head toward the door. "Come, Mouse," he said. "We who are about to die . . ."

"Die, sir?" Mouse blinked.

"Never mind. Let's go."

They rode in separate covered palanquins through the early morning streets of Bijapur. Palanquins always made Da Gama ill at ease. Bearers were rarely in the best of health. You could pull the curtain and hide them from your sight, but you could not escape their phlegmy breathing and the constant stream of their whispered curses. Unless the bearers were well matched in height and stride—and they never were—the *palki* rocked nauseously, worse than any boat. They moved as slowly as the oldest, weakest bearer, who invariably was the elder and in charge. All this for some ill-defined prestige, as if you were too grand for your feet to touch the ground.

Through the curtains Da Gama could not see much, but he guessed they were heading east. The buildings here seemed newer, plainer, more utilitarian. They had a raw, embarrassing nakedness, like a man showing his pink and flabby belly to a doctor. Da Gama knocked the side of the *palki.* "Where are we going?" The elder bearer lifted his grizzled chin to a long, windowless building with a tile roof. A twist of faded cloth hung limp from a pole above the single door. It took Da Gama a moment to recognize the flag of Portugal.

ಆಿ

With a puffy, scaly hand, Victorio Souza stroked his eunuch's cheek. "What do you think of my gelding, eh?" he asked Da Gama. "We all must have them, now—every household must have its gelding, that's the new rule, isn't it, Mouse?" The eunuch lowered his eyelids and shrugged, but pressed his head closer to Victorio's palm. "Well, it's turned out better than I ever thought. He's a great comfort to me, and he's smart." He turned to Mouse and said in Hindi, "Four hundred and twenty-eight from one thousand three hundred nineteen."

"Eight hundred ninety-one, uncle," Mouse answered, crinkling his nose.

"How do you like that, eh?" Victorio said in Portuguese. "Does sums in his head."

"How do you know if he's right?" Da Gama asked. Victorio merely glared in reply, and pressed his fat fingers on Mouse's withered hand. The old man had aged since Da Gama had last seen him. His cheeks sagged as if weighted; his watery eyes nearly hid by flesh that bagged from his eyebrows. His nose drooped now, blue and fissured, even gray in places. Instead of a distinguished silver, his mustache had turned yellow. Victorio wore an old man's knit hat for warmth though the air was hot, and his body filled the chair like a bag of sand.

It was going rather well, all things considered, Da Gama thought. Victorio heard the story of the bandit attack with a mournful reticence. None of it shocked or disturbed him; it was as if he'd already heard the news. But he lifted his heavy head each time Da Gama mentioned Lucinda. "And she is well? She is well?" he asked each time Da Gama said her name. Mouse's eyes never left Victorio's lips when he spoke. He's trying to learn Portuguese, Da Gama guessed.

Despite the early hour, Victorio's swollen hand, its skin peeling like an old snake's, cupped a flagon full of sherry. "What do you think of this factor?" Victorio asked nodding vaguely toward the building where they sat.

"I can't rightly say, sir. I've seen so little of it." For Mouse had brought Da Gama straight to Victorio's tiny office as soon as they'd arrived.

"You'll see more. You'll see it all. I'll have Mouse show you. I don't walk so well these days; I let Mouse be my eyes and ears. He's very clever." His hand stroked the eunuch's withered fingers. Da Gama wondered if the wine were drugged. Victorio tilted his head so his eyes looked deep into Da Gama's. "But I need more than a eunuch now, Captain."

Da Gama looked up, hearing an invitation in Victorio's words, or a warning.

"Have you not grown tired of soldiering? Are you ready to settle down? Take a woman, build a house? Get a gelding of your own?"

"The thought has crossed my mind, sir," Da Gama answered carefully. Except the part about the gelding, he thought.

"My brother Carlos is dead." The news slapped Da Gama like an unexpected wave. "My brother-in-law, I mean. Poisoned, from all accounts. Died the very day you left. He improved for a little while before your caravan left Goa, then died a few hours later. In great pain. Typical of poison."

"Dead? Poisoned?" It took a moment for Da Gama to process this information. "Who would poison him?"

"We may guess. When Carvallo, his secretary, sent news of Carlos's death, he said the valet had found Lucinda's box of *arsênico* by the bed."

Da Gama felt as if his heart were twisting on a blade. "She could never . . ."

"You know about her mother, don't you?" Da Gama shook his head. "Brain fever. She spent her last four years chained to her bed, screaming. God, I was glad when she died. She poisoned her first husband, you know."

"I had no idea."

"No, we kept it quiet. Even Lucinda thinks she died in Lisbon. Same with my Lucinda's aunt, my wife. Jumped to her death from a church tower. So we've been watching for signs in the girl, because, well . . . You never know, do you? Carlos should have been more alert." When Da Gama gave no answer, Victorio leaned forward. "I need to trust you, Da Gama. You are a relative, though a distant one. I need to trust our ties of blood." Victorio looked at him, pressing the question with his eyes.

"I am your servant, sir."

Victorio looked toward some distance only he could see. "I don't need a servant, Da Gama. I need a partner now, a friend. I need your help." He looked at him earnestly. "Did Carlos send any money?"

"Only the rials I used to bribe the bandits," Da Gama answered bitterly. "That's gone."

With a great sigh Victorio slowly lowered his hand to the arm of his chair. Da Gama tried to show no reaction when Mouse placed his face against it like a pillow. "Matters are delicate at the moment. The finances of our family are . . . well . . . complicated. Extended. Speculative." He looked at Da Gama significantly. Beside him, Mouse raised his dark-lashed eyes.

You're broke, Da Gama realized. Da Gama remembered Shahji's comments about Victorio's gambling. He said nothing.

"Our fortunes are enmeshed with those of the sultanate. It's not yet clear who will be regent to the young heir. Whoever gets the post will rule Bijapur for eight years at least. He will be the master of our fortunes. We've thrown in our lot with Wali Khan, the grand vizier, but his path is by no means certain."

"Wasn't the bayadere bought as a gift for him?" Da Gama asked.

"A bribe, you mean? Yes. Another of Carlos's schemes. He does not know the man. Did not, I mean. Wali Khan is subtle, and to influence him, we must be subtle also. I play Fives with him and lose. It's more effective than a bribe." Victorio's face grew dark. "But that bayadere cost us a fortune. We are stretched to our limits and beyond. Every hun that Carlos could borrow or beg."

"What did she cost?" Da Gama asked.

"Half a *lakh* of hun."

Da Gama gave a low whistle. Fifty thousand hun! Da Gama was not poor by any means, and in a typical year he made two thousand hun. A servant might make fifty. Half a *lakh* was a fortune.

Victorio continued. "News of Carlos's death has brought many creditors to our door. Now that you're a partner, you'll buy us some time. They don't know you. They'll guess about your resources. It will take time for them to sort things out. But when Wali Khan becomes regent . . ."

"If he becomes regent . . ."

A cloud covered Victorio's face at these words. Da Gama looked away.

"In any case, that whore could be our salvation." Victorio brightened a little. "Someone wants to buy her from us."

◉◉◉◉

Mouse helped Victorio rise, gently holding his arm as he shuffled from the office through the crowded aisles of the factor. "You can see that I've been busy, Captain," Victorio said, nodding to the goods stacked against the walls in disordered confusion—great rolled carpets, bales of silks, baskets of spice, barrels marked in some strange tongue. Atoms of dust swirled in the sunbeams that leaked through minute holes in the tile roof. "If only we could trade them, only get these things to Lisbon, our troubles would be over. But we must hold everything here because we lack the funds."

"Sell something," Da Gama said.

Victorio's gurgling laugh became a cough, and he had to stop to catch his breath. "Never sell in weakness, son. First rule of trade. Once it's found that we need cash, then the vultures and jackals will rip out our insides. We'd be lucky to get a quarter of what our goods are worth." Worried by his agitation, Mouse patted Victorio's shoulder. "This factor holds all the Dasana fortune. As a trustee, I must act responsibly. And now so must you." He leaned forward and spoke softly. "What do you know of Whisper, the sultan's Khaswajara?"

Mouse's ears perked at the word, and his large eyes glistened.

"Not much," Da Gama replied.

"He's the buyer I spoke of. It's he who wants the bayadere." Da Gama could not hide his surprise. "Yes, strange, isn't it? A gelding who wants to buy a whore?" Victorio continued his shuffle through the factor. "And he wants her delivered to some special place, not the palace. And in secret." Victorio turned his head and whispered, his hooded eyes glittering. "These conditions give me reason to hope."

At the end of the factor, light poured through a single window. Da Gama could see that a part of the floor near the window had been cleared and swept, and covered with carpets and cushions and silks. A bony silhouette sat there in silence.

"I'll do the talking. Just nod when I tell you," Victorio whispered.

ᏳᎧᏩᏤ

With the light behind him, Da Gama could scarcely see the Khaswajara, but could sense his dry, malignant presence. Mouse fell to his knees at Whisper's feet.

"Up, up," the Khaswajara said to him, but only after waiting for a long time.

Victorio merely nodded. "Senhor Whisper, this is my partner, Senhor Da Gama."

Da Gama unfurled his arms in a sweeping farang bow, which elicited, as he expected, an amused smile from the Khaswajara. "My Hindi friends call me Deoga, senhor."

"How happy I am to meet your partner, Senhor Victorio. We all need helpers, do we not? Helpers, and friends." Whisper's thin voice rattled like a dying man's fingers clutching at gravel. "Sit, sit. Let us talk."

Mouse eased Victorio to a cushion to Whisper's right, then caught Da Gama's eye and gave a brusque nod to a place on Whisper's left.

How about some respect for the new partner, bastard, Da Gama thought as he took his seat.

Whisper tilted his head. "So much more friendly here, is it not? So much more private than the palace. No unwanted ears." Each time before he spoke, Da Gama noticed, Whisper slid his dry gray tongue across his yellowed teeth.

With his good hand, Mouse carried a tray with pitcher and cups, all of bright silver. Whisper waved at the tray like a priest giving blessing, but he did not take a cup, so Victorio and Da Gama refused as well. The sun moved higher and the light from the window softened. Victorio and Whisper were just beginning the dance, discussing the health of one notable after another, and then smiling or shaking their heads before moving to the next.

ᏳᎧᏩᏤ

Da Gama's eyes drifted around the room. This part of the factor was crammed with odd lots. A row of life-size idols leaned against the near wall in a tangle of painted arms. Behind Victorio lay a wooden bird with the head of a man.

Further back Da Gama saw a gilded arch. The arch framed Victorio so that he seemed to be sitting on a throne. On the floor nearby the arch, Da Gama saw a line of dolls propped up in special stands. Then he realized what he was seeing, and he was even more confused to find it here, in a factor in Bijapur.

He was looking at a rich puppet theater, such as a nobleman from Lisbon might have in his palace. From the window, the sunbeams caught the silky orange fur of the fox prince, his puppet robe glittering with jewels, his toothy smile open but sly, his eyes black and empty as night. Beside the fox hung a delicately painted Columbina, hanging from her stand as if defeated, her serene face staring at the floor.

The black eyes of the fox absorbed Da Gama's attention far more than the endless talk of Whisper and Victorio. After a night of little rest, his thoughts began to drift. The fox seemed to lift its head, about to speak. Da Gama jerked up, but neither Victorio nor Whisper had noticed him drowsing, though Mouse glared at him, full of disapproval.

But while he'd drifted, the two had reached the heart of the matter. "Still, Senhor Whisper . . . a nautch girl?" Victorio lifted his hands as if confused. "What would you need with a nautch girl?"

Whisper's head wobbled on its reedy neck. "That is my business and none of yours."

"But it is my business . . . you seek not just the girl, but our silence also."

Again the beardless gray-haired head wobbled. "Silence would be included in my price," the rasping voice replied. "Name a figure."

Victorio frowned. Beneath his sagging eyebrows his little eyes moved to and fro. Mouse looked up at him with worry, for he seemed unable to speak.

"Ten *lakh* hun." Da Gama said. Then he blinked and looked around as if someone else had spoken.

All eyes stared at him. Whisper grew even paler. Victorio's mouth worked but no sound came. Mouse seemed about to burst.

"Ten *lakh*?" Whisper turned to Victorio. "For a simple nautch girl? This is your price? Does your partner speak for you?" Victorio raised his hands helplessly, his voice gone. Whisper glared at Da Gama and then moved his unblinking eyes to Victorio. "Seven *lakh* hun. No more. That is my final offer."

"Done!" Victorio managed to croak.

"In gold," Da Gama said.

Without a look, the Khaswajara rose gracefully to his feet. His bones were as fragile as a bird's. "When I have her, you shall have your gold." His rasping voice seemed more raw than ever.

"She's in Belgaum," Victorio said as Mouse helped him rise. "I'll send for her at once."

"Send him." Whisper's lizard eyes did not leave Da Gama's face. "Send him to fetch her. And not a word, farang. Not to Wali Khan, not to anyone. Is that clear?"

"Of course, of course!"

"Also, I may send one of my brothers with you. To look after the nautch girl's comfort. Of course you may refuse me this favor." A quiet fell on the room. Whisper did not move, but he held the floor. He had something to say. "There must be no mistakes. Forgive my rudeness if I emphasize this point, but we speak different languages and we come from different worlds. We must finally understand one another." Victorio lifted his hands as if to acknowledge the wisdom of Whisper's concern. "Do not mistake me. No word of this shall be said, not ever. Silence means silence. It means the silence of the dead."

Victorio seemed not to notice the threat beneath Whisper's words, but Da Gama's eyes narrowed as he listened.

The eunuch's voice got softer than ever. "I may even put it about that she has died. Of course it will only be a story. Of course she will not have died. But that might be the story that I tell." Whisper turned from Victorio and his eyes bored into Da Gama's. "You will say nothing, however. Nothing."

"Or we'd forfeit the price, I know." Victorio forced a chuckle.

"Oh, you would forfeit more than that," the rasping voice replied. "Bring her soon. Keep me advised of your travel plans. Mouse, see me to my palanquin."

With Mouse holding Whisper's arm, the Khaswajara disappeared amidst the shadows of the factor.

ⓈⓈⓈⒶ

As the bearers rose to help the men into their palanquins, Mouse drew close to Da Gama. "He will speak with you."

"Who will?"

"The Khaswajara." Mouse's face squeezed into an tight ball. "It's arranged." Glaring, he nodded to Da Gama's bearers, and stalked off, leaving Da Gama to stare after him bewildered. At last he climbed into his *palki*, and with grunts, the bearers hoisted him up.

Not far from the factor, the other *palki*s went straight on, but Da Gama's peeled away north. Da Gama worried a little, and checked his *pistolas*, wondering about what Mouse had said. "It's arranged."

Through the curtains he saw a huge white building, fifty feet high at the corners, and over all, a colossal dome. A temple or palace of some sort, Da Gama guessed. The bearers stopped near the arched entranceway and the fragile form of Whisper emerged at the door. The eunuch tilted his head for Da Gama to come. As Da Gama mounted the steps of the building's plinth, the clatter of his boots echoed from the towering walls.

When he reached the door, Whisper frowned until Da Gama understood, and pulled off his boots. "What do you think of this *rauza*?" Whisper asked; but Da Gama, hopping on one foot while he tugged the heel of his boot, could not answer. "It is the Gol Gumbaz, the great tomb of our late, dear sultan Adil Shah. The largest dome in the world, they tell me, greater than any the Moguls have built, or the farangs, or even the Turks. So grand, so immense, and yet this is not the greatest of the sultan's follies. Still it makes a perfect place for us to speak, don't you agree, farang? Come in and I will show you."

In his stocking feet, Da Gama followed Whisper. He was unprepared for the dreary letdown of the tomb's interior. The enormous vault of the dome could hardly be seen in the darkness—only shadows marked its loftiness, only echoes revealed its magnitude. The air, stale and still as in any sepulchre, pressed down upon them.

Even the sultan's casket seemed insignificant, pitiful. Dwarfed by the oppressive emptiness around them, it rested on a low plinth under a humble wooden pavilion. "Is the sultan buried there?" Da Gama asked.

Whisper frowned. "Are you really so ill-informed, or do you simply enjoy annoying me?" Da Gama did not know what to answer. "This is his cenotaph, of course. The real tomb is beneath our feet. None but the sultana goes there." Again his clawlike hand took Da Gama's arm and he led him further, to a dark, narrow staircase whose basalt steps could just be made out in the thin light of the hanging lamps. They climbed many flights, and the risers were high, so that by the end Da Gama was puffing. But Whisper seemed to float up the steps, looking back at him from time to time and shaking his head.

At the top they came to a narrow gallery at the edge of the round dome. "They call this the Whisper Gallery," the eunuch said. The sibilant echo of his words raced around the dome, as though spoken by a hidden army of eunuchs. Whisper flashed his eyebrows at Da Gama. "I must say I find the name amusing. Don't you?"

But he did not give Da Gama a chance to answer, though the question echoed a dozen times.

Instead he led Da Gama to an outside door. They stepped out to a crenellated wall a dizzying height above the ground, in the tiny space at the corner of the roof. Like the walls and dome, the roof and floor were painted white, reflecting the sun so Da Gama had to squint. A constant breeze whipped past the enormous dome beside them. The air was hot and clear, and Da Gama could see the whole city shimmering in the sunlight. Below, one of the bearers stepped out from the shadow of a tree, caught sight of them, and waved.

Whisper looked up at the dome and pursed his lips in disgust. "What an ill-favored design. Is it not a monstrosity? That dome. That dome. He must have that dome! It's just too big, you see? A smaller would have been so much more graceful. Yes, so much more poignant."

Da Gama turned to consider this, but suddenly Whisper was beside him, close to his ear. "This is the most private place in Bijapur. No one can hear us." Da Gama shivered as Whisper's hand slid gently along his back. "Your partner is a fool," the Khaswajara continued, his lips so close they brushed the hairs of Da Gama's big ears. "You, it appears, are not. I don't mind. I enjoy the company of so many fools, I'm pleased to deal with an exception."

Da Gama turned to speak, but Whisper hissed in his ear like a snake. "Be still," the eunuch said. "Already too many men have fallen to their deaths from here. Now look at me." Da Gama faced Whisper, surprised by his implied threat. In the sun the eunuch's skin looked bloodless, thin as parchment; even his eyes were pale. "So . . . you knew the value of that whore. Well, good for you. If you had not been there, I might have had her for less, but you win this hand. If she is who we think, if she has what we think, then what's seven *lakh* hun more or less?"

"Who are 'we,' sir?"

Whisper scowled at him. "Please don't bore me. I shall die too soon to waste time in foolishness. You know who we are." But Da Gama's face was blank. "One of our Brotherhood has been searching for that girl for years. He found her at last. Obviously you already knew this, or you guessed."

Da Gama's face betrayed nothing. Slipper, he thought. But the whys and hows of the situation eluded him.

Whisper shook his head. "That's good. Remind me not to gamble with you, Deoga. For a farang your face reveals little. I pray you, stop trifling with me. You'll get your gold, but I must have her intact, you understand? Complete and unmolested. Both her *and* her effects—entire. Do you understand my words?"

Da Gama nodded, and the eunuch's lipless mouth spread to show his long, stained teeth. The wind gusted, tugging Da Gama's hair and coat. It seemed not to touch the eunuch. He was about to answer when Whisper shook his head. "Do not talk, farang, but listen. That old man gambles, farang. He loses often. He gambles now—on the succession. He has placed his stake on Wali Khan. He gambles with his life. And yours. You must consider if his bet is sure. Perhaps you wish to gamble differently."

The eunuch stretched his lips as if affecting a smile. "I told you we will be sending a brother with you to fetch the nautch girl. I think you know him? Slipper?" Da Gama's eyes widened and Whisper struggled to contain his amusement. "Yes. Slipper has come up in the world, Deoga. Rings on his fingers now. You must treat him with respect."

Raising his nearly hairless eyebrows significantly, Whisper then pointed his chin toward the open door. "You go down first, farang. Join your partner at the palace." As Da Gama slipped away, he heard the eunuch say, "Entire, remember!" As Da Gama stepped into the gallery, Whisper's words echoed inside the shadowed dome.

❦❦❦❦

When the bearers set him down at the entrance to the Gagan Mahal a few yards from Shahji's "cottage," Da Gama looked up with a start. His head was still reeling with Whisper's news of Slipper. How did that damned eunuch fit into this business?

The citadel buzzed with activity. Peasants and merchants streamed toward Da Gama on foot, for the short public audience of the Sultana was complete, and they were no longer welcome. In their place came a stream of generals and jewel-draped lords on palanquins and feather-bedecked horses. Too fine, too great to grasp a rein, they rode with arms folded or reading the Koran, the horses of even the humblest lords led by tall grooms chosen for their imposing presence. The greater lords had a whole procession: umbrella carriers, fan-wavers, liveries and valets, guards with long spears.

When the bearers finally heaved his simple palanquin from their shoulders, Da Gama stepped out to find himself surrounded by buildings so high they blocked the morning sun. Tallest of all was the Gagan Mahal, where he was now to stay as Victorio's guest. A change had come over the bearers; he felt them staring at him with a palpable distaste. Why? wondered Da Gama. Do they now compare me to these rich lords? Or has my talk with Whisper given them some sign?

When no one moved to help him, Da Gama took his saddlebags from the palanquin and set off. The elder bearer waved him toward the entrance of the palace, and told him that his room was on the seventh, the highest floor.

Once again, Da Gama began to mount flight by flight of narrow stairs. When he reached the final flight, he came upon Victorio, slowly working his way up the staircase, grunting with each step. Mouse, holding the old man's arm, glared at Da Gama. "Let me help you, sir," Da Gama offered.

"No, my boy, I'm nearly there," Victorio wheezed.

Their rooms looked out over the courtyard, and from the balcony, Da Gama could see the old city. In the distance he saw the bloated dome of the Gol Gumbaz. Mouse was fanning Victorio, who had settled into a big wooden chair, the only farang element in the room. Exhausted, Victorio with a feeble wave of his hand motioned for Da Gama to take the cushion near his feet. His breath came in short bursts, and his face was pale.

Da Gama sat where he was told. Without moving his head, Victorio turned his gaze on him. "You disobeyed me, sir. I told you not to speak." Da Gama merely stared back. "You wrecked my strategy."

"Forgive me, sir."

Victorio snorted. This interrupted the rhythm of his gasps, and his face grew pale before he found the strength to speak again. "I had planned to demand seventy thousand hun. I would have taken sixty thousand, but I had hopes of seventy. But you interfered. Now we will get seven hundred thousand hun for the nautch girl, thanks to you, ten times what I had hoped." He gasped at the effort of saying this long sentence. "What made you name such an outrageous figure?"

Da Gama thought about telling him about Slipper, about the secret headdress, but decided against it. "A man of the Khaswajara's stature coming to your factor, all alone? Something big was up."

"Yes, you're right. Very observant. Very good." Victorio licked his dry lips, and Mouse patted his face with a white kerchief. "I have decided to make you a partner." Da Gama looked up in surprise. He thought he had already been made a partner. Rich men had no honor, he thought with disgust. He wished he were back on a horse with his *pistolas* tucked into his belt. "Yes, a partner. And when you bring her here, you'll get your first commission. What do you say to twenty thousand hun, eh?"

Da Gama lowered his head. In fact it seemed a paltry sum compared to Victorio's profit; on the other hand, it was ten years' wages. "Whatever you think best, sir," he answered with as much gratitude as he could muster. "That will be more gold than I have ever owned."

"Exactly," Victorio said. A little yellow was returning to his cheeks, and he began to sit up straighter. "That is why I will keep the money safe for you, in an account that you may draw upon at will."

And that you may turn on or off as you like, Da Gama thought bitterly. "I'll have it now, sir, if you please. And in gold, if you please. Otherwise you can find another man to fetch your nautch girl."

Victorio blanched. Seeing this, Mouse glared at Da Gama. "What have you said to my master, you lout!"

But before Da Gama could reply, Victorio placed a heavy hand on Mouse's arm. "Quiet, son, quiet. It is just farang talk. Do not worry." To Da Gama he said in Portuguese, "You must mind your manners around him, sir. For love of me he'd put a dagger through your heart while you are sleeping, whatever I may say. Give him a smile, sir."

But though Da Gama did as he was told, Mouse eyes shone with a murderous gleam. "I still want the gold, sir," Da Gama said with his most polite tone and another glance at Mouse.

"I have no gold to give you."

"Surely . . ."

"Listen to me. I've made you a partner; now you must share my secrets. We have no cash. None. Mouse buys my food on credit." Victorio patted the eunuch's withered hand. "I must ask you to fund your own journey to Belgaum. Bearers, palanquins, horses, and so on. I expect it will be only seventy or eighty hun, but that is more than I have at the moment."

Da Gama remembered Shahji and the loan he had nearly refused. He nodded and Victorio continued.

"Also ten or twenty hun for me. I must keep up appearances. The important part's the girl."

"The nautch girl," Da Gama agreed.

Victorio frowned. "Her? She's nothing. Seven *lakh* hun? I'm speaking of Lucinda. How much do you think she's worth, eh? The heir to the Dasana fortune—how many *lakhs* do you think that's worth, eh? How many *crore* of hun? You saw the factor. How much do you think that's worth, eh? Carlos and I have been busy. And it all belongs to her."

Da Gama let out a low whistle. "Someday, you mean, when she comes of age. But you're her guardian, so it falls to you . . ."

Victorio, now fully animated, raised his hand. "As a partner you must now share this information, but *in confidence.*"

Now what? thought Da Gama, who realized that he was only a partner whenever Victorio had bad news to tell.

Victorio glanced at Mouse, and though he and Da Gama spoke in Portuguese, still Victorio whispered his next words: "She came of age a year and two months ago."

Da Gama looked up, shocked. Victorio nodded his heavy head. "We kept this secret from her, Carlos and I, so that we might better order her affairs. Hers is the third greatest fortune in Portugal." Victorio enjoyed seeing the amazement on Da Gama's face.

"I had no idea."

"No one was meant to know. Now bring her here, and swiftly. We cannot afford to lose a moment!"

Da Gama nodded, though he did not understand Victorio's sense of urgency. "What do you mean to do, sir?"

"Do? Why marry her of course!"

Not even Da Gama could hide his amazement. "I thought she was pledged . . ."

"To that fool Oliveira? I arranged that match. It is easily disposed of."

"But, sir, your health . . ."

"You think I'm too old? You're wrong. I'll have an heir in no time, if she's fertile. It still gets hard, believe me. You can ask Mouse if it doesn't."

Da Gama's brain was swirling. "What if she objects?"

"She's still my ward. She has no choice!"

"You just said she's come of age!"

Victorio shook his head. "She doesn't know that, though, does she?" He raised his eyebrows until his jet eyes showed, black as a night without stars. Then his head slumped, and Mouse hurried over to straighten his knit cap and pat the beads of moisture from his brow.

"You must rest, uncle," he whispered, stealing an angry glance at Da Gama. "You exert yourself too much."

"But I shall exert myself a great deal more when Lucinda gets here." His wet laugh became a wheezing cough.

Da Gama tried to be a soldier. Ignore your feelings and just do your duty, he told himself. But his mind's eye saw that sweet blossom bouncing beneath this old man's sorry ass. Think, he told himself. There must be a way out of this.

"You have no choice, *soldado*," Victorio said as if he read Da Gama's thoughts. "Not if you want those twenty thousand hun."

Da Gama's cheeks grew hot. "What has that to do with you? It's her money now. I could just as easy get them from her direct."

Victorio's heavy lips lifted into a sly, cruel grin. "How? I'll be her husband soon, so the fortune comes to me. Also she's a murderess. Also she's mad, or going mad like her mother. I have friends everywhere, in Bijapur and Goa, and in Lisbon. You are a nobody. You don't know business or trade or the law. What chance have you against me?"

Victorio leaned forward in his chair, and patted Da Gama's hand. The old man's swollen flesh looked rough and raw, cracked and scaling at the knuckles. "You may try to go against me. Perhaps you have the determination, perhaps even the skill. Perhaps. Or you can be my partner, sir. My partner, and a rich man. Very rich."

Da Gama weighed his options. "All right," he answered softly. Victorio smiled and held out his hand. Cursing himself, Da Gama reached to take it. But as he did this, the old man gasped.

"What are you doing, sir?" Victorio demanded.

"I thought . . ."

"I want those twenty huns we spoke of. Give."

After digging in his pockets, Da Gama took out a few of Shahji's coins. The old man's palm was dry as sand.

Victorio leaned back in his chair, contentment and exhaustion on his face. Mouse took the coins from Victorio, kissing the old man's fingertips. Da Gama turned his head.

Part Five

Arrangements

In the gardens of Belgaum palace, a wide platform swing swayed gently under two enormous mango trees. The platform hung from ropes as thick as a woman's wrist, and the ropes had been covered with cotton batting and silks of many colors. The ropes were tied to the corners of the platform, so it stayed perfectly flat as it swung in the shadows. Cicadas droned outside the garden walls beneath a lazy sun.

The platform floor was padded, creating a large, gently moving room. Three women drowsed among the bolsters and cushions of the swing. The blind woman hummed, first one note, then another, as the swing sawed back and forth, back and forth. Her dry voice mixed with the creaking of the ropes and branches. Another woman sat propped against a cushion reading a long, palm-leaf book.

The last of the three floated with eyes half-closed. Shadows and sunlight danced on those dark lids like silent fireworks. She felt deliciously adrift, tetherless, suspended; as though she were a baby who had not yet learned to speak, not yet even learned her name.

As she sailed in the soft garden air, the blind woman said, "Lucinda." And when she did not answer, the blind woman said again, "Lucinda!"

"Who is Lucinda?" the young woman answered. "I do not know her anymore." And the other women smiled as though she joked.

She recalled a woman named Lucinda. But that woman now lay scattered in pieces on the banks of a stream, at the bottom of the chasm beneath a treacherous road. Some pieces of her might still be found, the woman guessed, in the trunk that had tumbled from a bullock cart. But Lucinda, that poor farang woman, was now lost forever.

Lucinda had been a lifeless thing, like the Colombina puppet in Tio Victorio's gilded theatre: a doll dressed in corsets and frocks and hose and drawers; all animated by another's hand. That had been Lucinda's life; a life of squeezing: squeezing into slippers too small; into corsets too tight; into roles that had only made her sad. But that Lucinda, that puppet, was scattered in pieces at the bottom of a ravine.

The woman who once had been Lucinda hoped never to see her again.

Lucinda had spoken of this to Lady Chitra who had of course understood at once. "The dew on the leaves before the sun rises," she answered in her dry voice. "The silence before the cock crows. The eggshell not yet broken by its chick." So Chitra said, patting her hand. Her black eyes, sightless as stones, wavered aimlessly. "Not what is, but what might be."

The woman who had once been Lucinda was now wrapped in saris, in yards of crisp silk. Red saris, green saris, black saris shot with gold. Her long hair fell in a soft braid. On her hands she had patterns painted with mehndi.

Now she walked differently. Maybe it was the way her twisted ankle had healed so quickly; or maybe because her tender feet now were cradled in sandals and could feel the ground. Without a corset, she could see the swell of her breasts as she breathed. Air flowed around her bare legs when she moved; silk teased her nipples. Her pale face flushed sometimes with all the new sensations, and she'd clasp her arms around her chest and swallow hard, hoping no one saw.

People still called her Lucinda—she called herself Lucinda—but it was a stranger's name—repeated two or three times before she remembered— yes, that's me. I am that one, Lucinda.

Here no one knew her past. Aldo alone might guess what she'd been like, a young Portuguese woman living in Goa. But she and Aldo had barely met before the changes began, and Aldo himself had started wearing *jamas,* just like a Hindi.

Maya only knew her as the woman who'd shared her howdah—not a little girl who had grown up in Goa, but the woman Lucinda had become since she left her home.

Lady Chitra's young serving girl, Lakshmi, sat on a stool and tugged the towing rope of the big platform swing. The women glided on it, lost in silent thought.

Far away, at the bottom of a deep ravine, Lucinda's dresses and corsets caught the breeze and tumbled over wet rocks. In a tiny pool of gravel, the stream swirled over her miniature portraits of her mama and her papa, and of the gray-haired Marques Oliveira, her fiancé. Beside them in the clear water lay her pot of vermilion, and her delicate silver box of *arsênico,* and the shattered blue glass bottle that had held her belladonna. A mongoose had taken one of Lucinda's silk slippers to her den and laid her four pink, hairless babies in its toe. But on the swing the woman called Lucinda, now newly born, opened her eyes and looked around as though waking after a long sleep.

ᘓᖇᘓᖇᘓ

"Come see, come see!" a man's voice called.

"Who is that?" Chitra whispered. "It is that man Geraldo!" She sat up, turning her sightless eyes toward the sound. "Go out, go out! This is the women's garden!"

At that moment, Geraldo appeared at the gate, and with him a tall man who held back even as Geraldo laughed and pulled his arm. "Look who I have brought!" Geraldo called.

Lucinda didn't recognize him. A glance at Maya's delighted face made her look once more. Dear lord, she thought, it's him! Captain Pathan! To think I'd nearly forgotten him.

"Go out, go out!" Chitra scolded.

But Geraldo ignored her. "Look who's just come from the doctor's. All better! Good as new!"

Pathan seemed embarrassed by the attention. He saw the little girl staring at him from her stool, and gave her a wink. She covered her mouth to keep from giggling.

But Lady Chitra hissed between her teeth. "This is a woman's place, farang. Go elsewhere."

"Nonsense!" Geraldo answered. "Mistress Chitra is happy that we've come, aren't you, dear? We are General Shahji's guests after all. That gives us some rights. And Da Gama left me in charge! So I shall do what I want—and what I want is to be here!" Geraldo laughed. "Well, Captain? Can you even recognize my cousin?"

Lucinda was pleased to see Pathan peer at her and blink before he answered. "Madam . . ." he gasped.

"Now you must call me Lucy, Captain. We've been through so much, we must be friends." For a moment she was about to extend her hand, but then she remembered where she was, and how she was dressed, and instead held her folded hands to her lowered forehead.

But she looked up at Pathan all the while.

He did the same as he bowed to her. Their eyes locked. Without a turban, his dark hair fell around his shoulders and framed his face. This time he did not seem so arrogant. Lucinda held his gaze, and wondered how she must look to him. A brightness like an ember glowing in his dark eyes was her answer. Lucinda found it difficult to breathe, like a corset tightening, and she looked away and blushed.

The garden suddenly filled with raucous trumpeting, as two grand peacocks strutted toward the swing, fluffing out their iridescent tails. "Now you have disturbed my birds," Chitra chided the men. "They are the only males permitted here! You see the effect you two are having!"

"Yes, we see," Geraldo answered. His mocking eyes glanced at Lucinda with a dark, wicked gleam.

◑◐◑◐

"I'm surprised you don't have more questions, Captain. You've been kept in the dark for nearly a week."

The two men ate supper, seated cross-legged on a white serving sheet placed over the dense, patterned carpet in Geraldo's room. The fare was simple—rice, dal, vegetables, chapatis, *dahi*—but fragrant and tasty. Near Pathan's hand rested a goblet of water, but Geraldo's was filled with a sweet wine he'd managed to find in the town.

"In the dark, truly, sir," Pathan replied. "My head was in such pain from my injury that the hakim kept the window shuttered and the doors shut. And as you know, the hakim allowed me no visitors."

"However did you stand it, Captain? I should have lost my mind."

Pathan's dark eyes blazed. "In truth it was a comfort. I meditated, I prayed. I recalled the words of the poets and the wisdom of the sheiks."

"Good lord, Captain . . . you're not a Sufi? Those men are quite mad!"

"Some may appear mad."

"What, spinning around, and howling at the moon? Do you do that?"

"I know some men who do that. But let's speak of other things. What has happened in my absence, sir? I was pleased to see that you and the women appear well. What about Slipper? And more to the point, sir, where is Deoga?"

Geraldo sat up straight. "I'll first answer your last question. My cousin Da Gama has gone to Bijapur."

"Alone?"

"He went in the company of Commander Shahji. They should be reaching Bijapur today, perhaps."

"But Bijapur is only a three-day ride from here . . ."

"Maybe, but Commander Shahji was making a tour of his western forts. Snap inspections, no warning, just arriving at the gates, him and his honor guard." Both men shared amused glances. "Shahji and Uncle Da Gama got along very well."

Pathan asked, "Did Shahji recognize me?"

"I don't think so. Should he have?"

"He was a friend of my father. I met him as a child, but I haven't seen him since my parents died. Still, one hopes—that is the way of things, to hope."

Geraldo had nearly forgotten the dark melancholy that hovered around the burak. "Anyway, before he left, Da Gama put me in charge. 'You're in charge while I'm gone, Aldo,' that's what he told me."

"And what have you done with your authority, sir?"

"I'll tell you what—I got rid of that goddammed eunuch."

Pathan reached for another chapati, keeping his eyes turned away from the farang. "And why would you do that, sir?"

"I'll tell you why. He was beating the nautch girl. Beating her! I told him stop and he kept on! So I kicked him out."

Pathan's thoughts flooded with a thousand questions, but he held them back, and spoke as simply as could. "You found him, you say, beating the nautch girl. Do you know why?"

"I know what he said. He pretended that Maya had stolen something."

"You call her Maya, now?"

Geraldo's eyebrows puckered. "It's her name! She's very friendly once you get to know her."

"Is she?" Pathan left Geraldo's comment floating in the air. "Did the *mukhunni* say what she had stolen?"

"She had stolen nothing! He's crazy. He's jealous, or delirious, I don't know." Geraldo frowned and he whispered his next sentences. "He said that Maya had something that belonged to him. Would he tell what it was? No! He said he tracked her down for years. He said he'd seen her with it during the bandit attack." Geraldo shook his head. "Again and again I asked what it was. 'She knows! Ask her!' he kept repeating. I had to stand between them—he kept swinging at her. He can hurt, too. You wouldn't think it. He looks soft, but he can hit when he wants to."

"He hides much, sir," Pathan agreed. "What did you do then?"

"I overpowered him. You smile, but it wasn't as easy as you think! Then I pushed him outside the wall and made them lock the gates." Geraldo took a long drink of wine, and then stroked his mustache. "Now your smile's gone."

"What did the *mukhunni* do?" Pathan's eyes betrayed nothing.

"What could he do? He ranted and raved. He can shriek like a cat! He pounded on the gate for a while. A long time, actually. Then he slunk off across the lake, and no one has seen him since." Geraldo laughed. "Don't look so shocked. I heard from the servants that he'd found a ride to Bijapur in some farmer's cart."

Geraldo took another draught of wine and looked very pleased with himself. "When I went for help that day—only a week ago!—what good fortune that I stumbled on Commander Shahji and his honor guard. It was he who sent you to that doctor or hakim or whatever he's called. He was very worried about you, though you looked fine to me. Uncle Da Gama had managed to keep Maya safe; just as you managed to keep Lucy safe. Slipper . . . ," here Geraldo laughed and took another drink, ". . . Slipper was a bloody mess. Completely hysterical. He was perfectly all right of course, not a scratch on him. But he'd managed to shoot Da Gama's horse through the eye and got covered by horse blood. He was sure he would die. No such luck! Shahji sent him to the doctor along with you. Just to be rid of him, I think."

"The others?" Pathan's voice was tight.

"They did not live, Captain. Did you know them well?"

"Only the mahout, and his elephant. He used to give me rides when I was a boy. The horsemen were Wali Khan's men; I had not known them long."

"Shahji ordered that they all be buried, not burned. He thought they were Muslims."

"He was right to do this."

"He knows his stuff. Reminds me of Uncle Da Gama in some ways. Old soldiers, I guess." Again a drink of wine. "But you wanted to know about this palace. It is a summer home of Shahji, Belgaum palace. That blind woman lives here permanently. Chitra, her name is. She knew Shahji from someplace; I think maybe she's his sister. Nobody really runs the place, I suppose, it's just her and a few servants, and that little girl, Lakshmi."

"That little girl by the swing?"

Geraldo nodded. "She's Chitra's favorite; she runs around everywhere, whispering to Chitra about everything she sees. They're a pair and no mistake."

❧❧❧❧

For a while, the two men talked about the attack on the pass. Geraldo, having missed the action, wanted to know every detail, but Pathan held back, not wanting to reveal what might embarrass Lucinda. Even so, Geraldo pieced the scene together, and looked at Pathan with admiration and gratitude. "I see now why Uncle Da Gama admires you. My family owes you a great debt."

Pathan tried to change the subject. "Look at you, sir. Dressed like a Hindi!"

Geraldo laughed. "Yes and Lucy too, as you saw. When the packhorses ran away, our trunks were broken and their contents spilled all over the ravine. All Lucy's things, my things. Slipper's too, but I care not a fig. These *jama* robes are Shahji's—quite fine, I think! And Lucy is wearing saris now—but you saw that. You could barely keep your eyes off her." Geraldo drank, amused by Pathan's embarrassment.

"The difference is quite striking, sir. And the nautch girl?"

Geraldo chuckled. "She's a wonder. She was the only one who kept her head. You saw her travelling bag? She never let it go. The only one of us whose luggage was not lost."

"*Ahcha,*" Pathan said. "So that's what Slipper looked for, I suppose. Did he not find what he expected?"

Geraldo's eyes were lazy now with wine, and he leaned close to Pathan and whispered. "Maybe Maya had given it away." He lifted his hand in a parody of a teacher. "She gave something to Uncle Da Gama before he left with Shahji."

"Did you ask about it?"

"Of course I did. I saw her give it to him, didn't I? So of course I asked."

"And . . ."

"And she wouldn't say. Not right away. But we've had . . . time together. Private time." Geraldo lifted an eyebrow, hoping that Pathan would understand his unspoken boast. "Just some cheap jewelry worn by dancing girls. Her guru gave it to her; some such thing. She wanted Da Gama to keep it safe." Geraldo shook his head. The wine was strong. "That Slipper. To go on and on so, and then all it was some cheap trinket. There's a lesson in there, Captain."

"As you say, sir. But I see you are weary. Let me not keep you any longer." He and Geraldo exchanged a half-dozen pleasantries, and at last Pathan stepped out into the colonnade and beneath the star-strewn sky.

The night air tingled in his nostrils, fresh and moist with lake fog. From the garden he heard the peacocks trumpeting hopefully to the hens. As he walked to his room, he saw a shadow move in the darkness.

It pleased him that his senses were still sharp despite his injury. It was a woman in a sari and a long shawl, slender and graceful, slipping through Geraldo's door.

Of course he thought of Maya. But then he remembered—Lucinda now wore saris, too. Which one was it? he wondered as he closed his door behind him. Maybe it was someone else, a servant girl perhaps. But his thoughts were troubled as he fell asleep.

Pathan was proud of his sharp eyes, and yet he had not noticed in the shadows near his own door another woman, slender and graceful in a sari and a shawl, hugging herself against the coolness of the evening air.

ʘʘʘʘ

In Goa one hot summer afternoon, Lucinda had watched a fighting kite fly off across the ocean.

Kite fighting was popular among the poorer children. Kites were small and cheap. You twisted the string with rubber glue and bits of glass, Lucinda had been told. Then you looped your kite around your opponent's string and then began to saw. The loser's kite then fell to earth.

The kite that crossed the ocean had been parrot green, the Goan sky a hazy turquoise. Lucinda had noticed the contest when she rose from her siesta. The cheering of street children drew her attention. She came to the window just in time to see a red kite cut the green kite's string.

But the green kite did not fall.

Without a string, the kite had a will of its own. For more than an hour it swooped and whorled, sometimes so close to her window that Lucinda almost caught it.

Below her window, a small crowd formed—a common occurrence in Goa. Men started betting on when the kite would fall. But whenever the kite stalled and began a plummet to the street, an updraft would catch it. Dancing away from the jumping, snatching children, soaring again into the brilliant, hazy sky.

Finally as the sun set, a westerly breeze blew the kite across the seaweed waves of the ocean, never to touch earth again.

Here in Belgaum Lucinda felt like that kite, untethered, buffeted by every breeze.

At home flowers had long stems and servants placed them in vases. Here loose rose petals were strewn over the cushions of her bed. Who brought them before she woke each day she never found out nor who swept up the petals each night before she slept. She braided tuberoses in her long dark hair.

Her feet grew sensitive. Her toes could wiggle in her curl-toed slippers; she felt the roughness of the tiles through the thin flat soles. She took off her shoes to enter a room, and her bare feet pressed against the cool, smooth stone floors, the scratchy warmth of the carpets. Her bare thighs rubbed each other as she walked.

Here in Belgaum she sat cross-legged on the floor and ate with her fingertips, resting a banana leaf and not a plate upon her knees. It had taken her no time to discover that she liked the taste of rice. For dessert, instead of cake, she followed Maya's example, mixing a little rice and *dahi* with her hand, and slurping the cool, soured milk from her fingers.

Goa, she realized, was a noisy place; but the lake palace of Belgaum was quieter than a Goan park before sunrise. Perhaps the lake damped the sounds. Only the singing of birds and the caws of crows disturbed the quiet, and the raucous peacocks strutting for the hens. Rarely did Lucinda hear a servant, and more rarely even see one. At first the silence made her uneasy, and she found it difficult to sleep, but once asleep often it was nearly noon before she woke.

Somehow, moments after her eyes opened, her own servant would appear, Lakshmi's auntie, a fat old aya called Ambika. Lucinda assumed that Lakshmi was spying on her, but she never found out where.

Ambika had only three teeth left, but she loved to show them. Once she'd spoken her name, Lucinda had never heard Ambika's voice again. Using her eyes, her eyebrows, a tilt of her head, Ambika expressed every thought. For the first two days, every time she saw her, Lucinda peppered Ambika with questions, chattering away despite the woman's silence. Ambika's fat cheeks glowed with amusement, but she never answered.

Finally Lucinda grew used to her silence, and began not only to accept it, but to treasure it. She too grew quiet. For the first time she heard the music of her heart.

ꙮꙮꙮ

The day after Pathan returned, after Ambika had helped her dress and then vanished without a word, Lucinda wandered through the empty palace. She strolled the garden; she sat on the cold stone rail of the pavilion and watched the bustle of the town on the other shore. Maya wasn't in her room. Aldo's room was empty; Lady Chitra and Lakshmi were nowhere to be found.

At last she passed Pathan's room. Through his door, she saw the captain leaning comfortably against the columns of his balcony. He wore no turban; his black hair hung in a long queue, tied now with a piece of string.

Pathan bowed when he saw her, but his face was frozen. His eyes were cold again, as distant and haughty as the first time Lucinda had seen him. Had that only been a few days ago?

"You're feeling better, Captain," Lucinda said.

"Madam, please let us go elsewhere. It is not right for you, to be alone here." Swirling a shawl around his shoulders, he strode past her. "Let us go to the pavilion," he said with scarcely a glance, and without waiting for a reply walked off.

He's just as bad as ever, Lucinda thought as she followed a few steps behind. At the pavilion he sat on the stone railing and motioned for her to sit on the cushions at his feet. Only then did his face soften, and even then, only a little.

"Maya has gone to some temple with the blind mistress, madam," he explained. "Senhor Geraldo has crossed the bridge to town. He hopes to find some sport."

"Gambling." Lucinda shook her head. "Why didn't he tell me he was going?"

"You slept, madam. He asked me to give you word." He paused. "Farang women do not gamble?"

"Some do."

A faint light came to Pathan's eyes. "But not you, madam?" He looked out over the hazy valley. "I have not expressed my gratitude for your help." Lucinda felt her face grow hot. "The hakim told me he'd given me up for dead. You and the nautch girl worked some magic to keep me alive."

"It was Maya, only Maya," she answered. "I just kept her company."

"Your company was a treasure, madam." His voice was almost sad. "At the road, when I was struck, I felt the soul leave my body." Pathan then told her how he rose to a great height above his body, toward a far-off light that drew him.

Lucinda was silent for a long time. "Maybe that was God, Captain."

"Maybe. I don't think so. Maybe that is your idea of God, madam, but it is not mine."

So it started, innocently enough, a conversation that lasted all the afternoon, as bit by bit Pathan unfolded for her the mysteries of his faith.

Sometimes what he said seemed so obvious, Lucinda almost giggled; or so implausible, she nearly choked. Occasionally she argued with some point, which seemed to surprise him. But then he would answer with a precision and subtlety of thought that quite astonished her.

Twice as they talked the muezzin called from the distant minaret, and Pathan kneeled in prayer, bowing to the west. He explained the significance of Mecca, and the Qaaba, the black stone that Allah had sent from the sky as a sign to Abram.

"Not Abraham from the Bible?" Lucinda asked, incredulous.

"That same man, madam. The grandfather of Issa, who you call Jesus, the scion of the Jews." As he said this, she saw him smile for the first time that day, that smile so open, so rare. She felt herself uncovered by it. Without wanting to, she turned away, trembling. "You are cold, madam," he said, placing his shawl around her shoulders. The smell of him lingered on it like spice.

ᐁᗧᐁᗧ

Later Geraldo joined them on the pavilion. There overlooking the shimmering lake the three of them ate supper. Geraldo barely spoke to her, but she felt his stare like a dark heat. He told her goodbye so strangely that Pathan looked up at him, his brow furrowed.

After Geraldo left, Pathan waited several minutes before speaking. "Is there some trouble between you and your cousin, madam? Can I offer any help?"

She studied his face before she answered. Maybe he couldn't help the look of disdain that seemed his constant expression. "Are you married, Captain?" She was surprised by her question; she had simply blurted it out. She nearly apologized but then realized that he wished to answer.

"Married? Yes, but when I was but a child. She had been my playmate. A few months after we were married, she died."

"I'm sorry, Captain." He shrugged in reply, his eyes looking into the darkness. "You loved her."

"I was learning to love. We were children, but even the heart of a child is full of mysteries. But you know how love is, madam. Are you not to be married?"

"Only pledged for marriage," Lucinda explained. "And I have never seen him, Captain. He is in Portugal." She looked at the town lights twinkling in the distance. "He's an old man."

"It has been arranged? I thought farangs believed in love marriage."

"In my case a fortune is involved."

"*Ahcha,*" Pathan sighed. Fluttering moths danced around the flickering butter lamps. His dark eyes reflected the flames.

"Do you ever hope to find someone else, Captain? Someone new? Someone who loves you and you love back?"

Pathan's eyes shifted to the courtyard where Geraldo had walked off, then bored into hers. Lucinda raised her face defiantly, as if answering an unspoken question. He looked suddenly uncomfortable and rose, saying as he bowed, "I will pray for your happiness, madam," and then wished her good night.

❧❧❧

She could not sleep that night. With Pathan's shawl wrapped around her, she crossed the moon-silvered courtyard. At the stairs that led to the pavilion she hid in the shadows. Pathan was there; he sat on the stone rail, gazing across the lake. For a long time, she watched him, then she returned to her room and stared at the ceiling until dawn.

❧❧❧

The next day she found him once more alone at the pavilion. Today his turban was wound tight, and he wore crisp white robes. His eyes lit up when he saw her. He deflected most of her questions, but asked her many, particularly focusing on her faith. He was fascinated by her descriptions of the mass, though Lucinda, as she answered him, winced at her own ignorance. From time to time he compared some element she'd mentioned to the teachings of Islam. His observations were often so subtle that Lucinda would frown as she tried to follow them. When Pathan saw this, he would change the subject for a while, which annoyed her.

After his noon prayer, he looked as though he'd finally made up his mind about something. "Shall we take a walk?" he asked.

They stepped outside the palace gates and walked the narrow causeway. She recalled again that untethered kite. In Goa, she had rarely left her house, and then only to visit a nearby friend or go to mass, and even then always in a covered palanquin or a carriage. To walk on this strange road— it seemed terrifying, tantalizing, and forbidden. Lucinda stopped at the end of the causeway; there in the sour-smelling mud of the lakeshore she saw a hundred lotus blossoms lifting from the black water, their petals brilliant purple edged in white. Pathan stood beside her, so close she could feel his breath on her bare neck.

The town of Belgaum was a beehive. People everywhere, in streets and shops and standing in doorways, alleys, and windows. Her ears, grown used to silence, rang with the shouts of shopkeepers and the laughter of children. Instead of flowers and incense the air was heavy with spices and sewage, animals alive and slaughtered, sweat and dust and rotting vegetables. Once an old gray cow came up behind her and nudged her with his nose. Most stared as they passed. If Pathan had not been beside her, she might have panicked. He did not alter his stately, graceful stride; he answered their stares with a haughty nod. He did not notice her hesitant steps. She worried that her sari would come undone.

He seemed certain of his way, but Lucinda quickly became lost. Once Pathan stopped and pointed to the palace behind them, hoping to orient her. "Just don't leave me, Captain," she whispered. "I'd never find my way." As they turned again to go, she saw another of his smiles, and his hand brushed against her elbow.

Lucinda could not fathom the twisting complexity of the town, so unlike the thoroughfares of Portuguese Goa. Here in Belgaum, houses and shops sprouted like weeds to form a labyrinth of narrow alleys.

At one intersection, they stopped for a moment to watch a noisy procession of men standing in a double line, passing a shrouded body from shoulder to shoulder. The body seemed to float above their unmoving heads as they handed it forward from man to man. A crowd of women followed, wailing.

As the corpse left their hands, the men at the line's end would peel off and rush to the front, like an elaborate dance. The shroud was parrot green, and billowed in the breeze.

Pathan bowed his head and Lucinda watched in morbid fascination, not moving even when he said her name. "That might have been me, Captain," she said.

"Or me," he replied. "Our lives are loaned us for a moment only. No one knows when the angel may knock upon our door demanding payment."

At last they came to a walled courtyard, standing in the midst of what Lucinda guessed was a Muslim graveyard. Pathan nodded toward her head, and after some uncertainty, Lucinda pulled the end of her sari over her hair, which seemed to satisfy him.

A few steps into the courtyard, Pathan removed his shoes. Lucinda placed her slippers next to his. He motioned for her to wait while he washed. "All mosques have tanks, as men must be clean before they pray," he explained as he splashed his hands, feet, and face. He gave no sign whether Lucinda should follow his example. He's not very helpful, she thought.

Still dripping, Pathan led her to a small building with a whitewashed dome at the far end of the complex. "We have come to the dargah of Yusuf Chisti, a great saint," he whispered. A couple of old men rose as they approached. To these Pathan gave long bows. Lucinda had never seen him so humble. The old men glanced at her and gave Pathan amused looks. "These are the great-grandnephews of the saint," he explained softly. "Their family tends his tomb." Lucinda lifted her hands to her forehead.

She stood with Pathan at the door of the dargah and slowly her eyes adjusted to the darkness inside. Pathan nodded toward two flat tombs beneath the dome, each covered by heavy dark-green velvet strewn with flowers. "The large one is Yusuf. The small one is his son, who died young." His face was more solemn than she had ever seen. "Will you wait for me here?"

What else was she going to do? "Of course," she answered. Pathan knelt and kissed the threshold before he entered, followed by one of the old men. He sat near the larger tomb for a long while, the old man standing silently beside him. Lucinda wondered if there were some prayer that she was supposed to be saying.

At last Pathan crawled to the foot of the tomb. Kneeling, he buried his head beneath the velvet cloth. When he emerged, Lucinda saw tears in his eyes.

The old attendant sighed as he bent over the tombcloth and picked out a few of the scattered flowers. He embraced Pathan and pressed the petals into his hand. As reverently as one might eat the Host, Pathan ate them one by one. Meanwhile, the attendant took a long peacock-feather fan, and patted the tomb of the saint as if dusting it.

Then he came out of the dargah, and motioned for Lucinda to come near. She glanced behind him to Pathan and saw him nod, and hesitantly stepped to the doorway, her bare feet on the cool flagstone walk, a gentle breeze kissing her face.

Then the old attendant began to pat her head with the fan. The air was dense with rose oil; each bat of the fan wafted a cloud of scent into the air around her, sweet and musky, like an avalanche of roses. Lucinda was surprised by her reaction. With each touch, she felt lighter, as if she was being dusted clean, as if sadness was being brushed from her shoulders. The old man lowered his head to her. *A salaam aleichem*, he said.

Pathan had taught her this Muslim greeting. *Aleichem salaam*, she replied.

They put on their shoes and walked in silence toward the palace. "Is that how you worship, Captain?"

"No, madam." Pathan seemed to consider his answer carefully. "To worship means to feel a distance. But God is not distant. He is closer to you than this." With that Pathan reached out and pressed his fingertips against Lucinda's jugular. She felt her heartbeat pulse beneath his touch. "So close is God to you, madam."

He lowered his eyes then, as if he too sensed the warmth that rose in her face, and slowly dropped his hand. "What we do in there is prayer, not worship. At the feet of a saint, one may place one's heartfelt wish. Who knows what will happen? Maybe that wish will come true." His dark eyes bored into hers.

"And what was your wish, Captain?"

But Pathan would not answer.

❀❀❀❀

Maya once more ate with Lady Chitra, so that same night, Geraldo again joined Lucinda and Pathan for supper. They spoke of Slipper, of Da Gama, and many times, of Maya. Geraldo's eyes darted often from Lucinda to Pathan and back, as though he was reading a troubling story in their faces. Lucinda shifted uncomfortably.

"Well, good night," Geraldo said at last, looking pointedly at Lucinda. She waved her hand to him in reply—a gesture that caught Pathan off guard, something Hindi women never did.

"Won't you be going to your room, Lucy?" Geraldo once more glanced from Lucy to Pathan. But Lucinda did not answer, and Geraldo's ironic smile had slowly disappeared. "Have a care, dear cousin," he muttered, walking off.

Lucinda had brought Pathan's shawl, and now she pulled it over her shoulders, though the evening air was still balmy. She stared at Pathan as if willing him to speak. What he finally said surprised her. "He lusts for that nautch girl." He said this as if it were obvious.

"Captain!"

"He lusts for you also."

"Surely not!" Lucinda could no longer stay seated. She rose and paced along the railing. The last rose light of sunset hid behind the dark mountains.

Pathan eyed her gravely, then spoke as if to a child. "Who could blame him, madam?"

Lucinda raised her face. Her belly trembled as if his voice had touched her there. His eyes seemed deep as night.

She felt a wildness stirring inside her: something beautiful and dark unfolding, glistening as if with the waters of its birth.

Later she could not remember who moved first. Her pulse raced and her ears roared. She was in his arms, pressing her lips to his.

Warmth suffused her belly and became a fire. Pressing herself against him, she felt her dark mysterious wings unfold.

❦❦❦❦

Kama, the god of desire, shoots a sugarcane bow, but his arrows of spun sugar can pierce the hardest heart.

They are not plucked out easily, those sweet, fragile arrows, and once they lodge they infect and cause a fever. The brain begins to heat, the sight to shiver, hands grasp out longing to be held. The lips tremble; the eyes burn. Sleep disappears: the nights ache past, and the days ferment with dreaming. So the heart grows sick from Kama's darts.

Here was the flaw in Maya's plan. She longed to hate Geraldo, or to feel nothing. Instead her heart was squeezed until it wept hot tears. Did she love Geraldo? No. But she wanted him, or more precisely, wanted what he gave her. She drank his love like saltwater, which slaked the dryness only for a moment before her thirst began again.

How was she to know? He had seemed to her as lifeless as a well-groomed doll. Empty words fell from his pretty lips, clanging at his feet like hollow tin. His eyes flickered like a hyena seeking something dead to eat. But Geraldo was handsome enough, and slender, and he did not smell bad for a farang. He seemed to her the perfect foil for her plan.

A farang, a base farang, more unclean than a nobody. Geraldo would be a defilement for her yoni, and no more. A thrust or two, a spurt, a groan, and all Maya's worth as a nautch girl would disappear. For who would plow a nautch girl's furrow once a farang had sullied it? Even the nobodies would shun her if they knew, as they shunned the *hijra.*

Maya made up her mind to live a living death of foulness, to become the ready vessel for his farang's pollution. Lady Chitra's words had shown her; Maya would blacken every part of herself with his polluted lingam; every orifice, each inch of her soft skin. She would reek of him, reek of farang, and no man of honor ever would come near.

She would be free.

That was her plan, her plan that fell apart so quickly.

She had not reckoned on those spun-sugar arrows, on blind Kama and his bow of cane.

Who could have guessed that Geraldo's tin words fell from lips so succulent? Or that his hands could stroke and glide and make her gasp, or that the sight of his dark eyes devouring her nakedness would churn her to a boil?

The *sadhus* who had used her for congress had studied tantra for years. Desire makes us slaves, the *sadhus* said. They had focused all their desiring on the Goddess, so they had become slaves of the divine. Now they could mold shakti to their will: stiffening their lingams on command, spending hours in congress with the *devadasis.* They had entered Maya slowly, reverently, and in the course of motionless hours embraced the goddess that

Maya became for them. Next to them Geraldo seemed as innocent and harmless as a child.

To her surprise she found that all of Geraldo's wisdom resided in places she had never thought to look: in the tips of his fingers and the palms of his hands, in the black hairs that curled on his chest No *sadhu* had such nipples, which felt hard as seed pearls when he embraced her, or a tongue that danced across her skin, alive and wet, slipping between her lips, between her legs. His whole body moved and coiled on her, around her.

He was no saint: he had flesh, and blood, and breath. He was, in fact, an animal. And so, she found, was she.

In the ripples of his belly, along his hard thighs and firm shoulders, she discovered that Geraldo owned a wisdom not of words but of touch; a poetry of stroking, of fondling, of embraces, of caresses dry and wet. His hands tingled against her, awakening her skin; she sighed at the warmth of them upon her breasts and flanks, the sudden empty coolness as they glided to her shoulders and her thighs.

Desire makes us slaves, the *sadhus* had taught her. Desire makes us slaves, she had mouthed in reply.

But she had never known desire until he entered her, bold as a lion, until she felt the yearning in her hips as her yoni lunged against his thrusts, until the gasping spasms took her and she squeezed her thighs against his sides and bit his lips till she drew blood, until her belly seized and seized and seized again and pleasure washed across her like sheets of monsoon rain. Until she felt him burst inside her, until she heard him groan her name, and thought: I did that to him. I did that. Until she held him as the moment passed for both of them, until she felt his heavy grateful drowsiness, and her own, as his lingam softened in her yoni, until their breathing once again grew calm and she felt his whispered kisses tickling her ear.

Desire makes us slaves, the *sadhus* had told her, and suddenly she comprehended.

She became his slave.

ꀂꀂꀂ

She had never seen a lingam so soft and shriveled before; for the *sadhus* always had made theirs hard before she even joined them. Geraldo's seemed like a pale worm, a blind, hairless mouse. She giggled when her rubbing made it pulse with life. She savored the way Geraldo's breath grew ragged as she stroked it, the way his head leaned back, and his eyes fluttered. Clean, unclean: these words had for her no meaning now. She wanted to hear him sigh, and scream, and beg her mercy.

In no time her lips enveloped him. Geraldo's hands gripped her shoulders, and his thighs tensed. Maya felt his lingam swell against her tongue. Biting the Sides, Sucking the Mango—with each of the eight forms of the congress of the mouth that she had only read about, Maya cataloged with wonder the subtleties of his moans. I did that to him, she thought. I did that.

Her mouth tingled as she thought it. He tasted warm and bitter.

She had planned a single act, an hour, no more. They spent all night together.

After, the filmy curtains billowed and emptied as the night breezes sighed. She heard faraway chanting. Purnima, she thought, the all-night festival of the full moon, and here she was pressed up against a sleeping farang, covered with his sweat and kisses, instead of at a temple dancing for the Goddess.

The next day she dreamed only of the sunset. She braided flowers in her perfumed hair, and as soon as it was dark she found his door.

She tried with him the five kisses, the four embraces.

He showed her arts her books had never taught, from the land of tea, a thousand miles away. His tongue coaxed her yoni until her thighs quaked. She bit a pillow so she would not scream. He wouldn't stop, not even when she begged.

When he at last looked up, she begged again—this time for more. He smiled, and stroked her hand, and leaned in to kiss her. She could taste the ocean when she sucked his tongue. Then he disappeared once more between her legs.

After she could breathe again, Maya turned him on his back. He was long and beautiful. The flowers in her hair hanging loose, her smiles broken by her hard breathing, she pressed her breasts against his chest. His dark eyes burned. Together they breathed the dark perfume of night, of flowers and incense and desire. In the candle moonlight their perspiration glistened. She moved her hips creatively, and soon his breaths melted into moans that mingled with her own. She embraced him in the wild moment—the thumping, throbbing, lunging of their hips; his hungry mouth devouring her eager tongue; the eruption of their bodies, like a great cloth ripping in two; and finally the exhausted quiet of their collapse. I did that, she thought. I did that.

Oddly, in the daytime, when she saw Geraldo on the verandah, or passed him in the courtyard, she did not even glance his way. She had nothing to say to him. The very thought of speaking with him annoyed her. When she saw him in the sunlight, she saw only the pale vacuity of his expression, the self-important vanity of his dress. It had been her plan to tell everyone of her defilement at his hands, but now, now she wondered if he could keep the secret. He had, she now realized, the look of someone who gauged his indiscretions, and might parcel out a secret to suit his own ends.

In the daylight, when she saw him, she was horrified by what she felt. She despised him, and she despised her own hunger, but she could not stop desire from tugging at her yoni. As she watched the sun descend with aching slowness her eyes drifted despite her will to his closed door and she nearly wept. She longed for Aldo's hands upon her breasts, and his lips upon her neck, she longed to squeeze his swollen lingam while he nibbled that spot on her forearm, just above the elbow, she longed to pull him inside, to press her calves against his shoulders as he thrust deep, longed for the cloudburst, and the drowsy, peaceful melting of their joined bodies. Like it or not, she could not stay away from him. The night would find her knocking softly at his door.

In the dark at least, her feelings for him were pure. In the dark, it did not matter what he was; only what he did to her, and she to him.

ﻌﻌﻌﻌ

The next morning, Lakshmi found Maya on the verandah, and took her by the hand to Chitra. Together they left the palace complex, and the three crossed the causeway and walked to a temple at the lake's edge.

The temple of the goddess Mahalakshmi was small but elegant; endowed by Lady Chitra's generosity, it reflected the same aesthetic as the palace: clean, serene, and quieter than any temple Maya had ever visited. They sat at the griha, the inner temple, taking the darshan of the Goddess. She was exquisite, a small deity made of flesh-white marble, her features painted with a delicate hand. When time came for *puja*, the brahmins accompanied their whispered chants with tiny finger cymbals instead of the crashing gongs and big bronze bells Maya was used to.

At the temple, Chitra lost her palace melancholy. She teased the brahmins like a girl. Some of her jokes were so bawdy that Maya found herself giggling uncontrollably.

Over lunch beneath a shady tree in the outer courtyard, Chitra rocked side to side as she gossiped.

"You seem much more cheerful, sister," Maya observed.

"Oh, how I hate that dreadful palace. So full of tedious memories, hanging about the place like impolite ghosts."

"Why don't you leave, then?"

"Hmm," she asked, turning her filmed and sightless eyes toward Maya as if she hadn't heard. "Well, I have no choice, do I? Besides, it's mine." Lakshmi whispered in the woman's ear. "Yes, yes," Chitra nodded to the girl, and then turned to Maya. "I understand the farang woman has feelings for the *darvish*."

"Who?"

"That *darvish*—Captain Pathan . . ."

"Pathan? You say he is a *darvish*?"

Chitra's eyes drifted in their sockets. "Of course, he's a *darvish*. Couldn't you tell? He's one of the quiet sort, apparently. Thank goodness. We've had spinners visit from time to time. They're bad enough, whirling around all night, but the howlers are worse, of course."

"Howlers?"

"Goodness, haven't you heard them? Count yourself lucky—they're all over Bijapur, howling at the top of their lungs."

"What, singing? Captain Pathan?"

"Some *darvish*es sing. Those, perhaps, one can tolerate. The ones I speak of simply howl like dogs. All night long." She demonstrated, and all three took to giggling uncontrollably. "Who knows why they howl?" Chitra said, when she had caught her breath. "In any case, you should tell your farang friend that it's hopeless. He'll only ignore her. It's one of their vows, I think." She looked toward Maya, her blind eyes drifting. "Lakshmi tells me, however, that the farang gentleman is very attractive."

Maya was glad that Chitra could not see her face, though Lakshmi could. She leaned to whisper in Chitra's ear, but a glare from Maya froze her and she sat down again. "Some may find him so, sister." She tried to make her comment sound offhand, but Chitra's face showed that she had failed.

"You should be careful, little sister. Farangs are no more to be trusted than *hijras*."

"Well, perhaps we are too harsh." Maya replied. "I don't like *hijra*s myself, sister, but really what have eunuchs done to you, or to me, that's so terrible?"

Chitra grew so agitated that Maya worried someone would overhear. "They robbed me, that's what! Robbed me of my love, and then robbed me of my flesh and blood. Did I not tell you eunuchs stole my child?"

She had said some such thing, but Maya had assumed she was exaggerating. Now as Chitra's face tightened with anger, she saw that it was a central part of Chitra's story. "*Hijras!* They tried but they could not conquer me! I loved the man they sent me to betray. I gave my heart to him, the sultan himself, and they could not stop me! I opened myself to him! I gave him a son, his only son!" Chitra seemed to be speaking to the empty air, no longer conscious of Maya, nor of how her voice echoed from the temple walls. "The *hijra* destroyed everything, and stole anything they could not destroy. They could not allow the sultan to have a son borne by a Hindi. They took him! Took my baby boy and drove me away. If not for Shahji's protection I should now be dead."

"I'm glad that farang drove away that *hijra*! I hate them, hate them all! They are all the same!" Chitra lifted the end of the sari to her face, whether to cover it or sob, Maya could not tell. Lakshmi patted Lady Chitra's shoulder. "I was delivered in that palace. The eunuchs told the sultan I had miscarried, and needed rest, and they had kept me there as in a prison." Chitra grew very quiet. "The day after my son was born, a *hijra* stole him away, a fat little *hijra* with no breeding. He had the servants say that the boy had died, but I found out the truth." From Chitra's filmed left eye, tears flowed. "I made enquiries. They made him a eunuch! My poor boy, my poor maimed, innocent boy. I knew he would have bad luck, poor child. He too had the sign."

"What sign is that?"

"The evil eye. Surely you've noticed?" Chitra opened her left hand, and displayed her palm to Maya. The dark streak stretched from her index finger to her wrist. "I have it, too. It is a mark of my family. For me bad fortune came when I was older, but his began when he was born!" She squeezed the hand into a tight fist and clutched it to her chest. "Now you've seen it, you will be afraid to speak with me."

"I don't believe that you are cursed, sister."

"How else to explain all that has happened?" Maya looked into her face so full of pain and did not answer. "Make me a promise, sister. When you go to Bijapur, look for my son among the eunuchs. Find him. Get word to me somehow." She reached for Maya with her uncursed hand.

"Of course I promise," Maya answered.

Slowly, surrounded by frangipani and tuberoses, beneath the shade of the spreading mango tree that towered over the temple steps that led to the lake, the two of them again grew calm. They napped in the temple court-yard through the heat of the day, just as the goddess slept in the *griha* until the brahmins pulled aside the curtains and woke her. After whispering hymns and garlanding the Goddess with fresh flowers, one of the brahmins came to Lady Chitra. "Sister," the blind woman said to Maya. "It's time for you to dance. That is why I brought you here."

"Now?" Usually one danced in the temple only in the morning to wake the Goddess, or at night right before she went to sleep.

"We must return to the palace before sundown. It is the rule. But the Goddess will not mind the time."

Whose rule, Maya wondered as they mounted the stone steps of the temple. At the doorway to the *griha*, the brahmins shuffled to one side, giving Maya room.

The little girl stared as Maya stretched in the corner. "Would you like to be a *devadasi*?" Maya asked. Lakshmi nodded with eyes wide. "It is a difficult life," Maya smiled. "You're named for her, you know," she added as she tightened the skirt of her sari, nodding to the *murti*. "Lakshmi. The goddess of wealth."

But Lakshmi, her eyes now nearly popping, dashed off to whisper into Chitra's ear.

There was no music, but using one of her gold bangles, Chitra tapped the *tal* on the flagstone floor. Teen *tal*, twelve beats, the most challenging of dances. As Maya's bare feet slapped the tiles, she began to forget. The bandits disappeared, Slipper disappeared, then Lucinda and Pathan, even Chitra and Lakshmi. It took time, but as she leaped and whirled with her eyes locked on those of the Goddess, even Geraldo's face began to fade, and at last she forgot even the touch of his hands upon her thighs. The stones beneath her feet became as soft as clouds, the flickering lamps of the temple grew bright. The *mudras* of her face and hands, each one carefully practiced and executed, required no more thought: they flowed from her like water now, the absolute expression of Maya's heart.

When she finished, she held the last pose for a long time, seeing only the Goddess's serene gaze. Slowly Maya became aware of her surroundings; her breath echoing from the dark walls, her sweat falling on the cold floor. Little Lakshmi stared in awe at Maya. The brahmins bowed to her as they returned to tend the Goddess.

"You are a great *devadasi*," Chitra said, as they walked back to the palace arm in arm.

"How can you know, sister?"

Chitra stopped and placed her hand on Maya's cheek. "I know." But her face was full of sadness. As they came to the palace gate, Chitra pressed Maya's arm. "Will you go to him again tonight?'

"What do you know of it?" Maya asked when she had caught her breath.

"Only that you are a woman, and that you are young," Chitra answered. "What will you do, sister?"

But Maya could not say, or would not.

☙☙☙

Geraldo once again had astonished her. That night Maya practiced with him the arts of pressing, and marking, and scratching with the nails, and biting. She could feel along the inside of her thigh the imprint of Geraldo's teeth, the Line of Jewels.

She had laid awake all night, but not from the tingling of his bite, nor from the memory of her body's fire. She was thinking of Chitra's simple question, and her thoughts roiled. "What will you do, sister?"

In the morning she found Geraldo gone, so she must have slept. Her side where he had laid against her now felt hollow, as if a part of her was gone.

As she dressed, as sometimes happened, a memory erupted in Maya's thoughts with such completeness that it was almost like a vision. She saw with exquisite clarity the face of her mother dying in the forest.

It was as though the room had disappeared, and all that she could see was that pale face, the lips turning gray-blue in the dawn. Maya had been about three years old, yet the memory was fresh and painful as a burn.

She'd felt her mother's body growing cold though she covered it with leaves, watched her beautiful face grow slack though she kissed the cheeks. At last a fat man had come through the woods, a big fat man with a bear. He led her to the temple where she would end up living out her childhood.

No one there believed her story. They thought she'd run away and that someone would come for her. When no one came, the *shastri* put her to work in the kitchen. One day by fate, she'd met her guru, Gungama, who'd taken one look at her and set her dancing.

Even Maya had come to think she'd made the story up, of her dying mother, of the stranger and his bear. Even so, whenever she got the chance, she'd wander through the forest near the temple, hoping.

Years passed. She grew up slim and graceful, became a dancer, became beautiful. The *shastri* taught her tantra and promised that one day she would be the vessel for *sadhus* seeking the divine.

❀❀❀❀

On her last day as a virgin, Maya had stepped still dripping from her river bath to find the saint named Twelve Coats waiting for her, seated on the bank beside his brown bear. The bear looked up and yawned at her, and she saw that it was old, its teeth yellow and its snout gray. The saint held a leash of knotted rags around the old bear's neck. He was thin, she saw now, but he wore a dozen coats, one pulled over the last, so he looked fatter than the bear.

The old man nodded to her silently and motioned to her with his twiglike fingers. He then gave the leash a tug and vanished with the bear into the leafy shadows of the woods.

Without a word, she followed.

It was nearly dark when the bear sat down near a mound of rocks and leaves. The saint gestured toward the mound and nodded. Maya's fingers as they touched the rocks were tender as a child's kiss. Then she touched a bone, dry and hard, and she stopped, and patted back the leaves and wept.

She looked up to find Twelve Coats rummaging at the end of a hollow log, from which he took something: dirty, cobweb-covered; Maya could not tell what. He placed whatever it was on the ground, and with his hand brushed off the cobwebs. It was a parcel wrapped in an old ragged coat, and inside the parcel were two plain wooden boxes, one long and thin, one small and square.

Twelve Coats pointed to the mound, and then to the boxes, and then to her. He gave the boxes to her, and then pressed his bony hand against her head. When he let go, she sat dumbfounded. This made him smile, and for a while he stared as an uncle stares at a charming niece. The bear scratched behind his ear like a dog. At last, with a tug at the bear's leash, he and the animal set off, leaving her to find her own way home.

The night watchman at the temple gate had stared at her as if she were a ghost. "We thought you'd died," he said, looking disappointed. "There's been a bear around."

By the dim light of a butter lamp, she opened the boxes in her room. The long one held a bright, broken sword, the small one a wedding head-dress, a net of glass beads, some clear, some white. She hid both boxes, but had at last a clue then who she was, or at least who she once had been.

Over the years Maya had managed to pack that memory away, burying it in some dark place, just as she had hidden her treasures from the *shastri*'s sight. Sometimes, though, like today, her mother's cold, pale face emerged unbidden. She remembered, and as she remembered, wept.

Even while she twisted her hair into a soft braid, she wept. Her tears spotted her dusty sandals as she walked. She found a quiet place in the garden, amidst the dew-wet rose leaves, pushed the end of her sari into her mouth, and cried until her throat ached. Even muffled, the sound of her sobs scared the crows that rested in the mango tree. They burst from their branches, finally fluttering down to prowl around her, their caws so loud they hid the sound of her weeping.

಄಄಄಄

She never heard Lady Chitra's footsteps, or those of Lakshmi leading the blind woman through the garden. Chitra turned toward Maya for a moment as though her blind eyes actually saw, and then she shooed Lakshmi away. Hesitantly, feeling her way, she came to where Maya sat, scattering the crows as she walked.

She sat beside Maya for a long time before she spoke. "Those *shastris* are bastards, sister," she said at last. "A girl should grow into a woman, but they turn her into a plaything. They toyed with you as they toyed with me. They told us that we served the Goddess, but we served them only."

Maya sniffed, but could not answer. Chitra's eyes drifted as though watching the movements of something far away. "Did the *shastris* ever tell us of desire? Did they tell us of the ache of yearning? Did they tell us of the feel of a man, or the smell, or of his weight on our breasts as he thrusts? No . . . They gave us *sadhus,* dried twigs of wood, not men. A man is a bonfire, a feast of agony and pleasure. It's such a nuisance."

Chitra stroked Maya's hair. "When you dance, sister, you feel in your heart the blessing of the Goddess, her peace, her kindness. But when you are with him, then the power of the Goddess is in your heart, crashing through you. The Goddess is no thing of stone. The Goddess is breath, desire, despair. She is the green of the bursting leaf, the baby's cry, the lover's bite, the fragrance of the rose. You feel the Goddess moving through you."

"It is horrible," Maya said, her voice choked.

"Yes," Chitra said.

"I enjoy it."

"Yes. Yes." Chitra dropped her hand into her lap. "Now what will you do?"

"I don't know." She tried to say more, but sobbing once more overwhelmed her. Pressing her hands to her face, Maya ran off.

ᘓᘔᘕᘖ

By now, Lucinda could wind her sari by herself. She placed kohl in her eyes, and touched vermilion to her forehead. When she stepped into the morning sunlight of the corridor, she saw Chitra's young guide, Lakshmi. "Are you looking for Maya?" Lucinda asked kindly. Lakshmi shook her head. "For who, then?" The girl's eyes grew wide, and she lifted her hand and placed it in Lucinda's.

Lakshmi led her down a corridor, and then a hall, and then across another courtyard. "Where are you taking me?" Lucinda asked, and though the girl looked at her with fear, she did not answer.

They had come to some part of the palace that Lucinda had not yet seen. The girl led her to a pair of ornamented doors that creaked when she pushed them open, and led Lucinda inside.

The room was completely dark except for the faint light that came in through the still-open door. The air was awash in fragrance, with the tang of Persian roses and jasmine, and a thick smoke of incense burning.

"Who is that?" said a soft voice, but Lucinda could not tell where. The girl dropped her hand, leaving Lucinda standing in shadows, too uncertain to move.

Slowly Lucinda's eyes adjusted. The room was as large as her uncle's hall in Goa, the beamed ceilings high. Where the light struck, Lucinda could see bundles of flowers heaped everywhere, like the stalls of the flower-wallahs in the market. Though full of perfume, the air felt still and stale.

In the shadows, Lucinda could just make out Lakshmi, now whispering in the ear of Lady Chitra, reclining on some cushions on a low dais in the center of the room. From the ceiling hung a white parrot in a cage, which cocked its head and whistled.

"Come here, Lucinda." Her voice came from the shadows. "Is it thought polite among farangs to stand at such a distance?" Lakshmi jumped from her seat and brought Lucinda forward. For the first time, she did not look terrified.

Lucinda had formed the impression that Chitra was ancient. Here, alone with her, with time to reflect, Lucinda saw that in truth Chitra was younger than she thought. Her face, though soft, was not that wrinkled, and her hands when she gestured appeared vibrant and young. Maybe her blindness had made her steps appear infirm. And although Chitra liked to assume the haughty authority of a matriarch, Lucinda now saw that she was just another woman, no longer young maybe, but not yet very old.

She held some tidbit to the birdcage, and the parrot snapped at it. "You are wearing a fine sari of heavy silk, light taupe in color, embroidered with gold and silver thread. Stolen from me."

Lucinda was silent for a long time. "I assumed you lent it to me." She said at last.

"Apparently I've made you uncomfortable." Lady Chitra sounded very bored. "Keep it. I like you. Besides, what good is it to me? My life has ended. Why does a corpse need another sari?" Lucinda waited uncomfortably. "I would know more about the farang. He troubles me."

"You mean Geraldo? How, lady?"

"It was he who expelled the *hijra* from my palace. I despise the *hijra,* so I thought he had done me a good turn. You know that a *hijra* stole my baby?"

"You have often said so, lady."

Chitra sighed, and for a moment Lucinda thought that she might cry. "I have found out that the *hijra* he expelled was the demon Slipper himself, that very *hijra* who took my baby from me nine years ago. I should have killed him! I might have torn out his eyes. Had I known, I would have strangled him with these hands!" Lucinda watched Chitra squeeze her hands, and then drop them to her lap. "Does he mean to marry you?"

"Who, lady?"

"Who? That farang, Geraldo, of course. Whoever did you think I meant?"

Lucinda gulped. "The man is my cousin."

"Then why does he look at you so?" Chitra demanded, holding another tidbit for her bird.

"How?" Lucinda asked.

But the woman's thoughts seemed elsewhere. "The lengthening shadows, the brown leaves on the rosebushes, the air so cold at morning that one needs a blanket," she said, her eyes drifting again. "Soon the summer ends. Do farangs marry their cousins?"

What business is that of yours, Lucinda thought. "I'm betrothed to another."

"And where is he?" asked the woman.

"Far away."

"*Ahcha.*" The woman raised her sightless eyes to Lucinda. She lifted another tidbit and for a moment, Lucinda thought that the woman meant to feed her with it. "Listen to me first, then leave me as one leaves a corpse. Is that too much to ask?" The woman held the tidbit just outside the parrot's reach, and was quiet for a long time.

At last she said, "A young woman far from home, a young woman alone among strangers, a young woman in a different world. A young woman who has looked at death and knows now how fleeting life may be. A young woman, beautiful, curious, and trusting."

Lucinda's face grew hotter. "You think I am a fool?"

"You see my parrot? Suppose I left the cage door open and the bird flew off. Which of us would be the greater fool? How long would he last outside his cage? He would fly into the open sky and fall to earth, blinded by the sun."

Lucinda drew herself up stiffly, feeling as stern as when she'd argue with Helene. "If you think to tell me how I should . . ."

"Oh," the woman sighed. "Forgive me. I did not speak of you."

"You don't pretend that you were speaking of your parrot?"

"No," the Chitra said, lowering her head. "I spoke of my sister, Maya."

"Of course anyone could tell," Pathan told Lucinda later. "She is mad for him. You alone did not notice because you are too pure, dear Lucy."

Lucinda had just told him about her conversation with Lady Chitra. His long fingers twirled a raisin, which he examined so minutely that Lucinda knew he wished to avoid her gaze.

"I'm not so pure," she answered.

Pathan lifted his dark eyes to hers and she felt the power of his searching look, as though he squeezed her heart with those elegant fingers. "Do you think this time will last forever?" The look between them deepened. "For Maya, I mean?"

But they both knew. "Maybe it will last," she answered.

"You know it cannot. Here in this old palace, untouched by the winds of change, here maybe some magic happens, for a little while. But the day must come when she will walk the road across that lake, and on that day, in the sad, heartless world on the other shore, you know it cannot last. She is a slave." Pathan looked away sadly. "Maybe she has forgotten."

"Maybe she makes it her purpose to forget."

Pathan was silent for a while, examining the raisin as one might examine a pearl. "Maybe you should remind her, Lucy." He popped the raisin in his mouth, and gave her an offhand smile. But Pathan's eyes were troubled when Lucy looked at him; he was trying to display that foolish courage men hope to show when their hearts are breaking, Lucinda saw, but like all men, he only ended up looking callous.

She could not bear to see him so, and turned her face away. "My heart is not yet so dry as yours, Munna. I think that she should be happy while she can. Even if it is only for a moment."

"Lucy, I would make her happy forever if it was in my power. But so much stands in the way."

"What?" Lucy looked at him with that defiant, open vulnerability that Pathan had seen on no other woman's face. For all her apparent softness, Lucy was as keen as a knife's edge. "What stands in the way of her happiness?"

"A fortress, Lucy, dear." He had been using that softer name for days, and it seemed to him it suited her . . . just as Lucy had begun to call him Munna, baby brother, the name his family had called him years ago. "A fortress built to stand against an unsuitable love."

"And whenever is love unsuitable?"

The sun reflected off the lake like a shower of diamonds. They stood at the far end of the balcony, two shadows framed against the endless sky, standing apart from everyone except each other, with only the sounds of the peacocks in the distance, and the soft clang of a far-off cowbell, and the lonesome barking of an unseen dog. Their heads leaned so close that Pathan could feel Lucy's breath against his ear. His hand stole to her arm; he found her hand; his dark fingers pressed hers, so small and golden.

"All I meant to say, dear Lucy, is that her heart's wish is unattainable."

"What about Aldo? Do his wishes mean nothing?"

Pathan answered with a sigh. "Maybe he loves her. Maybe he wishes to have her forever, maybe he wishes that she could be his bride. Even then he might lose much to be with her—his properties, his position. But next to his love for her, what meaning do they have? He would be a fool to treasure dead gold more than a live heart."

Lucy looked hard at Pathan, at the face of the man she now called Munna. Aldo had no property, no position, no treasure—they both knew this well. If Lucy had had any doubts, she now knew certainly that Pathan was not speaking of Maya and Geraldo.

"But what can that poor man do, Lucy? She belongs to another, not to him. He may only borrow his time with her, or steal it. She can never be his truly."

"She can give her heart to him. That no one else can take from her. That is hers alone to give. And her body, too. If he does but ask." Her fingers stroked his hand, and then the length of his arm.

"You say this, Lucy? Can you know her heart so well?"

"I know her heart, Munna." Her trembling hand lifted his and placed it on her breast, she could feel its warmth through the silk. "We are not so different. Her heart beats like mine."

"Lucy, this is not right," Pathan whispered hoarsely, his eyes burning into hers.

"I no longer care."

At the end of the balcony, framed against the endless sky, two shadows merged into a single form.

ᏇᏇᏇ

That afternoon, Lucinda swayed, reclining against a velvet cushion on the platform swing in the ladies' garden. Her thoughts flowed in wordless shapes, formless as the shadows of the leaves that flickered on her half-closed eyes.

The sound of approaching footsteps roused her. Lady Chitra, guided as always by Lakshmi, had come to the edge of the platform without her noticing. "Well?" Chitra said. "What did she say?"

Lucinda turned aside guiltily, and fiddled with the pleats of her sari. "I have not yet spoken to her, lady."

Chitra's eyelids lifted so wide they revealed the misshapen whites of her blind eyes. "Not yet? When, pray, do you mean to?"

After a moment's hesitation, Lucinda answered. "I do not mean to, lady. It is the movement of her heart. I cannot presume to guide it." She smiled, but realized how useless this gesture was with one who had no sight. "Maybe you will speak to her yourself."

Chitra's face was taut. "I tried. Did you think I would not try? She hears but does not listen. It is the folly of the young." Chitra grasped Lakshmi's shoulder. "You will betray me, too," she said sadly. Lakshmi pulled away, and rolled her eyes to Lucinda like they shared a secret. But Lucinda realized that Chitra spoke the truth. "It is in the Goddess's hands now. So. Never mind," Chitra sighed. Then she nodded to the girl, and Lucinda saw that Lakshmi carried a small cloth bag, which she now handed to Chitra. "Some people of mine found these things in the river. I showed them to the young farang. He said that they belonged to you."

The woman held the bag in the vague direction of Lucinda, who took it from her and set it in her lap. It was, she discovered, a big kerchief of dun-colored cloth, tied at the corners. When she undid the knot, she said nothing for a moment. Tossed in disarray on the dull cloth lay a set of vaguely familiar shapes. Then she gasped.

There were pieces of her blue glass bottle, which had held her belladonna. There was her golden locket, the cover bent on its hinge, which held the miniature portrait of her fiancé, Marques Oliveira. His nose was black, eaten away by water.

And last, a little silver box that she had by now almost forgotten. It seemed to vibrate in her hand.

She touched the latch, and the fine lid snapped open, revealing the red paste inside, glistening as fresh as the day she left Goa. It seemed less full than she remembered. Before she realized what she had done, Lucinda swept her finger over it and touched a tiny dab to her tongue. The familiar feeling spread through her, a coldness on her heart and a dullness in her limbs.

"That box with the snapping lid. What is in it?" Chitra asked.

"A medicine that farang ladies take, lady."

"Hmmph. Your cousin kept some for himself. He seemed very pleased about it."

Although she was surprised to hear this, Lucinda didn't feel like answering any more of Chitra's questions about her *arsênico,* and decided to change the subject. "I never expected to see these things again, lady."

"They are a sign." Chitra's black, ever-roaming eyes rested once again on Lucinda. "The yellowing leaves of the rose in drought, the well so low the bucket brings up mud, the grain jar filled with maggots. A sign, sister, of troubles, and of worse to come." With that she and Lakshmi moved away, leaving Lucinda with her shadowed, wordless thoughts.

ॐॐॐ

Perhaps Chitra in her blindness saw what Lucinda had only sensed, the way one senses a coming storm in the wind's change or in the sounds of rustling leaves. But by the time the sun set behind the mountains signs were everywhere: in the whispers of the maids and the glances of the cooks. As she waited for supper, Lucinda found herself drawn to the balcony near Geraldo's room, and found Maya there already, talking with Pathan, who wore a long, formal *jama* robe and a tight turban, as a man might wear to meet an elder. She could not tell from his dark eyes what he was thinking.

Maya reached up her hand, and pulled Lucinda to a nearby cushion. "What's happening?" Lucinda asked. Maya shook her head, and Pathan had already turned his eyes away to the shadowed mountains.

She did not recognize the sound at once. It had been so long since she had heard it: the click of leather bootheels on white tile, echoing like shots along the sandstone walls. Geraldo appeared, dressed again as a farang. He had worn only *jamas* since the bandit raid at the pass. This change, Lucinda thought, was not for the better. She wondered if his coat and pants had always fit so poorly, whether they had always made him look so furtive and squashed down.

He came with loud, broad strides to the edge of the carpet where the women sat. "A gift from Uncle Victorio," he said without a glance at Maya, and dropped a large flat parcel at Lucinda's feet. It landed with a thud. Lucinda stared at the ribbons that tied it, but did not move.

"So," Geraldo said, straightening his shirt. "I've had word. A parcel from Bijapur as you see," he said with a smile toward his new clothes, "and a letter from Da Gama." He reached into his doublet and took out a sheet of stiff, ivory paper.

"And?" Pathan gazed levelly at Geraldo, as though his thoughts were calm and elsewhere.

"And there is much news. His letter concerns each one of us. Since you ask, Captain, let me read that part concerning you."

"I myself will read it, if I may." Pathan reached out and after hesitating, Geraldo handed him the letter. The Muslim held it out and frowned.

"It is in Portuguese, Captain," Geraldo said, trying not to smile. "Allow me."

But Pathan turned away. "Lucy, you read it to me." He held the letter toward her.

She did not raise her lowered eyes. "I can't, sir."

After looking at her for a moment, Pathan passed the letter back to Geraldo.

"Here is the news for you, Captain. It concerns the bayadere as well." Maya's eyes shot up at the word, but Geraldo kept his focused on the letter. "My uncle Victorio sends his compliments and informs you that he will not complete the arrangement made with Wali Khan."

"What! Why not?"

"He has made a different agreement. The bayadere is to be sold to another party."

"This will not do!" Pathan exclaimed. "He has not the right!"

Geraldo shrugged.

"Who?" asked Maya softly.

Again Geraldo hesitated, as though realizing how his importance increased with each silent passing moment. "I should not say . . ." he murmured.

"Who!" Pathan demanded.

"To the Khaswajara, if you want to know."

"What? A eunuch? What need has a eunuch for . . ." Pathan managed to recover his calm and let the question drop, but Maya's face had drained of color.

"The letter says that Da Gama, and Victorio, and their suite will come to Belgaum soon, and escort the bayadere back to Bijapur. Da Gama says, Captain, that you are welcome to come with us or go on alone as you may wish. He reminds you that with this new arrangement, your official capacity as *burak* is ended."

"We shall see," Pathan muttered.

"Ended," Geraldo repeated with emphasis, "but our family will always remember your rescue of Lucinda, and therefore hold you in the highest regard."

"And this is how your family displays its regard?" Pathan glared at Geraldo, and then turned to Lucinda. But he found he could not maintain his indignation at the sight of her downcast eyes, and so frowned at Geraldo once more. "Who will act as *burak* for the Khaswajara?"

Geraldo could not conceal his amusement. "An old friend of yours, Captain. Slipper, the *mukhunni*." Geraldo enjoyed Pathan's astonishment.

☙☯☯❧

Lucinda felt Maya grasp her hand when Geraldo said the name. She looked up for the first time since the package landed at her feet. Maya's other hand was covering her mouth, and tears trickled from her gold-flecked eyes.

"And what of me, cousin?" Lucinda whispered.

Geraldo once more hesitated, looking Lucinda over before he spoke.

"I hope you find it pleasant news, cousin. Your engagement to Marques Oliveira is ended."

Lucinda's shoulders sagged in relief, and she tore at the bent locket she had replaced around her neck. "Thank god I will not marry that disgusting old frog!" she cried, and threw the locket with all her might. It landed near the railing of the verandah, skittering over the marble floor.

"There's more, cousin. Another suitor for you, a different husband. One you know quite well," Geraldo said with eyes gleaming. "Da Gama says Uncle Victorio means to marry you."

"No!" Pathan blurted out the word, but no one looked at him.

Lucinda's eyes widened, and her mouth gasped open. "Uncle Victorio? He must be eighty!"

"I doubt he's much older than seventy, cousin." Geraldo's eyes glittered.

"How dare you take enjoyment in her suffering," Pathan burst out.

"You are a heathen and know nothing," Geraldo answered. "Apologize."

"I will not."

"Then never speak to me again." Geraldo eyes gleamed as Pathan began to stand. They looked at each other for a moment, the tension crackling between them, until at last Geraldo without a further word spun on his heel, and strode from the room, the clack of his boots echoing into the twilight.

"Lucy," Pathan said, reaching toward her, but she shook her head and did not stir. Maya placed a hand on Lucinda's shoulder, and Pathan watched with a sad envy.

"Things may yet work out, Lucy," he said softly. "The road is not certain, and the end of the journey cannot be seen." Lucinda could not look up. Pathan reached out again, then shook his head, stood tall and drew back his hand. He then spoke in a low voice, staring into the distance because he could not look at her for fear of weeping. "Why, the poet asks, is my road so drear? Why do the stones give me no rest? Why is my way so hard, Lord, when my brother's way is so pleasant? That is your task, the Lord replies. It has no joy, but it is meant for you. Only do your best, the poet says, then close your eyes and see God's face." With silent steps Pathan turned into the shadows.

"I hate his poems," Lucinda whispered.

Maya thought Lucinda would be weeping, but her eyes were dry. "Sister," Maya said, her face close to Lucinda's ear. "He is right. We must take the road prepared for us, however hard—there is no other way." At last, Lucinda nodded silently and squeezed Maya's hand. They sat quietly, each thinking her own thoughts. Maya at last sighed, and tried to change the subject. "Whatever is in that parcel?" she asked.

In answer, Lucinda only slid the package toward Maya's feet. "Open it if you like." As Maya began to tug at the knots of the sisal string, Lucinda spoke, almost to herself, "Once you said I was a slave, and I denied it. But now I see that I was wrong."

Maya pulled aside the strings, and unfolded the cotton cloth to reveal a new-made dress, and a pair of hose, and silk slippers, and a stiff corset. "What is all this, sister?" she asked.

"Those," Lucinda answered, "are my chains."

☙☙☙☙

It seemed to Da Gama that they would never leave for Belgaum. He had sent the letter and clothing to Geraldo a week ago, promising to be there soon. How long could it take to find some palanquins, some horses, and a few guards? By himself, he could be in Belgaum in two days if he traveled hard.

He had not counted on the stubborn slowness of Victorio, or the ways that Mouse would find to make the simplest tasks impossible. Packing took forever: clothes could not be packed until they were clean; and the old trunks must be newly painted, and so on and on. Victorio went along with anything the eunuch asked.

"But we should move quickly. We don't know what's happening in Belgaum," Da Gama told him angrily.

"You worry too much," Victorio answered. "You'll become old before your time." Victorio motioned for Da Gama to come close, as though to whisper a secret. "Be attentive to my eunuch. Listening to Mouse has made me young. By the Virgin, I woke up hard as a rock this morning. He has some marvelous potions! I can't wait to get that little murderess to my bed. Pleasure is the best revenge!" Da Gama took a moment to realize that Victorio was speaking of Lucy. He tried to hide his face.

And suddenly there were eunuchs everywhere, it seemed, Slipper in the lead. The fellow had come up in the world, it appeared, for he had servants of his own, even a little black African boy who followed him like a puppy. For a while, Slipper pretended to make suggestions, to ask polite favors. It took only a few days before he was telling Da Gama how to make arrangements, and turning red if his words were not accepted.

Slipper had decided to go along to Belgaum. The eunuch had observed how Pathan had traveled with the caravan, and intended to follow the captain's lead. "After all I am Whisper's *burak*, you see, just as Pathan was the *burak* for Wali Khan. But in my case, I shall finish the job and we will have the settlement. Then I shall be a settlement man myself, Deoga! You must look out or I shall have your job!" His servants all laughed at Slipper's jokes, except for the African boy, who did not speak Hindi, but was as beautiful as a doll.

Then Victorio, old and slow as he was, decided he must also go to Belgaum. What should have been a simple suite quickly became a caravan. Da Gama would have traveled light, sleeping under the stars on the way to Belgaum and stopping in dharmsalas when he returned with the women. But Slipper would have none of it: Tents, he demanded, and of course, Victorio, under Mouse's influence, went along. Tents meant assemblers, of course, and bearers, and cooks and serving women, and soon a couple of dozen men were required, and schedules and deposits and all the rest.

When Mouse had demanded that in honor of his master's betrothal a wedding parade accompany the caravan, complete with horses and musicians, Da Gama had enough. After arguing with the eunuch for a quarter hour, he took out a *pistola* and began to clean it with his handkerchief. "Not to worry," Da Gama told Mouse as the eunuch eyed the wavering barrel nervously. "I'm sure it's unloaded. In any case they don't go off when I clean them—not unless I'm very, very careless." Mouse had to run to the latrines to keep from soiling himself. After that, Mouse's suggestions dwindled to a trickle.

Slipper let it be known that he once more was Whisper's second-in-command. No one knew why after leaving in disgrace Slipper was so honored on his return. But Da Gama knew, or thought he did. The answer lay hidden in Shahji's house, and with mounting delays, a plan began to form in Da Gama's mind.

One day he went back to Shahji's palace. Shahji had gone out, which suited Da Gama. He gave the servants an apologetic story and a little *bak-sheesh,* and in no time he was in the guest room where he spent his first night in Bijapur. He pried up the loose wall panel he had found that night, and retrieved from its hiding place the headdress that Maya had given him.

Then he went to the bazaar. He walked, because it cleared his thoughts to walk. People turned to stare at a farang striding in long boots through the streets, *pistolas* shoved into his belt; Da Gama ignored them. Every few yards he took his bearings and asked directions, for the center of the city was a warren of shops and alleys. The advice he received was cheerful, enthusiastic, and usually wrong.

Each street had a different character. After passing the meat markets with their abominable smells and fly-blown carcasses on iron hooks, he found stalls of fruits piled into pyramids. Beyond these were the working boxes of the flowerwallahs, who strung garlands as they sat cross-legged in piles of roses and marigolds. Next came the opulent, pillow-covered stalls of Gold Street, where jewelers hung earrings and necklaces on velvet boards, and weighed out their value on tiny scales. In one of the stalls, a woman in translucent veils stretched out her wrist while a goldwallah fitted it with heavy jeweled bangles. Nearby, her husband stood and frowned.

He kept walking. After a few yards the stalls grew less grand; here the merchants sold silver. In the street beyond that, Da Gama found what he was looking for; the shabby stalls of traders in gilt and lead and glass, where barefoot women peered at jewels that gleamed as no real gem had ever done.

Da Gama glanced at the faces of the proprietors of these stalls as they sat and worked tailor-fashion, at miniature anvils. He chose one who seemed both busy and dull. He sauntered over to the counter, pulled off his boots, and sat cross-legged on the floor. "Let's do some business," Da Gama said.

"I won't like it," the proprietor said. He put down a pair of tiny pliers and rubbed his eyes. "Whatever you're here to ask me for, I won't like it. Farangs only come here by mistake. They want only gold, or what can pass for gold. I make baubles for the poor to wear when they marry. I have nothing you could want."

"This is what I want," Da Gama answered. He took Maya's headdress from his pocket, wrapped in a white kerchief, and tossed it casually into the proprietor's lap. "I need a copy," Da Gama told him. "Fast."

The proprietor lifted the headdress and whistled. "This is quite good. Quite good. For a moment I thought it was real." His hands played through the web of gold. The pearls and diamonds caught the light.

"Sure. Those are real jewels. It's the Web of Ruci."

"The what?"

"Never mind. If it were real, would I be here? How much for a copy?"

The proprietor looked at the design. "For this, three hundred rupees."

"Fifty. And I need it tomorrow."

"Impossible. Two hundred, and it will take me a week."

Back and forth a few more times until, as they both knew from the start, the price was set at a hundred rupees. But still the jeweler shook his head and said, "Look, I'm telling you like my own brother, I need at least a week."

"It must be sooner."

"The copy will suffer. Even a eunuch will see that it is a fake."

Da Gama's eyes opened wide. "Why do you say that . . . about a eunuch seeing?"

The proprietor snorted. "They are famous for their bad eyes. Surely you know this. By the time they are forty, they can barely see, most of them, if they live that long. Have you not heard the expression?"

"There are few eunuchs among the farangs," Da Gama answered.

"Lucky for the farangs," the jeweler answered. "Listen, sir, for a very bad copy, three days. Maybe two. I'm telling you a child would know."

"I'll will see you in two days."

"I'll need something on account."

"You've got my headdress; is that not enough?"

"Not if you're willing to leave it." Da Gama parted with a few rupees and found his way back to Victorio's apartment at the Gagan Mahal.

❦❦❦❦

Two days later he went back to the sad-faced jeweler, and took back both his original and the copy. As the proprietor had warned, the copy was not very good. "Your original was very fine. The workmanship was very fine," he told Da Gama sadly. "The pearls looked almost real. Too large, of course, for real pearls, but very nicely done otherwise. The glass of the diamonds, that too was very good, very hard and clear. My reproduction is shabby in comparison. You should have given me more time. Who made that headdress, sir? I will give you two hun for it."

"It has sentimental value," Da Gama told him as he pocketed the original and the copy. But when he examined them later, Da Gama saw that the proprietor was wrong. The copy was good. At least, it was good enough.

ᎬᎭᎬᎭ

Da Gama stayed in touch with Shahji. The general helped him select reliable guards for the journey. The night before they were to leave, Shahji invited Da Gama to his house once more. Over cups of raisin wine, Da Gama told him everything, except about the headdress. He wanted Shahji's insight.

But the general could make no sense of it. "What do the *hijra* want with a nautch girl? It can't be for congress, and at that price, she would need to dance like a goddess. Anyway they care nothing for dancing, except for the rude sort with others of their kind." By the flickering light of a dozen butter lamps around his apartment, Shahji stared at Da Gama. "What do you think, Deoga? Does she know some secret?"

"She's an orphan . . ." Da Gama said.

"*Ahcha,*" Shahji said, brightening. "Maybe a lost princess whose parentage the *hijra* have discovered?" Shahji shook his head, dissatisfied. "But who? No princesses are missing. And I would guess that she is part farang, with her skin so fair, and eyes so light and flecked with gold." Da Gama smiled. "Don't tell me you haven't noticed," Shahji scolded him. "If I had more money I might have bid on her myself! Anyway, for that much money, a treasure must be involved, but I can't imagine how."

Da Gama quickly changed the subject. Fortunately Shahji was entirely happy to discuss his own concerns: the politics of the court. Who would become the young sultan's regent? The court spoke of little else, it seemed.

Neither Wali Khan nor Whisper had won the regency. The Sultana, who would make the choice, wavered constantly between the two. "In the end, I think that Whisper shall be regent, and then Bijapur will be in much difficulty. Already the *hijra* stand behind the thrones of many countries, dark powers in the shadows. A eunuch as regent here will bring them one step closer to dominating us all."

Before Da Gama might have chuckled at this notion, but as he came to know the *hijra* better, he found himself considering whether Shahji's feeling might not be justified. "What will you do if Whisper wins, General? Will you leave Bijapur?"

Shahji looked sheepish. "Well, that's the odd thing. We see eye-to-eye on most matters, Whisper and myself. I find myself arguing with Wali Khan, not Whisper. And if Wali Khan were regent he would force me to resign, and would then make the Sultana's nephew commander in chief." Shahji shrugged. "What is best for my country may not be what is best for me. What is a soldier's duty then, eh, Deoga?

Da Gama looked at Shahji and realized that they were not so different. "I ask this same question of myself, General."

"And what do you answer yourself, Deoga?"

Da Gama shrugged. "I tell myself to have another cup of wine, General."

Shahji smiled and passed the pitcher.

After a few more cups, their tongues grew looser. Shahji told Da Gama of the darkest gossip at the court— that the young heir might not even be the sultan's son. "He doesn't look like the old sultan, and in truth, not at all like the Sultana either, or so they say. But who knows what the Sultana looks like, hidden as she is behind those veils? Still, the maids have seen her face, and the eunuchs, and it is from them the rumors come."

Da Gama felt compelled to reveal some secret in return, and found himself telling Shahji about Victorio's marriage plans. "But he is so old! And the farang girl is so young and pretty. What a shame!" the general cried.

"Maybe it is for the best." Da Gama then told him about the madness and murders of the Dasana women.

Shahji took another drink. "You farangs are as bad as Turks," he said. There was a darkness in his eyes when he looked at Da Gama, a look Da Gama recognized: a secret Shahji wished to tell but could not; would not.

Eventually servants came and took Shahji to his bed. Da Gama stumbled back to the Gagan Mahal beneath a black and moonless sky where even the stars glittered like unfriendly eyes.

CICIC

One flight, two, three . . . and Victorio's rooms were on the seventh floor! Rats skittered past Da Gama's feet as he clambered up the stone staircase of the Gagan Mahal. Outside, the crescent moon was rising—soon it would be dawn—but the only light in the passage came from pierced shade lamps at every landing. Their tiny flames made the rats' eyes glow.

Up, up, step, step. Da Gama was too tired to think—he could barely plod to the next stair. In the dark, half-drunk and drowsy, his mind fell into a dismal reverie.

At the top, he nearly fell when he lifted his foot, for there were no more stairs. He stepped onto the long verandah that led to the apartments. He had a perfect view of the crescent moon rising and the bright morning star. Below him, far, far below, such a drop that made his head reel, he saw tiny figures: guards who had stayed awake all night, and cooks and servants rising before dawn: half-asleep passing half-awake. The sound of Da Gama's boot heels echoed softly down to the street below. There was little noise; this was the time of whispers; soft greetings, nods, small waves. Even the dogs passed each other silently.

A few feet from Victorio's door Da Gama looked out over the whole sleeping city. The rising moon lit the white facades of Bijapur. He realized that at this moment in the Gagan Mahal he was the only one awake and watching, that only he and God and the night birds could see the unfolding of the morning from this height. It made him feel special, and small.

At that moment however, a clatter arose from inside Victorio's apartment; the door banged open, and Victorio himself staggered out. Barefoot, in his nightshirt, his wispy hair flying, Victorio lurched to the edge of the balcony, not noticing Da Gama. Mouse crept out behind him. "No, master, please, no!" the eunuch whispered, but with a grunt, Victorio waved him off. He hitched up his nightshirt over his wide, sagging belly, and leaned against the stone balustrade. "Please, no!" whimpered Mouse.

But Victorio had already begun to pee, a thin trickle that glittered in the moonlight and splashed like rain on the walls and street below. Mouse moaned softly. Then with a resigned shake of his head the eunuch took the old man's hand. Victorio shook his *fonte,* and let go a thunderous fart that echoed against the quiet walls. With a snort, blinking and smacking his lips,

Victorio thumped back to bed. Though the old man never saw Da Gama, Mouse did, and gave him a sad, helpless shrug as he followed Victorio back to his room.

ⓢⓈⓈⓈ

Da Gama sat cross-legged near the glowing embers of the hearth wearing only his nightshirt. He could not sleep. His mind would not stop.

He had arrayed his *pistolas* in a neat line before his bare feet, and now rubbed them one by one with coconut oil and lampblack, and thought. He faced his future as one faces a wall about to crumble. He liked to think of himself as a man of action, a soldier. But he had not counted on his present situation. This plan of Victorio's would be difficult to manage, maybe impossible. One by one he considered the tasks that he was undertaking: Double-dealing with Wali Khan. Selling that young girl Maya to god-knows-what fate at the hands of eunuchs. Victorio wedding Lucinda. A failure was hard enough, but the results of success made his stomach churn.

What is a soldier's duty?

You pledged your service to the Dasanas, he reminded himself. You gave your word.

Then why do I feel sick?

Because they are all a bad lot, and Victorio the worst. How was I to know I'd end up here, a partner in his scheming?

Da Gama tried to ease his mind by polishing his *pistolas*. He tried imagining himself a wealthy man. But his thoughts kept drifting back to Lucy, and the nautch girl. Their faces blended in his mind until he could not recall precisely what either looked like.

Even when the last *pistola* had been cleaned and oiled, he still felt too upset to sleep. He pushed some more wood chips into the fire, and took from his shoulder bag a little kit: a knife, a casting mold, a small pig of lead, and a cup of scorched copper with a screw-on handle. While the flames blazed up, he whittled chips of lead into the cup. He blew on the flames until the embers glowed bright orange, then thrust in the cup. As he waited, he unlatched the iron mold—it hinged opened to reveal a pattern like a cluster of grapes—and picked out some stray bits of lead with the tip of his knife.

Da Gama liked casting shot: the smell of the hot metal melting, the swift motions of the hands, the concentration to keep from being burned. Involved with his task, he did not notice Mouse approach. "What are you doing, master?" Mouse whispered, wide eyes flickering in the reflected firelight.

"Ever seen anyone cast shot before?"

Mouse shook his head, and Da Gama motioned for him to sit. The eunuch lowered himself with silent grace, unconsciously moving his good right hand to shield the crippled left hand from Da Gama's eyes. Boiling up from his loneliness and uncertainty, and in truth, from too much wine, Da Gama felt an unexpected tenderness for the eunuch, and he smiled at him as one might smile at a favorite nephew. The gratitude in Mouse's eyes when he saw this nearly broke Da Gama's heart.

Da Gama showed him everything; all his tools; how to pour the molten lead over the lip of the red-hot copper cup into the iron mold, taking care to pour slowly, taking care not to spill too much; how the mold could be opened nearly at once, and the lead, shaped like a flat cluster of grapes, dropped into the hand warm but not hot enough to burn; how one could break the balls from the cluster as one plucks fruit; and then how one shaved the shot with the knife to smooth any roughness. Mouse watched in fascination, and asked a dozen whispered questions. Da Gama let him fill the mold a couple of times, but he could not use the knife with his bad hand.

Da Gama saw that this saddened the eunuch. "Never mind, Senhor Mouse. There is a different way to cast shot that does not require two hands." So he told Mouse about dropping hot lead from towers; the best way to make shot, Da Gama assured him. Mouse wanted to know more, and Da Gama told him of men with tongs who held red-hot iron crucibles over the balconies of high towers; the clever mechanisms for measuring out the drops of lead poured from the crucible into the air; the round shot that formed as the lead fell to earth. Mouse seemed eager to learn, and soon Da Gama found himself describing the drumming of the shot as it rained on the taut canvas sheet at the bottom of the tower, and the young boys who swept the warm rounds into boxes, watching the tower for fear more shot would fall on them.

"But how does the shot get round?"

"It's just round, that's all. Just from falling through the air. They add a metal to the lead . . . *arsênico* we call it—I don't know its Hindi name . . . The *arsênico* hardens the shot and makes it rounder."

Mouse asked more questions about *arsênico,* trying to guess from Da Gama's description what its name might be in Hindi. His eyes brightened when Da Gama told him the metal smelled like garlic. *"Ahcha,"* Mouse smiled. *"Haratala!"* Without another word, Mouse moved to his small trunk in Victorio's room. He returned to Da Gama with a shy, happy smile, holding in his hand a small wooden box. "Here, master."

Da Gama lifted the lid, saw the shiny, delicate red paste, and smelled the hint of garlic. *"Haratala,"* said Mouse happily.

"Why do you have this?"

"It is a medicine, master. Some of the brothers use it."

"For what?"

"I should not say," Mouse said, his face suddenly clouding. "Our health is not so good, you know. The making of a brother causes problems all his life. Also . . ." Mouse seemed embarrassed. "Also old men use it. It gives them back their . . . vigor."

"Old men like Victorio?"

Mouse nodded.

Da Gama scowled. "It's poison."

Mouse chuckled. "I've seen a pitcher from China, carved from the raw red stone. Exquisite. One of the brothers used it to pour wine for his enemies. He stored it in darkness . . . light, he said, would make it crumble to dust. But *haratala* is not always poison. Not if you are careful, master. Even farang women use it."

"But even a little too much . . ." Da Gama shrugged.

"Too much of that . . . ," Mouse lifted his chin to indicate the shot, "also can kill. Senhor Victorio says they call you the master of death."

Hearing those hard words come from Mouse's tender mouth, Da Gama felt tears welling. You must be drunk, he scolded himself. You know they've called you that for years. Da Gama looked at his hands, no longer sure he could control his face. "It's true. I've seen too much death. At my age a man discovers regret, Senhor Mouse. I pursued blood instead of beauty. My memories are all of killing. I've forgotten the rest. Sometimes I cannot sleep."

"Ah . . ." Mouse sighed. "You wish for peace." His eyes flickered as he watched the melting lead begin to bubble in the fire. "But to bring death . . . Surely that must bring peace, master? Is not death the greatest peace of all?" Mouse slid closer. Da Gama shifted uncomfortably, but then he realized that Mouse was in many ways no more than a child. Suddenly the eunuch held out his wooden box of *arsênico*. "Let's try it, master!"

Da Gama looked up startled. "What? Eat some?"

Mouse laughed. "No, master. Let's make shot!"

Though by now Da Gama was exhausted, to please Mouse he melted more lead, this time with the *arsênico*. They cast a few more dozen rounds. Mouse was so happy, he clutched Da Gama's arm and laid his head on the farang's big shoulder. Da Gama made sure he kept his thoughts focused on making shot.

"Enough, senhor," Da Gama said at last. "I must try to sleep." He took a few of the newly cast balls of shot and placed them in Mouse's hand. "Here. You made these. Keep them." Da Gama looked away so he would not be troubled by Mouse's reaction. The eunuch's hand was very soft.

After a moment, Mouse placed the shot into his pocket, and then scurried to help Da Gama pick up his tools. But when Da Gama tried to give him back his *arsênico,* the eunuch refused. "Keep it, master, and when you use it, think of me. Find peace in your memories of our time together." Mouse bowed so low his good hand swept the floor, and without looking back, he stepped into the darkness and curled up on the threshold of Victorio's door.

Da Gama slipped the box of *arsênico* into the bag with his *pistolas*, then lay down on his bed and stared at the ceiling until the first dim light of morning.

ଓଓଓଓ

Of course they were to leave at dawn, but the muezzin had called the second prayer of the morning before Victorio lumbered down the stair, holding Mouse's arm for steadiness.

Da Gama tried to curb his frustration at the endless delays. The only place large enough for the caravan to assemble was in the street outside the Gagan Mahal, and it was a disaster. A farmer led a long line of donkeys right through Da Gama's group; a skinny cow with a dripping nose nearly tipped over one of the palanquins; dusty dogs chased a pig through a nearby sewer. To this confusion the gods of chaos added jalabeewallahs and panwallahs crying out for men to buy their wares; a line of pretty nobody women carrying patties of cow dung in great baskets balanced on their heads; little boys herding goats with long blades of sword grass.

Tired of the delay, Da Gama's *palki* bearers were already demanding extra pay. A number of his guards had drifted away to the Mosque of the Hairs to say prayers.

"Well, what are we waiting for?" Victorio grunted as he reached the bottom stair. "Let's be on our way. My bride awaits!"

"We're waiting for that damned *hijra*," Da Gama said. At a look from Mouse, he regretted his word. "We're waiting for Slipper. I have sent messengers. Three or four of them. He can't be found."

"Then the hell with him. We leave without him."

Da Gama blinked. "You can't be serious!"

Victorio drew himself up, pulling in his belly and puffing his chest. "This soldier is very rude, don't you think?" he said to Mouse in Hindi. "I have half a mind not to make him a partner."

Mouse agreed emphatically, then glanced at Da Gama and blushed.

"I won't tolerate insubordination, sir," Victorio said in Portuguese, turning to Da Gama.

"We're partners, though, so I'm your equal, not your subordinate," Da Gama replied softly.

An exasperated sigh puffed out Victorio's cheeks. "We're partners when I say we are partners!" Da Gama was about to answer, when from around a corner, a row of soldiers wearing formal turbans of palace green trooped directly toward them. They carried ebony maces bossed with silver.

The leader glared at the farangs. "Are you Victorio Souza and Jebtha Da Gama?" His tone was impolite and his pronunciation intentionally terrible.

"What business of it is yours?" Da Gama bristled.

"You're to come with us, of your own will. The grand vizier wishes to speak with you."

"He's in Golconda!" Mouse piped up, clutching Victorio's hand.

"He returned last night." The guard's eyes narrowed. "If you cannot come on your own, we are to assist you."

Victorio wanted to take a *palki*, but the guards wouldn't allow it. Furious, he trudged along a slowly as he could. "You created this problem, Da Gama," Victorio hissed. "I expect you to solve it."

"I merely offered a price! You decided to sell the nautch girl to the eunuchs, not I," Da Gama protested. "Did you think the vizier would do nothing?"

"You are the settlement man. So settle this! If you sincerely wish to be a partner, then you'll handle this."

◎◎◎◎

They entered the vizier's residence through a rude-looking side door clearly meant for servants. A sentry told them to leave their swords. He then carefully removed each of Da Gama's *pistolas,* placing them gently on a table as one might handle a sleeping snake. Da Gama considered protesting but held his tongue. The sentry found fourteen guns, but missed the small one Da Gama strapped to his thigh next to his *fonte.*

The lead guard walked swiftly through the dark palace corridors. Da Gama worried that Victorio would collapse with the effort of keeping up.

At last the narrow corridor opened into a grand room. The walls sparkled in the sunlight that streamed from a pair of high windows, for they were covered in a bright mosaic of colored stones and pieces of mirror. At the far wall of the room, steps led to a platform, like a huge block of mirrored stone, its canopy closed in with red velvet drapes.

"Come forward," came a deep, tired voice. The guard nodded toward the dais, but hung back to let the farangs approach on their own. When Da Gama glanced back, he had already left the room.

As they approached, a small black eunuch boy pushed the heavy drapes aside. "Come, come," the voice said. "Closer." Victorio and Da Gama now stood only a few feet from the platform, and because of the angle, they could not see its occupant.

Victorio made a mighty sweeping bow, seen only by Da Gama and the boy, and rose with a long sigh. Clearing his throat, he began to intone, "O, mighty effulgence of Allah's wisdom . . ."

"Shall we dispose of all that nonsense?" the deep voice said. "I had enough flattery in Golconda. And for your information, Senhor Victorio, the Dutch flatter much better than you." For a moment, Da Gama thought that the vizier meant this remark as a good-natured joke. This might not be so bad, he thought. The moment did not last long.

"What makes you think I'd let you sell my nautch girl to the *hijra*?" the vizier barked.

Victorio too glowered at Da Gama, nodding for him to answer, wagging his eyebrows impatiently. Da Gama could not think what to say. Victorio scowled.

On legs as thick as an elephant's, Wali Khan, the Grand Vizier, inched down the steps, completely naked. He looked as though he had swallowed a giant egg. His dark skin stretched tight across his wide, round torso, and his taut, round belly hung so low it hid his *fonte*. Sadly, however, his back had no equivalent covering; as he turned to take the final step, his bare, flat ass quivered as he moved. He slapped his small round hands together. "Where's my bath? Fetch my bath!" Instantly the dark eunuch boy dashed through a door.

Wali Khan frowned after him, and then turned to his guests. "Did you think to toy with me, Victorio? Did you think I wouldn't care? I, the grand vizier of Bijapur? You would steal my goods?"

"Lord Vizier . . ." Da Gama said softly.

"I did not speak to you, Deoga, but to this pathetic old fool. What have you to do with this matter, in any case?"

Da Gama was about to answer when Victorio jumped in. "He's my partner now. You want to know who made the deal with the *hijra*? It was him. Blame him if you want."

Wali Khan took a step toward Da Gama, thrusting his belly nearly against the farang's. Da Gama tried to keep his eyes focused on the vizier's face, not on his gray-haired chest, or worse, his belly. "What about this, Deoga?"

Da Gama stared evenly at Wali Khan, who was a few inches shorter. "I don't see that anything's been stolen. She was never in your possession. A thousand calamities might have caused this same result. You never had the girl; you only had the hope."

The vizier's eyes gleamed. "I had more than hope. I had a promise. Your promise."

"While I understand that there's been some talk about offering you the nautch girl, Lord . . ." Da Gama said, choosing his words carefully and hating himself more each moment ". . . has anything been put in writing?"

Wali Khan squinted at Da Gama, and a jackal's smile spread across his face. He was close enough for Da Gama to see the beads of sweat that clung to the hairs of his chest. "Writing, is it? Has it come to that? To writing?"

Through the door of the great chamber came a short procession of nearly identical eunuch boys: three carrying steaming silver salvers, three with white muslin sheets.

Wali Khan lifted his arms while the boys circled around his naked torso, but he kept his frown pointed at Da Gama. Those boys with salvers placed them near Wali Khan's feet, and began a strange dance, bending to dip their hands in the steaming water, then reaching up to rub Wali Khan's thick flesh with their bare palms. As soon as they had scrubbed a place, the three boys with sheets reached in to wipe it dry. They stepped back and then the washing boys approached once more. But despite their work, Wali Khan's full attention was only on Da Gama.

"Which is worse, Deoga? Stealing, or breaking promises? Stolen goods might be recovered . . . but how will one recover one's broken word?" Wali Khan looked at him almost sadly. "I was giving you the benefit of the doubt. Why did you not take it?" Da Gama hung his head.

The boys finished their ablutions, and now scurried to fetch Wali Khan's clothing. While they arrayed him in his *jamas* and long robe and turban, in his ceremonial girdle and outer skirt of delicate gauze, the vizier never stopped speaking to the farangs. "Do you know what I was doing in Golconda? That city is under siege by the Moguls. I visited Aurangzeb himself, that cunning son of a whore. And with no more than a promise, I secured a peace."

Wali Khan pushed his face just inches from Da Gama. "With just my word, Deoga! No money. No guns. Only my promise! That is the value of a promise. That is what you lost." Da Gama nodded, feeling shamed.

"Promises, Deoga! I promised to send that nautch girl to the Mogul prince Murad. He has a fondness for nautch girls—he likes to watch them. He can't do much else. Aurangzeb suggested it—a sop for his dullard brother—and I agreed. I gave my word! She's far, far more than a nautch girl now, Deoga! Now she's the seal on a peace treaty!"

Wali Khan's eyes were bright, and though he was not yet shouting, his voice echoed from the jeweled walls. "And I come back to find that you've sold her? To the Brotherhood? Shall I now tell Aurangzeb that nothing was in writing?"

The eunuch boys who had been dressing him scattered and now pressed against the walls in fearful silence. Finally outfitted in his regal robes of turquoise silk, and his enormous gold-shot turban, Wali Khan seemed no longer silly and fat, but vast and powerful, a truly grand vizier with endless resources available, should he but clap his dimpled hands. "I assume you now mean to keep *your* word," he said, so softly that Da Gama now had almost to strain to hear. "I assume . . . that you have reconsidered."

"He has not!" Victorio burst out. Both men looked up in surprise. The old man began to laugh. "Look at him, Da Gama. You've got him scared stiff!" Victorio lumbered toward the vizier, still chuckling and shaking his head. "What were you doing, Wali Khan . . . selling what you don't own? Did the Sultana know of this treaty? Did she?" He fixed the vizier with a bright, sneering eye. "And what else did you promise Aurangzeb, eh?"

Victorio shook his head at Da Gama. "He's pathetic, my boy. Pitiful." He turned again to the vizier. "What will Whisper say to all your plans?"

Da Gama was surprised by Wali Khan's reaction. He bent his head, and his shoulders drooped as if from a thousand, thousand doubts. "I will make it work. I will think of something," the vizier whispered, and turned aside from the farangs.

"Wali Khan," Victorio said gently. "Send the baby spies away, and let us talk." Da Gama realized Victorio meant the eunuch boys. Wali Khan seemed too weak to do more than flutter his fingers, but the boys saw the small gesture and jostled for the door.

When the echoing thud of the heavy wood door had faded from the glittering walls, Victorio motioned to a carpet and bolsters, as though he were now the host. "Wali Khan, Wali Khan," he said as the men sat, placing a heavy hand on the vizier's thick shoulder. "Did you think your best friends would abandon you?"

"I need the girl, Victorio. I'll have the girl, by the Beard."

"Of course you will! Of course! Do you think we have no honor?"

Wali Khan stared at Victorio. "But I heard . . . and then Deoga said . . ."

Victorio laughed politely. "He didn't know any better. I kept him in the dark. I alone knew the truth, Wali Khan. If Da Gama knew my true plans, how could he have convinced the *hijra*? We merely toy with them, for our own advantage. I would never betray you . . . you are our friend— our best hope." He lowered his voice. "You haven't forgotten, have you?"

"No, of course not. The Dutch are out—the trade monopolies are yours, Victorio! . . . If I become regent."

"Surely you mean *when* you become regent, old friend."

Da Gama saw that sweat had formed on Wali Khan's round face,

though it was still morning cool. The vizier looked at Victorio with shame-
less gratitude and then grasped the old man's hand. "Senhor, I lost my
head . . ."

"Wali Khan, in these times rumors fly everywhere. The girl is yours,
old friend. We will settle with the *hijra*. Believe nothing you may hear!
Now we must go . . ."

"Yes, yes. Go now. Bring the girl, as quickly as you can." Wali Khan
stood and lifted his hands in salute, then waved to Da Gama. "I have a message for you, from some friends of mine."

Da Gama's eyebrows raised. The morning had been so full of strange-
ness he scarcely knew now what to say.

Wali Khan pulled Da Gama's shoulder to speak into his ear. "My friends
are from the Three-Dot clan. It can be helpful to have such friends, Deoga.
They send a message to you. They too were betrayed, as you were betrayed.
They told me of the trouble at Sansagar pass. Those messengers you met
with were killed by a rival gang, the Nagas. It was the Nagas who attacked
you." Wali Khan pulled Da Gama toward a small box near his sleeping platform, and took out a small purse, and spread some of its contents in his thick
round palm: a pile of golden rials. "Here, they return the *baksheesh* you gave
them." Da Gama took the purse with a bow of his head.

Wali Khan raised his hands. "Don't let my anger disturb you, Deoga.
That old man is a viper, and not the dullard that he pretends to be. He plays
us all for fools." Standing a little way off, Victorio stared into space. "We
must hang together until the regency is decided. I'm glad Victorio has made
you his partner. You are known to be a practical man. I see great things for
you."

"But what will become of her . . . the nautch girl?"

Wali Khan looked at him as if he could not understand the question.
"Go, Deoga. And don't worry about that *hijra*, Slipper. My friends"—Wali
Khan looked significantly to be sure that Da Gama understood that he
meant the Three-Dot clan—"will be nearby throughout your journey.
They do this at my request, but it is their pleasure. . . . They feel an obligation to you after the troubles you endured. If you need help, just give some
signal."

"You're sending bandits to protect us? You expect me to ask bandits
for help?"

Beneath his enormous turban, Wali Khan's dark brow knitted. "Are you unhappy with my arrangements, Deoga? That's rather harsh. Anyway, if you don't signal, you'll never know they're there."

"What sort of signal?" Da Gama blurted out, struggling to keep his voice low.

"How should I know?" The question clearly annoyed the vizier. "Wave a lamp three times. There." Wali Khan turned his head to fix Da Gama with an angry eye. "I took some trouble on your behalf, Deoga, and I expect your appreciation. Shall I tell all this to him, instead?"

Tell Victorio? "No," Da Gama said. He bowed and joined Victorio. *Do you want me to tell this to him?* It was how a child might threaten another.

What sort of men am I dealing with? Da Gama thought, not for the first time, nor the last.

ೞೞಜಿ

"That went well," Victorio said at the sentry's table as they strapped on their swords.

"You think so?" Da Gama answered. He examined each *pistola* carefully before pushing it beneath his wide belt.

"My dear fellow, yes!" Victorio seemed to be feeling expansive. Da Gama wondered whether Mouse had cooked up some new concoction for the old man, for his face was flushed and his eyes bright. "Look at our situation. On his own the vizier discovered about the eunuchs. He must know what they've offered us."

"What difference does that make? You just told him . . ."

Victorio sneered. "Don't pretend to be naïve. I lied to him, of course. Don't tell me *you* believed me, too? It was a brilliant move on my part. Now he's forced to match any price the eunuchs name, isn't he? What choice does he have, eh? Before the girl was nothing—a bit of *baksheesh*. Now she's Wali Khan's ticket to the regency. Best of all, he's already promised her to Aurangzeb. Can you imagine what old Prince Tiger Claws would do if Wali Khan reneged? What won't Wali Khan pay to keep his promise? And as for the eunuchs"—Victorio sighed and spread his hands—"they think . . . well, they want her, too. I shall watch the bidding with amusement." Victorio clapped Da Gama on the shoulder as they passed through the side entrance and began walking back to the Gagan

Mahal. "It's a game, my boy; it's all a game! You must not frown so! Get into the spirit of the thing or you'll go mad! We play one side against the other until someone blinks."

Or until someone cuts our throats, Da Gama thought. "What about the girl?"

"The nautch girl? What about her? It is my welfare that concerns you, not hers. Besides, you have other problems."

"Like what?"

"Like that *burak*. He's not going to like these arrangements, is he?"

"Pathan? I expect that he may have an opinion," Da Gama acknowledged, realizing that Victorio seemed surprisingly circumspect today.

"And that *hijra* Slipper. Best to keep him in the dark as well. Those two are dangerous. They have their ways . . . even if you say nothing, they'll get information. You must misdirect, persuade, confuse. If you wish to be a partner, you must use your brain now, not just your *pistolas.* That open face of yours is a real liability." Again Victorio laughed. "By the Virgin, I adore the game! It makes me feel ten years younger, squeezing those bastards! If we keep this up, I'll have an heir in no time. By the Virgin, I could rut like a fox!"

With a sudden burst of energy, Victorio strode off, leaving Da Gama to make his worried way alone.

ᏯᎲᏯᎲ

Soon they were off. Slipper had arrived while they were gone, and had rearranged things to his liking, and was full of questions. Da Gama let Victorio do the talking.

The caravan was small—two *palkis,* one for Slipper, one for Victorio. Bullock carts piled high with rolled-up formal tents, tent poles, ropes, and cooking gear. Another bullock cart for camp servants. On horses, Da Gama and a half-dozen guards handpicked by Commander Shahji. They would get more *palkis* when they got to Belgaum.

What would Shahji say if he knew that Wali Khan was in league with the Three-Dot clan, the most notorious bandits in the Southern Deccan? Da Gama wondered.

"Where am I to travel, Deoga?" Mouse asked, staggering beneath the weight of his pack. He still had the grateful look Da Gama had seen the night before.

"Who asked you to come?" came Victorio's voice from behind the curtain of his *palki.*

Mouse looked up, shocked. "Master . . ."

"You're to stay here. I don't need you, Mouse." The eunuch looked as though he'd been stabbed. "I'm going to fetch my bride, aren't I? I can't very well bring *you* along, can I? Wait at the factor. I'll introduce you to her when the time is right." With that, Victorio's scaly hand swung the curtain of his *palki* shut. He never saw Mouse's shattered look, or how he crept away like a broken puppet. But Da Gama did, and cursed Victorio beneath his breath.

All at last was ready, but once again Slipper was nowhere to be found. Finally he appeared, smoothing his robe, from a nearby latrine. "It's so uncomfortable to stop out there in the wilderness, don't you think, Deoga?" he said with an intimate smile as he walked past to his *palki.*

Slipper refused the *palki*wallah's assistance. "Deoga shall help me," he said, loud enough for all to hear. Da Gama shook his head in disbelief, but Slipper simply stood waiting.

At last, with a frustrated grunt, Da Gama got down from his horse. Only when he had offered Slipper his hand would the eunuch step into his *palki.* "You are very kind, Deoga," the eunuch said. Then the eunuch leaned close and whispered in his ear, "Mouse told me about the *haratala.* You nasty man. Do you have an itch you cannot scratch? My dear fellow, you should have told me! I have many poultices. *Haratala* and lots of others. We can share them anytime you wish." Slipper's breath tickled Da Gama's ear.

Da Gama fixed the eunuch with a cold stare. "It's not what you think," he grunted. But Slipper's raised eyebrows and knowing smile were what the company around him saw, and they drew their own conclusions. Da Gama strode back to his horse with his ears burning.

"Let's get the hell to Belgaum," he shouted.

The caravan began to move.

Part Six

Regret

"You alone," Lady Chitra said to Pathan, "appear to have kept your reason."

Even if Chitra could see him, Pathan would have kept his face just as blank, his head as motionless. He sat for the first time in Chitra's vast rooms, where the fragrance of a thousand roses filled the air, tugged to that place by Lakshmi's tiny hand. The little girl peeked at the *burak* from behind Lady Chitra's shoulder, and for a moment Pathan considered winking at her, just to see her reaction. But the moment was somber, and his mood also, so instead he merely mumbled something to let Chitra know that he had heard.

"Although you are a Muslim, you have acted civilly in my palace. I have decided therefore to place some trust in you." Chitra's pebble eyes glided beneath her half-closed lids. "I want you gone from here, all of you, before those monsters come."

Pathan could not hide his surprise, though only Lakshmi saw it. "I don't understand, madam."

Chitra sighed, but her back, straight as a ramrod, did not move. "You do understand, sir. Only you pretend not to. Many men employ this strategy." Lakshmi whispered into Chitra's ear. "She tells me you're offended."

"No, madam. I am indebted to you for your courtesy. We all are."

Chitra snorted. "It is Commander Shahji's courtesy. I am but his hostess, a guest here myself. He has been kind to me as well." She leaned in closer. "He said he knew your father. He said your father was a good man." Pathan did not answer. "He told me I could trust you."

After a moment, Pathan answered. "Yes."

"The fragrance of the roses wet with dew, the peacocks' cries, the wet smell of the lake breeze. You alone maybe have truly understood how special this palace is."

Again Pathan paused, then as if casting off a mask, he answered. "Yes."

Chitra smiled. He had never seen her smile, and the sudden beauty of it as it burst on her soft face struck him like a blow. She was not old, he saw now that she smiled, and she had been beautiful—more than beautiful— not that many years ago.

"I am glad you don't dissemble now. There is no place like this, not for many miles. In Kashi, maybe, near the Ganges, or on the shore of Pushkar Lake, or at the confluence of the rivers at Nasik, or in Puri maybe, or in Kanyakumari which is my home. Here as in those places old Hindustan still survives. Like a fragile flower, I maintain it here by my will. Do you understand me?"

"Yes. I have felt it."

Chitra sighed. "I could tell that you too were special, Captain." She lifted her hand before Pathan could say a word. "I was worried when you came here, you and the farangs." Pathan looked uncomfortably at Lakshmi, who whispered at that moment in Chitra's ear.

"Leave us," Chitra said to Lakshmi. The girl seemed shocked by this command. She stared at Pathan as she strolled away with exaggerated slowness. "You must speak frankly to me, Captain." She reached into the empty air, searching for his hand. Pathan watched as she sought him, and with a look of resignation, came closer to her. Her fingers closed around his wrist.

Her touch unlocked his heart. Suddenly he found himself telling Chitra everything. "What are you doing to me, madam?" he asked, as tears spilled from his eyes. He could not stop himself or even slow his words.

The bandits' deaths, the rescue. His awareness and growing feelings for
Lucy. His disgust at Geraldo's seduction of Maya. All this he told while
Chitra stroked his hand and sat unmoving, except for the wavering of her
sightless eyes.

She asked Pathan many questions about Geraldo and Maya. His every
answer seemed a needle that pricked her, but she kept on. At last she asked
no more, but sat silent, rubbing his hand. Lake birds cawed outside, and
that set the peacocks wailing.

Then she said, "Have you not loved before, Captain?"

He felt as though her hand were squeezing his heart, and once more his
tears began to flow. But he choked back his sobs and did not answer.

"When Kama shoots his arrows, Captain, no heart is safe, for their
sweetness is full of poison. Have you told the farang girl of your love?"

With the back of his free hand, Pathan smeared the moisture from his
cheeks. "She knows, madam."

"Don't confuse the issue. Have you told her, yes or no?"

Pathan swallowed his tears, ashamed to show such weakness. "Not like
that, madam."

"And of course she would not say such words to you."

"But I can tell. There are other ways than words."

"Not to the blind, Captain. And have you not heard that the heart is
blind?"

Pathan looked up at Chitra. "You are different than I expected,
madam."

"The Goddess keeps me so, Captain, not my own will." She sighed and
let go his hand. "Now, Captain, to the point. I don't want those others
coming here, that caravan from Bijapur. Deoga, maybe, I would not mind,
but not the others. Not that *hijra,* and not that old farang. I don't like what
little I've heard about him. He sounds too much like an aged version of the
farang Geraldo, and that one is a poison. I'm depending on you."

"But precisely, madam, what do you want?"

"I want you to go—take yourself and the other guests—and leave here
before the caravan arrives."

Pathan considered this. "My family's estate is not far from here. We
could meet the caravan there."

Chitra again gave that sumptuous smile, but this time Pathan could see that there was pain behind it. "Yes. If you don't mind, Captain. Do that as a favor for me. Leave me now, as one leaves a corpse . . . with regret, and memories, but without a second look."

Pathan rose and bowed, full-knowing that Chitra could not see.

"One thing more, Captain. Tell your love. Tell before you step across that bridge. The power of this palace will propel your words so that they land deep inside her heart. She does love you, Captain, and she would be happy."

⊙⊙⊙⊙

Maya spent most of her time with Lucinda now. They talked little and thought much, but each took comfort from the other's presence.

Maya had stayed with Lucinda for a while after Da Gama's letter had been read, but finally she left, and found her way once more to Aldo's room. She slid through his door as soft as moonlight. He looked so different in farang clothes. Before, he would have looked up right away, sensing her arrival, but he had changed. Now his attention totally focused on whetting the blade of his black sword.

After waiting for a moment, she whispered his name, but he answered without turning. "We have nothing to say now, you and I. What once was has passed away. It's best that you leave now. Best that no one sees you here."

Maya felt her face go pale. "You must tell about us, Aldo. I can't be sold to the *hijra*. You can't imagine what they'll do to me. You must tell what passed between us."

Only now did Geraldo look up, and a faint smile passed his elegant lips. "Now I see how it is. You played me. You meant this from the beginning, didn't you? You meant to use our pleasure to your advantage."

"Did you not do that very thing with me?"

Geraldo gave a snorting chuckle. "Tell them yourself. I will say nothing." He turned back to his sword.

"But you must tell them. They won't believe me."

"You are right—they won't believe you. And without my word to back you up, it's as though nothing ever happened. Oh, don't act innocent. You got what you wanted."

"Aldo, I beg you!"

"Save your weeping. I'm sure it starts and stops at your command. Unlike you, my dear, I have no desire for a painful death." He smiled, but did not look at her. "Anyway, what difference would it make? Perhaps a Muslim would be disgusted to know that I had plowed your furrow, or even a Hindi. But what would a eunuch care? Aren't they lower even than farangs? Besides, I think they have other plans for you."

Maya's skin grew cold. "What plans?"

"That box you carry with the sword inside. How does a nautch girl, a *devadasi*, come to have a farang sword, one worth a *lakh* of hun? That makes one think, that does. And then there's that bag, the missing bag, the bag you gave Da Gama. What's in that bag, I wonder? I'd guess the eunuchs wonder, too. About those things, and about what else you own. And about what else you know." Aldo's lips had stretched into a grin, but his eyes were cold. "You don't look well. Do you want some air?"

"But I don't have it anymore . . ." she whispered.

"Yes, I know. You gave it to Da Gama; dear, trustworthy Deoga, everybody's uncle, everybody's friend." Geraldo snorted. "Be careful who you trust, my sweet. Has no one ever warned you to be careful?"

Before she even realized it, Maya had fled from Aldo's room. She was halfway across the courtyard before she stopped and clutched her head and wept. She managed to contain herself enough to reach the ladies' quarters. There she burst into Lucinda's room, fell down beside her, and sobbed. Lucinda cradled her and asked what had happened, but Maya would not say.

She slept on a carpet near Lucinda's bed. Neither woman got much rest . . . they spent the night tossing fitfully, scared of what they might dream.

The next morning Maya helped Lucinda tighten her new corset and put on the heavy, rag-stuffed skirt Victorio had sent. "This is how poor women dress," Lucinda told her. "They can't afford stiff silks to hoop their skirts, so they fill the channels with rags."

"But you can barely see the difference," Maya lied. Lucinda's face, like Maya's, was a blank: she was full of thoughts too deep for speaking, thoughts that made no dent upon her face.

After she had dressed, from a little chest beside her bed, Lucinda took out her silver box and flipped the lid. "Do you want some?" she asked Maya, holding out the *arsênico*.

"Why do you have this?" Maya asked. "Why do you offer me a *dravana*?"

Lucinda blinked. "This is *arsênico*, to pale and purify the skin. What is a *dravana*, sister?"

"You don't know? It means a drug for passion, to make congress more pleasurable. Your cousin offered this same stuff to me."

"Surely not," Lucinda said.

"Yes, I say. It looked just the same. And had that same smell, just like garlic. It only made me dizzy. He said I had not taken enough, but I wanted no more."

Lucinda's eyes widened. "You did right. This is the poison I told you I had. A little makes you pale. Too much . . ."

Maya's face grew serious. "Give me some."

Lucinda held out the box. "Just a small bit, placed on the tongue."

"No!" Maya's eyes burned. "Give me what you promised me. Give me enough to kill."

Lucinda thought about saying no. She thought about asking what Maya meant to do. But she knew already, she knew by Maya's bright stare fixed upon her, for Lucinda's own thoughts also were dark. Having *arsênico*, having power, having hold of one's fate. *Arsênico* gave freedom, though the harshest kind of freedom. And she had promised Maya, after all.

"Bring me a cloth," Lucinda said at last.

Maya found a small silk handkerchief, and on it Lucinda scooped out half her *arsênico*. With some care she used an edge of the cloth to wipe the excess from her finger, and then tied the corners of the kerchief, and handed it to Maya.

Lucinda saw that there remained a few small dots of red upon her finger. She reached up and touched the tip to Maya's lips, and then her own. "Now we are sisters indeed," she said.

The next morning, Lucinda found Pathan in the courtyard, saddling his horse. She could not stop her feet from hurrying toward him, and when he noticed her, he gave the cinch an angry tug. She watched the change that crossed his face as she approached—how the brightness left his eyes, and his mouth grew harsh. He stiffened to a soldier's posture. In short he looked as distant and as haughty as the first time she had seen him in Goa. What happened to my Munna, a voice cried in her heart. But the heaviness of her skirts and the tightness of her corset whispered the answer: Lucy too had disappeared.

Even so, his gaze found hers and never wavered until she reached his side.

"You're leaving?" Her voice sounded harsher than she wished.

"You've heard my plans. I'll be back tomorrow night with *palkis* and horses. You heard all this last night, did you not?"

"I thought you'd tell me goodbye." His coldness chilled her. Lucinda felt the few feet of space between them like a chasm. Looking at his face she remembered the moist pliance of his lips against hers, and the press of his long fingers on the bare skin of her waist; she remembered the slippery, unexpected twisting of his tongue; and she had to turn away. "I wanted you to say goodbye."

"I could not bear it," he whispered back.

She realized that the stony blankness of his face was held there by the hard force of his will. Oh, the child, she thought. He believed it pleased her that he did not show his pain.

The fullness of her skirts kept a distance between them. He could not casually come closer without pressing against the bulky clothing. "Will you remember me, Munna?" she whispered, stretching out her hand. From where she stood, she could not quite touch him.

He looked at her pale hand, and her chalk-powdered face, and her cumbersome clothing, and peered at her as if to see behind a mask that she'd put on. He lifted both his hands, and cradled her outstretched fingers as gently as one holds a bird. "You are closer to me than my breath," he said. His eyes, for just a moment, lost their coldness, and she saw that he was frightened. "Must you marry him, Lucy?"

"I have no choice, Munna."

His face grew hard. "You say this? When you were pledged, then I could understand. But that pledge is broken."

"Another pledge now takes its place."

"It means nothing! I see that now. It is not your pledge, Lucy! This is another's will, not yours!"

"I have made it mine. I am a Dasana, and my will is not my own." She lowered her head. "I am no more than a puppet, Munna. Another pulls the strings." She pulled her hand away. "Listen, Munna. It is my duty to my family. But he will have my body only, but not my heart."

"Have I no family? No duty? Yet I would cast them all aside—for happiness, for love. For you."

Lucy looked up as if seeing him for the first time. "You are not a Christian, or a Portuguese. We are so different, you and I."

His face grew hard. "Suppose I put on farang clothes, and drank blood like a Christian, then would I be suitable?"

"No!" Lucinda cried. She stepped away for him, recoiling at the thought.

"Did I really mean to give my heart to you? Damn you then, and damn all women!" Pathan shouted, suddenly on fire. She had seen such a fury in his eyes once before, when he had killed her attackers at the pass, when his hands were stained with bandit blood. Without another glance Pathan slapped his horse, and mounted it even while it ran, and galloped out the gate, across the causeway.

"Munna!" Lucinda's throat was so tight, she could barely hear her own words. She tasted the ocean—her own salt tears, she realized—and then cried out once more, "Munna!"

The word echoed against the palace walls. He was gone. From nowhere, a bloated cloud edged past the sun, and the courtyard darkened in cold shadows. "I never meant," she whispered toward the empty gate. "I never meant for you to change, dear Munna." Her throat closed in a sob. "Come back. Let me tell you so." Lucinda shivered, and straightened her skirts, and pressed the pins more deeply in her hair, and turned and walked away unseen except by one, and he could only chuckle at what had passed.

☙☙☙

"Until we leave here, won't you wear your sari, sister?" Maya asked. She and Lucinda had come together to the wide platform swing in Lady

Chitra's garden. On their backs they lay as the corner ropes creaked, staring through mango-leaf shadows at the clouds and sea-blue sky; lying so
their heads just touched, and the closeness comforted them both. Maya had
told Lucinda of her conversation with Geraldo, and Lucinda then had told
Maya about Pathan and the courtyard. They had no secrets now.

"I dare not think about it, sister. I must set my thoughts on what is, not
what might have been."

"There's yet time." Where Maya's head touched hers Lucinda felt the
subtle vibrations of her skull with every word. It tickled. It made Lucinda
smile. She felt her head buzz as Maya asked, "Do you ever think of
dying?"

Maya's question hardly shocked her. They both possessed *arsénico*
now, and when one carries poison, thoughts of death are never far away. If
Lady Chitra had been there, of course, Maya might not have said a word,
but Chitra had not come out for days, not since Da Gama's letter came. "In
truth I think more of killing than of dying, sister," Lucinda answered
softly. "But you asked if I ever think of it—and I tell you: yes."

"How do you imagine it?"

Lucinda thought but did not answer for a long time. Maya waited and
then spoke again. "I think it is a coldness, like a shadow." Maya paused.
"That's how it was when my mother died."

"Then what?" Lucinda asked.

"I think it is a sleep. There's darkness for a time. Then you see your
next body glowing for you, lighting the way, waiting for you. You put on
the baby's body, as one slips a sandal on a foot. Then another life begins."

"Is there no end?" Now Maya did not answer. "When I die," Lucinda
continued, "I want an end. I want arms around me, holding me. I want to
see his eyes with my last sight, to taste his kiss with my last breath."
Lucinda's voice grew so soft that Maya could barely hear it for the groaning
of the swing against its ropes.

Maya reached her out hand until she touched Lucinda's face. "Sister,
have you no hope at all?"

Lucinda grasped her fingers. "There is nothing for me now but death. I
myself shall die, or walk among the living with a dead heart. Or maybe I
will kill."

"Who?" Maya asked.

"Who would you kill, sister? Who has destroyed your life?"

A half-dozen faces flashed across Maya's thoughts. "I must not think this way," she whispered.

"And I," Lucinda answered, "must not wear a sari. It is just the same, you see: some thoughts are too painful to be borne." The swing moved in its long slow arc while the branches swayed. In her warm clothes, beneath the afternoon sun, Lucinda's thoughts began to drift.

As if from inside her, Lucinda heard Maya speaking. The sound of each word, vibrating where their heads touched, formed a brilliant image in Lucinda's drowsy brain.

"I had a dream last night," Maya said. "I went in spirit to the Guru planet, where my dear teacher found me. She took my hand and we began to fly. There she lives atop a mountain island, in an ocean of pure milk. The sky was bright, but filled with brighter stars. We flew so high I thought to touch the sun, when suddenly we began to descend. I thought we were falling, but my guru held me close and gestured to the ocean. We dove into the milk.

"I saw that the ocean was the very void from which all creation springs. It sat completely placid, in abundant readiness, and as we two swam through it, the milk assumed a million forms—bubbles turning into objects that in a moment melted and were gone.

"My guru drew us toward a giant structure white as bleached bone. A great temple tower, so it seemed. Against its endless walls the milk swirled. Carved there I saw a million bright white figures: men and women—not gods but humans just like us—pressing and touching and coiling round each other. They were locked in couples, all of them, embracing, kissing, having congress in every imaginable way.

"Then I saw that the carvings were alive: thrusting and twisting in furious embrace—a million, million couples locked in endless passion, as far as any eye could see.

"At last my guru took me back, farther from the churning waters and the churning couples, until at last I saw the structure in its fullness—they formed the surface of a tower so enormous that it stretched into the endless sky and down into the endless depths, and every inch of it alive with forms of passion and desire.

" 'What have you shown me, my guru?' I cried. But for answer she only took my hand, and we began to plummet down, deliriously down along the length of that enormous spire. It was so huge that we were small as mites beside it. My guru then held out her hand to show me, far below, that the tower's base was ringed round with a circle just as vast and grand, pulsing like an annulus of light. And I gasped, for I realized at last what I was seeing.

" 'This is desire, daughter, the endless piercing that informs the universe throughout eternity,' my guru told me. 'Here is great Shiva's lingam, the source of all creation, and there the boundless fertile yoni of the Goddess which embraces and envelops it. Their endless longing creates through time the three worlds. Do you wonder that you yearn to feel this very pulsing in your soul? Desire is the essence of the gods, my daughter, and we ache to feel that godhood stirred within us.' "

Maya's voice softened as she ended the telling of her dream, and Lucinda's breathing was already deep and long. Together they rocked and slept beneath the long dark boughs and the bright sky, and together dreamed.

❧❧❧❧

Next afternoon, Lucinda stood alone on the verandah, staring over the lake to where the shore road met the causeway. All along the far shore, fullers spread long bolts of bright, fresh woven silk on the sword grass for the sun to dry. The silk billowed in the breeze like the feathers of a giant bird. But the scene hardly distracted Lucinda. Her eyes never wavered from the road.

She hardly noticed when Geraldo sat upon the railing next to her. He must have found some way to quiet his noisy boots. But there he was, his eyes as bright as ever, his mouth as ironic and suggestive as ever. "So, cousin," he said cheerfully. "Now you will be married sooner than you thought." Lucinda glared at him, which made Aldo's laughing eyes dance. "Once your old uncle, now your husband. Dear old uncle Victorio."

"I should be very glad when you stop repeating 'old,' cousin. Are things not bad enough?"

"At least your future is secure. You at least know what will happen to you. Your uncle is your future now."

"We shall see," Lucinda said, after a pause. "What do you want from me, Aldo?"

Geraldo leaned back. He reached out a hand and placed it on her shoulder. "I understand you, Lucy, dear. I more than anyone understand. Are we not the same in many, many ways? Strangers. Homeless. We are alone, and lonely. The ones we love desert us."

"It is you who deserted my sister," she spat back. Geraldo raised an eyebrow. "Maya, I mean!"

Sadly Geraldo shook his head. "Is that what she told you? She must have her pride, I suppose."

"Are you saying she's a liar?"

Geraldo looked injured. "I am a gentleman, cousin. Never would I say such a thing. Don't you understand, though, that she used me, too?"

"I didn't see you fighting her off."

"Of course not. I am a man. I have desires. Just as she does. Just as you do, cousin . . ." Geraldo looked at her significantly ". . . exactly as you do."

Why has the air become so still, Lucinda wondered. Birds had been playing tag just inches above the ripples of the lake; but suddenly they'd disappeared. Only the growling of frogs in the mudgrass could be heard, and her own pounding heart.

"What will your life be like, without a real man, cousin? Are you ready to give over all hope of pleasure? For old uncle Victorio? God knows he'll probably mount you once or twice before his spirit wanes entirely. Once, twice, and then what? Months? Years? Then what hope will you have, cousin? That some day Tio Victorio will mange to stay awake long enough to come to your bed? You'll be a wife, but will you be a woman?"

Lucinda wanted to scream out, to slap Geraldo's smug face, but her lips were frozen, and her arms. He knew she could not stop listening to his voice.

"What will you do? The harem women have devices. Will you find a way to get one? Would you use one? Or would you find yourself a gelding, with a long soft tongue? Slipper, for example—though he's come up in the world, I understand. Slipper as he was, then, when he was so ready to shampoo you. Many women like the *hijra* more than husbands, so they say."

Though Lucinda's ears grew hot and her cheeks burned, she could not find a word to answer.

"But there's an alternative—me, cousin. Think of what I offer. We are family. Our language, our habits, our temperaments so similar. In this land of strangers, you and I have much in common. Even common needs, cousin."

At last her tongue could move. "Go. Go away."

Geraldo smiled then, and stood, and seized her by her shoulders, and leaned toward her face. But he only kissed her forehead. As if by chance, his fingers slid across her breast as he stepped away. "Ask your friend— your sister, as you call her. Ask her if it was not pleasant, our time together. Ask her if she was not satisfied. Often. Ask."

"Go."

"When dear old Tio Victorio flops upon you like a gasping fish—when you're trapped beneath that sagging, ancient body—think of me, dear cousin, think of me. Think of me, as I will surely think of you." With that Geraldo walked away. This time his boots clacked brutally upon the tiles. Lucinda turned and stared across the lake once more, and cursed the memory of her last words to Pathan.

☙☙☙☙

Pathan did not return that night, but crossed the causeway to the palace the next morning just as dawn broke. As soon as he and his suite entered the courtyard, he sent word that they would depart immediately.

Maya and Lucinda entered the courtyard arm in arm, heads close together. They needed no servants to help them, for they had little left to pack. Geraldo watched with cold amusement, tracing with his eyes the shape of Maya's shoulder bag.

"Ready?" Geraldo asked. The ironic smile that had seemed so attractive in Carlos's study in Goa now irritated Lucinda, and she would not answer. Geraldo chuckled and turned to Pathan. "The palanquin for these two, Captain?"

Pathan nodded. Geraldo with exaggerated formality escorted them to the eight-man palanquin that Pathan had brought. Neither woman looked his way. He bowed with a flourish when they reached it, and walked off with a chuckling nonchalance.

"Are you comfortable, madam?" the old *palki*wallah asked as they settled in the cushions. "And you, madam?"

The women told him yes. Maya slid and sat in a corner, took out her palm-leaf book and set it in her lap while Lucinda fluffed her skirts and petticoats. "Now all we need is Slipper," Lucinda said ruefully.

"We'll have him soon enough," Maya answered.

The *palki*wallah gathered his men, and they took their places at the bearing poles. Maya leaned out past the curtains of the *palki.* "But what about our hostess, Captain?"

"She will not come, I think," Pathan answered from his horseback.

"You are wrong, sir." There came Chitra, as they first had seen her, her gold shawl billowing in the breeze behind her, her long walking stick banging step by step upon the tiles, and Lakshmi, tinier than ever, holding her hand.

Pathan dismounted, and to Geraldo's amused surprise, knelt to place his head at Chitra's feet. "Get up, my boy," she said. She found his sleeve and tugged him to his feet, and whispered in his ear. Lucinda saw him shake his head and whisper, "No." Chitra smiled indulgently, the way a mother smiles at someone else's misbehaving child.

"The girls," Chitra ordered, and Lakshmi tugged her to the *palki*'s side. Lucinda slid around to embrace her. While Chitra's cheek touched hers, Lucinda heard her whisper, "Be brave, sister, be brave. Do not forget me." When she opened her eyes, she saw Lakshmi staring at her.

A sudden impulse struck her. "Come here," she told the girl while she searched in her bag. She found at last her miniature locket of Marques Oliveira, still on its fragile golden chain. She coiled it into a tight bundle and pressed it into Lakshmi's hand. "Keep the chain and throw the rest away," she whispered. But she knew from Lakshmi's face that the girl would keep everything as a mysterious souvenir.

By this time Chitra and Maya had nearly finished their embrace. Chitra stood back. "Now go, in the Goddess's protection. Do not forget your time here, and remember me!"

Chitra stepped away from the *palki,* and once more the bearers took up the poles. Lucinda felt the lurch as they stood. She looked to Chitra and was surprised to see her waving at Pathan as though she could see him. "Come, come, Captain. Do your duty!"

Pathan, it seemed with great reluctance, stopped mounting his horse, and came with slow steps to the *palki,* and at last to Lucinda's side. He glanced at Chitra, who stared nearly in their direction, and then looked into Lucinda's eyes. The force of his glance was so intense she felt her belly tremble. At last he leaned close to her, placing his lips near the place where her ear met her cheek. She felt his breath, like a silent whisper, but he did not speak. Then he stood, searching her eyes.

"*Eu desejo tu*," she said, answering his silence. She spoke without intending to—the words slipped from her as if by their own will. Lucinda trembled. He looked at her strangely—though he had heard, of course he had not understood. Pathan straightened and then walked slowly, stiffly, back to his horse. She watched each step. He did not look back. From his horseback Geraldo had seen it all, and could barely contain his amusement.

"We go!" Pathan shouted when he'd mounted. He waved his hand, and led a slow procession through the gate. Behind them Chitra and Lakshmi stood and waved.

As they reached the long lake bridge, Maya slid next to Lucinda. "What did you say?" But Lucinda could not answer.

The bearers tried their best not to walk in step, and mostly they succeeded. When by chance their different paces merged into unison, the *palki* bounced and lurched, but then would settle down once more into a gentle bobbing as the bearers mixed their strides once more. "It's not the same as an elephant, is it?" Maya smiled, but Lucinda's thoughts were too busy to reply.

As they reached the other shore, Maya turned to look one last time at the Lake Palace. "I wish I had danced more at the temple," she murmured to herself. "I wish I had spent more time with Chitra, and with Lakshmi. I expect I'll never see them again."

"*Eu desejo tu*," Lucinda said. Maya looked up. "That's what I said. It just came out. I had spoken before I realized." Maya lifted an eyebrow, waiting. "He didn't understand. How could he?" she said softly. "It means, 'I desire you.'" She turned to Maya, and her tears brimmed over. "Why did he say nothing?"

Maya reached over and took Lucinda's hand. Behind them, the palace hid behind mists rising from the lake. "But could you not tell from his look? From his breath?"

"Why was he silent?"

"He is a man. I'm so sorry, sister."

"What will become of us?" Lucinda whispered. But Maya only shook her head.

ↄ෮෮ↄ

Lucinda Dasana's future husband belched.

This was his hour. This was his caravan; these were his men. The fire that lit their faces was his fire. The wine they drank was his wine. As if to prove his point, he belched again.

"You ate too fast, Senhor Souza," Slipper smiled across the flames. "Or ate too much, maybe? Perhaps the cook Senhor Deoga hired is not agreeable?"

"No, Senhor Gelding"—Victorio lifted his arms expansively, sloshing wine from his flagon—"you mistake me. My digestion has been bothering me, that's all."

"Perhaps you have a cold, sir?" Slipper piped, his voice like honey. "Your eyes are rheumy, I see."

"Only the smoke." Victorio caught another burp, which puffed out his cheeks. He rose from his folding camp chair and mocked a bow, spilling a little more wine. "Gentlemen . . . gentle people . . ." Victorio corrected himself with a nod to Slipper, "I'll be back soon. I need my . . . my medicine." He staggered toward the tent.

"Medicine?" Da Gama muttered to himself. "Is he sick?"

"*Dravana*s, Deoga," Slipper said smugly. "Didn't you know? Can't you tell?"

After a tiresome day's travel out of Bijapur, the caravan had set up for the night in a wide pasture outside Sunag, about a third of the way to Belgaum. The night sky glittered with a million stars. Bats danced in circles through the sparks and smoke rising from the campfire.

Da Gama gave Slipper a hard look. "*Dravana*s? Whatever do you mean?"

Slipper smiled. "Really you are so ill-informed in some ways, Deoga. You should be more attentive to me, my dear friend. Just think of all you'd learn." Da Gama turned away so he would not see Slipper's insinuating look. "*Dravana*s, if you want to know, are medicines of desire. The brothers have master hakims trained in the Kamashastras. Why do you think Mouse had that *haratala*?"

"You don't mean *arsênico*?" The word burst out without Da Gama's meaning of it. "Why would Victorio . . .?"

"You needn't believe me. Here comes Victorio to rejoin us. Let's ask him."

Slipper seemed quite amused by Da Gama's horror at the suggestion.

But Victorio minded not at all. Though tears ran from his blinking eyes, though he winced as if his belly griped, still he laughed as he answered. "Of course I'm taking *dravanas*. Whatever would you expect? I go to meet my bride. What would she say if my *fonte* didn't show an interest, eh?" He grunted, and winked a wet eye, and moved his arms suggestively. "She'll be satisfied, believe me."

Da Gama tried not to look. Slipper and Victorio noticed this and laughed at him together.

After a while, they grew quiet, and stared into the fire, each thinking his own thoughts. At length, Victorio cleared his throat. "Da Gama, that boy, our cousin . . . what's his name?"

"Geraldo . . ." Da Gama answered, though he saw that Victorio remembered it, and simply didn't want to say.

"Yes, whatever his name is. . . . Would you say that he's attractive?"

"Ask him, why don't you?" Da Gama nodded to Slipper, who turned away as if blushing.

"He's a nice-looking man, senhor. But I don't approve of his personality. He has a violent nature that he keeps hidden. I think he is dangerous."

"But good-looking, you say," Victorio repeated sadly. Slipper's head wobbled indecisively, as though reluctant to go this far. "Would Lucy notice him, do you think?"

Slipper's discomfort disappeared. "Oh, sir, I don't think he's her type; no, not at all. She is so gentle—not a violent or wicked bone in that fair body." Victorio flashed his eyebrows at Da Gama at these words, cautioning him to say nothing. "That Geraldo is not a gentleman, sir. He is a villain! And he owes me money." Slipper finished by giving a big, bewildering wink to Da Gama.

"What! Owes you money? I say, that does sound wicked!" Victorio chuckled and wiped his eyes with his cuff. "But you're sure? My dear fiancée, Lucy, is so innocent . . . What if . . ."

"You misjudge her, senhor. She has the taste and refinement found in all members of your family, save that one man only, that miserable villain who proves the rule. Besides, senhor, what woman would not prefer a man like you? With your experience? And with your wealth? She's loved you all her life, and now you'll be her bridegroom. She must be delirious with joy! You'll have an heir in no time!"

Victorio shifted uncomfortably. "You're right, Senhor Gelding, of course. It's just that Geraldo is a distant heir to the Dasana fortune . . ."

"Not so distant," Da Gama broke in. Victorio frowned at him. "You haven't noticed? A lot of the Dasanas are dead, sir. In fact, there's Lucy, and there's you. You two are all that's left. After you two comes Geraldo. He's that close!"

Again Victorio blinked his watery red eyes. "Now you sport with me," he scolded.

But Da Gama, with careful seriousness, counted out the names on his fingers. This cousin, dead. That uncle, dead. His brother, dead. And on, and on.

Victorio's face grew more and more concerned. "I hadn't realized. He could end up with everything. I shall have to be more polite to the boy next time. He stands to inherit everything, it seems, unless I have an heir."

"What about your partner?" Da Gama said.

"Partners come and go, sir," Victorio replied. "Only family is eternal."

Slipper had listened to this conversation, growing more and more frustrated. "All you farangs talk about is relatives," he complained at last.

"Family is everything, senhor," Victorio replied, nodding for Da Gama to agree.

"Please excuse my rudeness, Senhor Eunuch. Genealogy is a study of mine," Da Gama said.

"Yes, Senhor Gelding, here he speaks the truth. Da Gama has the most annoying ability to remember everybody's family tree. Get him started and he talks of nothing else. He's like a tax collector's book—every little item noted and recalled in triplicate. He's quite astonishing that way. It's why everyone despises him." Victorio smiled to show he meant no harm.

Da Gama smiled. "I'm sure it's the same everywhere. I'm sure the nobles of Bijapur . . ."

"Oh the nobles . . . who cares a fig for them? The brothers give genealogy no thought."

"Don't you wonder about your parents?" asked Da Gama earnestly. "Your brothers and sisters, whether you have them? You may not have children, but you might have nephews, nieces . . ."

Slipper put up his hand in an imperious gesture. "Families betray, Deoga. Families are poison. The first thing the brothers learn is to forget. We have no parents, not really. Our parents died, or sold us, or were slaves themselves. And the brothers have no offspring. So we only have each other, and that not for very long. The brothers are like flowers; some bloom, some wither while we watch, others live on in memory, for a while at least. At last all will be forgotten, as I will be forgotten. For this I thank Allah who made me."

Slipper looked at Da Gama seriously. "Things are best that way, Deoga. Forgetting, not remembering. You farangs become encumbered with your past. The past drives you mad. It keeps you from acting sensibly."

⊘⊘⊘⊘

When the others went to their tents to sleep, Da Gama spent a long time gazing at the fire. After making sure that no one watched him, he reached beneath his pillow and took out a letter, and two similar cloth sacks. He smoothed the letter on the ground to catch the fire's light, and read it once again.

He'd received it from a courier, who'd found him after they'd stopped to make camp—a letter from Pathan. The *burak* wrote that he was taking everyone away from Belgaum, as Lady Chitra had requested. He planned to make for his family's estate at Konnur, then to proceed on toward Sunag, and hoped to meet Da Gama there.

Of course Da Gama had no map—only the image he had formed in his head from travelling in these parts. But he had not traveled here long, and so had only a vague notion of how far it was to Sunag.

Da Gama did some calculations. If all had gone as Pathan planned, then Lucinda and Maya and the rest were at this moment at Pathan's home in Konnur—a cottage on his farm, Pathan had called it. Da Gama wondered how everyone would be comfortable there.

They might reach Pathan and the others by tomorrow, if they traveled quickly. Da Gama made up his mind to start at dawn. They would be turning west tomorrow, into the Gokak hills, and the going would be slower.

Tomorrow, he thought. Tomorrow we meet them. Tomorrow the reckoning begins.

Or the day after, he thought ruefully. For such reckonings are never prompt.

He folded the letter, and then drew the two twin bags close to the fire. Only a few flames licked the glowing embers. Da Gama glanced in all directions. Nothing. He wondered if the Three-Dot clan were really nearby, watching from the shadows. He listened and heard nothing but tree frogs and the screech of owls. Not even a dog's bark, nor a jackal's wail. The silence unnerved him. Then a rattling snore began in Victorio's tent, and Da Gama smiled, feeling suddenly at ease.

He opened the bags casually, as though unconcerned that anyone should see. He poured their contents into his hand, and spread the empty bags near the fire. Then, with some care he arranged them on his bedroll: two headdresses, pearls and diamonds woven by gold thread into a delicate web. That at least was how it looked a first glance.

How easy would it be to tell them apart? A eunuch could tell—isn't that what the jeweler had said?

The plan had been percolating in his mind for days now. Should I do it? Da Gama wondered. After all, he said to himself, now I'm Victorio's partner.

He shook his head. Partners come and go, he repeated ruefully. Why do I hesitate? None of them would hesitate to cheat me.

Da Gama knew what was holding him back. The real headdress, which he now felt certain was the long-lost Web of Ruci, belonged to Maya. How could he bear to hurt her, she so innocent, so beautiful? He tried to think of her face; he tried to imagine her blank hatred if he put his plan in action. But he found his faulty memory could not even recall her perfection. Instead he thought of Lucinda and recalled her with uncanny clarity.

Won't your plan hurt her as well, he asked himself.

She's a murderer. What difference does it make?

A murderer? Because Victorio says so? And you believe him?

Da Gama squeezed his eyes tight, suddenly furious.

He scooped the twin headdresses into their bags and shoved them in his pockets.

Who is looking out for *me*? Da Gama thought. Who can't sleep for fretting about *my* welfare? The world is cruel, and I'm old enough to know that I too must be cruel. It's time I begin to think of myself.

Then the thought occurred to him: his plan would hurt Victorio worst of all. While he savored this, he stomped the dying fire with his big boots, and the embers showered in all directions, flying in the air like stars.

৩৩৩

Pathan and Geraldo rode ahead of the *palki*, two abreast. They never spoke.

From the *palki* Lucinda's gaze rarely left Pathan, though he never looked round toward her. The rigidity of his posture, usually so fluid but now so unyielding, convinced her that he burned with anger.

After rounding the Palace Lake, their road led through the town of Belgaum, and passed the dargah where Lucinda had gone with Pathan. It seemed to her now as if that had been someone else's life.

The whitewashed dome of the saint's tomb could just be seen above the compound walls. As they approached, Pathan placed his right hand on his heart, and bowed his head. Lucinda felt certain he would then break down and glance her way, but instead he straightened and looked steadfastly ahead. It struck her as a gesture of insolence, as if he hoped to show how little he cared for her, or for anyone.

Beyond the town, the road twisted through a mountain pass. Though not so dramatic and terrifying as the Sansagar pass, both women stirred with memories. Without a spoken word, they shifted their seats until they pressed against each other, and Lucinda curled her fingers around Maya's wrist. In that way they rode for miles as the sun soared in the cloudless sky; Lucinda staring at Pathan, Maya pretending to read.

On the plateau beyond the pass they stopped for lunch beneath a neem tree beside a tiny stream. While the women dipped their hands and washed, the *palki*wallah spread out blankets for them, with packages of food wrapped in banana leaves bound up in twine. Pathan ate standing near his horse, apart from everyone.

"He hates me," Lucinda whispered.

"No," said Maya.

"Why won't he speak to me, or even look at me?"

It took a moment for Maya to reply, while parrots in the neem tree chattered and the small stream laughed. "He is a man, and helpless. It must be you who acts, sister."

Lucinda lowered her eyes. "Then it's hopeless."

☙☙☙☙

As they rode east, Geraldo guided his horse closer to Pathan's. "I haven't been to this part of Hindustan before, Captain," he remarked casually.

"I understood you no longer wished to speak to me, sir."

"Forgive me, Captain. I spoke in haste."

Pathan considered the farang, then turned his face once more to the road. "I understand." But still they rode in silence for many miles.

At last Pathan turned back to Geraldo. "*Desejo.* What does it mean?"

Geraldo looked surprised. "It's Portuguese. Where did you hear it?"

"What does it mean?" Pathan insisted.

"It is a woman's word. Men would not use it." Geraldo watched Pathan's expression carefully before he added, "Hate. *Eu desejo tu*—I hate you. What a woman might say to a lover before she abandons him forever."

Pathan stared at Geraldo for a moment, his eyes burning. "I understand."

"Did Lucy . . ."

"If you were to forget I ever mentioned it, sir, I would be in your debt."

"Of course, Captain," Geraldo replied with a sweeping gesture. "Even so, I'd like to know . . ."

But Pathan had spurred his horse, and now trotted ahead. He rode apart from the others for the rest of the day's journey.

☙☙☙☙

As the sun lowered in the west and their shadows lengthened on the road before them, they reached the crest of a gentle rise. Lucinda's fingers tightened around Maya's arm when she saw what lay ahead, and Maya looked up, and her book fell from her fingers.

In front of them spread a great verdant valley. Aside from tall groves of ancient trees scattered here and there, every inch of soil burst forth with grapevines.

Now with the monsoons past, the vines exploded with new life: leaves of bright, clear green; flowers and tiny fruits of butter yellow; and fresh tendrils twisting in such profusion that from a distance the plants appeared like a mist above the ground. The least imaginative *palki* bearer looked around and sighed, for in those vines, those leaves, one saw the celebration of life by life. Silent, enthusiastic and triumphant, from the soil and the sun the vines made fruit. The valley pulsed; it sang with life.

"Hey, Munna," called the *palki*wallah. "We're almost home!"

For the first time that whole trip, Pathan looked back. His face was radiant. Lucinda could not remember the last time he had smiled so. Munna, she thought. That is how they know him here. This is how he wished for me to know him. She forced herself to look away, so she would not see his smile fade if he should glance her way.

"Is your home near here?" Geraldo asked. Pathan nodded. "Da Gama said your family had a farm."

"This is my farm, sir."

"What part is yours?"

Pathan said nothing, but swept his open hand before him across the whole wide vista. Geraldo let out a low whistle. "And a cottage, he said."

Again Pathan nodded, and lifted his hand toward a place below them where a dark row of trees extended from a dogleg in the twisting yellow road. "My cottage is down there, sir, amongst those trees. We shall be there soon."

The *palki* bearers walked more briskly now; home was close. As they trotted down the hill, the *palki* bounced. Lucinda found it oddly exhilarating.

Here the vines grew up to the very edge of the road: she could look through the rows of trellises as they passed and see the dark green shadows cast by the bright leaves. The air held a perfume reminiscent of wine and honey.

They made good time now, for the way was easier, and their bearers' hearts were lighter. At the bottom of the hill, in the valley's most fertile part, the vines were tall and the grapes already prominent. A few hundred yards ahead, Pathan turned down the drive of sweeping neem trees that sheltered the path to his home.

At the end of a tunnel of overhanging branches, they saw a long colonnade of graceful stone arches. As they came closer Lucinda realized that the arches were of marble of a pale pink-golden color. It reminded her of the color of her own flesh, and Maya's.

Pathan dismounted briskly, and came to Geraldo. "See that the women are comfortable, out of courtesy." His face looked so distraught that even Geraldo understood—he couldn't bear to face Lucinda. Pathan introduced him to his housekeeper, Shaheen, just as the *palki* bearers reached the clearing.

ଈଓଓଡ଼ଓ

Shaheen looked as if she ate only bitter food, Lucinda thought, and not much of that. That would explain Shaheen's prominent collarbone and sternum, and the ropy veins on her thin arms, and her pursed and frowning lips. She eyed the visitors suspiciously.

Sour-faced Shaheen led them through the colonnade, which wrapped around the house. A servant carried the women's simple baggage. She gave a polite summary of the history of the family, and the house, and the vineyards surrounding. Lucinda got the impression that she did not like being so polite. She wondered what Pathan had told her.

From time to time they passed vaulted halls that led to an inner courtyard, and caught glimpses of its formal garden and splashing fountains. On the far side of the house the hill dropped away, and the verandah overlooked the valley rich with grapes.

"With all these vines, you must make wine—and yet the captain does not drink?" Geraldo said. He smiled to Lucinda and Maya, as if inviting them to share the humor of his ironic observation.

Shaheen tried to look pleasant, though in truth her face seemed unused to the expression. "It is the business of this family for many generations, sir. But Munna is a sheikh, so naturally he does not drink." She opened a doorway to a spacious, airy room. Through windows on the other side came the sound of water splashing in the fountains. "This will be your room, madam," Shaheen said to Lucinda.

"We would stay together, if that would be convenient," Maya said. Shaheen frowned but shrugged acceptance. "I'll show the gentleman his room and then come to see that you are comfortable." Geraldo gave the women an amused, ironic look, and followed Shaheen. They heard the fading echo of his bootheels against the stone tiles of the colonnade.

"His home is so beautiful," Lucinda said when Shaheen had left. Against the polished plaster walls, the room had two low beds. The floors were marble tiles set in a Persian star, and a half-dozen lamps with pierced shades hung from the high beamed ceiling ready for lighting. Lucinda felt tears welling as she moved to the courtyard window. A hummingbird whizzed past as she approached, and darted for the safety of a nearby rose bush. Water cascaded down a stairstep fountain, babbling cheerfully.

There was not much to unpack. Servants brought salvers and basins, and delicate towels of lawn. As they finished washing their hands, Shaheen reappeared. "I didn't mean to be abrupt. That man made me uncomfortable."

"He is my cousin, madam," Lucinda said.

Shaheen's face, so sour before, softened as she looked at her guest. "Munna told me a little."

"Who is Munna?" Maya asked.

"Pathan," Lucinda answered, and then looking at Shaheen, she blushed.

"The older servants still call him by his boyhood name," Shaheen said with a glance toward Lucinda. "I took care of him mostly, after his mother died. He is as a son to me." Shaheen again considered Lucinda. "Would you like to see his home?"

"Yes, please," Lucinda said. Then she blushed again.

ↄ৹ↄ৹

Once alone with other women, Shaheen appeared much more at ease. Still her gaze kept drifting toward Lucinda. Lucinda supposed that Shaheen had not had much contact with farangs.

It was unusual, Shaheen reflected, for a woman to steward an estate like this, but her father had been steward to Munna's father, and the role had passed to her hands so gradually and completely that no one seemed to notice exactly when the change had happened. Some had voiced their disapproval, but her Munna had soon silenced them.

For Shaheen each tile, each column, each nick and crack in the polished plaster had a history attached. As they walked, Shaheen gave the house a voice. Pathan's house, Lucinda soon realized, held much of Pathan's memory, and that of all his family. From time to time Lucinda's fingers strayed to brush against a wall, as though the impressions lodged there might flow directly through her hands.

They spent a long time in the garden, where Shaheen named each flower and shrub, and often recalled whose hands had planted it. The low, gold light of the sun cast mysterious shadows. Bees and hummingbirds whirred past, attracted by the perfumed nectar everywhere.

Shaheen halted near some white roses to show them the very tile where Pathan's elder brother had tripped and broken his skull. "He died a few days later. My Munna was inconsolable. They had been playing, you see, running and shouting against their father's rule of quiet. My Munna felt responsible for Abu's death. It made him serious, and very melancholy." She glanced again at Lucinda, who grew uncomfortable beneath her gaze and turned her face.

After seeing the whole house, Shaheen guided them to some outlying buildings. "Have you a husband, Shaheen?" Maya asked.

"It was not my portion in this life." But she smiled and then said, "But I have my Munna. That must be enough, yes? I suppose I miss having a husband"—she gave a sly look to Maya—"but not so much, I think. My Munna is such a fine young man, I would always be comparing, I think. And who could compare, I wonder?"

Though she did not look toward Shaheen, Lucinda could feel again the housekeeper's gaze. She wondered at it, and guessed that Pathan had spoken of her to Shaheen. What had he said?

Shaheen showed the two the winepress, configured so an ox could power the squeezing of the grapes, and the storehouse—a long man-made cavern where by the flickering light of butter lamps they saw row upon row of red clay jars. "Here the wine is made. These jars will be sold soon." She glided past many racks of jars. "It's always cool here. Munna would come here and sit for hours in the summer. He said it reminded him of a tomb. But I think he simply wanted to avoid the heat."

They clambered up the stairs at the other end of the storehouse, and emerged in a kind of park—a wide lawn shaded by the great branches of old trees. To the east, the sky was darkening, to the west, erupting with color from the sunset. Shaheen led them toward a whitewashed wall, and through an iron gate. "Here are the graves of many of the family. Most everyone is buried here, near the home and vines they cared for."

It made Maya think of Lady Chitra's garden—so many trees, so many flowers clustered around the stark white marble graves. Many graves were marked, as Muslim graves often were, with simple triangular prisms of stone, about the size of a person. Some stones had a soft, uneven look from years of weather. Some were draped with cloth, and one or two were sprinkled with fresh flower petals.

A kind of house had been built at one end of the compound. Painted panels on its walls showed pitchers, and cups, and leaves, and twisting vines. Shaheen was saying who was buried there, but Lucinda's attention was drawn instead to a small domed building at the other end of the compound. Without a word, she found herself walking toward it.

It was like a smaller version of the saint's dargah in Belgaum. Uncertain about the etiquette of the place, she did not pass the threshold, but peered into the shadowed interior. A wild notion popped into her mind that Pathan would be there, kneeling as he'd knelt at the dargah. But it was empty, though the grave cloth was heaped with fresh flowers, and the oil lamp's wick was newly trimmed.

"Come away!" Lucinda turned to see Shaheen behind her, frowning. "That is a saint's tomb, and women may not enter." Lucinda lowered her head, and followed Shaheen down the tile pathway, when she stopped and caught her breath.

She'd seen a figure kneeling, huddled by a grave, and supposed it must be a gardener. But when the man leaned back, she saw, of course, Pathan himself. He appeared not to notice her, nor anyone: his eyes were closed tight, and his folded hands pressed hard against his face. Shaheen raised a finger to her lips, and drew Lucinda from the place. She caught up with Maya, and then, still silent, led the two outside the gate.

As she hurried them back to the house, Shaheen whispered, "It is his wife's grave. He's never gotten over it, I think. She died giving birth. It would have a been son, if he'd been born alive. She was too young . . . so pretty, so willing, but too young. My Munna made them place the baby in her arms and bury them together. His heart is very tender. He doesn't like for anyone to see him mourn, or even to know that he has visited her grave."

☙☙☙☙

The women returned to find that the lamps in their room had been lit. They watched the last flames of sunset paint the twilight sky. Soon the flickering flames through the pierced metal shades were their only light.

Supper appeared. After they had eaten, Shaheen knocked, and asked if they had everything they needed. While the women expressed their gratitude Shaheen again turned prune-faced, and moved purposefully around the room, shuttering windows and straightening cushions. Maya, realizing from Shaheen's meaningful glances that she wished to be alone with Lucinda, told the others that she needed some fresh air.

When they were alone, Shaheen sat across from Lucinda, so close their knees nearly touched. "You leave tomorrow at the break of dawn, so I have no time to waste on pleasantries. I must know: What have you done to my boy? Why did you spurn his love?"

Lucinda felt as if Shaheen had stabbed her. "Who are you to ask this? Why do you accuse me so?"

"Do you know how hard it is for him to love? His is a great heart, and so it takes a great flame to heat it, and it then takes a long time to melt. Yet you have melted his heart. I know this. I don't know why he loves you. No matter. It is his great heart that matters to me. He is all the family I have left." Shaheen lifted her face to Lucinda, and its earnestness was unnerving. "He loves you. Do you love him?"

Shaheen's pronounced the question with such gravity that Lucinda could not answer. As she stared back mute, Shaheen's harsh face softened. "Oh, you are but a girl," she sighed. "You don't even know your power over him. He is in turmoil over you."

"How was I to know this?"

"Is such ignorance common to farangs? I ask you quite sincerely. Do you really not know?"

"How should I know it? He has not spoken to me all day . . . not even looked at me all day!"

Shaheen reached out and placed her hand on Lucinda's. "Even a farang should know. You should know it by the way he has not spoken to you . . . the way he has not looked at you."

"Did he speak to you about me?" Shaheen nodded, and was about to answer when Lucinda lifted her hand. "Don't tell me what he said. I could not bear it."

"They were most pleasant words . . ."

"Then even less could I bear to hear. Did he not tell you? I am pledged to another. I am on my way to meet my husband."

Shaheen sat straight and stared at Lucinda as if seeing her for the first time. Then she lifted her hands to her head, and began to rise. "I was wrong to come. I did not know."

Lucinda felt tears spill down her cheeks. "He is my uncle and an old man. That is my portion in this life."

Shaheen shook her head. "I will go now."

She had reached the door when Lucinda called after her. "Every day I will think of him."

She never found out if Shaheen had heard.

ᘓᘔᘓᘔ

"What did she want?" Maya asked when she returned.

"She'd never seen a corset," Lucinda lied. She had curled up on the low rope bed and drawn the blanket over her. Maya frowned at the answer—she thought about it for a while but then let it go. "What difference does it make?" Lucinda added later, as if she'd never stopped thinking about answering. "We'll be gone tomorrow, so what difference does it make?"

"I don't think we're going, sister. Not tomorrow. A storm's brewing out there."

The shutters rattled all night. Wind keened through the cracks around the doors and windows, and for several hours, the rain beat drumlike on the roof. Then thunder: sometimes like a rumbling snore; sometimes like the crack of great bones snapping.

"I thought the monsoon was over," Lucinda said.

"I've heard of late storms in the mountains."

"Just when you think it's over, it starts up again," Lucinda said into the noisy darkness.

"What's wrong with that?" Maya laughed. But Lucinda did not answer.

Maya was right; the storm rained so fiercely the next morning that they could not travel. Shaheen brought shawls of Kashmir wool, soft and warm. Her eyes never met Lucinda's. This is how she apologizes, Lucinda thought, coming round in silence, standing close but never looking at me. Shaheen's behavior explained much about Pathan's.

After breakfast she and Maya walked along the verandah. The wind blew fresh and wet and cold, and after a long night's fitful sleep, Lucinda felt refreshed. Rain danced across puddles that had formed at the verandah's edge, and sometimes Lucinda and Maya had to jump over one to keep their feet dry.

As they turned a corner, Lucinda saw Pathan. He stood with his back to them, looking over the verandah at the mist swirling through the valley. Lucinda hoisted up her heavy rag-hooped skirts and ran away. Near her door she passed Geraldo and with neither look nor word pushed past him, closed the door and threw her back against it.

She had barely caught her breath when she heard the gentle knocking. She could not stop herself from hoping, and so was disappointed when she opened the door and found Geraldo, with his ironic smile and neat mustache.

Reluctantly she let him in. "You must learn to trust me, Lucy." She sat on the foot of her low bed, watching as he walked idly around the room. "Who else is so honest with you as I? You know all about me now—I have revealed all."

He turned and faced her, and she saw the same attractive friendly face she had first seen in Goa a few weeks before. And it was true: he had never hidden his intentions, nasty as they were. She wondered what he was up to now.

"I know you have feelings for the *burak*. Do you want me to help?"

"Why would you help me?"

"We are cousins, are we not? And among these strangers, the only farangs. Surely that places a burden on us to help each other." He looked aside, and said as if casually, "Besides, some day you may be in a position to do me a good turn."

Lucinda's eyes closed slowly as she realized how much she had changed— no longer Aldo's baby cousin nearly grown up, now Lucinda had become another angle he must play; another source of wealth and power where he could beg favors.

So this is how it is, she thought. I will make the best of it.

"Yes, cousin. You might do me a good turn. Give Pathan a message for me." She then spoke Hindi. "Tell him that my feelings are the same as his. Tell him I regret that he ever thought differently."

Geraldo's eyebrows went up, and he gave Lucinda an approving look. "You have grown up, cousin." He bowed with a flourish and rose with his infuriating smile.

Lucinda glared at him. "Do not betray me, Aldo. Do this honestly or don't do it at all."

Geraldo tried to appear hurt. "Would you doubt me? Don't you know that in the future we shall be quite close? This confidence will bring us even closer. Besides, if I cared to bring your man a false message, I need not have even spoken to you."

"Tell him exactly what I told you."

In Hindi, Geraldo repeated, "That your feelings are the same as his? That you regret that he ever thought differently?" Then in Portuguese, he said. "Really, cousin, I'm offended that you mistrust me. I'll deliver your message just as you say. I shall do so right now."

"Then I shall be forever in your debt."

"That you shall, dear Lucy. I shall enjoy collecting what you owe." When he reached the door he smiled again, his even white teeth sparkling in his dark face. "With any luck, you'll enjoy it, too."

ඉලඉල

Geraldo easily found Pathan, for he had not moved since Lucinda saw him. Geraldo found a wall to lean against and began to chat with him. He focused all his charm on the *burak,* and even Pathan crumbled beneath it.

They spoke of everything: starting with the weather, they soon turned to trade, and politics; and to the personalities of people that they knew and did not know. Pathan paid special attention to Geraldo's description of Victorio. "An old man of nasty disposition—that's how I remember him, sir, though it was years ago."

The rain continued to fall, though the sun had risen enough to turn the clouds above them a painful glaring gray. And as Geraldo hoped, it was Pathan who first brought up Lucinda's name, and only after a few uncertain, diffident remarks did Geraldo begin to speak of her earnest.

"But you had feelings for her, sir," Geraldo said as if genuinely concerned, "Maybe you still do?"

Pathan looked at him, and his mouth worked before he spoke, as if the words were hard to say. "I did. I was . . . I was fond of her."

"How do you feel now, sir?" Geraldo asked. "Hateful perhaps? Hostile?"

Pathan's eyes flashed. "I feel"—he struggled to find the word—"indifferent. What is it to you?"

"Because I bring you a message, sir. From Lucinda. I wanted to understand your feelings first."

"Tell me!"

Geraldo gave Pathan a long, searching look that he hoped appeared sincere. "Remember, these are her words to you, sir. I promised I would tell them exactly as she told me. She says: tell Pathan that my feelings are the same as his. She says: tell Pathan that I regret that he ever thought differently." Geraldo lifted his hands and shrugged. "Cruel words, I thought at first—but now I see that you too are indifferent toward her. So maybe it is all for the best, sir?"

But Pathan turned to the swirling mists and stared silently into their depths until Geraldo slipped away.

ᘓᘓᘓᓀ

The storm moved off in the afternoon, leaving the air thick and cold with moisture, that dank cold that takes away all warmth and chills the soul.

Lucinda still had the shawl Pathan had lent her. That day now seemed far away. She pulled it round her shoulders, and sat on the low divan, and waited.

Maya, once more in a corner with the Gita on her lap, watched her. "But what are you waiting for?"

"Good news. Or bad," Lucinda answered.

When the knock came, Lucinda leaped to her feet, nearly tripping on her heavy skirts. But she stopped before she opened the door, to breathe, and pat her hair, and set her face.

Neither woman wanted to see the man that stood there. "This could make a fellow lose his confidence," Geraldo said, glancing at their faces. "I gave him your message," he then said softly to Lucinda. "As I promised you, I used your very words."

"And?"

"He gave no answer."

Time changed for Lucinda. Perhaps she waited only for an eyeblink, perhaps an hour before her thoughts began to work again. At last she managed to speak. "He said nothing?"

"Nothing, my dear cousin. He seemed . . . perturbed." Geraldo glanced at Maya, who had carefully buried her eyes in her book, and then took Lucinda's hand and kissed it. "He does not realize what treasure he has cast aside."

"Men are fools." It was Maya who spoke, without lifting her face.

"Yes," Geraldo said, looking uncomfortable. "Yes, we are fools." He nodded to Lucinda, and stepped out the door.

ᘐᘎᘐᘎ

That night instead of sleeping, Maya and Lucinda lay on their low rope beds and talked in the dark. Shaheen, along with supper, had brought news for them: they would leave Konnur tomorrow, and would likely meet Da Gama, Victorio, and Slipper by sunset. So in the dark, they talked, like sisters who would soon be parted.

They spoke of seeing one another in the howdah for the first time, of meeting Da Gama and Geraldo, of Slipper. They remembered Silvia, and Brother Fernando's long embraces. They remembered the bandits, and Da Gama's bravery and Pathan's. Lucy cried a little then.

They spoke of Belgaum, and the strange magic of the place—Maya's dreams, and blind Chitra, and Lakshmi, and the palace by the lake. And when they spoke of Geraldo, Maya wept.

They wondered what would happen to them now, and those thoughts were dark. Maya wondered what the eunuchs meant to do with her. She could not bear to say what she expected.

For her part, Lucinda tried to imagine Tio Victorio ten years older than the last time she had seen him. Then, aloud, she wondered what it would mean to be his bride.

It was hard to think such things, and they felt sleep call to them. In the dark cold air of night they could hear the sound of a lone voice singing a qwali. "That's coming from the graveyard," Lucinda said. The song poured out like the sound of a heart breaking, the far-off voice alternately quavering and strong, full of grief and triumph. Death seemed close, like an uninvited guest.

Finally one of them mentioned the word. And then they could not sleep.

Then they whispered, those two women, so young and full of life, for they spoke dreadful thoughts: Did it hurt to die by *arsênico*? How long would one suffer? To poison another, or to kill oneself—which brought the greater comfort?

And if another was to die, then who deserved it most?

At last they fell asleep, their dreams full of poison and of death.

ᗋᗌᗋᗌ

They awoke to find that Da Gama had come.

Shaheen brought the news with breakfast. After she set down the tray, she opened the shutters. Bright morning sun streamed through. She hurried them out of bed, saying Da Gama was waiting in the courtyard. She clearly liked him, even though he was a farang, and though she had never met him before. Maybe Pathan had given her some sign of his affection for old Deoga. As she left, she urged them to hurry.

Perhaps it was the way Shaheen's excitement lit up her sour face, or perhaps it was the brightness of the morning that dispelled last night's dread. They rushed like children: washed, dressed, packed up their few belongings, ate a bite of breakfast, and arm in arm hurried along the verandah.

"My dear daughters!" Da Gama called out when he saw them. He held out his arms as a father might, and they ran to him and embraced him. Then he stepped back and looked them over, shaking his head.

"Why, Deoga, whatever's wrong?" Maya asked. She had never seen his face so troubled; in truth she had rarely seen a man whose face showed so much anguish.

"Oh, nothing, nothing," Deoga said, turning away. "I am so happy to see you."

"We know why you cry," Lucinda answered. Maya looked at her, and was surprised to see how Lucinda's face grew taut and her eyes narrowed. "We have wept as well."

Da Gama faced Lucinda, and his voice trembled. "You know nothing about me, nor about my tears." Suddenly he turned gruff. "Get in the *palki*. We'll be going."

"Is Pathan going with us?" Maya asked.

"I didn't think you'd care, daughter." Da Gama shook his head. "Not with us. He says he'll follow later, on horseback. It seems he doesn't like the company."

ᏋᎧᏋᎧ

Pathan watched from the verandah. He only came forward when he saw that the women settled in the *palki*. He approached from behind where they could not see.

Da Gama realized his tactic, and went to join him. "What happened between you?"

"It is nothing, Deoga. They have mixed feelings about departure—why should I add more trouble?"

Da Gama stared at Pathan. Then he lifted his hands as if to show that Pathan could have his secrets. "You are kind to lend me your *palki* and bearers. I thought to hire one in Belgaum. I didn't expect to meet you so soon."

"You need not explain again, sir. It is the least a friend may do. Treat the bearers with kindness, as you would treat your own servants."

Da Gama laughed. "No, I'll have to treat them better than that!" Again he looked quizzically at Pathan. "Are you sure you are well?"

For a long time Pathan did not answer, but stared at the *palki*, "I would have done anything, you know, Deoga. In the end, I was ready to take on any burden, or to give up everything. My heart no longer cared for me. It had become hers. In the end I would have sacrificed all, but she spurned me. Why then do I still yearn for her?"

"What? Have you fallen in love? Not with the nautch girl?"

Pathan drew back his gaze from the *palki.* "You must be off, Deoga. Here comes your man Geraldo."

"Are you sure you're well, Pathan? Come with us, why don't you? At least say goodbye to the women?"

Pathan's face grew stern. "No. Let them go with no more intrusions." Then he drew himself up stiffly. "I shall meet you in Bijapur for the settlement, Deoga. Wali Khan's concerns must be addressed, sir, and I still am his *burak.* Until Wali Khan's interests are satisfied, I shall not be satisfied. If your master, Victorio, tries to renege, I myself shall settle matters properly!" Though he raised his voice, all this while Pathan smiled broadly at Da Gama as if business were now the only bond between them.

Da Gama felt suddenly weary. He shuffled his feet and at last looked up. "Look, Pathan, you've told me often that you owe me a favor . . ."

Pathan lifted his hand. "I love you, sir, but do not ask for what I cannot give. Take what you will from me—I offer all my wealth to you, even my life. But I cannot give what is not mine. Do not ask me to rob my master for you. Do not take away my honor."

"Very well, sir. We'll sort things out in Bijapur. We should be there in three days' time."

Pathan looked crushed. "Ask a different favor, Deoga. Let me repay you."

"Never mind. I've always said it was a trifle. Not worth all this fuss."

"Someday I will repay you. Until that time, *salaam.*" Pathan lowered his head and raised his hands in deep formality, and then turned and walked back to the long low stairs of the verandah. He did not turn, nor wave.

"*Aleichem salaam,*" Da Gama whispered after him, and then he turned to the *palki.* Whatever pleasure his arrival had brought initially now had faded: the women's faces were as grave as his own. Da Gama leaned in to Lucinda and nodded toward the house. "Don't you want to say goodbye, Lucy? He saved your life."

She took so long to answer, Da Gama began to wonder if she were well. "No," Lucinda said at last. "He took it from me." She pulled the curtain of the *palki* closed.

Da Gama's shadow appeared in the curtain as an unfocused silhouette. Maya leaned across the cushions to Lucinda. "It was not Pathan who took your life, sister. It was Victorio," Maya whispered. "I have not yet even met him, and he has taken mine as well."

Neither moved for a long time. Lucinda stared into Maya's gold-flecked eyes. It was as if they no longer needed words, as though in silence they had formed a pact.

ᏣᎣᏣᏓ

The rain had cleaned the air and the morning light sparkled sharp as diamonds. Puddles lingered in the road, reflecting the crisp blue sky. Cleaned by the rain, the sword grass poked from the ground glinting wet. Every green leaf glistened in the morning sun.

Da Gama mounted, and rode once round the courtyard, checking the *palki* and the bearers, and then drawing up next to Geraldo's horse. "Let's go," was all he said. The *palki* bearers grunted and hoisted the *palki* onto their shoulders; inside its railing, the women lurched.

"It's not far," Da Gama told Geraldo. "We made good time yesterday— it was all downhill from Sunag, or so it seemed." Geraldo smiled indulgently. "What happened, Geraldo? What happened to Pathan?"

Geraldo shrugged. "The man has problems, sir. He is lonesome and melancholy. It is a risky combination."

"Love," Da Gama said, with the same resigned horror that one might say the word "treachery."

"As you say, Deoga. The *burak* took it in his head that Lucy fancied him."

"What, Lucy?" Da Gama's eyebrows shot up. "Well? Did she fancy him?"

Geraldo shrugged again. "With women, who can tell, sir? Maybe for a day or for an hour. Such is woman's love. In any case, I steered him right."

"How?"

"I made up some story. Told him Lucy hates him. That cooled things down."

"But you say she fancied him?" Da Gama seemed genuinely confused.

"She hates him now!" With a satisfied shake of his head, again Geraldo chuckled. "She had me bring him some pathetic message. It was quite grotesque. Naturally I embellished it a little. I suppose she thought he'd come racing back to her. Nothing like. Not when I was done: he hates her; she hates him, and all is well."

Da Gama considered Geraldo with a frown. "It seems you have been busy, sir."

Geraldo's eyes flashed. "He's a heathen—and she's pledged! What would you expect me to do? Encourage them?"

"Calm yourself, sir," Da Gama answered, raising his hands as if he'd been attacked.

Geraldo's facile smile returned. "I begin to see that you are sentimental, Deoga." His face grew stern. "This was business."

"*Ahcha,*" Da Gama said.

❧❧❧

Once they had passed beneath the trees that lined the drive of Pathan's estate, and turned onto the Sunag road, Lucinda allowed herself to weep. She hid her face, and through her fingers watched the house and vineyards disappear into the distance.

Lucinda had stood by her mother's bed the moment she died. She had watched the long, slow sigh of her mother's last breath, and the stillness that came upon her; the fading of her face, already pale, as the color left her lips and cheeks; the way the delicate tissues of her nostrils and her tongue dried, like petals drying in the sun. Now as she watched Pathan's home fade behind her, she had that same feeling, as of a tearing; as of a bright, beating light ripped from her heart. Her throat ached from holding back her sobs.

Maya pretended not to see.

The sun rose higher, and in the cloudless sky bore down on them like a weight. The road grew dry, and then dusty. The *palki* bearers' shuffling gait raised a gritty cloud. The vineyards came to an end as they pushed up a hill. On the other side, the road was yellow and bare, and the ground rocky and untended, and there was no shade. Soon their eyes ached with longing for the cool greens of Konnur.

For lunch they stopped near a large broken rock, nearly as big as a house, and tucked the *palki* close to catch what little shade it offered. The air around the rock quivered with rising heat.

"We'll wait here for a while. Wait for the sun to fall a little," Da Gama said. No one ate much. The *palki* bearers squeezed next to the base of the rock. Geraldo found a shadowed niche and curled inside to nap.

Lucinda longed for the cool silk of the saris she wore in Belgaum. Dust clung to her hot skin. Maya had retreated to that quiet, imperturbable state that she found when she was traveling, and neither spoke, nor looked up. From time to time, she flipped the page of her palm-leaf Gita, while Lucinda looked on with envy. At last she lay on the cushions of the *palki* and tried to sleep.

After a half hour or so she saw Da Gama approach the *palki.* "This is yours," he said to Maya holding out a cloth sack. His voice was gruff, and his mouth tense, and he seemed more uncomfortable than Lucinda had ever seen. She pretended to move in her sleep to get a better look. The cloth sack that Da Gama now placed in Maya's lap was the one she had seen in Valpoi: the sack that held the wedding headdress.

When Maya began to open it, Da Gama laid his thick fingers on her hand. "Do you trust me?"

"Of course, Deoga."

"That sack—what's in the sack, I mean—that's what the eunuchs want. Not you."

"It's all I have left of my mother . . . of my history. If they take it, they take me as well."

Da Gama's hand closed on Maya's, and Lucinda realized that he was in love. It was such an unexpected revelation, she nearly sat up. Da Gama seemed very old to Lucinda, and Maya so young, but she saw that his heart smoldered for her. And she saw that he was timid and uncertain—him, at his age! She wondered if Maya saw it as clearly as she did.

"I do not like the part I'm forced to play." His voice was hoarse. "I'm doing my best, but . . ."

"We all must play our roles, Deoga. It is what my book says . . ."— Maya nodded to her palm-leaf Gita—". . . the song of God himself: play the role God gives you, knowing it is He in every heart." Her face was not innocent, but full of understanding: the face of one who had endured, without yet turning bitter.

Da Gama could not bear the compassion in her serene, unwavering gaze, and looked away, and stammered something, and stormed off.

After a few moments, Lucinda rose. Twenty yards away, Da Gama, with his back toward the *palki,* swung his fists at the open air, and they could hear him cursing. "What was that about?" Lucinda yawned.

Maya nodded toward the sack. She was not so calm, Lucinda realized, as she seemed at first. "May I see?" Lucinda took the sack and began to open it.

"Don't . . . not now." Maya's pretense of calm completely disappeared. "No, never mind what I say. Go ahead and look . . ."

Her expression puzzled Lucinda. At last she worked the knot loose, and lifted out partway the jeweled headdress she had seen in Valpoi.

"Stop . . . that's enough." Maya looked at the headdress, and then turned her head. "I've never seen it in the sunlight. Please put it back."

"It looked much grander in the lamplight. In the sun it looks so . . ."

"It looks cheap and false," Maya said, finishing her thoughts. "Children live in make-believe. I will be a child no more. Put it back."

Lucinda did as Maya asked.

"All these years . . ." Maya murmured, "I believed a fantasy. What did my mother really give me? False diamonds, and a broken sword. If that's what the *hijras* want, let them have it. Let them have me, too. I no longer care." She looked at Da Gama, who still paced angrily far off. "But I thought that somewhere in this world there still was . . . goodness." Her voice trailed off.

"You hoped for goodness, sister. So did I . . ." Lucinda gave back the sack to Maya, and then touched her hand. "I think we were very foolish, you and I."

ꙮ

A couple of hours after the sun reached its zenith, Da Gama got everyone moving once more. The road led upward now, ever upward, and the sun screamed down, and there was no shade. The bearers were silent, and their breath came hard.

The sun cooked Da Gama's thoughts. They bubbled in his mind like a stew on a fire.

He had felt angry at himself for miles, after he gave Maya the imitation headdress. He hadn't expected to feel so wicked. For a while he thought about going back to her, putting the original in her lap, saying sweetly that it had been an error.

Slowly his rational mind reemerged. No harm had been done yet, after all. There was still time to alter the plan if need be, after all. She might never even see the difference, after all. And who knew what fortune would bring for her? Why should the eunuchs have her headdress. Why should Da Gama not keep it?

Keep it safe, he corrected himself.

Yes, of course. Keep it safe, his rational mind affirmed.

Then growing weary of this introspection, Da Gama started to consider what Geraldo had said. It didn't hang together somehow.

Da Gama considered speaking with Lucy, but not now, he decided, not with Maya there to listen. But by placing sweet young Lucy in the center of his thinking, instead of Geraldo, the earlier conversation took on a different cast. Why had Lucy sent a message to Pathan? Why had Geraldo felt that he needed to embellish it? Why had he been so concerned about the two of them?

From Da Gama's slow imagination, the answers began to emerge. He wheeled his horse around and drew up next to Geraldo.

"You lied to me," he growled.

"Sir! Whatever do you mean?"

Da Gama lowered his voice to harsh whisper. "I mean about Lucy, and the *burak*."

Geraldo's face hardened. "It happened as I said."

"No. You left something out. She was fond of him. Admit it!"

"Fond?" Geraldo sneered. "Maybe, or maybe not. With a woman who can tell?"

"A man can tell."

Geraldo let the implication hang without a comment. "Well, if she was fond of him, what of it?"

"Then you had no business interfering. Her feelings are no business of yours!"

"Apparently you think they're your business." His dark, malevolent eyes denied Geraldo's sardonic smile. "She's my cousin, sir. I have a responsibility to my family, and I shall execute it as I see fit. Since you are my family's employee, I trust you know your place and you'll keep your opinions to yourself."

It doesn't pay to be his relative, Da Gama remembered saying of Geraldo in Goa. "I'm a cousin, too, you know. Distant maybe, but still family."

"You'll never be my family, sir. Besides, I had reasons for my actions, reasons that a man may claim despite the opinions of his employees."

"Like what?"

"What if I love her, eh?"

Da Gama's eyes widened.

"What if it cut my heart to see Lucinda throwing herself at some black-souled heathen? A man might do a hundred things in such a case, and who would blame him? Other than you, I mean. You who know so much about affairs of love."

"You . . ." Da Gama bit his tongue and chose his words carefully. "You are not suitable for her."

"Why? Because I am poor? I won't be poor forever."

"Because you are a liar, sir."

Geraldo broke into an unguarded laugh. "Unsuitable because I am a liar? By the Virgin, I always assumed dissembling was the very key to a happy marriage!" Once more Geraldo's eyes grew sharp, and his face now did not hide his anger. "Good lord, man—do you think Victorio will make a better match?"

"What can be done about that? He's her guardian!"

Geraldo's eyes hooded, and his face grew guarded. "We shall see what may be done. One thing's clear enough, however. You have no right to interfere. Say nothing! Especially to her!"

"Or what?" Da Gama bristled.

Without replying, Geraldo spurred his horse and galloped off.

Da Gama stared after him. He expected him to halt up ahead. Instead, Geraldo picked up speed, spurring his horse with a violent effort. "Wait for us!" Da Gama shouted after him, but maybe he didn't hear.

At last he disappeared, leaving Da Gama alone with his thoughts, remembering what else he'd said that night in Goa.

People die around him.

CRCAD

Hours later, in the late afternoon, the landscape changed. Instead of the long, endless rise they'd plodded up all day, here the road twisted over a series of craggy passes. The baked yellow grasslands grew suddenly green. Trees appeared again—how welcome was their shade! Gray-black rocks thrust from the soil, furred with tufts of grass.

The air grew cool and a breeze blew. They could smell the moisture in it like a perfume.

Da Gama halted everyone for a rest before the final leg. "There's a river near here," he told them. "We're close to Gokak Falls. Our camp's on the other side of those hills . . . not far, but the roads here are hard. Hearing this, the *palki* bearers groaned.

As the bottom of the orange sun touched the horizon, they mounted a final craggy rise. "There," Da Gama said. At the foot of the hill, they saw the camp amid the shadows of the trees: three large tents, and around a fire, a half-dozen smaller ones.

CRCAD

"Old friends reunited!" Slipper came toward them, beaming. He wore elegant *jamas*, and rings on every finger, but, as usual, the end of his turban had come loose, though this one was silk, heavy with gold thread.

"Where's Victorio?" Da Gama asked.

But Slipper walked right past him, though he chattered all the while. "Oh, he's in his tent with Senhor Geraldo. They have much to talk about, it seems. Where are my sisters?" He bounded to the *palki*. "Here they are, as beautiful as ever!"

He brushed the *palki*wallah aside, and held out his hand, bowing as he helped Lucinda out, and then Maya. "Dear me, you two look so serious!" he said. "You must have wine. We are all drinking wine! And tonight, a feast!" He held out his hand for Maya's bag, but she snatched it away. Slipper shrugged, but his small eyes gleamed.

Talking nonstop, he led them to the clearing, quiet and cool in the setting sun. When Slipper took a breath, they could hear from afar the sound of the river.

"See how grand our accommodations are!" Slipper spread his arms expansively, as if he himself had made the arrangements. The three large tents were laid out in the clearing like points on a wheel; in their midst carpets and cushions had been set near a campfire. A rough-looking cook nodded to them, and then returned to turning his spit; a goat sizzled, wet with juices.

Da Gama tethered his horse and started to take off its saddle. "Why are there no guards?"

"Oh, Deoga, you must learn to enjoy yourself. They're sleeping, most of them. One or two went to the falls. This is a picnic, not a battlefield!" Da Gama scowled at him, and Slipper shook his head. "Oh, don't be a grump and spoil everybody's fun! I shall show the women to their tent. You'll want to change before the feast!" Still chattering, though the women followed silently, he held the entrance flap of the large tent, and bowed them in.

Da Gama led his horse to where the animals were being kept. Someone had fetched a big tub of water, Da Gama noted with grudging relief, and the horses seemed well tended. But he wanted sentries. He had many reasons to feel uneasy, he told himself. Since the final hilltop, Da Gama had felt the tingling on his neck that told him he was being watched. There were eyes around them, unfriendly eyes. Da Gama remembered how Wali Khan had told him that the Three-Dot clan would follow the little caravan. Maybe he could feel their stares. Maybe it was all in his head.

Da Gama strode to the guards area and poked his head into the low tents. Finally he found a snoring guard, roused him. When he'd got the fellow standing, he told him to keep watch.

The guard sneered.

Da Gama acted before he thought. In an instant he had seized and twisted the man's wrist, pressing his full weight against it until the guard fell to the floor with a whimper, his cheek pressed against the earth. With his other hand Da Gama held a double-barreled *pistola* to the man's temple, and cocked both hammers. This all took a single heartbeat.

Holy mother, Da Gama murmured to himself. What am I doing. "Get up!" Da Gama said, releasing him. The guard rose slowly, his eyes widening as he realized how close he'd come to dying. "Next time obey me."

"Yes. Yes, sir," the poor fellow gulped. "Yes," he said again, even as he ran from the tent, buckling his sword.

What's wrong with me, Da Gama thought. He sat on the guard's bedroll, uncocked his *pistola,* and shoved it back in his belt. A man like me can't afford to lose his head, he thought. What is wrong with me?

There were so many things wrong:

Victorio and his double-dealing.

Victorio's lies.

Victorio's plan to marry Lucy.

Victorio and Geraldo.

Victorio.

Outside the tent Da Gama found a pot of water, and scooped some onto his head. As he dried his face with his dark kerchief, he saw the guard talking animatedly with Slipper. The eunuch nodded, listening intently, his eyes growing wide. At last he patted the guard's arm, as one might pat a child who has told a nightmare. Then, with a broad smile on a his fat face, Slipper came slowly, gently to Da Gama. "Senhor Deoga, your concern for our safety does you credit! How enthusiastic you are! Everyone says so."

"I expect obedience, Senhor Eunuch." He pointed with his chin to the sentry. "Nothing wrong with the occasional reminder. It builds discipline."

"Yes, yes. Exactly what I told the fellow. You must obey the farang, I told him, just like that. Deoga is paid to worry about our safety—the very words I said!"

Da Gama had never seen Slipper's oily grin so wide, nor so frightened. I must take care, he told himself. I really must not lose control. He tried to change the subject. "Tonight we have a feast, eh, Senhor Eunuch?"

Slipper gratefully followed Da Gama's lead. He fell in step beside Da Gama and gestured broadly to the cooking fire, and then to the trees beyond the guards' tent where a few camp followers were peeling a pile of red onions. "It is a grand day for your master," Slipper said. "A betrothal, and a homecoming. So much beginning! So much effort coming to an end! Too bad the *burak* would not come, too. We could recall our rescue from the bandits. Ah well, never mind. There's still reason enough for us to celebrate and feast, don't you think?"

Da Gama nodded, but his mind had seized the word *master* and was now considering it with horror.

"Oh, Deoga, did you hear? We received a visitor! Yes, the captain of the eunuch guards of Bijapur came here this afternoon, not long before you all arrived!"

"The captain of the eunuch guards? Why isn't he with the Sultana?"

"Ah, you see, now I have news!" Slipper's delight was obvious. He grabbed the end of his rich turban, which had again come loose, and shoved it happily back in place. "The Flying Palace has come. The Sultana wanted a change of scene. She and the heir came down to Gokak Falls. They're only a few miles from here. Also others, some friends of yours, I think: Wali Khan is there, and my master, Whisper."

At this news Da Gama's breath came short, and his heart beat fast. "Why have they come?" he glowered. "What mischief is this?"

Slipper stepped back. "Deoga, you must calm yourself. You'll die young if you keep this up!"

Da Gama looked away. "You're right. Please forgive my bad manners." Then a thought struck him. "Didn't you and Geraldo have a falling out. . . ."

A beatific light fell on Slipper's face. "The brothers don't bear grudges long. We have so few friends, we can't afford to lose any. Anyway, his interests and mine are the same. And did you hear? Victorio has made him a partner!"

"I had not heard," Da Gama answered.

"I know you feel concerned, particularly since the matter of the nautch girl is not yet settled. But this will pass . . . maybe sooner than you think! Whisper sent me word that he has brought along the nautch girl's price, in hopes of meeting us on the road." Slipper looked at Da Gama coyly. "She still has all her . . . her baggage?" he asked hopefully.

Hating himself, Da Gama nodded.

ଓଓଓ

Just as they reached Victorio's tent, Geraldo came out, looking very satisfied. "Congratulations on being made a partner, senhor," Slipper said delightedly. Geraldo lowered his head, but clearly was quite pleased.

"My own congratulations," Da Gama said, his face cold. "You appear to have been busy these last few hours.

Geraldo shrugged. "I am humbled by my good fortune."

They glared at one another silently until Slipper burst in: "I was just explaining to Deoga that you and I have made up our differences . . ."

"Yes, that's in the past. Senhor Slipper has graciously forgotten all about it." Geraldo swung his arm around Slipper's plump shoulder. "Master Victorio has decided to take dinner in his tent tonight," he said to the eunuch, ignoring Da Gama. "He wants to see Lucinda now, and then the nautch girl."

"I will fetch her," Slipper said and moved off, smiling warmly at Geraldo.

"What about me?" Da Gama asked.

"Oh, yes! I suppose you should go in now, before Lucinda comes." His offhand tone achieved its purpose: Da Gama bristled and with no further word strode into Victorio's tent.

The air smelled stale. Pierced shade lamps hung from the tent poles cast a soft light on the velvet walls. In the center of the spacious tent Victorio reclined barefoot on a camp divan. Da Gama noticed his yellowed, clawlike toenails. His gray hair fell loose around his shoulders; his linen shirt hung open, so low that it revealed his pale belly. But Victorio held a wine flagon in his thick fingers and appeared not to care. "Da Gama!" Victorio said in surprise. "What brings you here?"

"I'm the settlement man, remember? And your partner?"

"Of course, of course." Da Gama sat on the thick carpet at Victorio's feet. "Things have turned out well. Better than I hoped, in fact." He took a pull of wine. "What do you think of that Geraldo, eh?" Victorio didn't wait for an answer. "A true Dasana! The family blood runs in his veins, that's clear. A man with a future! So many excellent opinions! So many fine ideas!" Da Gama struggled to hold his tongue. "It's good you're here, Da Gama," Victorio said. His face was flushed, and his eyes red. "I've come to some decisions. I trust I can count on you." Victorio's thick tongue slid across his pale lips. "About the nautch girl . . . it's settled. She'll go to the eunuchs, as we agreed with Whisper."

Da Gama nodded. "What about the vizier?" he managed to say.

"Yes. Well, I leave that part to you. You're the settlement man, eh? You deal with it. You'll figure out something. Aren't you the master?"

Da Gama lowered his head. "I shall do my best."

"Of course, of course. I place the matter in your capable hands. After all, that is what your fee is for, eh? Even your usual fee, eh?"

In the flickering lamplight, Victorio's face looked thick and heavy. Instead of looking at Da Gama when he spoke, he leaned to fill his cup with wine from a brass pitcher. Da Gama stared at him in silence. It was nearly empty, and Victorio shook the last drops into his cup and took a long draft. "I'd offer you some wine," he said to break the silence, "but you see . . . it's gone."

"Yes." Da Gama rose and turned to leave.

"About that other matter—that special fee I promised?"

Da Gama turned and raised an eyebrow, waiting. The old man smiled wanly and then turned his head. "I may have spoken too soon. I must discuss it with my partner."

"Geraldo?"

"Of course . . . since he stands to inherit the Dasana fortune, you know, he must have some authority . . ."

"Aren't you forgetting Lucinda? Isn't the fortune hers?" Victorio flicked his hand in answer, as if batting away a fly. Da Gama's mouth tightened. "And I thought I was to be your partner."

Victorio spread his arms—as if he were helpless, as if he would embrace Da Gama, as if he could not care. "Yes, yes, dear boy, of course. I will discuss that with him, too." He turned away. "Just send Lucinda in, won't you? And we'll sort things out tomorrow. There's a good fellow."

Da Gama thought to speak, but Victorio had now looked away, and Da Gama did not trust his tongue.

☙☙☙☙

As they approached Victorio's tent, Slipper pointed out to Lucinda the many indications of his improved state: the fine clothing, the rich jewels, the guards at his command. "I am eunuch of the first rank now," he beamed.

"But I thought you already were of the first rank?"

"Oh, I said that. Once I had been, so it was not a lie. But now I truly am."

Lucinda gave a wan smile. The sunset faded on the horizon, and the darkening sky was filling with stars. She saw Da Gama coming toward them, and greeted him, but for the first time that she could remember, he did not answer her, not even to look up.

"What's wrong with Deoga, I wonder?" Slipper said as he held the tent flap wide for Lucinda to pass, and followed her into Victorio's tent.

Lucinda shivered when she entered, though the stale air of the tent was warm. She was glad for the dim lamplight, for she saw that Victorio had not aged well. She made a mental note to meet him only in darkness. "Lucy, dearest," the old man said, grunting as he stood to greet her. "How beautiful you've become. A grown-up woman now, and beautiful—quite, quite beautiful." Victorio's rough hands took hers. "You're bashful, I see. No matter, darling. Soon we shall be married, and there will be no more need for shyness." He glanced to Slipper. "Leave us," he said in Hindi. "And send in food."

When Slipper had bowed and left, Victorio beamed at Lucinda. "Some wine while we wait?"

Lucinda declined. While Victorio took another flagon and arranged himself on the divan, she stood and tried to make her face pleasant. "Too bad about your uncle Carlos," Victorio said. "Poisoned, you know. Or so the doctor said." Victorio raised an eyebrow significantly.

"I thought he died of flux," Lucinda stammered.

"Anyway he's dead," Victorio went on. "So when we are married, you and I shall have the entire fortune, you know. It's quite a lot. We shall be comfortable."

Instead of a servant, as Lucinda expected, Geraldo came bearing plates of spicy roasted goat, and another pitcher of wine. He gave Victorio an affectionate smile; to Lucinda, out of the old man's view, he rolled his eyes. When he left, Victorio motioned for Lucinda to sit near his feet. He poured more wine from the new pitcher, and this time did not bother to offer Lucinda any.

While he talked, Victorio stared past her, toward a panorama only he could see. He told her that he'd sent word to Goa for their banns to be announced, and that as soon as a priest had come to Bijapur, the marriage would be performed. "A small ceremony. Private. Only the finest people will be invited—the grand vizier, the Khaswajara. Perhaps Commander Shahji." Victorio rambled on. She should plan to make a household for them there in Bijapur, worthy of their station. "Only the finest will do. But don't spend too much, mind. Anyway, you'll have plenty else to do, soon enough."

Lucinda realized that Victorio was speaking of a baby. They would hire an ayah to help. Lucinda imagined the future he described: she and a baby

and a nurse in a strange house in a strange city, with a husband all too likely
to sicken soon and die. Suddenly Geraldo's offer did not seem as horrid as
it had a few days before.

"No." Lucinda found herself on her feet. "It shall not be as you say."
She turned and was nearly to the entrance before Victorio realized she was
gone and stopped his monotonous monologue.

"Lucy!" She turned. "What are you doing?"

"I'm leaving, Uncle."

Victorio chuckled, and then laughed so hard he began to cough. "And
where will you go, dearest?"

"You think I am without resources?"

"You are a child. You are my ward. You are my wife, or will be soon
enough. You are a Dasana and you'll do what you're told!"

"You are wrong. I have chosen a different path."

Before Victorio could say another word, she was gone.

ତ୍ରভଟ୍ର

Outside, Geraldo, Da Gama, and Slipper were eating near the fire. Farther
off, she saw shadows of sentries standing watch. Geraldo leaped to his feet
and joined her. "Well, dear cousin, how did you enjoy your husband?"

Lucinda passed him without looking up. Through the dark clearing
she hurried back toward her tent. She glanced behind her and saw that Slipper now followed her. "Leave me alone!" Lucinda shouted.

"I'm only coming for the nautch girl," Slipper whimpered as he followed her.

"Walk behind me, then," Lucinda said, and hurried on.

Maya looked up when Lucinda entered. "So," she said after a glance at
Lucinda's face.

"So," Lucinda answered.

Maya rose and took her hands. "It is my turn next." She embraced Lucinda and whispered in her ear, "Do nothing until I return. Do you understand me? Do nothing! There is time, sister, there is time. Wait for my
return. We'll talk and make a plan."

Slipper came in then. "This is pretty," he said. "You two have become friends." But he blanched when he saw the way they looked at him. "Do not harm me!" he cried, thrusting out his fingers as though to ward off the evil eye.

Maya stepped away from Lucinda. "Let us go then, master eunuch." She threw around her shoulders the silver shawl she'd worn as she left the dhow in Goa. "Promise, sister, that you'll wait for my return."

"I promise," Lucinda answered, her voice scarcely audible.

"What mischief have you two planned?" Slipper asked, barely able to contain his apprehension.

"The death of hypocrites," Maya whispered.

"What?" He gave a nervous giggle. "Oh, bless the Prophet, then I'm safe," he added, as if playing along with Maya's joke. But Maya did not laugh.

꧁꧂

"By the Virgin's tits, you're beautiful."

Slipper had just shown Maya into Victorio's tent, and the old man, stretched out on the divan, gazed at her with frank amazement. "To think I own you," he breathed.

"Until tomorrow, master," Slipper said brightly.

"Yes. But mine tonight, eh? Come closer." In the lamplight, Maya's silver shawl shimmered like the moon. "Turn." She did, and let the shawl fall from her shoulders so Victorio could see her golden skin. "You are trained in tantra?" Maya now faced him silently, her face blank, but her eyes shining. "Leave us," he told Slipper. Victorio's face was flushed, and his eyes were bloodshot. "Leave us now!"

"Now, you two *will* be *careful* . . ."

"Go now!" Victorio shouted, rising unsteadily from the divan.

꧁꧂

Slipper waited by the fire, too nervous to sit, glancing often toward Victorio's tent. Geraldo acted as if it were a great joke. Every time a muffled groan escaped the tent, he laughed, sometimes so hard he had to wipe his eyes. Beyond the fire, Da Gama had set out his *pistolas* in a line, and polished them, one by one, with his dark kerchief, never looking up.

At last Maya emerged, disheveled but no less beautiful. Her hair cascaded around her shoulders. She threw her shawl across her head. "Is he still alive?" Geraldo laughed.

"He was when I left him." As Maya walked past the fire, she for a moment caught Da Gama's eye, but both instantly looked away.

"Shouldn't we go with her?" Slipper asked.

"What for?" Geraldo said.

ෙ⊖ෙ⊖

"Tell me," Lucinda said when Maya entered. Lucinda lay huddled on a bed of cushions, wearing only her slip as a dressing gown, and a rough blanket pulled across her shoulders. She'd blown out all the lamps but one, which flickered behind its pierced shade and cast eerie shadows.

Maya did not look at her. She let the shawl fall from her shoulders to the floor. "He did not touch me." She laughed bitterly. "He made me wiggle for him . . . dancing, he called it. He said he preferred to use his hand." Slowly Maya unwrapped her sari, and stood for a moment naked before she slipped into a simple gown. Still silent, she pushed some cushions together to form a bed, and stretched on it with a sigh. At last she turned to Lucinda. "He wants me to train you, as I have been trained."

She said the words simply, as though they were not foul, but all the same Lucinda cringed.

"He's an old man," she continued, her voice carefully flat. "It will be quicker if you move; quicker still if you kick his buttocks with your heels, and nip his neck and suck his tongue." She said all this without a look at Lucinda. "This may not be pleasant for you, but it will get things over quickly. You might prefer quick. Or you can lie back, stiff and unyielding. Then it will take a long time to be over. But you will make him miserable. You will have to choose." Maya reached for her shoulder bag. "If it were up to me, I would make him miserable."

"Was it bad?"

"No worse than having congress with merchants in the temple. We spoke of that, did we not?" Lucinda nodded. "He could use a bath. Perhaps you can persuade him." Maya spilled the contents of her bag over the blanket in her lap. Maya found the twist of cloth that held the portion of *arsênico* Lucinda had given her. She pushed everything else back into her bag.

"I have mine, too," Lucinda said, holding out her silver box of *arsênico*. She clicked the lid open and the lamplight glinted red on the paste inside. "What shall we do?"

The women faced each other, eyes smoldering in the flickering light.

And then they heard the moans.

CRGCRG

Around the fire, the men had barely turned their heads from Maya's swaying shadow when they heard a clatter from Victorio's tent. "He's still at it," Geraldo joked. "He hasn't realized the nautch girl is gone."

More clatter, more noise, and Da Gama rose to his feet, shoving his *pistolas* into his belt. "Something's wrong in there."

But before he could do anything more, Victorio, wearing nothing but his pantaloons, came stumbling through the entrance, clinging to the guy ropes. "I have to take a piss," he grunted.

"You look like hell." Da Gama moved to help him, but the old man waved him off.

"Too much wine. Too much woman." He managed a leering wink before grabbing the rope once more for balance. "I just need the bushes, that's all." He lurched forward, half-stumbling, and then leaned against a tree. Then a few more stumbling steps, until he crashed into a sentry. "Who the hell are you?"

The guard helped him to his feet. "I am your guard, sir."

Victorio squinted at him; his eyes were so bleary he could barely see. "Thank God," he said. "I thought you were Old Nick come to take me straight to hell." He began to laugh, so hard he fell to his knees. Da Gama rushed to help him. "Thought he was Old Nick," Victorio told him as if confiding a secret. "Thought my time was up. Not that I'd mind. I could die happy. My God, her *calha* squirmed on my *fonte* like a fish!" Da Gama heaved him to his feet, and helped him stumble to the bushes. "By God I showed her what a real man can do. She'd only had Hindis before, you know. They have little *fontes*, like this . . ." Victorio held up his pinky, curled limply, and began to laugh.

The laugh became a cough, a cough so fierce it brought him to his knees, gasping. Da Gama clapped him on the back, knowing it was useless. Victorio could scarcely breathe. His eyes began to bulge. The coughing mixed with heaving. Vomit gushed from his mouth and poured over his chest. A rank puddle of the stuff formed at his knees. Da Gama tried to lift him, and got sprayed for his trouble. Victorio grabbed Da Gama's arms, eyes so wide they seemed about to burst, face red, neck veins roped and pulsing. Victorio's fingers squeezed Da Gama's arms tighter as his face contorted.

"Oh, God!" Victorio screamed the word, and it trailed into a high pitched squeal. His torso began to jerk, and he let go of Da Gama's arms to grab his belly.

Da Gama heard the sound like a tearing, and then smelled the foulness. Victorio tugged weakly at his pants but wasn't quick enough. His immense pale belly churned in the dim firelight; Da Gama could see it seething, like it was filled with eels. Victorio squeezed out more foulness. "Go get help!" Da Gama cried to the sentry.

"Yes, sir!" The guard turned, and then turned back. "What help, sir?"

"Geraldo, Slipper. Anyone!"

As his belly churned once more, Victorio gave an agonized, rattling moan. "Don't leave me, Da Gama!" he gasped. Then he moaned again. Da Gama knelt beside him. "I've been a fool," he whispered, and then howled in agony. "Da Gama, help me!"

۞۞۞

Oddly, Slipper seemed unfazed. When he saw Victorio, he clucked his tongue, rolled up his sleeves, and peeled off the old man's filthy pants. "Fetch water. A big basinful," he ordered the sentry. Victorio writhed naked on the ground, filling the night with moans, but Slipper knelt and stroked his forehead with a pudgy hand, humming a kind of lullaby. "He's dying," he whispered to Geraldo and Da Gama, but they'd already realized this.

When the water came, he made the farangs lift Victorio, and then sluiced him down, using his own hands to wash off the filth. Then, with Slipper's encouragement, they half-carried, half-dragged Victorio to his tent. By the time they set him on the divan, he was nearly empty. He heaved, and his belly spasmed, but he had nothing more to lose. "Dear me," Slipper sighed. "I knew I should have brought some opium."

They tried to keep him covered, but between the spasms and his anguished flailing, it was impossible. The sight of that old body squeezed by death's cold fingers made even Da Gama weep.

It took the old man a long hour to die.

Part Seven

Gokak Falls

They arranged the body on the divan. Geraldo, looking unusually serious, closed Victorio's eyes, and drew a blanket over his gray face. They stood in silence for a moment, and then Slipper snapped his fingers at a sentry. "Go to my tent and fetch one of my green plates. Now, oaf!" The sentry looked to Da Gama and Geraldo, but first one shrugged and then the other. At last the sentry made an uncertain bow and hurried off.

"The nautch girl was too much for him," Geraldo said as if in eulogy. "Poor fellow. Too much pleasure."

"Don't be absurd," Slipper answered. "It wasn't pleasure that caused his death."

Da Gama and Geraldo shared a glance. Da Gama suddenly realized how much the eunuch had changed since he'd first met him. He stood with his feet apart, arms crossed, staring up at them with grand authority. It was all Da Gama could do to keep from laughing.

The pewter dinner plates, the wine pitchers, and Victorio's empty flagon were scattered haphazardly around the floor. Da Gama stooped down and righted a silver pitcher. He looked at the blanket covering Victorio. What happens to us now, he wondered.

At that moment the sentry burst in and handed Slipper a pale green plate.

Taking it, Slipper hurried around the tent, picking up spilled pieces of mutton, laying them on the plate. Though he seemed completely sure of himself, Da Gama had no idea what he was up to. Slipper shook a few drops of wine from the nearly empty pitchers on the plate as well. "Look," he said, holding the plate close to a lamp.

A violet stain had formed on the surface. "Wine," Geraldo said. "The wine has stained the glaze."

Slipper glared at him, and then tilted the plate so its contents slid to the tent floor. Again he held the plate so they could see.

The pale green glaze was streaked—everywhere the food had been, the plate was stained. "This is Chinese celadon. The sultan uses it for his meals. Its property of darkening when touched by poison is well known. It even breaks in two if the poison is very strong."

Da Gama took the plate. "Someone poisoned Victorio?" he said, working it out.

"Deoga, yes. Someone poisoned Master Victorio's food and wine."

"But who?"

Slipper smiled. "Who indeed? I shall consider this tomorrow. For now, I'm off to bed. This episode has quite exhausted me." He made a great show of yawning. "There's nothing more to be done at the moment. Let's try to sleep." He bowed, but turned back just before he left. "Has anyone told the women?" Both men shook their heads. "Well, don't." With that he left.

Geraldo stared after him. He looked at Victorio, then to the plate in Da Gama's hands, and finally into Da Gama's eyes. "He suspects the women?"

"If they're suspects, then we must be, too," Da Gama said, pulling at his ear.

"Why should we be suspects? Why should I be?" Geraldo replied. "The eunuch had much to gain . . . what about him?"

❧❧❧❧

Later, of course, Da Gama realized his mistake. Geraldo slept in the men's tent, where Slipper was already snoring. Da Gama should have done the same. But he hated tents, and the night air was cool and fresh, and after his terrible day Da Gama wanted to be alone. A few yards from the campfire he found his saddle and his pack, and he spread a blanket on the ground. He stared at the immense bowl of stars above him, and his eyelids fluttered.

He was floating on his back in an ocean of milk. Clouds billowed in the bright sky, but then he saw that they were not clouds, but thousands of white cranes, darting through the air in perfect unison, like schools of fish. From their midst a star appeared, bright as a blue pearl. It fell toward him slowly, and opened to reveal an old woman not much larger than a child. Who are you? Da Gama asked.

The old woman's eyes shown blue as a twilight sky. "What do you mean to do with my daughter's headdress?"

Da Gama meant to say, What business is it of yours?... He meant to say, She's not your daughter. But unexpected words came from his lips ... "I mean for her to keep it. It is hers."

The old woman smiled. What teeth she still had were white as pearls. "You say well. Ask a favor."

Tell me your name.

"Gungama. Ask another favor."

Give me hope.

"I give. Ask another favor."

Give me respite from my loneliness.

"I give. Ask one more favor."

Help me set things right. It has all gone wrong.

Gungama lowered her ancient lips and kissed Da Gama's cheek. "You ask well. I give. I give. I give. But danger comes, Deoga. Wake up! Wake up quickly!"

Da Gama's eyes sprung open. Around his makeshift bed he found a ring of guards holding swords to his neck

Da Gama lifted his hands slowly to show that they were empty. Slipper pushed into the ring of guards with Geraldo at his back. "Take him up and bind him," the eunuch ordered. Two of the guards heaved Da Gama to his feet. One tied his hands behind his back, while the other took his *pistolas.* "Now put him in the tent."

"What are you doing, Senhor Eunuch?" Da Gama cried out. "I did not hurt Victorio!" The guards shoved him to Slipper's tent.

"Be sure that I believe you, Deoga," Slipper piped.

Once through the entrance of the tent, the guards pushed him to the floor. While one held a sword edge to his neck, the other bound his feet. After they checked his bindings, both left.

Da Gama struggled for a while, but the ropes were too tight. He seethed but could do nothing except wait. He heard noise outside the tent; grunts and shouts, and then a woman's scream.

After a few moments, the tent flap opened yet again. The guards who had bound him now led Lucinda in at sword point. Slipper followed. "There's your poisoner," he said softly.

"Lucy?"

"Even her, Deoga. I'm sorry to bind you up, for you have been so courteous to me, but if you decided to help her, who could stop you? You're much too dangerous, and she must not escape justice."

In her slip, her hair loose around her shoulders, Lucinda walked as one asleep. With her hands tied behind her, her young breasts were clearly visible against the cotton gauze. The guards leered as they led her to the divan and bound her ankles.

"What sort of game is this, Slipper?" Da Gama growled.

"Deoga, you surprise me. Should I ignore the murder of my friend? Maybe he was a farang, but was he not a man?"

"What do you want—money?"

Slipper's lips pursed and he blinked. "I want justice. And I shall have it."

"Let me see Geraldo."

"In time. We have some matters to discuss. Tomorrow I shall send messages to the Sultana. You are lucky, mistress," he now said to Lucinda. "I could execute you here and now—that is the law. There is no punishment for murder except death—even for women. But because you are a farang, there may be implications. Out of courtesy I must inform the Sultana. You Christians, I understand, say prayers? Use your short time well." Slipper gave Da Gama a sympathetic smile and then left with the guards following.

"Lucy . . . this is terrible," Da Gama said, struggling to get closer to her.

"Not so terrible. My life ended long ago." She sniffed but could not dry her tears. "I welcome death. Which is worse, tell me? Never to taste love, or taste it for a little while, and then have it disappear?"

"Don't talk of love at a time like this!"

Lucinda looked into Da Gama's face. "Why not. I'll be dead soon. What should I talk about? Have you never loved, cousin?" Da Gama could not find words to answer. His only thoughts were of escape. But Lucinda closed her eyes, and more tears spilled. "I was a fool. I hesitated. But my heart had become his, no longer mine. But when I finally made up my mind, when I was ready to give up everything—by then it was too late. He spurned me. He hates me. Now I shall give up everything anyway."

Da Gama pushed closer. "But Lucy . . ."

"We sleep in many tents, cousin."

Da Gama blinked. "What are you saying, little one?"

"Life is a caravan, and on this journey we sleep in many tents. Tomorrow I shall sleep in a different tent. Why should I care?"

"Who told you this?" Da Gama asked. But Lucy now hid her face and would not answer.

ᑑᑑᑏᑍ

Da Gama struggled with the bindings on his wrists. Struggling gave him a little comfort. At least it was something to do.

After a while, Geraldo entered with three guards. He carried a long-barreled pistol, one of Da Gama's. "Take her to Victorio's tent," he ordered.

"Why?" Da Gama shouted.

Geraldo answered without turning—his eyes fixed on Lucinda. "So she may view the man she murdered, cousin. So she may consider her misdeeds."

The guards strode to the divan—two took Lucinda underneath the arms, the other grabbed her feet, and like a sack lifted her. "Treat her with respect, or know my anger," Geraldo said, pointing with the pistol for emphasis. As Lucinda passed, he bent and kissed her mouth. "Oh, cousin," he sighed, "what a time we might have had."

Lucinda jerked her head and spat. He wiped his face and nodded to the guards. After they took her out, he collapsed casually onto Slipper's divan. "She has spirit, does she not?"

"You know she did not poison him," Da Gama growled.

"How insightful you can be, Deoga." Geraldo chuckled. "Of course I know. I poisoned him myself."

Da Gama's eyebrows flew up.

"Really, cousin, at times you can be quite thick." He toyed with Da Gama's pistol. "It has taken me years, Deoga. But tonight, my efforts are rewarded." He turned to smile at Da Gama. "To remove both remaining impediments, both Victorio and Lucinda in one stroke. You must admit the brilliance, cousin. With their deaths the Dasana fortune is mine."

Geraldo laughed at Da Gama's horrified expression. "Come, Deoga, you nearly figured it out. Victorio told me that you alone had realized my proximity to the fortune, how close I had come to being the sole heir. You can't pretend that you're entirely surprised."

Da Gama struggled with his words. "Maybe. I never reckoned on such audacity."

"Exactly!" Geraldo leaped to his feet. "Audacity! That has been the key! 'How could any man be so evil?' the good man thinks. 'Such a suspicion is outrageous!' So the good man walks smiling to his death with his eyes open, seeing nothing." Geraldo bowed to Da Gama. "You are the perfect example."

"You think you've won? Then keep your mouth shut and enjoy it. Don't talk about it, for God's sake!"

"Really, cousin—I need someone to share the fun." Geraldo leaned back comfortably on the divan, and pointed the uncocked pistol at Da Gama. "It's dangerous to keep these loaded. What if one went off by accident?" He pretended to shoot and chuckled to himself. "Do you want to know the best part? Slipper. I thought I'd have to poison the damned girl, or worse, marry her. Slipper solved all that for me. What a wonderful fool he is. A word or two whispered in his ear, that's all it took. When I told him I would be sole heir, and that I would always be his friend, he took the hint. At least Lucinda's death won't be on my head."

"You trusted Slipper?" Da Gama stared at Geraldo. Geraldo enjoyed the moment, basking in Da Gama's attention. But the moment passed and still Da Gama stared. Beneath that relentless gaze, he grew increasingly uncomfortable. Then Da Gama began to laugh. He laughed when Geraldo told him to stop, even when Geraldo raised the pistol and cocked its hammer.

"Go ahead," he said. "You're the fool, not Slipper! The Sultana just got rich tonight, Aldo. Not you."

"What do you mean?"

"Didn't you know that the property of a murderer is forfeit? Lucinda's fortune will go Bijapur—to the Sultana's privy purse!" Da Gama gave Geraldo time to work it out. "You should have killed her outright.

Your cleverness has been your downfall, Aldo! Tomorrow she'll be condemned of the murder. Tomorrow she loses everything—and so do you."

"But Slipper . . ."

Da Gama smiled. "Slipper will get a tenth part. He'll be rich. Not you." Geraldo was so pitiable, Da Gama tried not to laugh.

Geraldo's face was white. "I was a fool. My kind heart got the better of me. She hasn't yet been condemned . . . What if I killed her now?"

"You're too late. Slipper's smart. He expects trouble. That's why he restrained me. And even if you managed it, even if no one saw, Slipper would know it was you. Your fortune's lost."

"There must be a way," Geraldo said blankly.

"Never mind. You're young. You're dangerous. You could become a settlement man."

With his open palm, Geraldo clapped Da Gama on the ear. With that he stormed from the tent.

◐◑◐◑

It had only been a few minutes when the tent flap opened yet again, but to Da Gama the seconds passed like hours. He expected Geraldo again, and steeled himself for a beating, but instead, it was Maya. Quiet as a whisper she hurried to his side, and placed her cool small hand on his cheek. "Deoga, what have they done?"

"Have you seen Lucy?"

Maya shook her head. "They would not let me speak with her. It took all my efforts to be allowed just to come to you. They put her into Victorio's tent. She's tied to the tent pole, and she weeps. It is not good for her there, Deoga, in the company of a corpse. It will give her dark thoughts."

Da Gama's brow furrowed deeply. "Can you bring me a *pistola*?"

"No, Deoga. They are locked in a box, and the box has many guards. They think you are dangerous."

"They're wrong. Not without weapons. A sword maybe? A knife?"

Maya shook her head. "I don't know how to get one. And Slipper searched me before I came in. It pleased him to be very thorough."

Da Gama shook his head. "I thought it would be Geraldo who searched you."

"Geraldo watched." She moved her hand to Da Gama's, and pressed it gently. "Tomorrow we go to the Sultana's camp, and there Lucinda will be executed. Can we do nothing to help her, Deoga?"

"Nothing," he answered at last. He hesitated, frowning. "No—perhaps there's a chance for her."

"What?"

"Pathan." Da Gama peered past Maya, considering. "Under the right circumstances, he might manage. Did you learn what our route will be?"

"They say we shall pass under Gokak Falls. It is a hard route to the Sultana, they say, but much shorter."

Da Gama's eyes lit up. "That is excellent news. Perhaps there is a chance."

"But how can we get word to Pathan in time? How can we get word to him at all?"

So Da Gama in a rough whisper told her of the Three-Dot clan, how he'd seen their shadows following. He told her of the signal Wali Khan had set. Slowly he hatched a plan with her, slowly built the message that Maya was to say. He made her repeat it back to him, making sure of every detail. But even when she said it to his satisfaction, he shook his head. "This is impossible. This can never succeed."

"It must work, Deoga. And even if it does not, still we must try. She should not die. We must do our best, and leave the balance to the Goddess. I will make the signal. I will say your words to them. Pathan will surely save her."

Maya kissed his cheek as one kisses an uncle. Da Gama then remembered his dream of the old woman and ocean of milk, and meant to tell her, but already she was gone.

The sentries huddled around the fire and at the entrances of the tents that held the captives. She picked up a flaming branch from the fire. "I'm going to the bushes," she said quietly.

Once out of easy sight, Maya swung the flaming branch three times, saying her mantra with each pass.

Was that enough, she wondered? Should I do it again? What are they like, the Three-Dot clan? What if I bungle the message? Will they do what I ask, or will they . . . ?

She had just begun to spiral into worry when the bushes near her rustled, and two dark men appeared.

Before the dawn broke in the valley of Konnur, Pathan woke from a troubled dream. Though the memory of it faded as a mist, his unquiet lingered—like a fluttering of wings outside his window, like the coming of a storm, like the prowling of a wolf. He dressed and belted on a sword.

No one was awake except the old watchman, who sat on the verandah steps beneath a dozen blankets though the air was warm. Pathan waved at him and began his own patrol of the grounds.

Some premonition led him down the tree-lined drive. Birds trilled, and tree toads growled. But there was something else, some other sound just beyond the reach of Pathan's ears.

Then he recognized it. A faint, low sputter; a horse ridden hard, blowing his lips in the darkness. Slowly, so the steel would not ring, Pathan slipped his sword from its scabbard. Moving silently from shadow to shadow he found two horses tethered to a bush beside a low-branched tree.

He turned in the darkness, seeing no one, but now certain someone was there. "Speak now, and I will not harm you," he said in a loud voice. One of the horses looked up and snorted; otherwise there was silence.

For no clear reason, only a sense of being watched, Pathan spun around. Behind him, clinging to the great branches of a pirpal tree were two huge, dull brown cocoons. Before his eyes, they burst open—he now saw that the cocoons were merely blankets tied into the branches. Instead of moths, two men emerged and walked slowly to Pathan. Both carried bows with arrows notched.

"She said you were good. She said that you would find us, and you have." The cocoon men grinned at one another.

"Yeah, you're pretty good. We could only have killed you three or four times," the other said, and both men laughed.

"What do you want here? Who told you about me?"

"Calm down. We've got a message. Some farang who says he's your friend. Says you owe him a favor." The first man gave a leering grin. "Time to pay up, he says." The man paused, and his lips twisted into a gruesome smile. "There's some problem with another farang . . . about some other farang . . ."

"Farangs . . ." laughed his friend.

Pathan's face grew very still. "Why come to me? Why don't you help him?"

The two men shared a look. "He don't want us making a mess of things, Captain. His very words." Pathan raised an eyebrow. "It's true, Captain. He says you're the only one can help."

"Why? What is this special task?"

The bandits glanced at each other. "Captain, he wants you to kidnap a murderer."

ଡ୬ଡ୨ଡ

In Slipper's tent the lamps guttered and all but one went out. Da Gama dozed fitfully. Finally sunlight seeped in. Outside he heard muffled words he could not quite catch. He was hungry, and thirsty, and he needed to pee. For what seemed like an hour, Da Gama struggled with his bonds.

At last he gave up and fell back on the divan, and to his humiliation found himself sobbing. He choked back the sobs and cursed his weakness, but it took a while before he could stop. Then he slept. He woke soaked in sweat as from a broken fever. The air had grown hot and smelled of damp wool. No one came to bring him water. There was nothing to interrupt his dark thoughts.

At last his guards came in, and he was so spent from being alone, he welcomed them. They said nothing, however, but scooped him to his feet and blindfolded him. The guards marched him outside. At least they let him pee.

Around the blindfold edges, Da Gama could see a little: the yellow jet of his urine, and the brass tip of the guard's scabbard, and blue flowers crushed beneath his boots. As they walked he watched tiny patches of shade along the path. When they yanked him to a stop, Da Gama caught a glimpse of one of Geraldo's boots. After standing for a long silent moment the boot disappeared.

Then one of the guards grabbed Da Gama's shoulder, spun him around, and gave him a kick. He tumbled forward. He landed in a sprawl on a kind of bed. Gentle hands touched him and guided him onto it. Seeing a bit of scarlet pattern in a satin cloth, he realized they'd thrown him in the *palki.* He squirmed to sit up.

"Here, Deoga," came Maya's voice. She leaned over him to pull him forward by the arms.

"Where's Lucy?" he whispered.

Maya fussed with a cushion, trying to make him comfortable. "She's riding a horse."

"Idiots." Da Gama could just imagine the discussions between Slipper and Geraldo that had led to this arrangement. Scowling, he struggled, futilely pulling at his bound wrists. He gave up with a gasp.

"They're watching. I can't help you," Maya whispered. "And they see when we speak. Say nothing, Deoga. It is not safe. I pretend to cry, and speak from behind my hand. We're on our way to Gokak Falls, to the camp of the Sultana."

From every side came the sounds of a caravan forming up. "I know," Da Gama answered. "I mean, I guessed. Is Lucy in front or behind?"

"She rides before us. She neither speaks nor moves. Around her shoulders she wears one of Slipper's robes. They would not untie her even to let her dress."

The *palki* bearers grunted and Da Gama and Maya lurched into the air. The caravan was on the move.

❦❦❦❦

They traveled for more than an hour, uphill mostly. The bearers' breath grew short; they panted with their effort. Beyond them came the deep booming of the falls. At the camp they had heard the distant rush of water. Now the sound grew constantly louder, a dull thundering roar, and now and again the unexpected blast of water slapping rock. "We're close," Da Gama said.

Their pace had slowed; the path here was uneven—broken rocks beside the river's edge. The *palki* began to pitch as the bearers stumbled. They stopped often, and the *palki* heaved unexpectedly. At last Da Gama heard Geraldo's command to halt, and with a suddenness that confirmed their exhaustion, the bearers dropped the *palki* with a bump.

"Geraldo comes," Maya whispered.

"Let him."

A moment later an unseen hand yanked off Da Gama's blindfold. He blinked at the sunlight. To their left, a stark rock wall towered forty feet into the air; to their right the river Ghataprabha churned. White cascades broke over hidden rocks. The path was punctuated by broken cubes of stone, each about the size of a strongbox. In time the river had swept them into tumbled heaps, as a child sweeps aside toy blocks. One could walk the trail, but only by choosing each next step carefully.

Directly ahead they saw the edge of Gokak Falls. The falls fell fierce, swollen from the recent rains. Mist boiled from the canyon and rose into the blue sky. The river here was wide and shallow, its current treacherous. The other shore was a riot of plants, vines, and trees twisted in impenetrable confusion. A hundred yards or so ahead, where the falls had formed a swirling pool, mists rose around a temple so ancient that vines had grown through the colonnades, and its tower listed over the water as though about to fall. Parts of its ghats, the steps that led to the water, remained intact.

Without his blindfold, the noise seemed louder. Da Gama saw Geraldo speaking but had to strain to hear. "You're too big to carry, Da Gama. From here on you walk," Geraldo yelled. He took a knife and sliced through the ropes on Da Gama's ankles.

"Untie my hands," Da Gama shouted.

Geraldo merely smirked. He nodded to the falls. "Do you know anything about this place?"

Da Gama nodded. "I came this way once. It was in the dry season then. Not so big as now. This path."—He snorted at his own description—"this miserable trail, I mean, leads right through the falls."

"What?" Geraldo said. "Through the water?"

"It's easy enough in the dry season. You climb up there"—Da Gama pointed with his chin to the trail that clung to the cliff face—"duck through a trickle of water. It's just a little shower. Then you walk behind the falls. There's a big chamber right behind the falls, a sort of cave carved by the water. You walk through the chamber, get another shower, and then you're out. In the dry season you don't even get too wet."

Da Gama looked around, trying to act nonchalant. He took in Lucinda on horseback, the wide eyes of the anxious guards, the exhausted *palki* bearers. "This is dangerous, Geraldo. Why did you choose this way?"

Geraldo sneered. "The goddammed eunuch chose it. I wanted to go the long way, but he's beside himself to get to the Sultana by afternoon. I told him—let's get there tomorrow if it means arriving in one piece. He ignored me. I think we should turn back."

"You're right," Da Gama lied. A change in plan would affect Pathan—if he even showed up. On the other hand, Da Gama thought, a detour would buy Lucy a few more hours. "I'll speak to Slipper. Maybe I can talk some sense into him." Geraldo looked skeptical. "Look, Aldo, I don't want to die here." Geraldo at last closed his eyes and nodded.

With his hands still tied behind his back, it was hard going for Da Gama to navigate the broken trail. At the head of the procession a few guards stood next to Slipper's *palki,* only a few yards from the climb up to the falls. Behind it came Lucinda, mounted on Geraldo's mare; then the remaining guards. Maya's *palki,* where Da Gama had ridden, came last, with no guards at all.

"What did you do with Victorio?" Da Gama shouted over the roar of the water.

"Buried him near the tents."

Like so much garbage, thought Da Gama. When they passed Lucinda, who sat listlessly on one of the horses borrowed from Pathan, Da Gama gave her a brave smile. Her expression never changed. "Has she had any food?" he shouted to Geraldo.

"She won't eat," he shouted back. It seemed likely that he hadn't bothered to offer any.

They found Slipper speaking animatedly with one of the guards. So close to the falls, he had to shout, of course, and his high voice pierced the air like a trumpet. He greeted Da Gama with a warm smile. "We won't inconvenience you for long, Deoga. On the other side of the falls are the Sultana's guards. Once we hand over the condemned, I shall see you are released."

The condemned, thought Da Gama. "Look, senhor, this is folly. The path behind the falls is never easy. Look at the water coming down! With the rains, the force is gigantic!" Da Gama struggled to make himself heard.

But Slipper's mind was made up. "I'm sick of this foolishness. I'm getting back to civilized society, and as quickly as I can!"

"It's madness! The *palki*s will be swept away and the bearers with them."

"Who cares about some old bearers, Deoga?"

"You will, if you're in their *palki,* Senhor Eunuch."

Slipper pulled Da Gama by the arm, right to the river's edge. "Look, Deoga! Can you see the Sultana's guards, right over there?" Da Gama could make out their green turbans through the swirling mist. "I've been through the back of those falls a dozen times. The Sultana loves this place. It's easy!"

"Have you done it after the rains? When the water storms down? I don't think so."

Slipper's expression showed that Da Gama had guessed right. He glanced at the path behind the falls, then back to Da Gama. "You say a *palki* won't make it through?"

"A man on foot, maybe. But not a *palki.*"

Slipper considered this. His eyes kept drifting to the other side, to the green turbaned guards. He licked his plump lips, like one anticipating a feast after long fasting. "We'll go through on foot then, Deoga!"

"What about the *palkis*?"

"We'll send them back. Pathan's can go home, and ours can go the long way." Slipper sized up the falls and the procession with a surprisingly professional glance. "What about the horses?"

Da Gama squinted. All this worry made his brain hurt. "Maybe. Maybe they can make it. Those falls are treacherous, senhor! Look!"

Of course, by now Slipper's golden turban had come unwound, and it was soaked by the spewing mist. Water dripped down Da Gama's face, and from his queue along his back. "Well, we can't get too much wetter, can we, Deoga?" Slipper grinned. "The Sultana's camp is just a few yards from here. On the other side of those falls is safety, comfort, and justice. We can get a little wet and be there in an hour, or we can trudge uphill and down for a day, or two, or even more. I'm already wet, senhor. Let's go through!"

ভাঅঅভ

In drier times, the falls came down gently, like a sheer curtain. The trail of broken rock passed behind the curtain, where the falls had hollowed out a large chamber. In drier times, it was amusing and exciting to pass behind the roaring curtain, and to stand in the dark, carved-out rock and see the sunlight glittering through the water curtain, making a *lakh* of rainbows. Yet even in drier times, the falls roared in the chamber so loud that one felt terror—the way a child feels terror when his father tosses him in the air, that pleasant terror of knowing that the danger is not so very great.

But now the river above them had crested in a flood, and overflowed its banks, and water poured over the cliff's edge in a harsh deluge, and seeped across the haphazard trail of rocks, to make each step treacherous.

Slipper's eagerness would brook no more delays. "I will eat lunch with Whisper!" he announced. After sending the *palkis* away, Slipper arranged things: He himself would go first, with Deoga. Then the nautch girl. Then Geraldo would lead Lucinda on her horse. Then the guards. Da Gama made suggestions, but perhaps the falls' roar was too loud.

So they stood at the edge of the falls, the last remnants of the caravan that had set out from Goa a few weeks before. Da Gama, once their leader, now bound; Slipper once the butt of many jokes, now in command. "On the other side is safety, comfort, and justice!" Slipper announced, appreciating his turn of phrase. "A little bath, and then comfort, pleasure, and the Sultana's hospitality!" His voice was barely audible over the thunder of the falling water. "Come, Deoga! We two shall lead the way!"

Taking Da Gama's arm in his pudgy hand, Slipper stepped forward. Singly, the going was difficult, but to go together was nearly impossible. Slipper lurched one way, Da Gama the other. The overspray from the falls drenched all their clothes. The path climbed upward, about ten feet over the surface of the pool below.

"Don't look down, senhor," Da Gama shouted. "We're nearly there!" The roaring's loudness increased and its pitch grew higher as they approached the water curtain. Slipper's beadlike eyes grew wide, and he still clung to Da Gama. "Come, Senhor Eunuch!" Da Gama screamed.

It was not like water. It was like stepping into a shower of pebbles, so fierce was the pounding on Da Gama's head. He stumbled, and fell through the water. Slipper spilled beside him. "Oh, Allah," Slipper moaned.

They had reached the chamber behind the falls. Here it was dry, and oddly, the noise of the falls was dampened, though other sounds echoed. Each heard the other's sighs. "Oh, Deoga, what was I thinking. That was terrible! I thought I was dead!"

"Help me to my feet, senhor," Da Gama answered.

Slipper lumbered up, and then steadied Da Gama. "I should not have made you go through bound, senhor," Slipper said, almost weeping. "The force of it! Who could have imagined!"

"Unbind me now, then, Senhor Eunuch."

"Alas I have no blade! And your bonds are drenched—I'd never get the knots untied with these fat fingers!"

"No matter. We're nearly through." Da Gama took a moment to enjoy the place—the huge dark chamber carved by the water from the living rock; dry, spacious, lit with rainbows filtering through the water curtain that formed its outer wall. The place had the tangy smell of humid rocks. "Now we've had a little rest, let's go."

Slipper fell to his knees. "No! I can't go through it again!"

"Forward or back, senhor—the problem is the same. You might as well go forward! As you say, there's lunch this way." This time Slipper clung to Da Gama's arm as a bride to a bridegroom. The water smacked them like wet sacks of sand. A moment later, they stumbled into the arms of the green-turbaned eunuch guards of the Sultana.

"Look out!" one of them said, nodding to their feet. They had stumbled only a few inches from the edge of the path, and nearly fallen to the pool below.

Slipper pressed Da Gama in a sideways embrace. "I can't release you yet, Deoga. Not until the guards have custody of the condemned. Oh dear, senhor, you must forgive me this small insult. I never could have made it through without you!" Slipper made his way to the river's edge. Water spilled into the pool, sending a plume of mist into the sun. The eunuch leaned out, and waved to the others who waited on the other side of the falls. "It's good, it's good!" They could only see his broad enthusiastic smile.

ඏඏඏඏ

"I'm next, I suppose," Maya said. Geraldo came forward as if to embrace her, but she stepped away. She glanced at Lucinda, who stared with lifeless eyes at the rushing waterfall. Why must I go alone? she thought. Ah, she answered herself, at least I won't be going with *him*. She stared down at the mists rising fifteen feet below. At last she gripped her shoulder bag, said her mantra, and drove forward.

She didn't expect the power of the falls. The water drove her to her knees and poured upon her. She gasped for breath. I'll drown here, she thought. With all her will, she managed to stand, but the water came from everywhere. She stumbled right, left. Somewhere the falls must end! She pushed on, but stumbled ever deeper into the water, never out of it. Again and again she fell to her knees. She began to choke.

A hand reached through the water. A moment later she found herself sprawled on the rock floor of the inner chamber, coughing. At last she managed to look up. "Hello?" she called. "Deoga?" She stood, water poured from her clothes and hair. "Who helped me? Speak!" She wiped her dripping eyebrows with her palm. "Bless you, whoever you are!" she cried, when no one answered. "And bless me while I make for the other side."

Perhaps she was better prepared for the water's weight this time. She felt as though someone pushed against her back, thrusting her through the curtain. Then many hands reached out for her, and there was Deoga, laughing. "Quite a view from up here," he said, nodding toward the drop to the pool below.

"Did you help me in there, Deoga?" she asked. Then she saw that his hands still were tied.

Someone else had been in the chamber.

❀❀❀

On the other side of the falls, one of the Sultana's eunuch guards squinted through the mists. "Hey!" he called. "What's that on the other shore?"

"What?" Slipper shouted. "Where?" He looked across the pool and shook his head. "It is nothing. Deoga, do you see something?"

Da Gama peered through the clouds. On the other bank, near an old, decaying temple, two horsemen had appeared, with long, deadly looking bows. Maya reached Da Gama's shoulder and whispered to him: "Those are the men I saw last night!"

Da Gama nodded nearly imperceptibly. Then to Slipper he said loudly, "They are hunters, I think." But the eunuch guards now took an interest and peered across the water. "Damn . . . ," he said in Maya's ear above the roar of the water. "What're they doing over there—on the wrong damned shore?!"

❀❀❀

"Well, dearest cousin, it's our turn now," Geraldo said.

From one of his pockets, Geraldo took a large square of tawny wax-cloth, wrapped it around his long-barreled pistol, and shoved the package in his belt. Then he took the reins of Lucinda's mare and guided her to the very edge of the falling water. Geraldo walked backward, tugging the bridle, leading the mare with calming words. The mare walked on calmly—as calmly as Lucinda, whose empty expression never changed. At last, with the roaring waters to his back Geraldo took a breath, and pulled them through the deluge.

He felt the pelting weight of the water, and for all his blinking could barely see the horse's head. He gasped for air; he fell to his knees. Suddenly Geraldo felt someone take the reins from his hands, and pull the mare through. He stumbled after.

In the scattered rainbow light that filtered through the falls, Geraldo saw a figure gentling the mare: a tall man, dripping wet but slender and strong. When he had stroked the mare to calmness, he moved to Lucinda. He touched her bound hands.

Pathan!

Geraldo scowled as he pushed his dripping hair from his brow and found his breath. Lucinda's wet clothes clung to her skin, exposing every contour of her body. Water spilled down her legs and fountained from her slippered feet. But Pathan seemed oblivious; he merely touched her hands and searched her eyes.

"What are you doing here, *burak*?" Geraldo shouted. His words echoed from the chamber walls.

"I owe a man a favor," Pathan answered, not looking at him. "Now I shall pay my debt." He wore no turban, and his wet hair hung in dark, dripping sheets around his shoulders. A puddle had formed at his feet. Though his eyes never left Lucinda's, his hand stole to the hilt of his curved sword. With a motion so smooth the mare never stirred, he unsheathed it, and lowered it to his side.

"What do you mean to do, *burak*?" Geraldo got slowly to his feet; his left hand gestured with each word, while his right stole silently toward his pistol. "You know she is a murderer."

"Yes," Pathan said, still staring into her eyes. "For she has killed me." With his left hand, Pathan stroked Lucinda's fingers. "I do not dream anymore, nor do I sleep. My days are empty, my nights endless. My only thought is of her, this murderer. But despite what you say, she brings me life."

Lucinda's eyes stirred, and she looked into her Munna's face, and when she saw him gazing at her with such devotion, Lucy smiled.

"I ask again, *burak*. What do you mean to do?"

Pathan now looked at Geraldo. "I mean to save her from you. You have done a terrible thing, sir. Her only hope is to run. But now the Sultana and the Brotherhood will pursue her endlessly, seeking the Dasana fortune. Lucy will need to hide forever. Never will she know a home, a family. You have taken from her not just her rightful legacy—you have taken her life."

"Make him tell the truth then, Munna," Lucinda said. "I know what he did. Let him die for his crimes!"

"It will do no good, Lucy. Dearest Lucy, his lies have sealed your fate, even if he now confesses. They will ignore it. When has truth ever mattered to them?"

Geraldo laughed so loud the chamber rang. "He's right, Lucy. Truth is what the powerful decide. Like now, for instance . . ." Geraldo ripped the wax cloth from the pistol and pointed its dark barrel at Pathan's heart. ". . . This *pistola* makes me powerful. Now I shall make a new truth—a better truth." Geraldo moved toward the two of them, his eyes bright and his smile sharp. "Let's see. Jealousy, I think. Yes, the jealous *burak* cannot bear to be deserted by a woman, and a farang at that. He hides here, and cuts her throat. But he hasn't reckoned on me—I shoot him through the heart. Alas, too late. My dear cousin dies." Geraldo shrugged. "But with her tragic, unexpected death, she at least avoids condemnation! And so of course the Dasana fortune now comes . . . to me."

He cocked the hammer of the *pistola* and nodded to Pathan. "So . . . you first? Or her? The order of your deaths means little. My story will be believed in either case."

"Maybe I will kill you first!" Pathan whispered.

Before Pathan could even move, however, Lucinda scrambled from her stirrups, and leapt off the saddle with a shout. Her hands still bound, she could not guide her fall through the dark air, but even so she pitched against Geraldo and knocked him to the ground.

Geraldo recovered quickly, and lifted the *pistola* to Lucinda's forehead. Her mouth gaped and her eyes searched for Pathan.

As Pathan rushed from behind the horse, Geraldo pulled the trigger.

The hammer clicked, but instead of a shot, only a long green flame burst from the barrel, sizzling Lucinda's wet hair. Smoke belched from the strike plate, and Geraldo began to cough so hard he dropped his weapon. The pistol spun across the stone floor, into the curtain of water.

He turned to find Pathan racing toward him with his bright sword swinging.

"No!" Lucinda cried, struggling to sit up. "No more death!"

The arc of Pathan's sword did not falter, but instead of slicing through Geraldo's neck, he slammed the jeweled knob of his sword hilt against Geraldo's temple. Geraldo staggered, nearing the curtain of the falls. Blood pulsed over his fingers where they held his temple. At last he crumbled to his knees, then spasmed and collapsed on the stone floor.

"Is he dead?" Lucinda asked as Pathan stepped closer to him, sword point ready.

Pathan stood over him, sword raised. "Not dead," he said at last, lowering the blade. Then he knelt at her side, and began to cut through Lucinda's bindings. His sword blade sliced the leather thongs. Pathan rubbed her chafed wrists with his thumbs.

Lucy turned to him, eyes brimming with tears. "No, Munna, you must get away. They will kill you! Go while you can!"

Pathan lifted his head. "Then we will die together."

Again Lucinda leaped, again she knocked another to ground. This time it was Pathan who fell beneath her. But first Lucinda threw her arms around his neck, and as they fell, he pulled her close. On the stone floor of the inner chamber, she covered his wet face with kisses.

"If you love me, you will leave me and live, dear Munna," she whispered in his ear.

"Because I love you, I will stay beside you." Pathan sat up, and looked hard at her. "But we need not die. There is a way, though it is a hard life that I offer. They will pursue you because they want your fortune, and they'll pursue me to gain my family's estate. The Sultana may give up, but the Brotherhood will come after us, and they have people everywhere, and they never tire. Never can we rest, nor ever feel safe. A bandit's life lies before us. But you'll be alive, dear Lucy, and I'll be by your side. Will you go with me?"

Lucy's fervent kiss was her answer.

"We must hurry, Lucy."

"But how can we get out?" She nodded to the entrances to the chamber. "On that side are the Sultana's guards. On the other are Slipper's guards. Both will stop us." They could just make out shadows moving through the narrow veils of water at the chamber's sides.

He smiled, that rare smile that broke her heart with its clear beauty. Then he lifted her onto the mare, and swung up behind her. Then Pathan backed the mare to the very rear of the chamber, and faced the brilliant torrent of the main waterfall. Here the stone of the chamber's rear walls amplified the roar, and the sheet of water gleamed white ahead of them. "Hold on very tight." He spurred the mare. She reared up, and dashed forward through the white deluge.

☾☽☾☽

With the eunuch captain of the Sultana's guards, Slipper discussed the bowmen on the other shore. He then came back fuming to Da Gama. "He says to take no notice. They aren't hurting anyone, he says. If he had seen what we have seen, he wouldn't be so calm!" All this he shouted over the roar of falling water.

Da Gama forced a chuckle. "You now talk like a settlement man. Any thing unusual is cause for worry."

"Exactly! For example, what is taking Geraldo so long?" fussed Slipper.

"He's got the horse to think of, senhor. It can't be easygoing."

Slipper twisted his lip, glancing first to the exit from the falls, then to the other shore at the horseman. "I don't like it. Something's wrong. I'm sending someone in." Again he hurried to the captain, but was no more successful than before. "He says he doesn't want his men to get wet! Can you believe it!"

Da Gama, however, had noticed a streak of red swirling in the white water that flowed from the exit. He struggled to keep his face impassive, but then a pistol rattled to the nearby stones beneath the cascading water. He stepped between Slipper and the sight, hoping that the eunuch's bad eyes had not seen. What was happening inside that chamber?

Then Maya screamed.

A horse burst through the falls, crashing through the curtain of water. Swirls of droplets exploded in the bright sun, making trails of light. The horse's legs churned the mists as it vaulted into emptiness. On its back, two riders held tight as the beast soared and splashed into the pool below. Then they sank beneath the surface of the water.

"It is Pathan!" Maya shouted despite herself.

The eunuch guards crowded to the edge of the pathway of the falls. "He's drowned!" one of the guards yelled.

"Where is Geraldo!" Slipper screamed. "Where is the poisoner?" He neared the falling curtain of water, but could not steel himself to pass.

"They've come up!" shouted one of the guards. In a swirl of bubbles, the mare's head emerged, and behind it her two riders. "One's a woman!"

"It's her!" Slipper screamed. "Shoot them, shoot them!"

"We have no bows," the captain shouted back.

"You have spears, don't you?" Slipper's face was bright red, and his tiny eyes nearly burst from his head. "Use them!"

But at that moment, an arrow zipped past his face and clattered on the rock wall beside him. The bandits on the other shore had begun to fire. They were fast: a rain of arrows struck the rocks. One pierced the arm of a eunuch guard, who gave a wailing scream. He pulled at it desperately, yelping with each tug.

A dozen more arrows slapped against the stones. "Behind the falls!" the captain ordered. "Hurry! Take cover!"

The guards pushed against each other, some nearly tumbling down the rocks. One shoved Maya through the water into the chamber. Another grabbed Da Gama's bound arm.

He shook out of the guard's light grip and stared across the pool, despite the arrows that clattered all around. The mare stumbled up the other shore, Pathan and Lucy clinging to her back. Da Gama watched the mare stagger up the ancient temple ghats to the ground beside the bandits.

The guard tugged Da Gama's arm once more. He had only time to see the mare rear up as Pathan waved his bright sword, as they charged into the jungle.

The guard dragged Da Gama into the waterfall chamber. Everyone was soaked. Slipper knelt near Geraldo, who was shaking his head as if to clear it. When he saw Da Gama enter, Geraldo struggled to his feet. "You!" he shouted. "You planned this!"

Da Gama did not answer.

Geraldo wheeled suddenly and hurled his fist into Da Gama's head. Though Da Gama ducked, he still caught much of the blow. His bound hands threw off his balance: he fell to his knees and tumbled forward. The tip of Geraldo's boot caught his chin, and light exploded in his eyes.

As he lost consciousness, he vaguely felt his body lifting from the floor with the force of Geraldo's kicks.

၏ၜၜ၆

"Hey, Deoga. Time to get up. Get up, lazybones."

Da Gama blinked awake. Every inch of his body ached. In a moment his eyes adjusted to the dim light of a grand tent, and he recognized the face of Commander Shahji. "General!" he said. Or tried to. His mouth was caked with dryness and his teeth ached.

"Yes, that Geraldo fellow gave you a few good ones. The hakim's been in . . . you've nothing broken, and you'll live, though the way you'll hurt for the next few days, you might wish that you were dead."

"Where am I?"

"You're a guest in my tent, at the Sultana's camp at Gokak Falls." Slowly Da Gama's senses came awake. He could smell the musty tang of damp wool-tent walls, and hear outside the rumble of the river as it tumbled down the falls. "I volunteered to glue you back together. Slipper and the guards brought you here, you and the nautch girl. And Geraldo. They've set him with the *hijra* guards." Shahji chuckled as he said this. "That should teach him to behave, eh? Anyway, you're to stay away from him . . . otherwise, you're free."

That reminded Da Gama—he lifted his hands. They were unbound.

"So, Deoga, how do you feel?" Shahji said with real concern.

"Like hell."

"Too bad. You've got business—serious business, I think. Right now the Sultana is in audience, about to hear matters that affect you."

"An audience? Here . . . in the middle of nowhere?"

Shahji shook his head. "You really are a child, sometimes. Do you think the scheming would halt, just because the queen has left her palace? Everyone of any consequence has come along. In the Flying Palace, at this moment, the audience proceeds, and the Sultana wants you to attend."

Da Gama blinked, and chanced sitting up. His body screamed in protest and his vision went black, but then things settled down. "Where are my clothes?" His voice sounded terrible.

"So filthy that I had them buried." Shahji laughed. "You must make do with some of mine." He gave a single clap, and a grave old servant brought in a stack of carefully folded *jamas*. "You have worn this stuff before?"

"On occasion," Da Gama answered. "It makes me look a fool."

"At least you won't be a hypocrite. Hurry dressing." As Shahji was about to pass through the curtained entryway, he turned. "I put your belongings on that table, by that pitcher of wine. A cup or two couldn't hurt."

Before he dressed, a servant produced a razor and basin, and gave Da Gama a painful shave, then oiled, rubbed, and combed his hair. In truth, though he felt a fool in Shahji's clothes, the fit was good and the style flattering.

With Shahji walking beside him, Da Gama headed for the audience. Shahji's grand tent was one of about a dozen in a wide ring around the Flying Palace, which dominated in the center. Da Gama saw that a wide area had been set with ring after ring of tents; the grandest like Shahji's in the ring closest to the Flying Palace, then smaller and smaller tents until one came to simple peasant tents in the outer rings. Shahji pointed to a far-off stable tent where the elephants and horses all were quartered.

Before they went to the palace, however, Shahji took Da Gama's arm, and drew him a few yards away. "Look here, Deoga," he said. "That's the river Ghataprabha there. See that bridge? The Sultana always brings it when she camps here. They set it up right there, just a few yards from the falls. It's too fragile to carry any kind of load—so they bring the tents across a mile upstream. You stand on that delicate bridge, looking down into the rushing water, and in a moment you're convinced you'll tumble over. It's quite unnerving. The queen stands there each day at noon."

The bridge was a narrow wooden path stretched across an arching skeleton of wood. Despite its handrails, it struck Da Gama as a doubtful structure. "Most amusing," Da Gama said to be polite.

Shahji glared at him. "I don't show this for amusement. These things should indicate to you the character of the persons you are dealing with. They are bored and reckless and wedded to routine. A soldier notes such things."

Da Gama bowed. "I owe you much, General."

Shahji went on without acknowledging him. "The bridge is guarded by the *hijra*. It is the only access point to the zenana. You can see the private harem tents through those trees. They put up those tall muslin screens to keep things private. Those are the quarters of the Sultana and her ladies, and of course the *hijra* servants. That is where your nautch girl stays as well."

"You say that Geraldo is with the eunuch guards?"

"Yes," Shahji answered, "but those guards are quartered on this side of the river. They'd stir up too much trouble in the harem." Shahji said this with a straight face. "Enough. Let's face the battle like men." He led Da Gama toward the palace, and the Sultana's audience.

❀❀❀❀

The Flying Palace did not seem quite so huge once it had been set upon the ground. Floating above the road, its enormous bulk suspended in the air by straining elephants, one might assume that it was some sort of colossus. But once it rested on the ground, one saw that the palace was scarcely larger than some of the grand tents surrounding it.

Shahji passed the guards without a glance, though they lowered their heads to him. Da Gama also slipped behind without challenge, for Shahji's aura expanded to contain him. They strode up the wooden staircase—Da Gama grunted with his aching bruises—then crossed into the main hall of the palace, which had been set up for an audience, in imitation of the Diwan-I-Khas in Bijapur Palace.

It was a square hall. At the far end, away from the double-entry door, Da Gama saw a three-tiered dais: a silver railing around the first, a gold railing around the second, higher dais. Behind the silver railing, on a silver bench, sat Wali Khan, looking agitated. Behind the gold railing Whisper leaned over a cone-shaped pile of dark green cloth.

"What's Whisper doing?" he muttered.

"Talking to the queen," Shahji answered.

Slowly the picture came into focus. It was not a pile of cloth, it was a person, hidden under a vast, impenetrable array of robes and skirts and veils. Near the peak of the mountain of cloth—for so it seemed to Da Gama—he could make out a dark, horizontal slash, and if he stared hard, he could see in the shadow of the veils the eyes of the Sultana. "Why does she hide so?" he whispered to Shahji.

"She breaks tradition doing even this. No other queen had ever set foot outside the harem."

Shahji led Da Gama through the stares of the brightly costumed courtiers and to the polished silver rail, where he casually placed his hand. Wali Khan looked at it and grimaced, as if he'd placed feces there. "Highness," Shahji said in a calm voice that filled the room, "here as you requested I present the farang Da Gama, called by many Deoga."

"How do you come to have this second name, sir?" The muffled query of the Sultana was so soft Da Gama had to strain to hear.

Da Gama bowed, a deep and swooping farang bow that looked completely out of place in his borrowed *jamas*. "Your highness, it is a sort of joke. I once stayed in Deogarh, but I could not say the name right. Now this failure follows me wherever I go." The Sultana gave a polite laugh, like a soft cough.

"But he is too modest, highness," Whisper said, in his rasping voice. Only those close to the dais could hear. "This man single-handedly saved a dozen children from a fire at the mosque of Deogarh. Then he returned to brave the flames alone. He rescued the Koran of Nazamudin, and a hair of the Prophet's beard."

"Is this true?"

Now he knew what to listen for, Da Gama could more clearly understand the Sultana's muffled words. "The tale grows in the telling, highness. I did no more than any man might do under the circumstances. In truth I wish it were forgotten."

"And yet you persist in recalling it, by using that name." A silence fell, and Da Gama got the feeling that those hidden eyes were examining him. Da Gama took a moment to glance around the room. In a corner, near a eunuch guard, Geraldo stared at him. He was still wearing the clothes he'd worn at the falls, and they looked very damp. Once more the Sultana spoke: "We have heard some conflicting stories, Deoga. We would hear your version."

Da Gama gave another sweeping bow. "A nod will suffice, sir," Wali Khan whispered.

"You were the *burak* for Victorio Souza?"

"We farangs say 'settlement man,' your highness. We have not the subtlety of a *burak*, nor a *burak*'s wisdom, as your advisors surely have already told you."

"They told me, sir, that you were dangerous. Now answer my question."

Da Gama licked his lips and answered haltingly. "I'm a hired agent, highness, and my services were employed for a settlement arranged by the Dasanas. Victorio Souza was a trustee. In the end he defined my duties."

"You answer carefully, Deoga. Are you afraid of us?" Da Gama stirred uncomfortably. He disliked standing still. He felt the eyes of all the court upon him. "Never mind. An honest man has nothing to fear. Do you know who killed Victorio Souza?"

Across the room Da Gama saw Geraldo straighten. "I don't know, highness."

"Truly? It appears that you alone doubt the guilt of the niece. She had poison, and she had reason."

Without looking, Da Gama could feel Geraldo's eyes boring into him. "You did not ask for my opinion, highness, but for my knowledge. Many persons in that camp had poison, highness. Even I had poison. And many persons desired Victorio's death. But in truth, I do not know who killed him. Not for certain."

Across the room, Geraldo's eyes grew wide. Da Gama nearly smiled to see his reaction.

"We will not press that point for now. Another question concerns the ownership of the nautch girl. Your master, Victorio Souza had . . . a liberality of nature. In his generosity he promised that same woman to two persons." The thickly veiled head nodded barely perceptibly to Whisper and then Wali Khan. "Do not concern yourself with knowledge this time; this time, simply tell us your opinion in this matter."

Da Gama nodded to her, smiling a little, for he saw that she too was subtle. Feeling his way as a man in a dark place, he answered. "The girl had been promised to the grand vizier. Later Victorio changed his mind, and agreed to sell her to the Khaswajara. The vizier expressed his prior claim. I'm not sure how Victorio would have decided to resolve the matter."

"Lies!" Whisper fixed him with his old eyes. "Our brother Slipper was there. He had made up his mind right before he died."

"My master Victorio would say, I fear, whatever popped into his head. Had he lived five more minutes, he might have changed his mind again. Highness, it's my opinion, since you asked me, that he planned to play both sides against each other up to the final moment."

The Khaswajara pursed his lips, and Wali Khan scowled. The Sultana sat in silence. "So tell us: What is your interest in this matter, Deoga?" she asked finally.

"I have my obligation to the Dasanas; I must see that they are treated fairly."

"It's been said that you were Victorio's partner."

Da Gama saw Whisper glance quickly toward Geraldo. He could not see the trap, but sensed the danger nonetheless. "Your Highness mentioned Victorio's liberality. He made many more promises than he kept. He promised partnerships. More than once. To me, and to others. Settlement men don't believe in promises." He cast a glance toward Geraldo. "In my case, I suppose he merely wanted me to lend him money. He had many debts."

"Deoga," the muffled voice said slowly, "you are most surprising. Here is the Dasana estate, a great fortune, waiting only for you to reach out your hand. Yet you avoid making a claim. Others have not been so reluctant."

Da Gama lowered his eyes and shrugged.

"Tell us, Deoga—who in your opinion owns the nautch girl at this moment?"

"Until a settlement is made, she is the properly of Lucinda Dasana, highness, the heir of the Dasana fortune."

"That person is a villainess and a murderer, and her claim is forfeit!" Whisper coughed with the effort of his speaking.

"She may be accused, but she is not condemned," Da Gama answered. "And her estate, as I understand it, is forfeit only after her conviction and her death."

"That should be easy to arrange," Whisper rasped.

"Except that she is gone, Lord Khaswajara."

"Abetted, highness, by this man!" Whisper lifted his bony finger to the vizier. "Wali Khan's *burak* has betrayed your justice!"

The Sultana, hidden behind her wall of cloth, made no sign of having heard. When she spoke again Da Gama thought he heard a pleading in her muffled voice. "Deoga, to face difficulties is the lot of a settlement man, is it not? How would you settle this matter?"

What's she like in there? Da Gama wondered. Young? Old? Devious? Terrified?

He made up his mind to speak to her as to a sister, if he'd had one. "Highness, it is up to us to do our best, and then leave the rest to God. First

I would decide. Then I would enforce." Despite his aching body, he straightened. "Since no one has clear claim, maybe I'd begin by wondering how to do the most good. The Khaswajara—what is his desire here? Has he become a patron of the dance? Why does he want a nautch girl? Why this one? What does she have, eh?" Whisper glowered at Da Gama, but he said nothing. "And the vizier. Making promises and treaties with your enemies. Using that young woman as *baksheesh*." Wali Khan gave a worried look, not certain how to take this statement. "And yourself, highness. When you must choose between two men of such stature, how can you have peace? I would ask—is there any way to satisfy everyone? And if not, whose plea most benefits the cause of the heir?"

Beneath her veils the Sultana sighed. "Oh, you are dangerous, farang. You play upon us, mixing truth and doubt in equal measure. Like a conjurer, you gesture with one hand to distract us from the other."

Da Gama, regardless of the vizier's advice, bowed deeply. "You have seen through me, highness. But I say this with my whole heart—better you decide than I."

"Yes, there we agree, sir." She rose from her silver bench—she was so small it was hard to tell that she had stood. A pair of eunuch boys rushed to arrange her skirts so she could walk. "Our audience is at an end."

Wali Khan stood too. "But, Highness, what have you decided?"

"Nothing, sir. First we will speak to this nautch girl."

"Will Whisper be with you when you do?" the vizier said accusingly.

"That is our concern, sir, not yours." Without another word, she moved to the door, trailing yards of cloth behind her. Whisper and the eunuch boys followed close behind, and after them a half-dozen eunuch guards. All around Da Gama, courtiers bowed so low, they swept the floor with the backs of their hands.

When the courtiers began to depart, murmuring to each other, Da Gama approached the vizier. "You are not satisfied, sir."

"I am not. But at least you did not speak against me."

"I thought I spoke in your favor, sir, but who can tell." Da Gama lowered his head. "Someday I might need a job, sir. Your *burak* is gone."

The vizier hmmphed. "When that day comes, you'll know how to find me. But who knows—maybe I too will need a job."

As he walked off, Geraldo came over. "Why did you not betray me, Da Gama?"

Da Gama eyed him, wondering if he'd done the right thing. "I had my reasons."

A shrewd look came into Geraldo's eyes, and his handsome smile reappeared. "You're afraid of me!"

Da Gama's face was blank. "Remember that I did you a favor."

Geraldo considered a response, but finally merely shook his head. He hurried away, asking for Whisper.

Shahji came up behind Da Gama. "Neither good nor bad," he said. "If it had been me, I'd have spoken in favor of the *hijra*. Seven *lakh* hun! You may have thrown that away. And you might have said you were a partner—who could dispute it?"

"I was not meant to be a rich man, General." They walked across the painted wooden floor of the Flying Palace.

But Shahji appeared not to have heard. "She's going to decide the regency. That's why she came here—to get away from all the pressure. As though this place were any less a nest of snakes than Bijapur." Shahji looked carefully at Da Gama. "She asks my opinion. I hope I speak as well as you have done."

"What have you decided, General?"

"Much as I hate to do so, I must side with the *hijra*. Wali Khan's the better man, but he'd instantly replace me as commander. He owes too much to Afzul Khan. But I hate the *hijra* . . ." Shahji shook his head. "They will squeeze and squeeze and squeeze me. And how will I resist them?" Shahji forced a laugh. "You don't need to hear my problems, though. At least not sober. Let's find some wine."

ତ୨୧୨

Behind the muslin purdah screens that shielded the traveling zenana from unwanted eyes, Maya sat beneath a tree in a field that had recently been mowed and raked to make a lawn. The short grass felt stiff and slightly moist, and still gave off the fresh perfume of mowing. The grand tent of the Sultana, brightly colored, with gold bossed poles, rose in the center of the lawn. Around it were a dozen lesser tents, where maids and eunuchs napped.

She had taken the Gita from her bag, and struggled to concentrate on it, but her eyes drifted toward the sound of the river. On the other shore, the Sultana sat in audience, deciding her fate. She knew whatever happened next would be the working of the Goddess's will, but still she wondered. She could not help herself.

A few women and eunuchs made their lazy way through the encampment, some with water jugs on their heads, others carrying great heaps of laundry. Somewhere a flute was playing.

A few yards away, a pretty eunuch boy tossed a silver ball into the air, and caught it. He looked very bored and unconcerned, but each toss brought him a few steps closer to Maya. She focused on her book.

When the silver ball rolled a few inches from her feet, Maya looked up. The boy came toward her, scooped up the ball, and stared. She stared back for a while, but he said nothing, and at last she turned away. Then, of course, he spoke. "What are you doing?"

"What does it look like?"

"Women can't read."

"I can."

The boy flipped the ball into the air a few times, and then sat a few feet from her. His clothes were very fine, and he wore many rings. A *hijra* boy being trained for royal service, Maya guessed. The boy moved closer. "What's that language?"

"Sanskrit. It is the language of the gods."

"You're a heathen," he said brightly. "I worship the one true god." When Maya did not answer, he tried again. "I can read. Persian and Arabic."

"Very nice."

"Play ball with me?"

There was something in his eyes that caught her off guard; a look of eagerness and resignation, of hopes dashed. She saw, maybe, her kinship with him, that of slave to slave. Instead of telling him to go away, she closed her book, and folded it in its silken cover, and stood. "I'm not very good."

"That's all right." He tossed the silver ball to her. It was expensive, hollow silver, heavy with engravings. "Do you like it? You can have it if you want."

"Let's just play." She threw the ball, so swift and hard he laughed.

"Who said you weren't good? Girls can't throw that hard."

"I can."

Back and forth they tossed the ball. He kept stepping back, challenging her, laughing when she reached him all the same. Soon they were both laughing, running to catch it as the ball glittered in the air. Sometimes he made a diving catch despite his fine clothing.

"What's your name?" he asked after they'd played a while.

"Maya."

"Mine's Adil. You're the new nautch girl. Slipper told me."

Maya's face grew cold at Slipper's name. For a moment, she'd forgotten. "I'm tired," she said, and sat again beneath the shade.

The boy came over to her, and pulled a shiny pomegranate from his pocket. "Want some?" He pushed his thumbs in the end of the fruit and split it in two, revealing seeds as bright as rubies, and offered her half.

That's when she saw it: the scarlet mark on his palm—the mark of the evil eye.

The same mark as she had seen just days before on Lady Chitra's hand. "How old are you?" She tried to mask the urgency in her voice.

"I'm nine." The boy looked up. "Damn. I can't play anymore. I have to work." Maya turned, and saw what he had seen: a woman moving toward them like a walking hill of cloth, followed by a few more eunuch boys, and a skinny old eunuch, dry as a dead branch. "Maybe I'll see you again." He raced off to join them.

Having seen the return of the Sultana, Maya could not be calm: she tried to read, she stood, she sat, she folded up her book again.

After a little while, a maid appeared. "The queen wants to speak with you. Follow me." Maya picked up her shoulder bag. As they walked toward the Sultana's tent, the maid chatted in a friendly way, telling her which tent was which, gossiping. "We saw you playing with Adil," she said. "He doesn't like many people."

"He seems nice enough," Maya answered. "Has he been a servant long?"

The maid stopped short and laughed. "Did you think he was a eunuch?"

"Isn't he?"

Again the maid laughed. "Are you not familiar with our ways? Boys of royal blood stay in the harem with their mothers until they are married. The eunuchs teach them. Surely you knew this."

Maya shook her head. "Is he of royal blood, then?"

"Dear girl, of course. He is the only son of the Sultana. He is the Heir." Maya's eyes grew wide. "He's the sultan of Bijapur, silly. You really didn't know?"

C®©©

Her way seemed so bright and offhand, that Maya only realized after she had
left that the maid had told her much useful information in their time together. What to call the Sultana; where to sit. And she'd told Maya to be
watchful of the Khaswajara: "Dry as an old bone, but crafty, with eyes like a
cobra that has lived too long."

The Sultana never acknowledged Maya's bow. She perched on a stool.
The thin old eunuch by her side was Whisper, Maya had no doubt. She saw
that he'd developed a habit of tilting slightly when he stood, first to one
foot, then the other. She wondered if he ever got to sit.

The Khaswajara had some business to discuss, some petition from a
courtier, which he spoke of endlessly in a low, husky voice. Maya could
not tell if the queen even heard a word. Piece by piece, two maids un-
dressed her, like servants unpacking some rare piece of porcelain wrapped
in layers of batting. Walking in endless circles around her, they unwrapped
the Sultana. They removed bolt after bolt of cloth and then started on the
next. Slowly the Sultana dwindled, smaller and smaller as each piece was
put away, until at last her face appeared, and then her tiny body.

She was younger than Lady Chitra, older than Maya—but though her
face was smooth, her hair was mostly gray. One of the eunuch boys
brought her a jade cup, and she drank it off in a gulp. She held out the cup,
and let it drop without a care. The eunuch boy retrieved it in midair.

The queen's eyes flicked toward Maya, and then turned away.

The maids clothed her in a simple dressing gown. Her movements and
the maids' seemed stylized, almost like a dance. The queen would lift her
arm or drop her heel as if certain that her maid would be in place to catch
it. It was more exquisite than dance, Maya thought, more disturbing—
movement without thought or feeling—like the clockwork figures she'd
seen for sale in Cochin's bazaar.

The Sultana at last took a seat among some cushions, which a maid had
plumped just moments before. "The heir must have his nap," she said to no
one in particular. "See to it. Then an hour of Persian study. Then his
prayers. Then bed. Now leave us." The servants bowed.

"Not you," she then said, her dark eyes at last finding Maya's.

When the others had gone, the queen indicated with a glance the place beside her. "You're very pretty," the Sultana said after considering her for a moment.

"You are kind, madam," Maya said, sitting.

"But those clothes of yours are dreadful. Never mind, we'll find some better." Maya inclined her head in thanks, but the Sultana had looked away. "We have a little time together to ourselves. Don't pretend shyness. We have not the patience. Why are you worth seven *lakh* hun? Can you tell me?"

"No, madam."

The Sultana stared at some place far away. "It can't be congress, can it? The eunuchs have no use for that."

"I dance," Maya said helpfully.

"All nautch girls dance." She gave Maya a long appraising look, as though reviewing every detail of her appearance. Maya felt the heat rise to her cheeks. "As far as Wali Khan, the answer's plain: sex. Sex obviously. You're young, well muscled. Of course you know the tricks? They all do."

Maya turned away. She whispered her mantra until she'd regained her calm. When she turned back, she saw the queen's expression, irritated and amused. "There, we've upset you. But now we can see—it is your beauty that the vizier covets. Those eyes, we think, that glow when you are angry, and those fine lips. They would drive a man like Wali Khan to some distraction. He's a connoisseur. He collects fine women, and makes a trade in them. He sends out scouts to find the best, the young ones not yet worn out." The Sultana looked away, as if for a moment wistful, jealous. So unguarded, she seemed to Maya very sad. When again she spoke, she whispered. "Have you no one in this world, child? Are you all alone?"

"My guru, perhaps. But she is lost. I thought she was dead, but I see her in dreams. Deoga has befriended me."

The Sultana rolled her eyes. "Never trust farangs. He's tossed you over, like an empty cup. You must begin to cultivate your own resources. It appears that we are now your only hope, child. And we don't know what we are to do with you."

"Tossed me over?" whispered Maya, but the queen was saying something else and did not hear.

"Now the vizier's already bargained you away," the queen went on, as if repeating facts well known to them both. "Do you know Murad?" Maya shook her head, not yet taking it all in. "He's the son of Shah Jahan, the

Mogul emperor. He's the Mogul viceroy in Surat. Wali Khan has made a treaty with the Moguls. And you, dear child, you are the seal on the contract. What do you think of that?"

"I am a slave, madam."

"Surely your brain still works? Let us tell you about Murad. He's harmless. He has a hundred wives, and never sleeps with any of them." She made a sign of drinking and nodded significantly. "Wali Khan is not to be trusted, but we could make certain that he sent you there. That would be best for you. Surat's hot, but otherwise no worse than Bijapur. Yes, that would be best." She sat up, as though a matter was settled. "But why does the Khaswajara want you? Why are you worth seven *lakhs*? What does he have in mind?" She nodded to Maya's bag. "What's in there?"

Instead of saying, Maya spilled the contents at the Sultana's feet. The queen picked up her things, item by item. "A book. *Dravanas*? Is that all? Surely you have more in there?"

Reluctantly, Maya took out her broken sword, the rough-sawed coin, and last of all the headdress. The queen examined each piece carefully. "There's a story here, isn't there? Come nearer. So many ears about. Nearer still." She motioned Maya to her ear. "Tell us of these things, but quietly."

CIOCIO

Despite the wine, Da Gama could not sleep. He hated tents. In the middle of the night he gave up and left his tent to walk beneath the stars.

A few fires burned, a few shadows moved in the darkness, but the camp was quiet. All that could be heard was the endless roaring of the nearby falls. The full moon burned so bright the grass looked silver, and Da Gama cast faint shadows as he walked.

Without a conscious thought, he found himself moving toward the river. As he left the circle of grand tents the crickets chirped noisily, and once in some bushes he saw the glowing eyes of a panther, but the beast darted off. Suddenly he wished he had his *pistolas*. No one in the camp carried weapons except the eunuch guards.

By the time he came to the river's edge his borrowed slippers were soaked through. The river still ran high, and here and there eddies that had formed along the shore glittered in the moon. Da Gama came to the narrow wooden bridge that led to the zenana camp. Across the river a eunuch guard lounged against the railing.

Here the roaring grew loud. He stepped onto the bridge. Even over the river noise, he heard the wood and lashings squeak with his every step. In the middle he leaned against the rail, which sagged against his weight.

The bridge was set only a few feet from the falls' edge. Da Gama could look over the drop. Mists swirled like ghosts in the moonlight. Below he made out the pool where Pathan's horse dove, and past that, the listing tower of the crumbling temple.

Suddenly Da Gama thought of Lucy. He wanted desperately to reach out to her, to wish her well, to give her his blessing and embrace. She had been a brightness, but she was gone forever now. He thought of the life ahead of him—of days spent on the move, of nights spent sleeping on the damp ground, of the company of men like Geraldo, Victorio, men who made his stomach churn.

Da Gama shook his head. These thoughts came from exhaustion, he told himself. He looked around, and was considering a chat with the eunuch guard when he saw across the lawn of the zenana a moonlit figure floating toward him like a sylph.

Maya.

She drifted toward the bridge. The eunuch guard stopped her, but she spoke soft words to him, and at last he let her pass. She came next to Da Gama, gentle as a whisper, in a sari more sheer than a moth's wing. Her face shown delicate in the brilliant moon.

"You're up early, Deoga," she breathed.

"I couldn't sleep."

At the end of the bridge, the eunuch guard watched suspiciously. "He thinks we're here for romance, Deoga," she laughed. The sound pierced Da Gama. She seemed utterly without a care, a living jewel, desirable and impossible for one like him to grasp. Even more than usual, he regretted his clumsiness, his gruff voice and thick body, his stiff whiskers, and his heavy thoughts. Like Lucy, Maya made him think of perfumes, and of the things that women keep around them; the delicate things they wear against their skin; the fragile things they hold in slender fingers and soft hands. Every moment with her heightened his despairing emptiness, yet he found himself longing for that despair. In that despair was his last joy.

Then Maya said something that caught him by surprise. "This is my last day of freedom, Deoga. The Sultana says I will be in purdah by the evening, in the harem, nevermore to walk again through the world of men."

Da Gama blinked as if newly wakened. "What did you say?"

"Purdah, Deoga. We all knew it would happen sometime. The time comes tonight."

"But, it can't. . . . When will I see you?"

She laughed at him. She was so beautiful when she laughed, he could almost bear the sting. "You silly. I'm just a nautch girl, a slave. Soon I shall be a whore—but whether for the grand vizier or the Khaswajara, the Sultana has not yet said."

He'd never seen her so open. Perhaps the final resolution of her fate brought relief. But his mind raced. "Listen, Maya," he whispered in a rush, interrupting whatever the hell she was saying. "We can get out of here. I can steal some horses. We can go into the forest, like Lucy and Pathan. . . ."

Her silence was her answer, and her lowered head, and her fingers, hidden from the guard, that crept across his hand where he gripped the flimsy railing of the bridge. She squeezed his hand, and her eyes drifted over the falling foam. Then she took her hand away. It felt cold now where her fingers had just been.

"It's impossible anyway," Da Gama said, suddenly hoarse. "That's a young man's fantasy. Time I act my age." He tried to force a laugh. He stared at the emptiness where the waters spilled away, and at the pool below, dark and impenetrable. The falls roared.

Maybe he was drowsy after all. His eyes grew fascinated by the sweeping river. Suddenly it felt as if the water were standing still, and that the bridge itself rushed forward like a ship racing on the wind, a ship flying toward the edge of the earth.

It would be so easy.

"Deoga!" Maya said, grasping his arm. "You were falling!"

The eunuch guard moved forward, but Da Gama waved him away. "I must have nodded off."

"But did you not hear what I was saying? The heir . . ." she lowered her voice. "I think he is the child stolen from Lady Chitra." This information made no difference to Da Gama. "Deoga, promise me you'll get word to her. She must be told. You must give me your word." But Da Gama made no sign that he had heard. "Deoga, promise me."

"Of course." He glanced at the falls, then away, forcing his mind to work. "There's something I have to give to you. How can I . . ."

"I'm supposed to dance at the audience later. That's when the queen will announce her decision about me. My last appearance in public before I'm sent to purdah. Give it to me then." A worried look flashed across her face for just an instant. "The Sultana gave me good advice. I must cultivate my own resources. I should have done this long ago. Oh, Deoga, I have been so very foolish! I must be hard as diamonds, and as cold." She then moved away, backward, her eyes on his. "Do not forget me, Deoga. Remember me as I was!"

She walked slowly to the end of the bridge. Da Gama watched until he could no longer see her shadow, and kept watching until the first pink light of dawn peeked over the horizon, and the river glistened. He turned to see the moon setting behind the ancient temple near the falls, where the swirling mists, now silver from the moon, now gold from the sun, churned endlessly over the roaring void.

ଈଓଓଈଓ

It was nearly noon when Shahji woke Da Gama. "Turn out, soldier. Your presence is required by the queen. And anyway, we've got to strike the tents. We break camp after the audience."

Da Gama grunted and got up. New clothes had been laid out for him—some of Shahji's *jamas*—and he dressed quickly. "Do you go back to Bijapur, General?"

"No, to Belgaum for a few days. What about you?"

"I have no idea." Da Gama drew on a long robe of tawny silk. "Perhaps you would do me one more favor, sir? I have a message to deliver to Lady Chitra." He told Shahji of Maya's discovery about the heir.

Shahji's eyes grew wide. "Is this true?"

"She has never lied to me, General."

Shahji's eyes darted nervously, like a soldier assessing a battle. "Deoga, if she's right . . . This could be the key for me."

Da Gama wrapped the wide brown sash around his waist. "Perhaps I'm missing something."

Shahji gave Da Gama a shrewd look. "I doubt it. I think you know exactly what this information means. Why you would pretend otherwise, I don't understand. This information gives me the power to deal with Whisper and the Brotherhood." Da Gama bowed as if confused, and again Shahji searched his face for a sign that he realized the import of his words. "The Sultana admired your subtlety, Deoga. So do I."

"Don't mistake my ignorance for cleverness, General," Da Gama answered.

Outside, tentwallahs scurried to pack the grand tents into a train of bullock carts. "Mine is the last to be taken down, you see? A favor for you, Deoga. I thought you'd need your rest." Despite Shahji's mocking smile, Da Gama lowered his head to acknowledge the courtesy.

Courtiers hurriedly made their way to the Flying Palace. Nearby, mahouts directed the placing of the huge yokes and harnesses on their enormous elephants. Large men tied the thick lifting ropes through the massive iron rings at the corners of the palace. "The Sultana's whim changes with the breeze," Shahji explained. "At dawn, she commanded that the camp return to Bijapur. Everyone's been hurrying since. It will take an effort to reach the gates by nightfall."

Da Gama glanced across the river. The muslin screens were gone, and only one harem tent remained. A few more men stood at the river bridge. "That bridge will be the last to go. The queen always takes one last look at the falls, and throws roses in the river in memory of the sultan," Shahji explained as they mounted the palace steps.

The audience hall teemed with courtiers, many more than yesterday, standing in small groups as they awaited the arrival of the queen. Wali Khan stood already behind the silver railing, speaking with a group of smiling men.

"Everyone is here, you see. With the tents being struck, there's nowhere else to go. You'll wish to join those fellows, I expect?" Shahji said, nodding to a cluster of men across the room. Whisper was among them, stroking his long chin, and talking earnestly with Geraldo—whose farang clothes were at last freshly pressed—Da Gama saw the eunuch Slipper.

"I'd prefer to stay with you, sir, if that's convenient."

"My dear fellow," Shahji answered.

They moved toward the place that Shahji seemed to prefer, near the right-hand corner of the dais, when Wali Khan rapped the floor with his silver-tipped staff of office. Once, twice, thrice the staff banged, and the hollow beneath the dais boomed through the hall. Conversations stopped, men straightened their robes and pressed their turbans into place. Whisper hurried to the highest step of the dais just as the queen glided in.

As before, she wore such a profusion of robes that no sign of her could be seen. She'd altered the color of her outfit, to a bright leaflike green; its gold embroidery glittered when the hill of cloth passed beneath the sunbeams streaming from one of the small, high windows. As the queen's form moved along the dais, all the courtiers in the room bowed at the waist, sweeping the backs of their hands along the wood floor.

Behind the queen, Da Gama noted not only the usual guards and eunuch boy attendants, but also Maya, wearing a brilliant sari of bright red and gold. As she turned through the door, Da Gama caught a glimpse of a boy behind her, maybe eight or nine, he guessed. He held Maya's hand, not as a child might, but with the formality of a royal escort. "That is the Heir," Shahji murmured into Da Gama's ear.

When they caught sight of the boy, the courtiers began again to bow, and some to cheer: *Jai, Jai, sultan. Jai, Jai Adil!* Whisper glowered at the noise, but it took Wali Khan, banging his staff once again, to bring it to a halt. The boy brought Maya to the Sultana's side, and then sat at her feet, not far from Whisper.

The queen, beneath her many veils, gave a barely visible nod, and Whisper spoke, so softly that the crowd had to struggle to hear. After a dozen flowery preambles, Whisper said, "At the request of the heir, Adil, our sultan, may he live forever, the queen brings to us today Prabha, the famous *devadasi* from the Orissa temple. Before she joins the women in purdah and takes her nautch name, Maya, she has graciously agreed to dance for us."

"This is unusual," Shahji said softly to Da Gama. "Why bring a nautch girl out in public?"

But before Da Gama could reply, he heard music. For the first time he noticed tall screens of wood and silver set near the dais; behind them unseen musicians played. Women, Da Gama guessed, nautch girls in purdah, and soon Maya would join them in the shadows.

But now she stepped forward, glorious in her brilliant sari and borrowed jewels. Over her bare feet, ankle bells jingled as she walked down the dais steps to the palace floor. She had wrapped her sari skirts to cover each leg separately, so instead of being hidden, her bare calves showed when she moved. Her skin glowed like rich cream, her black hair gleamed like polished ebony. She passed only a few arms' lengths from Da Gama, and the light that glistened in her gold-flecked eyes was as brilliant as diamonds, and as cold. She gave no sign that she had even seen him.

The courtiers pushed back to the edges of the hall to give her room. The boy sultan rose from his mother's feet and slipped beneath the golden rail as a child ducks under a fence. He stood next to Wali Khan, who placed a big hand on his small shoulder—neither said a word, but only watched.

Maya came at last to the very center of the hall. Every eye was on her. She held her folded hands before her heart, and then stood still, more still than Da Gama had ever seen a person stand, the way a tree is still, or a statue, or a stone. Her stillness filled the hall. Da Gama became aware of his own heartbeat, and the river's roar, and the grunts of elephants and shouts of men outside. Meanwhile the music curled through her silence: a flute, and the endless buzzing of the tamboura's drone.

Even after all this time in Hindustan, Da Gama could make no sense of the music. From simple notes that hung like clouds at first, the melody progressed to flow in intricate randomness, suggesting a pattern sometimes, but never a simple theme or rhythm.

A drum then joined the music. The time for dancing had begun.

At first Maya made small, simple movements, from her current place into a new posture. She held each in stillness for a moment before switching to the next.

Her face, which had been void of all expression, suddenly came into bright relief. The tilt of her head and hips, her eyes, her hands, her feet combined with each new pose. Each attitude gave voice to an emotion: happiness, alarm, and some that Da Gama recognized, but for which he had no name. With each trill of the flute and slap of the drum, Maya added another step, another move. It was as though she flipped through a book of paintings, revealing with each beat another page.

Her head turned, and now her eyes surveyed the room. She caught Da Gama's gaze in a kind of web, and with his eyes, his full attention. It was as though she danced for him alone. He knew it was part of her art, that every person there at this moment felt the same, but it made his feelings no less palpable for knowing.

Each pose came on now faster than the last. Sometimes now her feet moved four times while her arms moved three. She turned her head so quickly that her braid swung behind her like a whip; her hands cut the air like knives. Her steps became strides; her strides hops, then jumps. Soon she was leaping in the air, landing as lightly as a paper ball. The soles of her feet slapped the wood floor like a drummer's fingers.

The music swelled in intricate profusion as she turned. Da Gama himself began to sweat, just watching her exertions. It was not desire that he felt, at least not as he was used to. Maya did not flirt nor leer. But the power of each pose, each leap brought to his thoughts an awareness of the supple strength of her limbs. His heart beat faster as he watched, joining the music like another drum.

Da Gama could feel the swirling of the flute pulsing through his veins. As Maya danced, a strength, not only of her body but of her will, exuded from her. It stirred him to be her equal with his own strength and will. She seemed to him both childlike and godlike—divinity approachable by man.

What I might do, he thought as she soared in a leap. What I too might be!

☙☙☙

It took a while to realize that the dance had ended. The hall still echoed with the tamboura's drone even when the music stopped, and once again Maya stood alone and unmoving in the center of the hall. Her limbs shone with sweat, and her sari clung to her body. Her chest heaved as she caught her breath. But that same unnerving stillness hovered in the air around her. The bountiful nothingness from which her dance had emerged could be perceived once more. At last the moment faded like a mist before the sun. From outside the shouts of the tentwallahs could again be heard, and the bellow of the elephants, and over all, the roaring of the falls.

The boy sultan stepped out from behind the silver rail, and with him two of the eunuch boy attendants, one of them carrying a square of folded black cloth. The heir came to Maya, and raised his hands in a formal bow. Then the eunuch boys approached her, and opened the cloth with a snap, and lifted it over her. It floated through the air and fell in a billow over her head.

She was now veiled.

They led Maya up the dais. The cloth was dark, but sheer, and as she moved, it pressed against her and puffed out as if it breathed. Sometimes the curve of a hip might be guessed through the cover, or the outline of her chin or cheek. Before the hidden queen, Maya inclined her cloaked head, and the veiled queen bowed back. Then Maya passed through the door like a shadow.

The hall, which had been utterly silent, came once more to life. Courtiers again began to move, to talk. Nervous laughter filled the air; Da Gama got the sense of men making ribald jokes. If he had his *pistolas* he'd have shot a few. He saw Geraldo whispering with a leering grin to Slipper, who giggled at his words. Shahji, at least, had the courtesy to stand apart, watching Maya's departure as one might watch a passing funeral.

After a moment, as the talk crescendoed, Wali Khan once more tapped his staff on the dais. "The Sultana speaks," he announced.

After the quiet had returned, the Sultana's muffled voice began. "She has a rare gift. You have seen today what few will see hereafter. But what shall be done with her? That is the question we must decide."

As she spoke, the young sultan settled once again at her feet, lounging comfortably and looking pleased with himself and rather bored. Whisper made a show of giving him extra room. At last the queen continued. "Many men have laid a claim to her, and her circumstances are enmeshed with a family of farangs, and many of them are dead, and one, maybe, a murderer. So our deciding has been difficult. Hear then our will."

"First, the nautch girl Maya was given as a gift to our grand vizier. Wali Khan, therefore shall have her."

At these words, from across the room, Slipper squealed in pain. Wali Khan did his best to look serene despite the sudden envy of the courtiers. "Hear, though, grand vizier . . . You made a promise to the Moguls: that you would deliver her to Viceroy Murad. That promise has been a factor in our thinking. Do not disappoint us." The grand vizier lowered his head in obedience.

"Also, there is a later item that may affect you, Wali Khan," the Sultana said as if in afterthought. At this he looked up with a frown. Trouble came in the queen's second thoughts.

"Next, the matter of the Dasanas. We find that before he died, Victorio Souza, trustee of the estate, made Geraldo Silveira a partner. We confirm that now. One half of the estate belongs to him." The murmuring of the court grew loud. Geraldo beamed, and Slipper grabbed his arm happily. Da

Gama gave no sign that he had even heard. "Master Khaswajara, there is some small tax on transferred holdings, is there not?"

"Highness, your memory once again is perfect. I shall see to its collection."

"A tax indeed. Seven parts of ten, if I recall," Shahji whispered into Da Gama's ear.

"The remainder of the Dasana estate belongs to Lucinda Dasana, accused of poisoning her uncle. Until she is produced, and condemned, and executed for her crime, those assets shall be held in trust. Senhor Geraldo Silveira shall manage them as the crown's agent. Upon the poisoner's death, they shall revert to the state."

Slipper had been growing more and more impatient, and suddenly burst out, "But, highness! What about the claim of the Khaswajara?" After he spoke, he clapped his hands across his mouth.

The hall laughed, Wali Khan tamped with his staff, and the queen continued. "There is that matter yet to decide. We find that the Khaswajara has a certain claim on the nautch girl. He made an offer, the offer was accepted—even though no goods changed hands and no settlement was made. How shall we provide for his claim?" Whisper now bowed to her. "Do you have the money, Whisper?" the queen said in a voice that only Da Gama and a few others were close enough to hear.

"Of course, highness."

"Hear then our judgement. For the seven *lakh*s you promised, you may have the girl." Slipper slapped his hands across his mouth to keep from cheering. "Since she is now owned by Wali Khan, you must pay him."

Whisper could barely hide his delight. "Yes, highness! Thank you, highness!"

Wali Khan stared back, speechless. He was gearing up to speak when some of the queen's cloth moved as she raised her hand. "Whisper, we mean the girl only, mind you. None of her things, nothing that she owns, or wears. The girl, and only the girl, as is, naked as when she was born." Whisper's smile took a moment to fade, but across the room, Slipper gasped out loud.

"Or, if you wish, for those same seven *lakh*s, you may choose a single item that she owns. Any item."

Whisper's expression became difficult to read. The courtiers frowned at one another, squinted at the queen, some stuck a finger through their turbans and scratched their heads. Only Da Gama and a few others had any understanding of what the queen intended. He began to smile.

"May we inspect her things?"

The Sultana looked toward Wali Khan. "No!" he shouted, banging his staff.

Beneath her cloths, the queen's shoulder moved, making a tiny shrug. "You see how he says. And he is her owner now."

"But without seeing those items . . ."

"Never mind!" shouted Slipper from across the room. "It's fine! We accept!" He wagged a finger at Whisper, and this gesture, even more than his outburst, set the courtiers murmuring.

"It seems your brother agrees on your behalf, sir," the queen said. Da Gama thought he could hear the smile in her voice. "But how shall this settlement be made?" The eye slit moved to face Da Gama. "Deoga, will you not act as our *burak*?"

"Highness, at your pleasure." Da Gama nodded. "I will need a scribe."

"Use the *mukhunni* Slipper. Anything else that you require?"

"A second-at-arms would be useful, highness."

The Sultana took a moment to answer. "Arms? Do you really think arms will be needed? Among such men of honor? To settle a bargain made under our seal?"

Da Gama considered his answer, and several times stopped just as he was about to speak. At last he bowed his head. "Yes, highness."

"Then take Commander Shahji for your second, Deoga. Make the settlement within the hour. Then we depart for Bijapur."

ෙෙෙෙ

Despite being nearly beside himself with anticipation, Slipper had been gracious and helpful. Hurrying over after the Sultana left the audience, he pulled Da Gama to a side hall and into an alcove where there was a low table, paper, and a pen box. "We can do the settlement right here!" he said brightly.

"No," Da Gama answered. He'd had enough of the palace for the day. "Outside. By the harem bridge."

"Who would have guessed you had this streak of romance, Deoga!

What an exciting setting! The day shall be memorable indeed!" With that
Slipper found a servant, and dictated a list of items to be brought to the
river's edge immediately: carpets, cushions, tables, writing implements, re-
freshments.

"It's just a settlement, Senhor Eunuch," Da Gama said, trying not to
seem too surprised by Slipper's efficiency.

"It is more than that, senhor. For years I myself was unjustly maligned
for the loss of . . . of a certain item. For years I searched, not just to regain
that item, but also my reputation. Today that shall be accomplished. I shall
be vindicated!"

"Being a good Muslim, you should say 'Ishvar-Allah'—if it is God's
will."

"Yes. But God is often lazy. It is persistence that eventually triumphs,
Deoga."

Or evil, thought Da Gama. Or sometimes luck. But Slipper was too excited for a conversation, so instead of discussing philosophy, Da Gama set
about dictating the settlement documents to Slipper, based on the decisions
of the queen.

After half an hour, Slipper and Da Gama left the Flying Palace. They
passed the maids of the harem and the eunuchs of the first rank making their
way to the stairs. They would travel in the Flying Palace with the queen.

"Don't bother looking for her, Deoga," Slipper said with a knowing
look.

"Who?"

"The nautch girl. She won't be traveling with the palace, but rather
with Wali Khan's suite. I'm sure he'll want her in his howdah." Slipper
winked and wagged an eyebrow, and Da Gama resisted slapping him.
"Now she'll be just another nautch girl, Deoga."

"You must find her special, or you wouldn't be paying seven *lakh* hun."

Slipper snorted. "She just happens to have something we want. A monkey could have had it just as easily, and been worth just as much."

The palace field was now stripped bare of tents; now only *palkis* and
howdah elephants marked the places where the grand circle had been. Men
fastened tarpaulins over the heaping contents of the bullock carts. In the
distance the eunuch guard was forming up. By the harem bridge, a carpet
had been laid for the settlement.

They arrived to find Wali Khan and Shahji seated, sharing a pitcher of wine. Da Gama refused a cup, but Slipper accepted and swallowed it in a gulp. "Careful, senhor," Da Gama teased.

"This is too great a day for moderation," Slipper answered as he took another cup.

Da Gama, as was often the case before a settlement, found it impossible to sit. He paced around the perimeter of the carpet, trying to calm himself by looking at the scenery. The carpet sat close to the fall's edge, where the river surged over the lip of the cliff to the black pool below. The bright sun shone warm, so the mists were thin. Da Gama looked long at the ancient temple, and the shadowed forests, and hoped that Lucy was safe and happy with Pathan. But he must think of that another time, he decided.

"I'll go see about the nautch girl," Slipper announced. He staggered a moment when he got to his feet, which made him laugh, and the others. Then with exaggerated care, he set across the wooden bridge. It groaned beneath his weight, and he turned and laughed some more as he proceeded.

"Why so nervous, Deoga?" Shahji asked.

"Done many settlements?" Da Gama answered. Shahji shrugged. "They never turn out how you think. When there's goods and gold in proximity, and men with different memories of the deal, there's trouble. At least this time there are no weapons." He frowned. "There are no weapons, are there?"

"Not even I have a weapon, Deoga," Shahji answered. "And I'm your second-at-arms. Don't worry, if someone makes trouble I'll hit him on the head with my wine cup." They all laughed.

But their mood changed quickly as Whisper limped toward them, holding Geraldo's arm. Behind him came seven servants, each carrying a small wooden chest bound with iron. "I forgot to arrange some way to carry my gold back after the settlement," Wali Khan said softly.

"And it's lapses like that that make a settlement dangerous," Da Gama said to Shahji.

The men made space as one by one the servants set the chests in a pile in the center of the carpet near the table.

Whisper waved the servants off. "Where's the girl?"

"Slipper's gone for her. Have some refreshment, Senhor Whisper."

Whisper frowned and turned away from the others.

"I'll have some," Geraldo said enthusiastically. He moved next to Da Gama. "I told you you should have made a claim. Look at me! I'm rich!"

He knocked back his wine. "I suppose I must thank you. If you hadn't kept quiet . . ."

Da Gama glared at him. "Repay me by doing a good turn for someone in the future."

Geraldo was about to answer when he caught sight of Slipper. Beside him was Maya. The breeze pressed the dark veil against her face.

As they crossed it, the harem bridge groaned and listed. One corner of the bridge bounced off the ground. "Look! It's not attached!" Geraldo shouted. "Be careful, you two!"

"You're right, sir," Shahji said, getting to his feet. "Careful there!" he shouted. "The bridgewallahs have removed its stakes!"

But Slipper and Maya crossed easily enough, though the bridge lurched when Slipper stepped off its end. "Here she is," he announced. "And I made her bring her things."

Maya made her way to a corner of the carpet, and stood quietly. Perhaps it was her veil, but she seemed almost to fade from view. The river roared behind her, and no one noticed as she turned her back to the proceedings.

"I think everyone is here," Da Gama said. "Let the settlement begin."

"Should we have a prayer, Deoga?" Slipper laughed. "Or a cup of wine at least?" The eunuch helped himself.

"Actually it's good that you are here, Geraldo. You can sign that certificate of custody. Based on the Sultana's decisions, I'd say you are now the *devadasi*'s owner."

Geraldo sat down to the paper with a chuckle. "Her owner. Think of that." He plunged a feather pen into the inkwell and scrawled a signature. "Short, but very sweet."

"And now, sir, if you'll sign that you've received the goods." Da Gama nodded to Wali Khan.

The vizier looked at Maya, who stood at the carpet's edge, an amorphous shadow against the brightness of the sky. "I suppose I've received her," he murmured, and placed his own signature beneath Geraldo's. His was a complicated swirl of flourishes, impossible to decipher.

"At last," Slipper said.

Da Gama gave the eunuch a gracious smile. "I hope you get satisfaction, Senhor Eunuch. Senhor Vizier, by order of the Sultana, you must deliver to the Khaswajara either the girl, or any one of her possessions that he may choose. For this right, the Khaswajara must give to you seven *lakh* hun. Senhor Khaswajara, do you understand this? Senhor Vizier?"

"I've brought the money. What I want . . ."

"Please, sir, we must go in order. The money is for the right for you to choose and to receive. The vizier must receive your goods before you can have your choice."

"What nonsense!" scowled Whisper. "Very well." He handed Da Gama a ring of seven keys. Then, after standing ever since his arrival, he finally sat.

Da Gama picked a chest; the third key opened it. He swung back its lid: inside were rows of cylinders wrapped in silk, tied with blue ribbons and sealed with red wax. Da Gama chose one at random, and lifted it from the box. The silk tore easily beneath his thumbnail to reveal a stack of golden coins. He spilled the coins into his palm, examined a few, and began to count. Everyone but Whisper stared.

"Never mind, Deoga. Let's get on with it."

"Senhor Vizier, do you not wish me to count the money for you?"

"It would take all day, and besides, the Khaswajara's not that kind of a cheat."

"What kind of a cheat am I, then?" Whisper snapped back.

Da Gama stepped between them. "Sign here that you received your gold." When Wali Khan was done, Da Gama said, "Which do you choose, Senhor Whisper? The girl or one of her possessions?"

"Let me see her things."

"No!" Wali Khan shouted, pushing to his feet. "The queen agreed—no examining!"

"Yes, yes," Da Gama said, soothing him. "Not to examine . . . just to see, that's all. For seven *lakh* hun, he deserves the right to see, eh, senhor?" Wali Khan let himself be gentled back to his seat. Slipper was already moving toward Maya, but Da Gama pushed ahead.

"No!" Maya shouted from beneath her veil. "They are all I have. The few things that make me who I am. You shall not take them from me!"

Da Gama glanced at Shahji. They stood on either side of her. "*Devadasi,*" Shahji said. "You do yourself no honor this way." Maya bowed her head.

"You must give me your things," Da Gama said as gently as he could. But how gently can such words be said? She pushed her cloth shoulder bag from beneath her veil.

"Why are we taking so long!" Slipper said shrilly. "He's got the money; give me the bag!"

"Easy, Slipper," Shahji said.

"One item! One item only!" Wali Khan said at the same time, rising to his feet.

"Let us remember ourselves, senhors," Da Gama said. "This will soon be over," he whispered to Maya, but she did not turn. Then Da Gama knelt, and slowly spread the contents of her bag upon the carpet, next to the chests of golden hun.

Everyone had realized by now that the eunuchs had no desire for the girl. What did she own that was worth seven *lakh* hun?

Slipper watched Da Gama's actions with his small eyes glowing, scarcely able to contain himself. At last he saw the sack that held the headdress. "That's it! That's what we want!"

"Careful," Whisper murmured. "Let's be sure. Let's see the rest."

Da Gama slid the contents of the bag out to the carpet. It didn't take long.

When all was displayed, Slipper pointed again at the small sack. He could not stand still. "That's it, that's it! That's what we want!"

"Do you agree, Senhor Whisper? It's your decision, not his."

Whisper bit his lip, glanced at the seven chests of gold, and then back to the pitiful, small sack. "Brother, tell me you are certain." Slipper was now too agitated to reply, but he nodded so hard his jowls wiggled. "All right," Whisper sighed.

Da Gama scooped the sack from the carpet, and put the last settlement document on the table with a flourish. "Sign that you have received the item that you chose."

Whisper knelt to the table and was about to sign when Wali Khan stood over him. "No."

"What do you mean, sir?" Whisper spat.

"I mean that's two items. The sack and its contents."

"I take the contents, obviously," Whisper said. Watching Wali Khan warily the entire time, he wrote his emphatic, precise signature at the bottom of the document. "Now, Deoga, I think that it is mine."

"I agree." Da Gama swept up the signed papers. "The settlement is at an end. Senhor Vizier, the girl and gold are yours. Senhor Khaswajara, this is yours." With that, he opened the end of Maya's sack, and spilled out the headdress into Whisper's palm.

☙☯☙

"Give it me! Give it me!" Slipper cried. He snatched the headdress from Whisper's hand and waved it above his head. "The Web of Ruci! Mine at last!" Slipper wiggled his body in a kind of dance. In his fat hands the bits of gilt and glass sparkled in the sun.

"The Web of Ruci?" Wali Khan exploded. "It can't be!" He turned to Shahji. "Could it be?" He grabbed Da Gama. "It can't be the Web of Ruci!" Wali Khan began to chase after Slipper as he danced away.

Whisper brought his thin cold body close to Maya. He sniffed at her as if she were a piece of meat that might be rotten. "You've been more trouble than you're worth. I don't like you, and I will see to it that others dislike you, too. Beware the brothers in Murad's court."

Shahji stared after Whisper with disgust. "To think I must make a deal with that ruin." He moved about the carpet, picking up Maya's possessions and putting them in her bag, all except for the empty headdress sack, which seemed to him too pitiful to be included. He handed the bag to her. "I myself will tell Chitra about the boy. You have done me a good turn, *devadasi*. I will not forget it."

Maya turned her veiled head, and her small hand slipped from underneath the cloth. She took the bag, but made no reply. This Da Gama watched from the other side of the carpet.

"Now I see your game, sir!"

Da Gama looked up to see Geraldo coming toward him. He'd all but forgotten about him. "What game is that?"

"Isn't that the trinket that she gave you when you left Belgaum?"

Da Gama eyed Geraldo carefully. "Maybe." But at that very moment, near the river's edge Wali Khan had managed to snatch the headdress from Slipper.

"Give it back to me!" the eunuch cried.

Wali Khan shoved Slipper's grasping hand aside and peered at the headdress. "Why, this is a fake! This is nothing but cheap glass!" he crowed.

"What! What's that?" Whisper cried. He limped quickly to Wali Khan's side.

"No," Slipper gasped. "No, it can't be!"

Now Whisper seized the headdress. Wali Khan put up no fight. The old eunuch held it close to his eyes and squinted. "Shahji! General!" he called, hurrying toward him. "Which is it? Real or fake?" He held it up inches from Shahji's face.

"I couldn't say. It's very pretty. I suppose it's real."

"It's a damned fake," Geraldo said loudly. "I can see it from here."

"A fake!" Whisper wheeled on Slipper. "What do you say to this?"

Slipper took the headdress. "It can't be! It's heavy! It glitters!" He hurried to Maya and screamed at her dark veil. "Tell me that it's real!"

Da Gama reached past Maya's side, and pushed the eunuch away. He was about to give him a talking-to when something caught his eye. A few yards from where they stood, Wali Khan was doubled over with laughter, but Whisper hobbled toward him, in his hand a silver blade. "Shahji, help me! Come quick!" Da Gama cried as he raced for Whisper.

Shahji followed, with Geraldo at his heels. By the time they reached him, Da Gama had pinned Whisper's thin arms behind hs back. The blade lay in the grass. Whisper's tiny chest stuck out; under his silk shirt his ribs looked as fragile as a bird's.

"He cheated me, *burak*!" Whisper spat out in his rasping treble.

"I never did," Wali Khan snorted.

"He knew it was a fake! He knew!"

Wali Khan held up his hands. "By the Prophet's beard I swear I did not know. Is that not enough for you?"

But at that moment, Maya screamed.

ᏻᎧᎧᏻ

The men turned to see her sprawled on the grass near the river's edge. Slipper had knocked her down, and she scrambled to get away. They could see now by his walk that he had drunk too much; he staggered, and stumbled often. But despite his size he was fast, and when Maya struggled to her feet and began to run, he raced toward her and slapped her twice across the head until she fell again.

"You did this! You!" Slipper placed his feet astride her and brought his mouth down close to her veiled face and screamed. A string of spittle hung from his lips. Then he pounded on her breasts with both hands. She squirmed but could not ward off his blows After a moment, he rose as if exhausted. Maya crawled away.

Shahji pushed Da Gama aside: "I am your second. Leave this to me," he said and ran toward them. A few feet from the eunuch, he called out, "Senhor Slipper!"

Slipper stumbled, as if his rising had caused him to black out. He pitched toward Shahji, who reached out to help him. Whether by mistake or by design, however, Slipper's motion did not stop. He rammed his head into Shahji's. The general crumbled to his knees, clutching his nose. But Slipper rose unhurt. His turban unwound behind him, and he had a smear of Shahji's blood across his pale forehead.

Maya had made it halfway across the harem bridge when Slipper caught up with her. "You have ruined me!" he cried, staggering after her.

The bridge, no longer tied down, bounced beneath the eunuch's strides. Half-drunk, half-dazed from his bashed head, Slipper tottered from rail to rail. The bridge groaned and pitched with his every step. Maya clung to a rail.

Slipper advanced, waving the headdress and screaming. He'd long since stopped saying words.

Geraldo and Wali Khan ran to help Shahji. He waved them toward the bridge. When they reached it, Wali Khan started to run toward Maya. The bridge pitched beneath his feet, and Geraldo pulled him back. "Don't be a fool!" he shouted over the river's roar. "It's too flimsy! The bridge will fail!"

Slipper had reached Maya, and with the fist that held the headdress he struck her veiled face. She fell to her knees, but clung to the railing, though she could not stand. When she looked up, Slipper struck again.

Da Gama and Whisper had now joined the others at the bridge's end. "Brother!" Whisper called to Slipper. "Leave her! All will be well!"

Slipper turned. His face was a horror. It had collapsed beneath his fallen hopes. "All will be well when she is dead!" he shouted.

Maya wrapped her arms around the railing and started to get to her feet when Slipper's fat fingers grasped her neck from behind. She writhed but he would not let go.

"He's killing her!" Da Gama yelled. He grabbed a corner of the bridge and began with all his strength to lift it. The bamboo and wood lashings shrieked from being twisted. "Help me!" Da Gama screamed. For he had seen that Maya held the railing with her arms, and that Slipper had no grip. "We can shake the eunuch off!" The other men looked at each other, and obeying Da Gama's commanding voice, grabbed hold where they could. Together they heaved until, with a creaking groan, they spilled the bridge onto its side.

When the bridge upended, Maya and Slipper both tumbled into the roaring water. Maya's head ducked beneath the surface, but still she clung to the rail. At last her veiled face showed above the foam. She shook her head, and the veil slid slowly off. In an instant it had swept down the falls.

Beneath her weight and the current's force, the bridge twisted and flexed. "We can't help her," Da Gama yelled. "It won't hold! She'll have to come here!"

"Why doesn't she come then?" Wali Khan said. "What's stopping her?"

Then they saw.

Inches from the falls, Slipper's bulky form clung to Maya's ankles. In the water's rush he planed first one way, then the other.

"He'll drag them both in!" Whisper cried. "He will kill them both!"

ꙮꙮꙮꙮ

"Let go, let go!" Maya gasped as water surged across her face.

Hand over hand, Slipper walked up her leg, as one climbs a rope. Against the raging current, she held on for both herself and him. She felt the railing bow beneath her arms.

Water pummeled Slipper's eyes. The current twisted him so hard he spun like a fishing lure on a string. He reached up and grabbed her knee. "For God's sake!" he shrieked. "Give me your hand!"

As the white foam cascaded around her, she remembered. Slipper's insults, Slipper's beatings, Slipper's taunts. Slipper at the pass, tearing at her hurt arm, scrambling over her to safety.

I must be hard as diamonds and as cold, she had told Deoga.

Her sandal had long ago swept down the falls. With her bare toes she pried Slipper's fingers from her leg. He clung yet harder with the others. Through the crashing foam, his face grew wild with horror, and malice, and surprise.

She made up her mind to watch him die.

There was a moment of utter stillness when he at last let go, as though the river stopped. In the silence of that instant, she saw Slipper lift the hand that held the headdress. He mouthed some words—she did not care what.

Then the river surged again, and Slipper, screaming, plunged into the empty air.

෴෴

Slipper's final slide took but an instant. The falls swallowed him, and he was gone. Looking at the empty space where moments before the eunuch had fought the current, Whisper's face grew pale. "Gone! Gone!" he gasped. He staggered along the bank toward the falls' edge and looked over the cliff, bent with weeping.

Maya still clung to the railing, clearly growing weak. Da Gama leaped into the rapids.

"You farangs are madmen!" Wali Khan shouted to Geraldo. "We should hold the bridge for him at least!" But Geraldo moved more slowly than Wali Khan would have expected.

Da Gama edged along the railing until he reached Maya. It had been hard going, for the current was strong, and the bridge seemed on the verge of collapse. He reached out his hand, but she merely looked at him with eyes exhausted to the point of death. "Don't let go!" Da Gama screamed. He could not bear to lose another life. Not hers.

Maya shook her head. Da Gama inched closer. One of her arms slipped, and her head dipped below the foam. Da Gama begged the gods to help him. As her other arm let go, he swung toward her with his last remaining strength. His knees caught her hips. He managed to wrap his free arm around her breasts. Somehow he struggled until he had cradled her neck in his elbow, and could lift her head above the current. Her eyes rolled back, and her lips were blue.

The bridge railing finally cracked. Still held in Da Gama's embrace, they ducked beneath the water. He dragged her to the surface—her body felt limp and lifeless now. He saw the others staring at him desperately from shore. I'll never get there, Da Gama thought. I don't have the strength.

He looked at Maya. I should tell her that I love her, here as we both die.

But he never had the chance. With an ear-shattering bang, the bridge cracked in two. Da Gama watched the other half of the bridge pitch end on end as it bumped the river rocks. With a final heave, it swept down the falls. Da Gama looked to the shore. The men were struggling to hold on to his half of the broken bridge, straining to keep it from sliding down the falls as well.

Da Gama's part of the bridge began to move with the current. Like a gate on a post, pivoting where the men held it fast, the broken end of the bridge turned slowly for the riverbank.

It's a miracle, Da Gama thought. But he soon wondered if he had spoken too soon. As the bridge drifted toward the shore, the end to which they clung swung closer and closer to the falls' edge. The river's force grew even stronger as they reached the plummet. The end of Maya's sari flapped out over the falls. He held her tight with his remaining strength.

The men holding the bridge could not let go to help Da Gama, for fear that everything would be swept over. Finally it fell to Whisper, slowly coming to his senses, to wade like a bird into the river, and with Da Gama's help to drag Maya to the shore.

Then Whisper came back—Da Gama would never forget that he came back—and held out his bony hand for the farang. With his help Da Gama clambered out of the river, and then he kissed the ground.

Then the men let go, and the bridge groaned and fell in pieces down the falls.

Shahji reached him first. He heaved Da Gama to his feet. "Good job," he said. Then he ran to help Maya.

Wali Khan reached them a moment later. He clapped Da Gama on his back. "Marvelous, marvelous!" he laughed. "That, senhor, is what I call a *settlement!*"

ᏺᏺᏺᏺ

The camp, which had been moving swiftly toward departure, erupted into chaos. Guards were sent for. The hakim arrived, turned Maya on her belly, and slapped her back a dozen times. After sputtering and coughing up some water, Maya woke. Whisper sent for dry clothing and a veil.

Whisper sent a party of eunuch guards to the bottom of the falls, but though they searched the pool and the rapids leading from the falls, the headdress could not be found—nor any sign of Slipper.

After Da Gama had changed into dry clothing he went to thank Whisper. But the Khaswajara was less than gracious. He would not even nod in reply. "Gone . . . gone," Whisper had said, looking out at the falls, and turned away and never spoke again to him.

Wali Khan, however, made a point of finding Da Gama. After his servants loaded the seven caskets of gold onto an oxcart, he threw a thick arm around Da Gama's shoulders. "Take heart, farang! There's worse fates than being hated by the Brotherhood," he laughed. "You are quite a *burak*. I want to hire you! I'll be sending the nautch girl up to Viceroy Murad, and that will take a good man, a man like you, farang." He laughed and clapped Da Gama on the back. "No other will do, in my opinion! But that won't be for a few months, of course. In the meantime I've a few problems you could attend to. You could stay at the Gagan Mahal, in Victorio's old place. That was quite a settlement, farang! Quite a settlement!"

"You could do worse, Deoga," Shahji said to him when Wali Khan had left. He'd had the foresight to send for wine, and encouraged Da Gama to drink to restore his strength.

"What would you do if you were me, General?"

"I'd work for the Moguls. They love their farangs. They'd like a man like you." Shahji chuckled. "And if I were you, I'd find a wife."

Da Gama shook his head. "No woman could stand me, General. I'm getting used to solitude anyway. Why should I disturb things now?" The two men laughed. "All the same, I'll consider your advice about the Moguls. Maybe I'll take Wali Khan's offer—take the nautch girl to the Mogul viceroy. I can scout things out when I get there."

From the Flying Palace word came that the Sultana wanted to be on her way. Slowly the excitement faded back into the routine of readying for a journey. Shahji invited Da Gama to join him for a few days in Belgaum, and he agreed. Then Da Gama walked to Wali Khan and accepted his offer of a job and place to live.

As Da Gama came back slowly across the encampment field, the great elephants once more were harnessed to the hoisting ropes of the Flying Palace. He watched in fascination as they strained and grunted, as their mahouts calmly tapped their ears. Against their dark skin, their silver-studded livery gleamed. Suddenly, with the groan of wooden beams flexing, the palace rose into the air.

There was a flurry of excitement then, as when a great ship departs, and the dock is busy with last-minute comings and goings. Da Gama scarcely noticed when a small, veiled figure approached.

"You saved me once again, Deoga," her soft voice came from underneath her veil.

"I'm so glad you are alive!" He wanted to say more, to embrace her, something.

"I wanted to die, Deoga. But now I too find that I am glad to be alive. My old life is gone, Deoga. But at least you will remember me as I used to be."

Da Gama could find no words to answer. He glanced around, and saw that though they stood within the midst of much activity, no one gave them heed.

"I hoped I would see you," he said. He took Maya's headdress sack from his pocket, and discreetly pressed it toward her. He could hear her gasp beneath the veil. It was heavier than she expected. "Open it in private only," Da Gama whispered. "I had a copy made. That's what was lost."

But people were coming toward them then, and they could say no more. Maya floated away, toward Wali Khan's suite. Da Gama watched as she mounted the silver ladder to Wali Khan's howdah, and remembered a day in Goa. It now seemed long ago.

As he headed on his way to join Shahji, Geraldo caught up with him. Da Gama barely acknowledged him. "Something was up with that headdress." Da Gama kept walking and did not turn. "Slipper was a wrong sort, but he was no fool. I think she did some trick. Or you did. I think maybe both of you! Do you deny it?"

Da Gama stopped and stared up at Geraldo. "Listen," he said. "I'm getting to an age where I don't care what you think, or anyone. Men do things, right or wrong. Good men try to make up for their misdeeds. That's

my stage in life, cousin." Geraldo flinched beneath Da Gama's gaze.
"You're rich now. You've done some evil—maybe we all have. But you've
achieved what you set out to get. You're rich! Why not try your hand at
being good?"

"And keep my mouth shut, you mean?"

Da Gama shrugged. From the corner of his eye, he saw Shahji waving
for him, motioning for him to depart. "Where are you headed now, Geraldo?"

"To Bijapur. The Khaswajara wants to discuss some plans."

Da Gama shook his head. "Try being good for a change. Around that
eunuch it will not be easy."

"And you?"

"To Belgaum for a while, then Bijapur."

"We'll have to spend time together. Bijapur must be a lonely place for
farangs."

Da Gama looked at Geraldo with a sad smile, as if expressing sympa-
thy for a malady that Geraldo did not yet know he had. "For some men,
every place is lonely." Da Gama made a sweeping bow, and without another word, headed briskly to Shahji's horses.

There were worse things than loneliness.

Epilogue

Wali Khan proved a man of uncompromising honor: when he returned to Bijapur with Maya, he sent to Da Gama his full fee and Pathan's as well.

Da Gama took up residence in Victorio's old apartments in the Gagan Mahal and became reacquainted with Mouse. After a time, Mouse overcame his sorrow about Victorio's death, and resumed his genial demeanor.

Da Gama discovered for himself why Victorio was so fond of the eunuch. He was gentle and faithful and always anxious to please. For Da Gama, Mouse's subtle presence brought comfort, and later pleasure. One night when Da Gama could not sleep, Mouse brought out his *haratala*, and the two cast shot until morning.

Over the next six months while he waited to deliver Maya to Murad, Da Gama undertook a number of settlements for the vizier. While on the road, he wore his old outfit—farang clothes, big leather boots—but when he returned to Bijapur, he put on *jamas*. He found them more comfortable now, and anyway Mouse preferred them.

Word of Maya's skill and beauty spread quickly through the city, and an invitation to Wali Khan's zenana became a much-sought prize. Hopeful courtiers lavished *baksheesh* on the grand vizier; the lucky ones were asked to supper at his palace. After servants cleared the food, musicians played, and Maya danced.

Favored guests might meet her alone. Later some of these claimed to have had congress with the nautch girl. If they exaggerated, Maya did not say.

The Sultana had taken a fancy to her. She often visited the harem of the Khas Mahal, the most private palace. Oftentimes the heir would sit at his mother's feet as the women chatted, and when the conversation flagged, he would ask Maya to play ball.

As the time for her departure neared, the heir wrote a letter in his own hand, offering to purchase Maya from the grand vizier—he offered a *crore* of hun from the privy purse. Considerable discussion followed between the Sultana and Whisper and the grand vizier. In the end, Wali Khan was chosen to explain that Maya was the seal on a promise of peace, and that peace was worth much more than a *crore* of hun.

The heir hid in his room for days, and when at last he came out, he refused to see Maya anymore.

Geraldo thrived in Bijapur. He quickly established a household, and invited many courtiers to his home. Courtiers, of course, never refuse a free meal, and soon Geraldo gained many friends. He attended the Sultana's audiences and rode through the streets on a silver *palki*. But even though he lavished gifts on the vizier, he never received an invitation to see Maya dance.

The vizier in this took Da Gama's counsel. He had become friends with the farang, who visited him often. Da Gama made it a point to avoid Geraldo, and Wali Khan observed this.

"What's wrong with your young farang then, Deoga?" he asked one night while the two men sipped a sharbat.

"Maya does not care for him," was all Da Gama answered, and when pressed would say no more.

ↂↂↂↂ

About a month before he was scheduled to take Maya to Prince Murad, Da Gama worked a settlement in Sarat for a friend of Wali Khan. Unlike many settlements, this one had gone smoothly, and Da Gama was much disappointed. He had brought with him a new man, an Irishman who'd made his way to Hindustan from Persia, and he had hoped to show him how hard the job could be. Now whenever Da Gama described the difficulties of his role—the unexpected ways a settlement could explode into chaos—the Irishmen agreed politely, as one agrees with the old host at a dinner when he spouts some precious nonsense.

"You'll see," Da Gama told him. "It's not just easy money. Bandits no doubt saw us on our way to Sarat, and they will look for our return now our purses are full. They'd rather have the gold than goods. We must be very wary."

"Oh, yes, sir," the Irishman replied.

They slept beneath the stars as Da Gama preferred, in a grove of banyan trees near the Pratapghad road. As their campfire burned to embers, the sky hung so black and close it seemed the stars would drop upon them. Peacocks cried in the forest, and they heard a panther growl. Then silence settled, and the peaceful chirp of crickets returned.

Da Gama just drifted off when he heard a *thunk* in the ground beside his right ear, and in an instant another *thunk* beside his left. His eyes flew open to find two arrows jutting from his pillow, inches from his head.

He sat up, cocking his *pistola,* in time to see two huge cocoons unfold in a nearby tree. From their blanket hiding places, two bandits fell lightly to their feet. In the glow of the dying fire there was just enough light to see that one of them was tall and wiry, the other slight and young. Both carried arrows notched in strong short bows.

Beside Da Gama, the Irishman snored.

The tall one waved his notched arrow at Da Gama's *pistola.* He uncocked the hammer and lowered it to the ground as they approached.

"Hello, cousin," said the smaller. Da Gama blinked up, uncertain. The slight bandit's hands moved swiftly; the turban fell to the ground, and Da Gama saw the unexpected face of Lucinda beaming at him. He leaped to his feet, embraced her, and kissed her soft cheek before he realized that the other bandit, chuckling beside them, was Pathan.

"We're bandits now, Deoga," Lucinda told him brightly, keeping her voice low. "I wear *jamas* now. I ride horses, and I shoot."

"She's a dead shot with a short bow, Deoga," Pathan added with a note of pride.

"See there?" she pointed to the arrows in Da Gama's pillow. "I could have grazed your ears if Munna'd let me." Her look at Pathan was full of affection.

"No need for pride, Lucy," Pathan beamed.

"Are you married?" Da Gama asked, and instantly regretted the stodginess of his question.

Lucinda tossed her hair and laughed, and then grabbed her mouth for fear the Irishman would wake. "Married bandit style," she answered, and then reached to touch Da Gama's arm. "Did you worry about us, cousin?"

"Yes, of course. Every day—every hour."

"You are a good man to worry so, but there was no need. Munna is my husband, and lets no harm come near me. And anyway, now I can protect myself." She nodded to her short bow, and Da Gama saw that she held it firmly, and that her palms had gotten wider, and the fingers stronger, and her hands had the look of sureness that comes from practiced skill. She moved with a springing quickness. And her eyes, Da Gama noticed now, were no longer dreamy, but full of certainty and determination. Ruthless, Da Gama thought, then felt shocked that the word had come to mind.

"We asked for this job, Deoga, so that we might see you, and ease whatever worries you might feel," Pathan said softly. "Also so you might not be troubled too much by our brother bandits, who do not share our history."

"No, they would have taken everything," Lucinda said.

There was a silence then. Slowly Da Gama began to work things out. When finally he saw how things stood, he felt as if he'd lived too long. Wearily he placed his purse into Lucinda's outstretched palm.

Lucinda tucked her bow beneath her arm, and spilled Da Gama's gold into her hand. She put half into her pocket, and replaced the rest. "Remember the ties between the Three-Dot clan and Wali Khan, cousin," she said seriously. "This can be good or bad, but there is danger in forgetting. We will tell our brother bandits that we took all your gold. If you hide the part I've left you, no one will ever know."

The Irishman grunted in his sleep but did not wake. Da Gama gave no sign of what he felt. Pathan lowered his head and murmured, "We must do our best with the portion given to us by the Lord, Deoga. Now we are bandits, we must be good ones."

"The best," Lucinda agreed. Pathan moved into the shadows. "He's getting the ponies," she explained. She tiptoed to place a kiss on Da Gama's cheek. "I'm glad I saw you. Find peace. Joy hides in unexpected places. Be happy, as I am happy."

Pathan rode up, towing Lucinda's pony. "*Salaam aleichem,* Deoga," he said. Da Gama bowed. Then Lucy bounded from Da Gama's side to the saddle in what seemed like a single jump. She grabbed the reins and wheeled the pony close to Da Gama. "Don't be sad, cousin. Our paths will cross again." With that she spurred her pony into the darkness, and behind her followed Pathan.

"I do not think so," Da Gama murmured to the shadows.

Beside the fire, the Irishman snored.

ᝍᝍᝍ

On her last night in Bijapur, Maya sent an invitation to Geraldo.

He went to the zenana dressed in fine farang clothes, tailored in dark velvets and dense satins, rich with golden braid. Wali Khan's servants bowed low when he approached. A eunuch led him through the vizier's palace, and through corridors lit by a hundred butter lamps in alcoves in the walls. He opened a set of carved doors, and bowed Geraldo through.

A vast array of silver dishes spread on a muslin sheet in the middle of the carpet. Incense burned, and a dozen hanging lights flickered through pierced shades.

In cushions by the feast sat Da Gama, dressed in a dark blue *jamas*; to his right was Maya. She wore a sheer sari of soft silver that glittered in the lamplight. Her hair was covered, but not her face. Her gold-flecked eyes shimmered when she saw Geraldo enter.

"Come and sit, Aldo," Da Gama said.

They ate mostly in silence. There was too much to say, so they said little. Maya presided, offering the delicacies with a practiced grace. Geraldo stared at her lips, at her hands as they glided through the air. "You are more beautiful than ever," he whispered. Maya merely closed her eyes.

"I had this made specially, in the manner of farangs," she said at one point.

Geraldo tried the dish—mutton flavored with spices and much garlic. "It's like being in Goa," he told her, bowing his head. "You are too kind. Haven't you tried it, Da Gama?"

"My digestion is not so good these days," Da Gama answered without looking up. "You finish it."

Maids cleared the dishes and brought sharbats. Da Gama described tomorrow's journey for Maya. Elaborate preparations had been made; even a decoy caravan.

"Do you fear danger, Deoga?" Maya said.

"Always. You are more valuable than ever now. I've enlisted special guards."

With the sharbats finished, Da Gama rose. "You young people have things to discuss, I'm sure. An old man has no place here." He bowed to Geraldo, and then Maya. "Besides, I need my rest. Ahead of us we have long journeys."

"Make peace," Maya said to both of them.

So Geraldo rose and embraced Da Gama. "*Vá com deus,* senhor," he said as he leaned back.

"*E com você,*" Da Gama answered. He walked out without looking back, quietly closing the door behind him.

A feeling of anticipation filled Geraldo. His heart began to beat faster, and he felt heat rising to his face. He loosened the collar of his shirt. "So," he said to Maya.

"So," Maya answered. He could not read her face. "Why do the gods allow wickedness, do you think?"

"Surely you don't mean for us to discuss philosophy?" Geraldo laughed. Then he burped, and this made him laugh again. "Other subjects are more pleasant."

"Answer me."

Geraldo shrugged. The mutton sat like a lump in his belly, but he smiled in spite of the discomfort. "Perhaps the gods themselves are wicked. Perhaps there are no gods. Maybe we make our own fates. Maybe those who fear the gods are weak, and those who know the truth are strong."

"Then are you strong, Geraldo?"

Again he shrugged. Seeing her in the golden lamplight, her beauty even grander than he recalled, set his skin tingling.

"You have killed and robbed. You've cheated your own family."

Geraldo gave an uncomfortable laugh. "I've cheated death as well."

"Yes." Maya moved her hands to the veil that covered her hair. "I wanted you to see this, you of all persons."

She drew back the veil, and revealed a glittering web of gold and pearls and diamonds. Against her raven hair, the jewels sparkled like stars in a black sky. Geraldo gasped and stared. "This is what I am, Geraldo. This is what has become of the woman you abandoned. Men have fought and even died to have me."

"You are magnificent," Geraldo choked out.

"You could have had all this, except you wanted more." The golden highlights of her eyes now gleamed like fire. "This is what I wanted you to know. What you might have had, and what you have lost." Once more she veiled her head, and the light within the room appeared to dim. "You were a fool."

Geraldo gulped. He had begun to sweat. "I've made up my mind to be a better man."

"Do it quickly then. And when the tally of your life is reckoned, remember this moment."

Then she stood, as if dismissing him. For a moment Geraldo felt disappointment, and then relief. He was not at his best. His belly rumbled. With some effort he got to his feet. Maybe he'd drunk too much wine; his head swam. Geraldo tried to smile. "Business sometimes takes me to the court of Murad. Perhaps I'll see you." He burped again and tasted bile.

"I do not think so," Maya opened the door, and Geraldo, with as much dignity as he could manage, set his shoulders and walked through.

"Good night," he whispered. "You've shown me your secrets. I will not betray you. I will be silent as the grave."

"I depend on it," Maya answered. She looked into his eyes, and he saw a momentary flash of the girl that he remembered, of the first time he'd seen Maya's face—beautiful, distant, young, a little frightened. "Geraldo, do you pray?" she asked.

"Sometimes."

"Then pray now."

The carved door closed before his eyes, and the sound echoed through the lamplit hall.

◠◡◠◡

Outside the doors of the vizier's palace, Da Gama acknowledged the servants' bows. He stopped for a moment, and sighed, then slowly made his way down the stairs to the torchlit courtyard. He'd just decided to dismiss his *palki* bearers and walk back home, when he saw a form emerge from the shadows.

"Mouse," he said. "What are you doing here?"

"I thought you might be lonely, Deoga." His dark eyes were wistful.

"You are kind." Da Gama blinked. He hated tears.

Mouse looked up at him. "Why must you be sad? Many people love you." He lifted his hand to Da Gama's head. "You are a good man. You must be happy."

Da Gama sighed. "Let's go home," he told the *palki*wallah.

In the *palki,* Mouse laid his head against Da Gama's shoulder. As they rose into the air, Da Gama took the eunuch's gentle hand in his.